SUPER DUPER SERIAL

Harker McNair

This is a work of fiction. All characters, organizations, corporations, and events portrayed in this novel are products of the author's imagination or are used fictitiously. Any similarities to business entities or persons, living or dead, is coincidental, and is not intended by the author.

Cover Design By: Jeffrey Smith

Editing By: Jill Davies, The Deliberate Page

Name: McNair, Harker, author.

Title: Super Serial / Harker McNair

Description: First edition: 2024

ISBN: #979-8-9890336-3-8 *(ebook), 979-8-9890336-4-5 (paperback)*

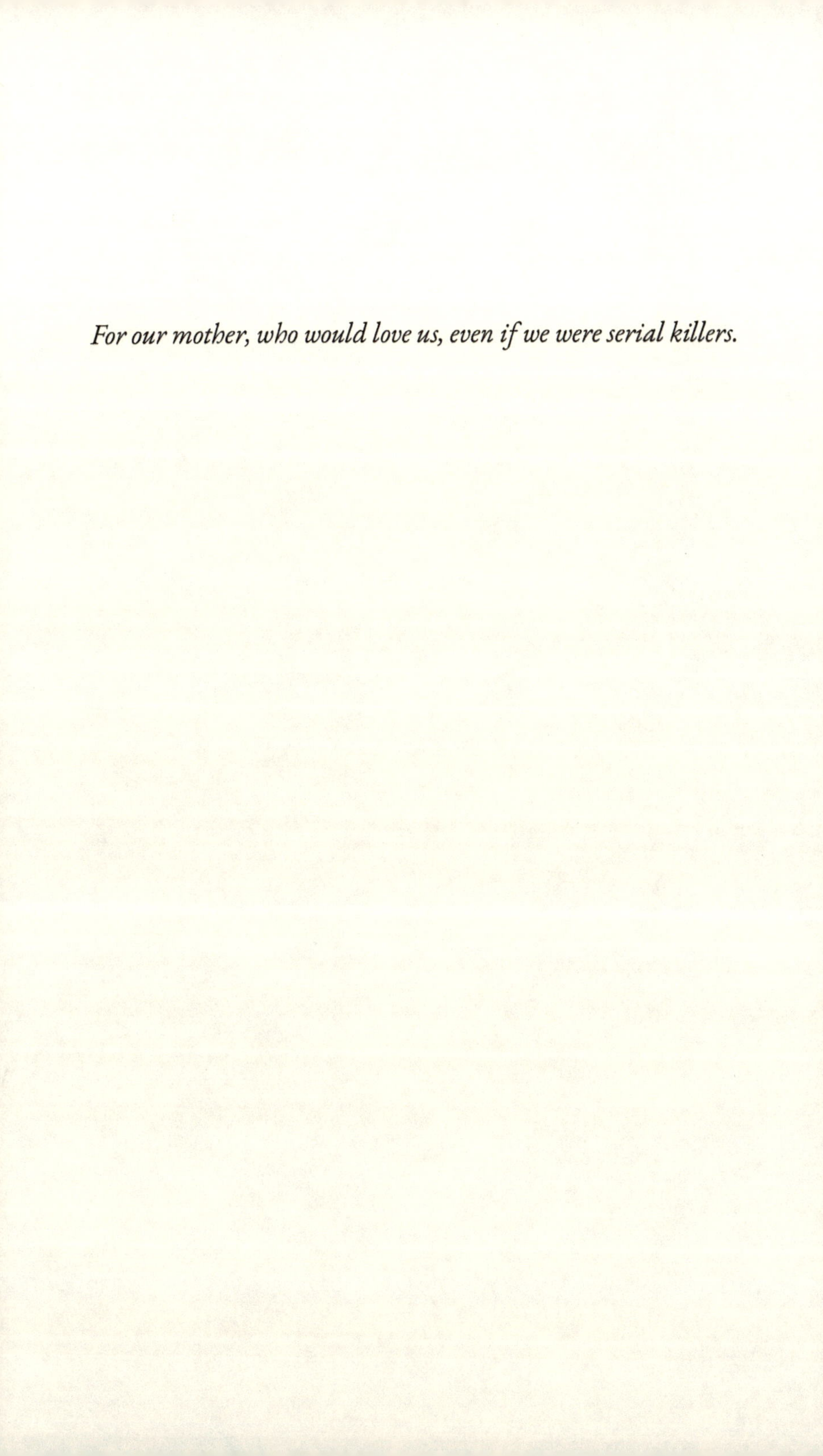

For our mother, who would love us, even if we were serial killers.

Contents

Content Warning

This book is about serial killers. It contains gratuitous violence, extreme gore, death, and discussions about serial killers and their methods of killing. Throughout the series, there are instances where characters who commit heinous crimes are celebrated in their fictional society. The purpose of this writing is to thematically address complex social issues, and does not convey the authors' personal viewpoints or opinions. Many details in this story are inspired by real people and events. Please proceed with caution.

<u>Potential Triggers are Listed Below:</u>

Gratuitous Violence and Gore
Torture/Murder of Pedophiles, Sex Offenders, and Criminals
Pedophilia and Child Death (Discussion, Not Depiction)
Attempted Sexual Assault
Radicalized INCEL (Offensive, Misogynistic Remarks)
Nudity
Animal Attacks, Abuse, and Death
Snakes

Ableism (Neurodivergence/Autism)

Ageism

Forced Labor (Discussion, Not Depiction)

Religious Trauma (Christianity)

Mental Illness and Personality Disorders (Not Specified)

Grief and Loss (Spousal, Parental)

Fatphobia

For a more detailed description of the trigger and content warnings found in this book, please visit www.harkermcnair.com

Chapter 1

Take Me Home, Country Rolls

Floyd McNut leaned in across the small dining table until his nose was mere inches from Ziggy's. "I knew it!" he exclaimed, a triumphant grin spreading across his face. "I knew you'd be here!" The faint odor of stale pretzels clung to his breath.

Ziggy was happier to see Floyd than he wanted to admit, but the feeling was snuffed out by a growing sense of alarm. "What are you doing here?"

Floyd waved his scrawny arms above his head, craning his neck toward the door to the lobby. "Pepper, it's him!" he shouted way too loudly, his oversized noise-canceling headphones still hugging his head. "Ziglar Ghostshade! Here in the dining room. Pep? Pepper Devoux!" He turned to Ziggy and shrugged. "I don't think she can hear me."

"Everyone on the whole damn beach can hear you," Ziggy said, pointing at the headphones Floyd had clearly forgotten he was wearing.

Realization dawned on Floyd, and he yanked the headphones off. "I'm so glad we found you!" he said at a lower volume, his eyes shimmering with emotion.

Ziggy leaned away by a fraction. "No, Floyd—" he yelped, but it was too late. Floyd flung himself over the table, wrapping Ziggy in an awkward, tangled hug. "I missed you!"

Unpeeling himself from Floyd's gangly embrace, Ziggy repeated his question. "What are you doing here?"

Floyd's mousy hair looked like a dandelion puff in the humidity. "I'm hugging you, Ziggy," he snorted as if Ziggy were dense. "And you're sunburned, but the way. You should really put on sunscreen. Frequent sunburn can cause skin cancer, premature aging, and skin lesions. If I had that much surface area on my scalp, I'd wear a hat every day."

Ziggy couldn't decide if he wanted to laugh or cry. "I bet you would."

"I sent your suitcase to your room." Pepper's commanding voice floated in from the front lobby into the dining room. "They said Ziggy was down at the beach. But my Portuguese isn't very—" She stopped dead in her tracks and her chinchilla eyes, sharp as ever, zeroed in on Ziggy.

Seeing Pepper in anything other than her trademark power suit and vibrant high heels was a pleasant surprise. But even in a sundress and sandals, she was the embodiment of a high-powered executive administrator—albeit a weary one.

"I told you I'd find him." Floyd's chest swelled with pride. He patted Ziggy's hairy arm, gripping it slightly as if he half-expected Ziggy to make a run for it.

"Hello, Pepper." Ziggy leaned back in his chair as if he'd never been more relaxed. "Didn't expect to see you here. Hope you brought your swimsuit."

Her expression was as thunderous as Ziggy had hoped. "Very funny," she said, striding over and setting her purse on the table. "You're well aware I had no choice but to track you down here. Why didn't you answer your phone?"

He tried not to squirm under her intense glare and feigned interest in a nearby pair of potted Bird of Paradise flowers. "It was disconnected," he replied, opting for a half-truth. Alexia Ito, the CEO of DipShip Incorporated, had cut off his phone service after firing him, and he hadn't bothered to reconnect it or get another phone. He told himself it was because he dreaded panicky phone calls from Pepper and Floyd, but his true fear was that they wouldn't care enough to call at all, so he'd dumped the phone in a trash can at the airport.

Pepper huffed. "Fine, where is it?" she demanded, holding out her hand. "Because I highly doubt it's hidden in those flowers you're staring at. Give it to me, and I'll reconnect it."

"It's gone."

"What do you mean, it's gone?"

A wave of heat crawled up Ziggy's neck. "I got rid of it."

Pepper looked as if she might breathe fire. "How did you expect me to get a hold of you without your phone? Carrier pigeon? Garbage gazer?"

"I didn't expect you to get a hold of me," Ziggy said, bracing himself for a tongue-lashing.

Pepper's fierce expression crumbled as the implications sank in. A brief silence hung in the air before she spoke, her voice tinged with regret. "I didn't know. I promise I didn't. Alexia never told me she was holding your husband's ashes for ransom."

At the mention of Gio, Ziggy's heart clenched. A salty ocean breeze blew through the dining room, tickling his sweaty neck, carrying a whisper of the soft, endless melody of Gio's memory. It wasn't heartache, just the memory of heartache. He looked at Pepper's limp curls and puffy eyes. She'd been worried about him enough to travel halfway across the world. Reaching out, he gripped her hand. "I know you didn't."

"I thought the contract between you was about paying off your GlutoBlock debt to Pill Depot." Pepper's eyes flooded with tears. "If I'd known she was forcing you to hunt serial killers to save something so precious, I would've..."

"I don't blame you," Ziggy assured her, swallowing past the lump of emotion lodged in his throat. "And you shouldn't blame yourself." Pepper was second-in-command to a soulless barracuda, but beneath her polished corporate exterior lay one of the most generous souls Ziggy had ever known.

"You should have told me," Pepper said.

"I should have," he agreed, releasing her hand. The tension level was unacceptable for the quaint dining room of a beach pousada. "It's good to see you again."

"You too."

Floyd's eyes scanned back and forth between them. "You seem upset," he said to Pepper. "I noticed when you started crying."

"I'm okay. Just tired." She rubbed the space between her eyes.

Floyd surged to his feet and grabbed a vacant chair from a nearby table. "Of course, you're tired," he said as Pepper sank into the seat. "You didn't sleep on the plane."

"We left DipShip on short notice." Pepper dabbed her eyes with a tissue from her purse. "I was too anxious to sleep."

"Your circadian rhythm is off because of the time change," Floyd said, returning to his seat across from Ziggy. "That's why I gave you a blackout sleep mask, a melatonin chewable, and noise-canceling headphones. Although, they should be called noise-reducing headphones, since there's no such thing as total noise cancelation. If you'd used them like I suggested, you wouldn't be so tired."

Pepper shot Ziggy a "please help or I'll kill him," look, so he cleared his throat. "How'd you find me this time?" he asked.

Floyd beamed. "It was easy. I tracked your flight. And once Pepper and I knew about the ashes, we went through Gio's records to find his home district. The Samurai gave us the rest."

"The Skidmore Samurai?" Ziggy asked as if there were miraculously more than one serial-killing Samurai in his circle of friends. An uneasy feeling crept through his veins. Not long ago, while on the brink of death, he'd made a blood oath with the head-hunting warrior. *A life for a life.* The Skidmore Samurai willingly joined DipShip's Super Serial team in exchange for the life of one of his greatest enemies—Alexia Ito. Ziggy wasn't sure what the Samurai expected him to do, but he knew he couldn't refuse without risking his head.

"He told us you'd be at Ipanema Beach because you promised to scatter Gio's ashes there," Floyd said. "I checked out dozens of hotels before realizing you likely skipped the big resorts and went for a smaller villa, which I guess is called a pousada here. I did a quick search for the place with the best pastries and found your reservation in a matter of minutes."

Just then, as if the universe had conspired to mock him, a server glided to their table, carrying a tray of Ziggy's favorite local pastries. Floyd's eyes flicked to the stack of delectable sweets. "Case in point."

Ziggy chuckled, his cheeks heating before taking a *bolinho de chuva*, which was basically a raindrop-shaped donut dusted with cinnamon and sugar.

"How did the Samurai know you'd be here?" Pepper asked, studying him closely. "Did you really tell a serial killer your travel plans?"

"Long story," Ziggy muttered, but the truth was he couldn't remember. At least not fully. He'd said a lot of things that night in the Skidmore Dump when he'd had one foot in the spirit world and nothing to lose. The Samurai had lurked in the dark, listening as Ziggy spilled his emotional guts, waiting to strike and spill Ziggy's actual guts.

In the end, they'd made an oath, and as their combined blood dripped into the trash, the Samurai had spared his life. Ziggy looked at the long puckered wound on his palm. It was healing, but he'd carry the scar forever. A jagged, fleshy symbol of a murderous promise he could never take back.

"Do we have time?" Floyd turned to Pepper.

Pepper blinked. "Time for what?"

"Ziggy said it was a long story. Do we have time to hear it? You told me before we left we had to act fast once we found him."

"There are some things we need to discuss first," Pepper said.

"What's going on?" Ziggy's gut knotted with fear, and for one terrible moment, he thought he'd forgotten to take his Gluto-Block. "It must be something pretty bad if you went to all this trouble just to talk to me."

Floyd nodded. "Oh, it's bad. Pepper said DipShip was a shit storm about to become a category-five shit hurricane."

Ziggy picked up a *sonho*, the closest thing in the area to a Boston Cream, and savored the sweet, creamy filling as he took a bite. The sweetness calmed him. "Seems like your story is more important than mine," he said.

"The Super Serial Preliminaries start soon," Pepper replied. "We need your help. Everything's been a disaster since you left. You have to come back." She buried her face in her hands and Floyd patted her shoulder, his wiry eyebrows pinching together.

"Come back?" Ziggy had known the request was coming, but it still landed like a punch to the nutsack. Alexia fired him less than two weeks ago, and they were already asking him to return to a life of corporate greed, ruthless CEOs, and homicidal maniacs.

"The killers we caught are becoming impossible to control. Even with added security," Floyd said.

Ziggy dropped his *sonho* on the plate and bit back a scoff. "They're serial killers. What did you think would happen?"

"I expected them to be difficult," Pepper said with a slight frown. "But more like the kind of difficult they were when you were in charge."

"I was never in charge." If being bribed by Alexia had taught him anything, it was that he was a flunky with zero power and even less control.

Floyd shrugged. "You were in charge of Pepper and me. Plus, the security guards and the killers. You have a way with them."

Ziggy let out a frustrated huff. "So what? Alexia wants me to come back and wrangle some misbehaving killers after she sent me packing? No thanks. I did my time in that snake's nest. Tell her to put on her big kid pants and use the kill-chip."

Pepper flushed, clenching the fabric of her dress. "There was an incident," she said after a moment.

Ziggy's eyebrow arched. "An incident?" He'd spent enough time at DipShip to know that their idea of "an incident" was usually a nightmare-fueled catastrophe.

"Actually, it's more like incidents," Floyd said, emphasizing the "s."

"Big Montana Ice killed the lead security guard before a team meeting," Pepper confessed with a grimace.

"Poor Joe," Ziggy murmured, but it wasn't really a surprise considering DipShip's lack of safety protocols.

"Not Joe," Floyd said. "It was a female guard. What was her name?"

"Jill, I think," Pepper replied. "Several other guards tried to help, but the situation was too out of hand. Alexia wouldn't trigger Big Montana Ice's kill-chip. She's unhinged."

"Big Montana Ice or Alexia?" Ziggy asked.

Pepper's lips pressed together. Her refusal to speak ill of her sociopathic boss was answer enough.

He rubbed his hand over his stubble. The first time he saw Big Montana Ice, she'd gifted him a severed head inside a cardboard box, asked him a bizarre, completely arbitrary question, and then beheaded the nearest security guard, Steve, with her bare hands. It wasn't a huge leap to assume she'd kill again. "Alexia would never sacrifice a killer to save a guard," he said. "Serial killers are an asset. She needs them to win a seat on the Associated Board of Corporate Directors. What about the integrated stun option? Did she even try to use it?"

"Stunning doesn't work on Big Montana Ice. She thinks everyone is in cahoots with Bazgoroch," Floyd said. "If they don't answer her questions right, she thinks they're possessed by the demon and fights through the pain."

"Don't the kill-chips also sedate? Did she try that?" Ziggy asked.

Pepper shook her head. "Big Montana Ice fights through that, too."

"It's actually very fascinating," Floyd said. "There have only been a few killers in Super Serial history who could fight through sedation. The combination of her obsessive focus and high pain tolerance creates an unusual transformation when she's sedated—she becomes a mindless, sleepwalking, killer zombie. District Mongaphalee requested data on her to try to resolve the issue before the Prelims."

"And now she knows no one will kill her when she attacks," Ziggy said. "If Alexia won't activate the kill-chip to save her own employee, it's like having a gun with no bullet."

"As if Alexia would give us guns," Pepper muttered.

Ziggy noticed the glazed look in her eyes, a clear sign she was reliving the trauma she'd experienced. He knew that feeling all too well. He'd seen Gio's murder a thousand times in his mind, and pulled the trigger on Red Judas, Gio's killer, a thousand times more.

"It's not just Big Montana Ice," Pepper sighed. "It's all the killers. Carol concocted some awful essential oil mix to help that did nothing but stink up the entire floor."

"It was horrible." Floyd's nose wrinkled at the memory. "Like lavender, rotten lettuce, and ammonia combined. It stung my eyes so bad I had to flush them with water for fifteen minutes."

"Lin Meihua is refusing to eat until you're brought back," Pepper went on, her breath a staccato of anxiety. "She's 105 years old. If she fasts for much longer, she'll die."

"She has tea with me almost every day," Floyd said, holding his finger in the air.

"Tea is not food."

Confused, Floyd countered. "Of course, it's not. That would be absurd. I was only pointing out that she's likely still hydrated. The human body can survive for months without food, but without liquids, she might not last a week. We should really…" Floyd trailed off, his eyes scanning the medley of dishes and desserts being brought out for dinner.

"Can we eat here?" He looked at the buffet with longing. "This food looks good, and the only thing I've had since we left DipShip is the terrible food on the plane. They gave us breakfast sausages with grilled tomatoes and a very dry and crumbly muffin. The entire plane smelled like sage and sweaty armpits."

"Go ahead," Ziggy said, and Floyd busied himself at the buffet.

Ziggy turned back to Pepper. "Apart from the hunger strike, what else is happening with our favorite murder of crows?"

"The Samurai does nothing but exercise and meditate in his cell," Pepper said, watching Floyd gather food. "Benedict's dogs have kennel cough, and the hired caretakers are too scared of getting mauled to treat them. The list goes on."

She slumped into her chair. She looked like a fading candle, barely burning on a stub of a wick. Ziggy had seen her tired before—they'd pulled all-nighters together trying to find DipShip's Super Serial team. But this was different. She was exhausted, body and soul.

"I didn't realize Alexia sent you on the red-eye," Ziggy said, and a shadow crossed over Pepper's face.

"She didn't. I paid for the trip here, out of my own pocket."

Ziggy scowled. "Alexia found money to pay off my debt, then turned around and tried to rehire me, but she drew the line at covering your travel expenses? That woman is utterly repulsive." He knew exactly how much the trip to Ipanema had cost Pepper. Probably most of her spare funds. A sense of familiar judgment smoldered inside him. Pepper's savings were a drop in an ocean of wealth for Alexia, but God forbid Alexia let anyone nibble at the corporate bottom line.

Pepper looked like Ziggy had punched her in the face. "Ziggy, do you think Floyd and I came all this way because Alexia wanted to hire you? We came because you're our friend and we need you. You belong with us."

Her emotional counter-strike hit him like a sledgehammer. "Oh," he murmured, realizing his folly. Years of self-loathing had made it difficult to imagine anyone wanting him around. "Does Alexia even know you're here?"

"She knows," Pepper said with a wince. "She agreed to let you come back, but not at her cost."

"*Let* me?"

"I didn't come for her," Pepper said. "I came for myself—and Floyd—and also for you. What if Big Montana Ice had targeted me instead of the guard? I can't stop imagining what Alexia's response would have been. Would she have let me die, too?"

Ziggy remained silent. Pepper already knew the answer. Alexia wasn't Pepper's friend any more than she was Jill's. In the ruthless world of corporatocracy, friends were expendable, but money and power were not.

From their first encounter, Ziggy had seen the cruelty lurking beneath Alexia's polished facade, but he kept his observations to himself around Pepper. She already carried the weight of Alexia's corruption and incompetence, and he didn't want to add to her burden.

"DipShip's failing, and Alexia doesn't care," Pepper said. "She's running the company into the ground for a shot at an ABCD seat, but she's more likely to catch the wind in a mesh net. You know our killers. Even on their best day, they can't win."

"And when they don't, Alexia will abandon DipShip just like she abandoned Jill," Ziggy said, his voice cracking with bitterness. "We're all expendable to her—assets, not people."

"We have to stop her, Ziggy." Pepper's dark eyes suddenly looked as regal as the Samurai's. DipShip was to Pepper as Skidmore was to the Samurai. It was more than just a district to her—it was her people, her home.

"What's your game plan?" he asked.

"Alexia's been painting herself as the sole financier of DipShip, but the sales documents tell a different story. Turns out, her father's investment holdings bankrolled the entire operation," Pepper said.

"Hirofumi Ito?" Ziggy asked, a dark sense of foreboding blooming in his chest. Prior to being plucked from his fugitive life of false identities and food comas, Ziggy had been forced into hiding by Hirofumi, CEO of Pill Depot, the most powerful corporation in the world. The mere mention of his name triggered Ziggy's fight-or-flight response. "If Hirofumi's involved, there's bound to be a bunch of shady backdoor deals."

Pepper nodded. "DipShip was basically handing out huge shipping discounts to Pill Depot and other companies in Hirofumi Ito's portfolio," she explained. "Seems like he had plans to use DipShip as a vertically integrated shipping platform."

"It was a strategic move, no doubt," Ziggy said, his mind shifting effortlessly back to his days as a marshal, analyzing corporate maneuvers with ease.

"I've been digging through their correspondence," Pepper said. "Hirofumi's furious with Alexia for using DipShip as collateral to fund the Super Serial entrance fees. If DipShip goes under, it could lead to major cost hikes that jeopardize his entire portfolio. I looked at the numbers, and Pill Depot shipments are decreasing every month. He's pulling his investments and siphoning money into other districts."

"Interesting," Ziggy said, rubbing his chin. "Why wouldn't he invest in Alexia, win her a spot on the ABCD, and double his family's influence on the board? With an odd number of board seats, you'd think having Alexia in his pocket would be a good strategy."

"I had the same thought," Pepper said. "But as soon as Alexia took ownership of DipShip, Hirofumi showed up in person, and I saw for myself the way he looked at her. I know it may seem like the usual rich family conflict—domineering parent versus defiant child—but I've seen it myself. Ziggy, he *despises* her. It's pure hatred. He treated her like she was some kind of vermin. He said he'd completely cut off support if she didn't quit Super Serial."

Ziggy's jaw tightened. "Hirofumi cares about money and power more than anything. Including family," he said bitterly. "He's the apex predator of the corporate world. He'd sooner sacrifice his own flesh and blood than risk his empire."

It was a chilling reminder of the ruthlessness that made Hirofumi Ito so terrifying. Ziggy had felt the weight of that ruthlessness firsthand on the day Hirofumi threatened his life. It wouldn't be worth it to challenge the seriousness of the threat.

He often wondered what Hirofumi thought about Ziggy's prior involvement with Alexia and DipShip. Being blackmailed by Alexia had left him no choice, but this time it would be different. Going back now would have nothing to do with extortion. He'd be openly and publicly defying Hirofumi.

"If we lose Hirofumi's business and DipShip tanks in the Prelims, we're screwed." She scrunched her nose, her resolve growing. "Our highest chance of survival is to lose in the Prelims but keep as many of our killers alive as possible."

The idea of being involved in Super Serial made Ziggy feel sick. It was nothing more than a gruesome spectacle fueled by the bloodlust of the mega-wealthy. The death penalty—with sponsors. Despite its sinister nature, Super Serial eclipsed the global popularity of soccer and cricket combined, captivating the insatiable public. An entire season was dedicated to cheering for favorite killers and teams, and Ziggy couldn't stand the hype.

Each year, corporate marshals hunted down society's worst criminals, but instead of delivering justice, they sentenced them to the games. Mega-corps paid exorbitant fees to take part in Super Serial, lured by the promise of fame, sponsorships, and outrageous prize money. This perpetuated a twisted cycle of murder for profit, all at the expense of their own citizens.

Pepper leaned forward, her voice dropping to a low tone, as if she didn't want her words to be overheard. "DipShip needs to create a sensation big enough to increase the market value of the killers, but not so big it puts a target on our backs. Alexia will be furious that we didn't try for the Championships, but it's better than the alternative."

"If the killers perform well in the Prelims," Ziggy said, envisioning the potential, "she could earn a pretty profit. Might take the sting off losing the ABCD seat."

"Exactly," Pepper agreed. "Some of the killers we captured already have the potential for a high return."

"Big Montana Ice?" Ziggy guessed.

Pepper nodded. "Her and the Samurai—if we can figure out how to market them. My hope is that she'll have no choice but to sell the killers on the open market in order to pay off DipShip's debts."

"That's walking on a razor's edge," Ziggy said. "Trying to deliberately lose without Alexia noticing the sabotage?"

"I convinced her that DipShip has a higher chance of making it to the Championships with you leading the team," Pepper said. "I know I'm playing her, but there's no other choice. Our real goal has nothing to do with her, but she can't know that." She swallowed, and Ziggy wondered if she felt ashamed for manipulating Alexia. He hoped not. Alexia certainly didn't lose any sleep over exploiting everyone else—including Pepper.

"What if none of the killers survive?" Ziggy asked. "The Prelims have hundreds of serial killers, thousands of criminals, and a million ways to die."

Pepper's confidence wavered, and she sank lower in her chair, a visible weight on her shoulders. "If we lose too many killers in the Prelims, or they survive but don't boost their market value enough, Alexia won't get her money back, and DipShip will be sold off in pieces."

"Divestiture?" Ziggy wished he could muster up some genuine shock.

"I'll lose everything," Pepper said, her expression turning somber. "All the work I've put into the district would be for nothing. And that's just the beginning. Hundreds of thousands of livelihoods, including ours, would be at risk. Jobs would be lost, families displaced, and sub-corps shattered. DipShip is the anchor for the entire district. Without it, everything will collapse."

Ziggy sat back in his chair, absorbing the gravity of her words. The stakes were higher than he ever imagined. DipShip wasn't just a mega-corporation—it was a lifeline for the people who lived there, and their futures hung precariously on the outcome of Super Serial. Even Sweet Sally's would be at risk if the landlord went bankrupt. He sighed—the last place he wanted to see go under was his favorite bakery.

"You're not walking on a razor's edge," Ziggy said. "You're dancing on it and praying you don't get sliced in two. Is DipShip worth saving? Is it worth that risk?"

Pepper's lips parted, but before she could speak, Floyd sat down at the table, holding two plates loaded with food. He slid one in front of Pepper.

"I didn't know what you wanted," he told her. "So, I guessed based on your eating patterns and past preferences. You're hungry, aren't you? You must be after such a long trip."

Pepper looked at Floyd. "Thank you," she murmured, picking up her fork, and Ziggy realized something had shifted between the two in the short time he'd been away. Floyd was the same as he'd always been, but there was a subtle softening in the way Pepper looked at him.

"I didn't get you any food, Ziggy," Floyd said through a mouthful of rice. "I could only hold two plates at once and you've already eaten some donuts."

"It's fine," Ziggy said, smirking at Pepper, who scowled. He motioned for a server and ordered a round of caipirinhas, a local favorite, then visited the buffet himself to give Pepper a chance to eat, returning to the table with a heaping plate.

"Say I do come back, and we somehow keep a few of our killers alive through the Prelims," Ziggy said, cutting into his steak. "Could Alexia still dismantle DipShip and sell it off?"

Pepper's hand froze on her fork, and he could see the very idea was making her stew. "It's possible."

"You want me to come back to work for a company that may be gone in a few weeks? That doesn't seem like a very smart move," Ziggy pointed out as he chewed.

"Because it's not," Floyd said, and Pepper nudged him in the ribs with her elbow. "You're already a famous marshal, and now you're out of debt. Plus, you have lots of GlutoBlock, which you're going to need if you plan to keep eating all that—Ouch, Pep! Why do you keep jabbing me?" he complained, scooting his chair closer to Ziggy's.

The drinks arrived, and Ziggy slid one across the table to Pepper and another to Floyd. Floyd lifted his glass to his face and sniffed the contents. "This smells like alcohol," he said. "I don't drink alcohol."

"You do today," Ziggy said, downing his drink. Pepper's was gone in two swallows. Floyd took a hesitant sip and grimaced, his face twisting as if he were swallowing poison, which, technically, he was.

"Another?" Ziggy asked, and Pepper finally cracked a smile.

Floyd coughed into his elbow. "Can I get some water?"

Pepper drummed her fingers on the table, her gaze fixed on Ziggy. "You asked me if DipShip was worth saving. It's a fair question. From the outside looking in, DipShip is a mess, but I've lived there my whole life."

Ziggy was taken aback. In a system designed to prop up the rich at the expense of the poor, it was rare to find someone who made their way to the top. It was yet another testament to Pepper's ingenuity and perseverance.

"My mother was a dreamer," Pepper said, her eyes softening with nostalgia. "She saved every dime from her job delivering goods for a sub-leased grocery store in the district. Eventually, she scraped together enough for a cheap lease and opened a bookstore—or at least tried to. In the end, it wound up being more like a library. The location was terrible, and the building was filthy, but she made it work."

"Seemed like every kid I knew found their way to that store," Pepper continued. "Some just wanted a quiet place to read. There's nowhere quiet in DipShip."

Ziggy murmured in agreement. It was true. The streets of DipShip were obnoxiously loud, even in the dead of night. That's why Ziggy found himself so often at Sweet Sally's. It was his eye in the swirling storm of toxic shit.

"But most of those kids came because they had nowhere else to go," Pepper said. "Nowhere they were wanted. Mom had a way of making everyone feel special. Many of the kids couldn't read, but she always took the time to teach if they wanted to learn. She taught more kids to read than the nearby schools, a blessing considering most families in our neighborhood couldn't afford to send their kids to school."

"DipShip employees work a shocking number of hours for very little pay," Floyd said.

"How can you afford school when putting food on the table is a struggle?" Pepper said, her eyes downcast. "Only white-collar workers from corporate sent their kids to school—and those kids moved away the moment they could.

"My mother gave the poor kids hope. Most of them ended up working at the loading docks for next to nothing anyway, but a few escaped DipShip. They wanted something better, and Mom gave them a stepping stone. When she died, hundreds of those kids rallied to save her store, but DipShip sold the lease to a sub-corp that wanted it for storage. We couldn't compete."

A surge of anger and helplessness washed over Ziggy. Mega-corps feasted on money and power, and the bigger they got, the more people shriveled and died in their shadows.

"I started off as an unpaid intern at DipShip," Pepper said. "It took everything I had to get to where I am today. But I did it because I believe in the people. They pull together when it matters, and they need someone at the helm who sees them as more than just a faceless commodity."

Ziggy met her gaze. "The corporation isn't worth saving, but the people are. I get it, Pepper. Truly, I do. But let me make sure I understand this. If I come back, and against all odds, we manage to keep even a few killers alive, we could save DipShip?"

"Correct," Pepper said.

"You realize these odds are slimmer than a wax cat's chance in hell, right?"

"We have to try."

"What's in it for me?" Ziggy asked, feigning churlishness.

"Well, DipShip would pay for your room and board," Pepper began, pausing when she saw Ziggy's smirk. "All right, fine. It doesn't directly benefit you," she admitted. "Sure, you could keep your job, but I know that's not enough of a reason."

Ziggy's throat tightened with a mix of emotions.

"I need you to do it because you're my friend," Pepper said. "Please, Ziggy."

He'd made his decision the moment he saw Pepper and Floyd, but hearing those words warmed him to the toes. Working with his friends had given him a sense of connection and purpose, which is exactly what Gio had wanted for him. For three years, Ziggy had been alive but not living, heart beating but soul empty, surviving, but with no purpose. No matter how many tantrums Alexia threw or threats Hirofumi made to stop him, he'd never abandon Pepper or Floyd if they needed him.

Out of habit, Ziggy waited for Gio's ghost to materialize and tease him or call him out on his bullshit, but the air was still. It had been from the moment Ziggy's shoes touched the Ipanema sand. Spreading Gio's ashes wasn't about releasing his grief. He would live with the blinding pain of that loss until his last miserable breath. It was about giving himself permission to exist in a world where Gio wasn't. It was time to go home. And the only home Ziggy had left was with Pepper and Floyd.

The soft melodic sound of a guitar playing "The Girl from Ipanema" floated on the breeze up from the beach and prickled Ziggy's ears. The song played often at the pousada, its familiar melody humming through the air. But this time, as he listened, something shifted within him, and his stony heart cracked wide open.

"Okay," he said, breaking the silence. "I'll come back."

Pepper flashed a bright smile, and Floyd couldn't contain his excitement, enthusiastically pumping his fist. "I knew it!"

Ziggy helped himself to another pastry. "I'd rather die than let Sweet Sally's go out of business."

Chapter 2

Flan the Road Again

DipShip's conference room was the corporate equivalent of prison toilet wine—smelly, unpleasant, and only slightly better than sobriety. The carpet, a nauseating swirl of hot pink and lime green, somehow looked both flamboyant and bleak. An overhead fluorescent light flickered, adding to the overall dystopian feel. Ziggy breathed in the familiar stale air. It was good to be home.

The night before had been a practice in jet lag and pizza-fueled anxiety dreams. As dawn broke, Ziggy surrendered to insomnia, spending the early morning hours scrolling through Super Serial competitor profiles from the other districts. The more profiles he looked at, the more screwed they became. Rival teams boasted deadly assassins, weapons experts, and ruthless executioners. DipShip's roster included a sanctimonious mother-of-six, a poison-slinging granny, a delusional juggernaut, a skeevy cockroach and his pack of stubby-legged mutts, and a Samurai nursing a revenge boner.

Compared to the other teams, they were careening down the pathway to destruction in a clown car on a road paved with banana peels and blood.

Arriving at the conference room, Ziggy found himself alone, greeted by a pink box, unmistakably from Sweet Sally's at the center of the table. Lifting the lid, he found the words, "Welcome Back, Ziggy!" written in Pepper's feminine scrawl. Of course, she'd beaten everyone else there.

He helped himself to a couple of Florentine cannolis and Boston creams before grabbing a cup of coffee and taking his usual place at the head of the conference room table. Fishing a bottle of Gluto-Block from his pocket, he downed two pills before even thinking about touching the pastries. Without GlutoBlock, he'd be hauling his gluten-battered colon out of the nearby bathroom in a blood-soaked sack. Gluten shredded his insides, and even though GlutoBlock was outrageously expensive, Ziggy couldn't imagine life without it.

He couldn't help but let out a satisfied sigh as he sank his teeth into the cannoli, savoring the creamy filling and the sweet crunch of the pastry. It had been weeks since he'd had Sweet Sally's, and it tasted even better than he remembered. He'd lost count of how many grief donuts he'd scarfed down, seeking comfort in their sugary goodness. But as time passed and he started to heal, something shifted. The experience transformed from a sugar-filled dopamine hit that helped him survive minute-to-minute to a genuine love for the amazing confections. Maybe now they were more like "cautiously optimistic" donuts.

"That won't work, Alan, and you know it!" Pepper stormed into the room like a disgruntled war general in a losing battle. She tossed a distracted wave in Ziggy's general direction before refocusing on her phone. "I understand that four security guards are enough for other districts, but other districts don't have a six-foot-eight gargantuan serial killer with superhuman strength." Pepper glanced upward at the ceiling as if silently praying not to turn into a serial killer herself, starting with poor Alan, whoever he was. "Well, if Alexia wanted to make the decision herself, she wouldn't have made it my responsibility.

"Look, if we have to kill Big Montana Ice, we can't replace her, and we'll get kicked out of the games. She's already killed three people, and it's not like we can afford the risk. Make it happen, or Alexia will have us both scrubbing latrines in the shipyard." Pepper ended the call, but looked like she might chuck her phone at the wall.

"Good morning," Ziggy said, and Pepper took a long, controlled breath, her cheeks puffing out on the exhale. He couldn't stop himself from grinning, and Pepper responded with an eye roll.

"Alan's the new security coordinator. And he's a real piece of work holed up in his office like a sweaty badger, crunching numbers on spreadsheets instead of actually observing the killers in person," Pepper said with a sour look on her face.

Ziggy chuckled. "Like someone who reads books about basketball but can't dribble worth a damn?"

"Exactly! I'm pretty sure he stole one of your Boston creams, too,"

"Unforgivable," Ziggy said with an indignant sniff.

"Fucking Alan."

During the plane ride home, Ziggy, Pepper, and Floyd hashed out their game plan for the Prelims, attempting the near-impossible feat of covering every angle. Ziggy quickly realized that managing a Super Serial team was like juggling flaming chainsaws while blindfolded. They had five killers to prepare for battle, each representing a different annual category, and to make it through the Prelims alive, they'd need to be top of the line...which was a problem because they were far from top of the line. More like ten feet below the line under a moldy rug everyone forgot about. But they were still murderers, and even a shitty killer could cut your throat when you weren't looking. They just had to convince the world the DipShip killers were worth a second look.

Carol Petersen, their Angry White Women killer, usually cooperated, but she had a strong obsession with Jesus and adamantly claimed innocence for any crimes. Delusion was her middle name, making it highly unlikely she'd ever touch a weapon, even if her life depended on it. Benedict Bork, the killer of the Pet Lover's category, was the biggest pantywaste on the planet, but at least his twenty-eight corgis were decent killers. Big Montana Ice, their resident Leo, was volatile, unpredictable, and prone to ripping the head off of anyone who didn't agree with her—literally. Lin Meihua, the Centennial killer, was a hundred and five years old; although she was adept with poisons, she was also too ancient to do much more than fart and fall asleep. Their Vigilante, the Skidmore Samurai, was as badass in battle as they come, but even he couldn't survive an arena full of serial killers on his own.

By Super Serial standards, the DipShip killers weren't even worth the energy it took to arrest them. It was like journeying through a haunted swamp, hoping that on the other side was the land of milk and honey. They were the underdog's underdog. But Ziggy's love for Pepper outweighed his hatred for the games. She had a vision for District DipShip, and with her leading the charge, he might be able to muster enough belief in the future to bother living in it.

Floyd arrived just as Pepper settled into her seat. Today he was sporting an orange shirt that read, "Facts don't care about your feelings." He pulled out his tablet from his backpack and connected it to the smartboard on the wall. "We have a lot to do today," he said, slightly out of breath. "Morning, Pep." He rocked back and forth on the heels of his shoes, oblivious to Pepper's answering smile. "Is everyone coming today? All the killers?"

"Yes," Pepper confirmed. "But first, Alexia's bringing in the publicist she hired. He wants to familiarize himself with each killer and decide how to present them to the public. Tomorrow, we'll discuss the strategy ideas we developed for the Prelims with the killers, and the next day is the analyst interviews."

"That's a terrible idea," Ziggy said.

"Which part?" Pepper asked, her fingers flying over her phone. "The press interviews, the publicist, or the room full of serial killers?"

"Take your pick." He could feel a headache creeping in already. "We're bringing in a pack of dangerous murderers, and I don't even have access to their kill-chips."

"I asked Alexia again, but she shot me down," Pepper said with a sigh. "She's the only one with access."

His jaw clenched. Alexia was a vile human being, willing to let them all die to protect her interests. In his book, she was as much of a psycho as any of their killers, and if she had picked the publicist, he doubted they'd be any better. "Why do we need a publicist?"

Pepper arched an eyebrow. "You're the celebrity marshal here. Don't you see the value in shaping public perception? A little positive press can go a long way in boosting our image."

Ziggy grunted, his cynicism prickling like a fresh insult. Being labeled a "celebrity marshal" grated his nerves like sandpaper on skin. The title felt hollow, a cruel irony in the wake of his ruined life. Celebrity his pickled ass cheek. The only thing he was celebrated for was executing the monster who killed his husband.

Gio, once dazzled by the idea of being the hero marshal who caught Red Judas, the worst serial killer of their generation, ended up kidnapped and tortured by Judas himself. And Ziggy, consumed by grief and fueled by vengeance, had hunted Judas for three relentless years. But when the moment came, he hadn't sentenced him to Super Serial like everyone expected. He'd put a bullet through his skull.

That act of retribution, the catalyst for Hirofumi's intense hatred, also became the reason behind Ziggy's quiet disappearance from the world. Not only had Ziggy already owed Pill Depot an enormous sum of money, he'd snubbed them further by executing a serial killer worth millions, if not billions, in product endorsements and sponsorships.

The only positive press for Ziggy was no press at all. Alexia had settled his Pill Depot debt as part of their initial agreement, but Hirofumi's animosity ran deep. Ziggy hoped his ire had faded over the years, but it would be foolish to draw attention to himself.

Pepper tapped on the thick transparent partition that cut through the room and over the conference table. "Mr. D'Chango should be perfectly safe. The barrier we installed before you left for Ipanema has been helpful. It separates us from the killers. Besides, it's not like we can talk strategy without them."

"D'Chango?" Ziggy repeated, dread pooling in his gut. Even the name sounded pretentious.

"Alexia hired Boomer D'Chango," Pepper said as if Ziggy would recognize the name. "He's an up-and-comer with a background in fashion. The D'Changos and the Itos are close family friends."

"He could be close family friends with Jesus and still not be safe if the killers rushed the partition."

"That's why we removed the chairs," Pepper said. "Alexia tried to bring in a publicist before, but Big Montana Ice chucked one at the wall and the publicist quit on the spot."

"Smart," Ziggy quipped.

"The partition isn't necessary if you're friends with the serial killers," Floyd said, absently rubbing his stomach. "I'm having some indigestion," he added when he noticed Ziggy watching.

"Maybe one of your serial killer best friends poisoned you," Ziggy joked.

Floyd looked puzzled. "Why would anyone poison me? And you're my best friend, Ziggy. Everyone knows that."

Internally, Ziggy glitched. The notion of having a best friend was alien to him. Besides Gio, he'd never really considered anyone else occupying that sacred space. But thinking back on the past few months, Ziggy realized he couldn't even count all the times

Floyd had been there—saving his hide, coming up with solutions to impossible problems, and even cheering him up when he was an ornery asshat. Floyd drove him up the wall and down the gutters, but there was definitely a bond between them. In the most unexpected way, Floyd actually had become his best friend. It was a surprising realization that must've crept up when he wasn't paying attention.

The door swung open, revealing Alexia arm in arm with a man who could only be Boomer D'Chango. Boomer was thin and wiry, with a broad face and hooded eyes smothered in black liner that swept up into his temples, giving him the look of an angry wasp. He was wearing a long sweater with billowing sleeves and a geographic print under black overall shorts, topped with sparkly thigh-high boots.

Fuck-a-duck. This was going to be a disaster. And not the usual DipShip disaster they were all used to. This was the kind of disaster that made Ziggy feel like he was staring down the barrel of a sawed-off shotgun.

Pepper shot to her feet, a confident smile brightening her face. "Welcome to DipShip, Mr. D'Chango—" she began, but Alexia cut her off with a flick of her wrist.

"This is our little team." Alexia gestured toward the group, her glossy black hair cascading over one shoulder. "I know they're not much to look at," she added, directing her words to Boomer as if the rest of them couldn't hear, "but I'm sure you can come up with something. Pepper?" Alexia's command cut through the air like a jarring screech from microphone feedback. "Coffee."

Pepper flushed, hurrying to pull out chairs and prepare coffee. Anger bubbled up within Ziggy as he watched Pepper droop under the weight of Alexia's condescension. She wouldn't have a business to ruin if it weren't for Pepper. He shot Alexia a glare burning with intense hostility. Just when he thought she couldn't stoop any lower, she found a way to prove him wrong.

Boomer, however, was taking in everything and everyone. His eyes roamed over Ziggy's bald head and paunchy middle. "Don't worry," he assured Alexia. "We can make this work. Boomer D'Chango is here."

Alexia clapped her hands, her rings and bracelets jangling together. "We are so lucky to have you!" she gushed.

"Who could resist the irresistible Alexia Ito?" Boomer preened, smoothing his wavy, dark hair, so perfectly coiffed Ziggy was sure it was a wig.

"You're the one who's irresistible!" Alexia cooed, and Ziggy stared at the ceiling, trying to tune out the rest of the compliment circle-jerk as they gossiped about their families and mutual friends.

"You must be Ziglar Ghostshade," Boomer said after a moment, and Ziggy grunted in acknowledgment.

"He likes to be called Ziggy," Floyd added, even though no one asked.

Boomer whipped out a pair of ridiculously tiny wire-rimmed glasses from his pocket and perched them on the tip of his nose to peer at Ziggy. "This is an obvious boon," he told Alexia after a moment. "Having Ziglar Ghostshade managing your team will give you a huge edge with the media. Especially once we clean him up a little. The public adores him, and they'll assume his return is a testament to your exceptionalism."

Ziggy was stunned, unable to decide which thought was more absurd—him believing Alexia was extraordinary, or him going anywhere near the media.

Alexia's cherry red lips curved into a silky smile. "Ziggy and I go way back," she lied, fiddling with a button on her shirt. "I was truly grateful when he said he wanted to come out of retirement to help build my team."

Boomer squinted as he studied Ziggy. "Well, the public does love a good comeback story."

A loud wheezing snort echoed through the room, followed by a smack as Floyd slapped his hand over his mouth, attempting, and failing, to stifle his laughter. Ziggy glanced at him, smirking in response. They both knew Alexia had blackmailed him into hunting killers for DipShip. Describing that as a comeback story would be like calling a sinking ship a glamorous cruise liner.

"Security's en route with the killers," Pepper said. To the untrained ear, she sounded composed, but Ziggy caught a subtle tinge of panic. Anything Floyd blurted out could cause trouble, and the stakes were higher for her than anyone. He made a mental note to play nice with Alexia and whatever fools she dragged into the mix—for Pepper's sake.

"About time," Alexia muttered, sipping her coffee and inspecting her flawless manicure.

"Sorry for the delay, Ms. Ito," Pepper said. "Security had some trouble waking up Meihua. Seems she had a cup of tea late last night and didn't sleep well."

"That's possible," Floyd said, "if the tea was caffeinated."

"Or maybe it's because she's a thousand years old," Boomer said, earning a giggle from Alexia. Ziggy inwardly cringed at the sound, which seemed so out-of-place coming from her—like a snake attempting a melodic tune instead of its usual hiss.

"Actually, Meihua is a hundred and five," Floyd corrected, prompting even more laughter from Alexia and Boomer, who huddled together, whispering behind their hands like snobby teenagers from the ritzy private schools near the Pill Depot city center.

Boomer perked up, eyeing Pepper near the door. "What's her role here?" he asked. "She could be attractive with the right style."

"She's my assistant," Alexia said.

"Executive administrator," Floyd interjected. Loudly.

Alexia's almond-shaped eyes narrowed into slits. "Excuse me?"

"Pepper's an executive administrator," Floyd repeated, oblivious to the mounting tension in the room. "You called her your assistant, but that's inaccurate."

A palpable silence hung in the air. "My mistake," Alexia replied with a saccharine smile, her tone glacial.

Pepper froze momentarily, but Ziggy noticed her gaze flickered toward Floyd, not Alexia. Suddenly, there was a sharp knock on the door, and Pepper opened it to a gaggle of security guards escorting the serial killers into place on the other side of the partition. Each killer wore a tan jumpsuit, but Big Montana Ice was in chains, with a short leash attached to her neck and a mesh spit hood covering her face.

"Ziggy!" she cried when she spotted him, straining against her restraints as she rushed toward the partition, pounding her massive fists against its surface. Alexia jumped, and Boomer gasped in shock. Big Montana Ice stood at a towering six-foot-eight and weighed a solid three hundred and fifty pounds.

"Hello," Ziggy said with a nod, feeling like a child at the zoo, watching the rhino exhibit. It was hard for him to digest the notion that a serial killer was genuinely thrilled to see him. They were probably more comfortable with someone familiar leading the team, but it felt a bit like saying he and Red Judas were "work associates."

Big Montana Ice gave up her attempt to break through the wall. "Thank the Goddess, you're back! I thought we were fucked up the turd pipe," she exclaimed. "Not one of these jabronis has a plan." She smoothed the frayed denim vest over her jumpsuit. While it was hard to see under the hood, Ziggy knew Big Montana Ice had ratted auburn hair in a mullet, greasy skin, and bushy caterpillar eyebrows framing her hooded eyes, giving her a permanent scowl.

"Try to breach the barrier again, and I'll have to restrain you," a burly security guard with a buzz cut warned sternly.

Big Montana Ice leered with a mouthful of yellow-stained teeth, lobbing her thumb at the officer. "That one's a smoke show, but between you and me, he needs to get railed," she whisper-yelled to Ziggy. "He's got a pole so far up his chimney I'm surprised he ain't breathing smoke."

Carol Petersen, standing nearby, gave a prim, disapproving sniff before waving in greeting. "Marshal Ghostshade," she said, batting her fake, bat-wing lashes. "I prayed every night for your return, and the Lord answered. He knew you were the only one who could grant me my freedom. The Bible says, 'Ask and ye shall receive, knock, and it shall be opened unto you.'" Her chin-length blonde hair was especially poofy today.

"Not this again," Big Montana Ice groaned. "Jesus this, God that. This one's probably humping the Bible under her covers."

Carol's small face screwed up. "Your crude words will never shake my faith."

"I don't want to shake your faith, Lil Biscuit," Big Montana Ice said with a wink. "Just your legs."

"Stop calling me Lil Biscuit! Heathen!"

"Crotch noob!"

"Harlot!"

Boomer burst out laughing. "We've got to get these two in an interview," he told Alexia. "They'd go viral in an instant."

"Good to have you back, Ziggy," Benedict's frail voice croaked, his neck ensconced in a bulky, white brace a result of playing bait in a sting operation to capture UltraChad. The failed ploy had left him with severe strangulation injuries and two black eyes, making him look even more pathetic than usual. His wounds were healing, the mottled purple fading to yellow patches. Benedict had nearly died in the process, but it all went to hell when District Taste-E Chicken stole UltraChad and recruited him to their Super Serial team. Sniffling, Benedict adjusted his thick glasses, sweat staining his armpits. If it weren't for the fact that Benedict was also a serial killer, Ziggy would almost feel sorry for him. Almost.

Floyd scooted closer to the partition when Lin Meihua, their Centennial killer, motioned for him. Meihua spoke in hushed tones, gesturing slowly with her veiny, wrinkled hand.

"Meihua's glad you're back to protect me," Floyd translated, and Ziggy waved in her direction.

"Nice man." She gave Ziggy a thumbs up. Besides a few English phrases and the occasional Mandarin word Floyd tried to teach them, Floyd was the only team member who could communicate with Meihua. She was a Super Serial icon, and Floyd was the most knowledgeable Super Serial fanatic Ziggy had ever known. He spent hours drinking tea and playing mahjong in Meihua's cell, listening to her tales from the early competitions. It was a bizarre friendship that both Ziggy and Pepper disapproved of, but Floyd argued that despite being a killer, Meihua was a good person at heart, and her experiences could give them an edge.

"She also mentioned you should have worn more sunscreen at the beach," Floyd added, flashing an "I told you so" grin.

"Lavender oil's great for sunburn," Carol chimed in. "Peppermint and Melaleuca work wonders, too."

"You've returned with honor, Ziglar Ghostshade," the Samurai said in the deep, hypnotic timbre that replayed in his nightmares. "No longer running from your oaths."

Ziggy's tongue turned to ash in his mouth, so he settled for a nod, a bone-chilling shiver skittering down his spine. *A life for a life.*

The Samurai stood so motionless he could've passed for a cardboard cut-out, scarred hands resting at his sides.

"He's sly, that one," Big Montana Ice said with a thick-lipped grin. "Like a scrappy little bullet lizard. I thought he might be the demon at first, but don't worry, Ziggy. He passed the test. More than once."

The reunion felt surreal, surrounded by a bunch of serial killers who, despite their heinous deeds, treated him like one of the gang. Ziggy had dived straight back into the blurry space between buddy-buddy and murderous criminal territory, but this time, he couldn't blame bribery. He'd come with his eyes wide open.

His thoughts drifted to the chilling encounters he'd already had with his "friends." Big Montana Ice's brutal takedown of four guards, tearing off one's head with her bare hands. Lin Meihua's lethal poisons killed a man without her even laying a finger on him. And the Samurai, sparing his life for reasons Ziggy couldn't even begin to understand.

In this twisted world of death and dubious morality, he's somehow stumbled upon a weird sense of belonging. Maybe it was because he'd spent so much time navigating the polluted waters of the corporatocracy that he could recognize the light for what it really was—a complete and total sham. Mega-corps looked like charming secret gardens, but the flowers bloomed from graves.

Alexia and Boomer approached the partition to get a better look at the killers. Boomer's manicured fingers danced across his tablet at lightning speed, jotting down notes and observations. He peered up at Big Montana Ice.

"Which category is this"—Boomer craned his neck to study her—"person assigned to again?"

"Leos," Pepper replied from behind Alexia. "The Zodiac sign from western astrology."

"Good Lord, how tall is she?" Boomer exclaimed, clearly feeling secure enough behind the barrier to sling insults at seasoned murderers. "I'm going to need a metric fuck-ton of fabric." Alexia stifled a laugh behind her hand.

Big Montana Ice's expression changed from mild to murderous in an instant. She leaned forward until she was at eye level with Boomer. "I've got a question for you," she snarled, her breath fogging the glass. The security guard yanked on her leash, but she didn't budge. "If a cloud takes a dip in a cup of tea, how many raindrops can it juggle?"

Boomer let out a nervous laugh, stepping backward so quickly he nearly collided with Alexia. "Uh, what?"

Ziggy surged to his feet. "No questions," he barked. "She'll get plenty in the analyst interviews." If Boomer answered incorrectly, Big Montana Ice would stop at nothing to kill him...which was likely because she was the one to decide if the answer was correct, and Boomer seemed to have made her shit list in record time.

"How'd you catch her?" Boomer asked Ziggy.

"She responded to an online ad we put out in search of killers," he replied, barely masking his grimace. "She came in voluntarily."

"Voluntarily?" Boomer blinked confidently over his spectacles, but Ziggy saw him swallow and wondered if he was more afraid than he let on.

"I came to DipShip to slay the shadow demon," Big Montana Ice glared at Boomer as if Bazgoroch might rip through his sweater at any moment and tromp around the room in his sparkly boots. "It can take any form, popping up when you least expect it," she growled. "Maybe even here in this room."

One corner of Boomer's mouth twitched as he looked at Alexia. "There's potential here. Maybe we could spin her as a wild warrior or a Viking berserker of sorts. What's her preferred method of killing?"

"My bare hands," Big Montana Ice snarled before anyone else chimed in. "The ancient Goddess Amriel made me a protector, armed with the power of Alaskan Thunder. No need for weapons to slaughter a demon."

Ziggy made a mental note to keep an eye on Boomer whenever Big Montana Ice was nearby. "Let's move on," he ordered. *Before things took a violent turn.* Alexia glowered at him as if he were a lowly peasant daring to make a demand in the queen's presence.

"What's the deal with this guy?" Boomer sidled around the table until he stood in front of the Samurai, who hadn't budged an inch except for his eyes, which were fixed on Alexia. Boomer could evaporate into thin air, and Ziggy doubted the Samurai would even notice.

"This is"—Pepper glanced at Ziggy—"well, we call him the Samurai."

"The Samurai?" Boomer arched an eyebrow. "He doesn't look like a samurai. More like a boring, middle-aged, run-of-the-mill dude."

"Obviously, he doesn't look like a samurai," Floyd said with a snort. "He's not wearing his *yoroi*. Did you think they slept in their armor?"

"He's our Vigilante killer," Pepper said, bypassing Floyd's comment. "We arrested him in the Skidmore Dumping District."

Boomer's eyebrow shot up. "What was he doing there? Throwing banana peels and lighting bags of dog shit on fire?"

"He was beheading corrupt CEOs and corporate board members with a homemade sword he made from rebar and a mezzaluna," Ziggy said, just to melt the smug look off Alexia's face.

It worked. Alexia scowled, absentmindedly sliding her palms down the sides of her black pencil skirt, studiously ignoring the Samurai. "This one's the killer for the Pet Lovers category," she said, nudging Boomer with her elbow and gesturing to Benedict.

Benedict shuffled back and forth on his feet, and Ziggy could tell his eyes would be glued to the ground if not for his neck brace. His brown polo shirt was soaked through with sweat.

"You've got to be kidding me," Boomer said as he scrutinized Benedict.

"This is Benedict Bork," Pepper said, sounding sorry about it. "He has twenty-eight dogs housed in a separate facility."

"Vicious dogs might be a decent angle," Boomer considered, rubbing his chin. "Even if the killer's a bit lackluster. What breed are they?"

"They're corgis," Pepper replied.

"Corgis?" Boomer repeated as if the idea were so ridiculous he must have misunderstood. "As in, those fluffy little dogs with the perky ears?"

"That's correct."

"Size doesn't always mean strength," Floyd said. "Corgis were bred to herd cattle, thanks to their muscular bodies and low centers of gravity."

"This one will be a nightmare," Boomer said to Alexia, his shrewd eyes watching Benedict's every move. "Too pathetic to pull off the wolf in sheep's clothing act and too unattractive to be the right kind of creepy. A total train wreck," he said, and Benedict broke into a hailstorm of snotty tears that dripped onto the cuff of his neck brace.

Boomer sighed before turning his attention to Carol. "Now, this is something I can work with," he said, eyeing her up and down. Carol beamed.

"She's relatively young and in decent shape," Boomer said. "With a makeover, we could spin her as our district sex symbol."

Carol's jaw dropped.

"Marshal Edwards captured Carol Petersen before he was murdered, and Ziggy took over as marshal," Pepper explained. "She's the killer for the Angry White Women category."

"Overworked, sexually repressed mommy finally snaps and goes on a killing spree," Boomer said to Alexia, nodding approvingly. "The press will eat it up."

Alexia looked down the length of her nose at Carol. "She needs a major overhaul if you're going to pull that off. Right now, she looks more like a backwoods librarian than a sex symbol."

"Excuse me," Carol straightened her spine. "I don't appreciate what you're implying about me. First off, I didn't snap. I'd never hurt a soul."

Boomer grinned. "Sure you wouldn't."

"Second," Carol pressed on, glancing at Boomer, "I don't think it's fair we have to take fashion advice from this"—she lifted her chin into the air—"*person,* when I'm not even sure if they're a man or a woman."

Boomer burst out laughing. "She's perfect. Ignorant, conservative, and wound tighter than a drum. It's like she stepped out of the 2030s in a time machine. Women will hate her, and men will drool over her. It's foolproof."

"We'll have to tread carefully, or it might come off as objectifying," Alexia said.

"Once we're done, they'll be convinced she chose it." Boomer's brown eyes glittered with excitement. "Then it'll be empowering. Especially with the rumors her husband was cheating on her."

"How dare you?" Carol's face twisted in anger. "My marriage is sacred in the eyes of God, something someone like you would never understand. Jeff is my eternal companion. To suggest that he would do anything to hurt me is pure evil." She peered around Alexia until she could see Ziggy. "Aren't you going to say anything? You're the one in charge here."

"I most certainly am *not* in charge," he said before Alexia could shoot him dead with daggers from her eyes.

"How could you let them treat me so horribly?" Carol spluttered. "I need to find a space where the Holy Spirit can dwell." Unzipping her fanny pack, she pulled out a bottle of essential oil. She put two drops into her palms, rubbed them together, and took a deep breath. "I release these lower vibrations," she murmured, turning her back on Boomer. "I accept only what serves to inspire and enlighten."

Boomer's eyes lit up with mirth. "She just gets better and better."

"Last on the list is Lin Meihua," Pepper said, seeing they weren't getting anywhere with Carol. "Lin Meihua is our Centennial killer. DipShip purchased her at a labor auction in District Yifu after Floyd recognized her from past Super Serial games." Floyd beamed proudly as if presenting Alexia and Boomer with a rare and precious gem.

"This one's a wash," Boomer shrugged, looking over Meihua's papery skin and milky eyes. "It'll be a miracle if she makes it five minutes into the Prelims. She can barely stay upright."

"Should I translate that?" Floyd asked. "Because it wasn't very kind, and it might hurt Meihua's feelings. She's actually a really excellent killer."

"Bùyòng fānyì. Cóng tā de biǎoqíng wǒ míngbái tā de yìsi," Meihua said, her voice a barely audible crackle.

"Wǒ wèi tā de bù zūnzhòng ér dàoqiàn," Floyd said, and Meihua huffed in response.

Boomer sauntered closer to the conference table to view the team as a whole. "The bad news? They're terrible," he declared, and Alexia glowered at Ziggy as if he were responsible for the D-minus quality of their serial killers.

"I knew it," she muttered under her breath.

"On the bright side, they're original," Boomer said. "No killer clowns or hockey masks here. So passé. Last I checked, there were already like five psychotic clowns registered for the Prelims."

Benedict whimpered. "Psychotic clowns?"

"I can salvage something with the giant, the ninja, and the sexy mom," Boomer continued, reading off his tablet, "but the creep with the corgis and the mummified corpse? They're a lost cause. He looks like a sweaty weasel, and she's like a squashed leather shoe with eyeballs."

"That's not very nice," Floyd said, his brows furrowing in concern. Pepper gripped her tablet, bending a little at the knees as if she might faint.

"You want me to be nice to the serial killers?" Boomer shot Floyd an incredulous look. "You're worried about hurting their feelings? They've killed hundreds of people. Maybe thousands. Get real."

"We'll discuss the details in my office," Alexia said, smoothly looping her arm through Boomer's. "Pepper," she called over her shoulder as they strolled away in a cloud of security guards. "Lunch. Now."

"Right away, Ms. Ito," Pepper answered as the door closed in her face.

Chapter 3

Show Me the Whey

The team was back in the conference room early the next morning, thankfully, this time without Alexia and Boomer. Floyd stood at the smartboard, tablet in hand, projecting the ominous Super Serial logo—a hollow-eyed skull above a shield adorned with two ornate Ss and a pointed dagger at the center. A sense of foreboding wormed through Ziggy. Failure would mean death for more than half the people in the room. Success might keep DipShip afloat, but they were sailing through an never-ending ocean of bloodlust and greed.

Serial killers who murdered innocent people were given death sentences by society—the very society that romanticized homicide and glamorized bloodshed. This never-ending cycle only bred more killers, who took more lives, tithing a system that made being a serial killer better than being poor.

"Good morning, Team DipShip!" Floyd said, flashing his trademark toothy grin. "Today, we'll be diving into strategies for the Preliminaries."

Ziggy had decided to let Floyd take the lead in the meeting. There was no use in him being the harbinger of doom. He'd already played that role when he'd handed out their sentences. Floyd was a huge Super Serial fan, and practically a walking encyclopedia of the games. Plus, his enthusiasm was infectious, spreading through the team like warm syrup on a hot pancake.

Pulling up a long list on the screen, Floyd squinted at the minuscule font. "Let's start by reviewing the rules. There are lots."

Big Montana Ice let out a groan, her handcuffs clattering against the table. She slouched in one of the ridiculous inflatable chairs Pepper had insisted on before the killers arrived, a guard at each shoulder.

"No one can stand for that long and still stay focused," Pepper had reasoned with Ziggy before bringing in the seats. "We'll just have to pray they don't deflate before the meeting's over."

"If you're looking for someone to pray," Ziggy had teased, "I can ask Carol."

"Ask Carol," Pepper had sighed, "and Big Montana Ice will probably chuck her at the wall instead."

Big Montana Ice moaned, the chair squeaking beneath her weight. "I hate rules."

"It won't take long," Pepper said. "Most of the rules are for me, Ziggy, and Floyd."

"Serial killers aren't really known for their rule-following," Floyd chimed in, sporting a cheery salmon-colored shirt that read, "I've got my ION you."

"Damn straight," Big Montana Ice said, perking up. She fluffed her mullet over her shoulder. "I make my own rules. Those corporate douchebags can suck a fat dick."

"Language!" Carol scolded from her seat next to the giantess, her posture rigid with murderous piety.

"Shut it, ankle-biter." Big Montana Ice raised her giant nicotine-stained hand, blocking Carol from view.

"I told you, it's about *respect*," Carol insisted, refusing to even look at Big Montana Ice, who was biting off her jagged fingernails. She flicked one, hitting Carol in the face, and Carol's eyes lit up with rage.

"Pipe it," Ziggy ordered before security had to intervene. "Unless you'd prefer to die in the first five minutes of the Prelims. In that case, carry on."

Big Montana Ice narrowed her eyes, and Carol sniffed, but neither of them argued, so Ziggy nodded for Floyd to continue.

"One registered competitor must qualify in each annual category," Floyd began, reading from the list, and Ziggy noticed he'd included text translation for Meihua. "The categories have been predetermined by the ABCD, and qualification is determined upon registration. Please see attached addendum forty-eight-point-one-D for a list of qualifying documents. But we don't need to go over those, right?" Floyd glanced at Pepper.

"No need." Pepper shook her head, still tapping away on her phone. "Our killers were qualified."

"Competitors must have a minimum of three confirmed first-degree murder convictions and be sentenced to the competition by a corporate marshal in good standing," Floyd continued, glancing at Ziggy. "Competitors also need to be listed on the Super Serial roster of active participants and registered with the ABCD. We've covered all that, so we're officially in the competition."

"I quite fancy being referred to as competitors," Benedict murmured to Carol, who nodded in agreement. "It does feel rather more civilized."

Ziggy huffed to himself. The ABCD could rebrand Super Serial however they pleased, but it was still nothing more than putting a fancy top hat on a turd. "Competitors"—competitors, his maggoty ass.

"*Yùsài shénme shíhòu kāishǐ?*" Meihua asked Floyd, her voice like a toad's croak. She was dressed in so many layers she looked like a living cocoon.

"*Wǔ tiān hòu kāishǐ,*" Floyd replied with a polite smile, and Meihua nodded in understanding.

"*Gǎnxiè Xiǎomèng, wǒ qīn'ài de péngyǒu.*"

Pepper tapped her finger on the table to get Floyd's attention. "Some of us don't speak Chinese," she reminded him.

"Sorry, Pep," Floyd said with a shrug. "I forget sometimes. Meihua wanted to know what day the Prelims begin."

"Let's see..." Pepper murmured, reading from the schedule on her phone. "Tomorrow Boomer will prep the team for the analyst interviews and upcoming press. The next morning, the analysts arrive, and interviews begin in the afternoon. Then there's a day of travel, followed by the Opening Ceremonies and the Serial Showcase. The Preliminaries start the morning after that."

"Five days," the Samurai spoke, his deep voice demanding attention. Benedict glanced at him nervously, and Carol sat up even straighter. Even Big Montana Ice fell silent, waiting for the Samurai to say more—he didn't.

Floyd highlighted a section of text on the screen. "On the morning of the Preliminaries, teams will enter the cityscape from a predetermined, undisclosed location," he read. "The moment the teams have entered the cityscape, they're considered active targets."

"What exactly is a cityscape?" Carol asked. Her skin paled, giving her massive fake eyelashes a haunting, gothic look—like a possessed porcelain doll. "Is that the arena? My family doesn't watch Super Serial. It's much too violent and promotes evil. None of us should watch it."

Pepper scoffed in disbelief. "Well, it's a bit too late to worry about that now."

"In the early days of Super Serial," Floyd said, his voice brimming with enthusiasm, "the ABCD would pick a host district from a pool of applicants, and the killers would battle in their city center. But as Super Serial gained popularity and more corporations formed teams of killers, it became too much of a hassle for the cities to keep hosting in their actual city limits. CEOs were paying too much on property damages and civilian transport. Plus, the Preliminaries lasted for too long because the city centers were large, and it was easy to hide."

Lin Meihua cleared her throat and raised her withered hand into the air. "Everyone quiet down!" Floyd commanded, even though no one was talking.

"*Dāng wǒ háishìgè xiǎonǚhái de shíhòu, Yùsài zài wǒ de qū jǔxíng le,*" Meihua said, her voice growing stronger as she spoke. "*Wǒ de jiārén líkāi le liǎnggè yuèle. Dāng wǒmen huílái shí, wǒmen de jiā bèi huǐle."*

"Meihua says she remembers some of the earlier games," Floyd translated for the group. "When she was a young girl, their home district was chosen to host the games, and the family left the city for over two months. When they returned, their home had been looted."

"Two months?" Benedict blurted out, his eyes misting with tears. "Are you mental? We can't last for two months!" He trembled like a gelatin mold in an earthquake.

"That's statistically unlikely," Floyd said. "The Prelims used to last for weeks, but now they rarely go longer than a few days. It all depends on how quickly the teams hit the qualifying point target. The shortest Prelims on record was just under two hours."

Benedict's glasses fogged as tears rolled down his pallid cheeks.

"Don't cry, Benny Boy." Big Montana Ice clapped her beefy hand onto Benedict's shoulder. "You'll be with me, and the Goddess gave me the power of Alaskan Thunder. A couple of heads ripped off, some blood spilled, a handful of murders, and lickety-split, we'll be out of there. No harm done."

"No harm done," Pepper repeated under her breath, and Ziggy snorted into his coffee cup. Only a serial killer would call gruesome murder "no harm done."

"Exactly!" Big Montana Ice gave Pepper a sunny smile—if the sun were filtered through a layer of nicotine. "You see?" She patted Benedict's sweaty back so hard the air whooshed out of his lungs. "Even Pepperoni gets it."

"Pepperoni?" Ziggy asked, his lips twitching.

"Just a little nickname for Pepper I came up with," Big Montana Ice said. "Because she's a little spicy, and when I asked she said she only likes sausage."

Pepper's face flushed.

"Host districts stopped using city centers," Floyd pushed on, ignoring the interruptions. "Cityscapes are battle arenas built specifically for the Prelims. They range in size, but the average is about a hundred acres."

"Who's the host district this year?" Ziggy asked. He hadn't watched Super Serial in years, but he knew enough to know that most of the cityscapes were frivolous and campy, designed for maximum gore and profit.

"The ABCD chose District Mongaphalee," Floyd said. "It's their second stint as host. Mongaphalee is a peanut production corporation near the Bay of Bengal. The theme is 'Mongaphalee Jubilee,' whatever that means."

"A jubilee is a celebration," Carol said with a self-important smile. "My son, Rykker, was part of a scout jubilee in our district. The whole family volunteered. We had a wonderful time. It was very festive."

"I'm sure this one will be just as festive," Ziggy said, and Carol's eyes narrowed into feathery slits, correctly sensing Ziggy's mockery.

Pepper tried to steer the conversation back onto the subject. "Can we make a decent guess about the cityscape based on the district's history?"

Floyd flipped to another document. "The host district sent this regarding the theme," he read aloud:

Hear ye! Hear ye! Ladies and Gentlemen, killers of all ages, gather round! The Mongaphalee Jubilee is coming to town! Get ready for a blood-soaked extravaganza of combat, slaughter, and gore that will leave you breathless... or heartless... or headless. Or more! A carnival of appalling attractions, revolting rides, creepy cuisine, and gruesome games awaits at the 119th Super Serial Games. See you under the Big Top!

"It's got to be a fair or circus," Floyd speculated, his hands fluttering with energy. "Ambitious and innovative. It's going to be so much fun!"

"Sounds like a real hoot," Ziggy muttered. "Bloodbaths and psychopaths are always more fun with carnival games."

"Do you really think there will be carnival games?" Floyd beamed at Ziggy.

"That reminds me," Pepper said. "They also sent a short info list. Let me pull it up." She tapped away on her tablet, connecting to the smartboard. "There are 309 teams competing this year," she said as the list appeared. "That's a total of 1,545 killers."

"And at least 309 pets," Ziggy added, thinking of Benedict's twenty-eight dogs. "Actually, scratch that. Probably more like a thousand."

Benedict gasped, his beady mole eyes growing wide with dread. "Are you having me on? They're sending my babies in with thousands of killers? What if something happens to them?"

"That's the point," Ziggy said grimly. "The ABCD wouldn't have chosen a Pet Lovers category if they didn't plan on including the pets."

Floyd nodded. "Plus, there will be at least five to seven thousand other criminals in the cityscape at any given time. Around twenty-five thousand overall. They keep a reserve depending on need."

"Besides the serial killers?" Carol asked, her mouth agape. "What kind of criminals?"

"Well, there's the standard pedophiles and rapists, of course," Floyd said, unfazed by the horrific subject matter. He began counting on his fingers. "Along with child abusers, thieves, burglars, larcenists, embezzlers, cyber-criminals, frauds, and racketeers. I could name some more if you want. And then there are debtors who voluntarily sign up. They're not criminals, but it doesn't matter in Super Serial. Their kill point value is the same."

Benedict's muffled sobs intensified, and Big Montana Ice patted his back so aggressively that his glasses flew into his lap. A muscular security guard with a slick ponytail had to tug on her neck leash to get her to stop.

"Voluntarily? Who would volunteer for that?" Carol asked, her lower lip quivering. "Unless it was their way of committing..." she trailed off.

"Suicide?" Floyd guessed, glancing at Ziggy. "I suppose it could be, but that would be unusual since there's about a nine percent chance of survival. Debtors volunteer to reduce their debts to their district. If they survive the games, their debt gets reduced or absolved altogether. Some do it to avoid being sent to a labor prison."

Ziggy suppressed the urge to squirm in his seat. Not too long ago, he'd been drowning in debt to Pill Depot. The grief at losing Gio, coupled with the staggering $5,784 per-bottle price tag of Gluto-Block, had plunged him into a financial crevasse so deep he thought he'd never crawl out. If Floyd hadn't found him first, he'd be rotting away in a Pill Depot prison, stuffing cotton balls into pill bottles—or competing in Super Serial himself.

"Debt is the shackles of the free," the Samurai broke in, his lip curled in disdain. "Corporations force humanity into poverty, then bind them with the desperation they created. Not one debtor forced into these games ever had the liberty to *volunteer.*"

His words hung heavy in the air, thick with the damning indictment of a system exploiting lives for profit. Only Pepper remained unphased by his words, a muscle tensing in her jaw. If anything, she looked more determined, and Ziggy wondered if she was imagining the DipShip employees being forced to leverage their lives in the games to pay off unavoidable debt.

"Let's not focus on things we can't control," she said. "We have plenty of clues to work with. If we combine our strengths, we can figure this out."

"Pepper's right," Floyd said. "We won't know what the cityscape looks like anyway until thirty minutes before the Prelims start. The killers won't know either until they're inside. We have to work with the information we've got. What else is on the list?" Floyd nudged Pepper with his voice.

She picked up her tablet. "Competitors should work with their teams to achieve the qualifying point target—2,000 points. The first thirteen teams to achieve the point target will advance to the Super Serial championships."

"How do we get points?" Big Montana Ice asked, licking her lips. She leaned forward in her chair, clenching her fists as if she couldn't wait to wrap them around someone's neck.

Pepper's voice was uneasy as she read aloud, "Points are awarded based on the total number of kills accomplished by the team. Points are allocated as follows. Rapists, pedophiles, child abusers, and child killer, including, but not limited to, filicide and infanticide—seven points, all other criminals, including single or double murderers—five points, voluntary debtors—five points."

Bile crept up Ziggy's throat. "Debtors and murderers are worth the same?"

"Correct," Floyd said.

Ziggy tried to wrap his mind around the horrific implications. "That would mean a sick cancer patient with medical debt is valued the same as a murderer." He glanced at the Samurai, whose brown eyes flashed.

"In Super Serial," Floyd confirmed, "that's accurate."

"Here's what I don't get." Big Montana Ice said. "The chomos and kid killers should have to fight, like us. They're worse than we are!"

"Serial killers often gain celebrity status," Floyd said. "Their corporate sponsors keep them happy, even in prison, because of the profit they bring in. Most of them have a fairly luxurious lifestyle."

"Why cater to them?" Carol frowned. "They're horrible!"

"Imagine the public outrage if a pedophile was living a life of luxury," Ziggy said wryly. "Even serial killers have standards."

Big Montana Ice slammed her fist on the table. "Damn straight! Fuck those creepy-ass perverts to the shadow realm!"

"Language!" Carol sighed but then added, "But Jesus did say it would be better to have a millstone hung around your neck and be thrown into the sea than it would be to harm a child."

"Anyone who perpetrates a crime against a child has a ninety-eight percent chance of dying in the Prelims," Floyd said. "Their higher point value makes them a guaranteed target. The districts want to get rid of them, so they're basically cannon fodder. The only criminals with a higher point value are sponsored."

"Sponsored?" the Samurai said, his face pinched in disgust.

"Pepper, anything on the list about sponsored criminals?" Floyd asked.

"Corporate or private sponsored criminals have a kill point value of thirty to fifty points," Pepper read. "Each competitor will also be assigned a ten through one hundred point value, determined by the assessors prior to the Preliminaries. These point values will be revealed during the Serial Showcase at the Opening Ceremonies."

"I'll be worth a hundred points," Big Montana Ice boasted. "Count on it."

The Samurai turned to face her. "Mastering others is strength; mastering yourself is true power."

"What does that mean?" she asked, chin jutting forward to scrutinize the Samurai's deeply lined face. "Why do you always talk in riddles? Are you trying to trick me?"

The Samurai didn't so much as flinch. "He who knows he is a fool is not the biggest fool; he who knows he is confused is not in the worst confusion."

Big Montana Ice clenched her fists. "Are you calling me a fool, Ninja Man?"

Sensing the tension, Ziggy noticed the security guard stationed at Big Montana Ice's shoulder inching closer, hand flexing toward her stun baton.

"He was trying to say you weren't a fool," Ziggy interjected, attempting to smooth over the situation before it escalated and the Samurai lost his head. Or Big Montana Ice. Or both. "He was… paying you a compliment."

The Samurai went unnaturally still, a jungle cat waiting to pounce.

Big Montana Ice blinked, the words taking a moment to penetrate her thick skull. "Well, I'll be damned," she said with a hearty chuckle. She slapped her palm on the table, and everyone but the Samurai jumped. "I thought you were making fun of me. My bad."

"So we enter the cityscape, and the killing begins?" Benedict asked in a wan voice. "Just like that?"

"The teams enter simultaneously from different locations," Floyd clarified. "The killing usually starts as soon as teams begin interacting with one another and with the point targets."

"One thing's for sure, without weapons, we're boned," Big Montana Ice said, cracking her knuckles. "We need to charge in there like a pickup truck full of motherfuckers and jack some shit up."

"Winning without weapons or armor is unlikely," Floyd confirmed, his brow furrowing. Ziggy could tell he was trying to decipher what Big Montana Ice had actually said. "Historically, I mean. When teams don't have brute force behind them, they usually try to craft weapons from their surroundings, but the cityscape planners know this, so they make it difficult. Using the system they've created is the best way to get weapons."

"Speaking of which," Pepper said. "The list also mentions that weapons and armor cannot be obtained with points, only through tokens awarded during special events."

"That's unusual," Floyd said, "but not unheard of. In the 74th Super Serial, the killers could only win tokens for weapons if they got enough votes from the viewers."

"Special events are usually traps," Ziggy said. "Maybe we should forget about competing for weapons. I saw what the Samurai was capable of when we were at Skidmore. He can make weapons and armor from anything. He made his sword from a pizza knife for crying out loud." Ziggy looked at the Samurai, who returned his gaze without prompting, his deep brown eyes always assessing.

"That's true," Pepper agreed. "I saw it, too. He's resourceful. That could be our edge."

"A true warrior adapts," the Samurai said, and Ziggy wondered if he'd ever even seen him blink. "Weapons are what we choose them to be."

"I don't even know how to fight," Carol said with a sniff. "Besides, I'm innocent. I shouldn't have to worry about where to get weapons." She tugged on the zipper of the fanny pack at her hip. She lined up her collection of essential oils on the table, selected one from the line, unscrewed the cap, and inhaled like a mafia boss snorting cocaine.

"Is this bitch being serious right now?" Big Montana Ice whisper-yelled to Ziggy. "None of you have told her she's a serial killer yet?"

"Oh, piddle paddle!" Carol whirled around in her seat. "I would never hurt a soul, and I never have."

Big Montana Ice guffawed. "Are you hearing this, Marshal?" She looked from Carol to Ziggy and back again. "Our Lil Biscuit is one ass cheek short of a full moon."

Carol flushed, but instead of replying, she took another bottle from the line labeled "Serene-Blend," put two drops into her palm, cupped her hands together, and buried her nose inside, breathing deeply. The smell of lavender and chamomile filled the room.

"Why don't we just find a decent hiding spot and wait 'til it's over?" Benedict suggested, turning his whole body to look at Ziggy past his neck brace.

"Teams have tried hiding in the past, but it rarely pans out," Floyd said, scrunching his nose against the odor onslaught. "They usually end up dead first, or their resale value plummets. Many teams prefer offense to defense, hunting others down. Catching someone off guard is better than being caught off guard."

"Now we're talking!" Big Montana Ice said. "Let's hunt down those rim-licking scum goblins."

Ziggy considered the possibilities. Stealth wasn't their strong suit. "Benedict's dogs will be with him," he pointed out. "Sneaking up on anyone will be next to impossible."

"Why?" Big Montana Ice argued. "Those mutts were quiet enough when they attacked all those people at the park. Those mean-ass bitches are as good as a weapon. One nearly bit off my finger when I tried to pet it."

"First Mother died, and now the babies could too?" Benedict burst into noisy tears at the memory of his oldest corgi, recently killed by UltraChad. "How can I bear it?" Snot dripped onto his neck brace.

"There, there," Carol comforted him, dabbing at his face with a handkerchief she pulled from the depths of her fanny pack.

"It may not matter. Animals are being separated from their killers upon arrival in Mongaphalee," Pepper said, her brow furrowing. "It was in the notice they sent this morning. We don't know why or how they're being used."

Floyd leaned back, intrigued. "Interesting. There have been animal categories in past competitions, but they've never entered the arena separately from their owners. I wonder what they have planned?" He turned and began translating for Meihua.

"Killers will just be running around in there with their pets?" Carol voiced the concern that hung in the air.

"They're not just pets," Ziggy said, watching Benedict blubber into Carol's bosom. "They're trained to kill, too."

"There will probably be large animals like bears, tigers, and mountain lions," Floyd said, raking his hand through his hair. "It's common for them to help with kills, then later eat the bodies of the victims to destroy evidence."

There was an airy gasp as Meihua spoke. *"Bié wàngle. Xǔduō rén yǎng yǒudú kūnchóng hé shé zuòwéi chǒngwù."*

Floyd nodded in agreement. "Meihua says not to forget about poisonous animals and insects like snakes, scorpions, and spiders. Many people keep them as pets."

Meihua rasped, *"Nǐ cānjiāguò yǔ dòng xù de bǐsài ma? Wǒ méiyǒu cānjiāguò yǔ dòngwù de bǐsài, dàn wǒ kànguò. Bǎohù jiǎohuái hé xiǎotuǐ hěn zhòng yào. Xǔduō dòngwù kěyǐ bǐ rén pǎo dé gèng kuài, yě kěyǐ pān pá."*

"Meihua hasn't been in any Super Serial that involved pets or animals, but she has watched a few," Floyd translated. "She says it will be important to protect your ankles and shins with sturdy boots, and reminds us that many animals can run faster than humans, as well as climb trees and structures."

"Bloody hell," Benedict whispered.

Floyd tapped back to the rules on the smartboard. "You'll be in the cityscape until thirteen teams have qualified for the Championships, or when only thirteen teams remain with a registered killer in each category. At that point, the surviving killers are sedated and taken out of the cityscape."

"Sedated?" the Samurai asked, his jaw tense.

"It used to be done with arm bands that triggered the kill-chip if removed," Floyd explained. "But the killers started using them as weapons to rack up points. So now, sedation is built into the chip."

"They tried to do that to me a while back, and it didn't work for shit," Big Montana Ice bragged. "Don't sweat it."

"Why are there thirteen winners?" Carol asked. "What's the significance of that number?"

"There are thirteen CEOs who sit on the board of the ABCD," Pepper explained. "Their teams, last year's Super Serial champions, face off against the thirteen Prelims winners in a head-to-head contest during the Championships. Killer versus killer. The winning CEOs gain a seat on the ABCD, plus marketing opportunities and a massive pool of money."

"Once we're in the cityscape, every decision counts," Ziggy said, "and every risk should have a payoff. You obviously need to stay alive, but if you spend the Prelims running and hiding, you won't earn points, and your resale value will tank."

"Who cares if our resale value is low?" Carol exclaimed. "I'd rather be alive."

"Exactly," Benedict murmured in agreement.

"When the Prelims are over," Ziggy decided not to mince words, "Alexia will sell off anyone still breathing to another district. The higher the resale value, the better the district."

"What?" Carol gasped. "But why can't we stay at DipShip? I don't want to go to another district!"

"Fuck that shit!" Big Montana Ice growled. "The Goddess sent me to DipShip for a reason. I ain't leaving."

"Dāng wǒ shì niánqīngrén de shíhòu, wǒ bèi mài dàole shíwǔ gè bùtóng de dìqū," Meihua said, and Floyd leaned closer to the partition to hear her.

"Meihua was sold to fifteen different districts during her active years in the games," Floyd said. "It's common practice to buy and sell killers like commodities."

Pepper caught Ziggy's eye. "They need to know," she murmured, taking a deep breath before addressing the killers. "This may come as a surprise, but Ms. Ito leveraged the district's value to pay the Super Serial entrance fees," she stated bluntly. "After the Prelims, she'll have no choice but to sell you off, or the district goes under."

The Samurai was the first to break the heavy silence. "What do you mean the district goes under?" he asked, watching Pepper with intense focus.

Pepper's brows furrowed, and Ziggy wondered if she was debating how much to reveal. "DipShip isn't financially stable," she said carefully. "Without assets, Alexia will have no choice but to divest."

Cold fury flashed across the Samurai's face. "She wagered the lives of thousands on a game?" Pepper remained silent, but her expression spoke volumes.

Shitballs. The last thing the Samurai needed was another reason to want to kill Alexia. "Performing well in the Prelims not only sets you up for a better future," Ziggy tried to redirect the conversation, "but it gives you a chance to do some good in the world." He didn't know if appealing to the humanity of serial killers was insane, but he knew, at the very least, their cooperation would help Pepper.

"Tāmen xiǎng zhīdào wèishéme huòshèng bǐ shēngcún gèng hǎo," Floyd spoke to Meihua, but his eyes were on Pepper. "I am asking for her advice," he explained to the group. "She would have better insight than any of us here."

As Meihua spoke, the room hushed, allowing Floyd to translate. "She said that everyone wants to reminisce about her glory days in the games," Floyd relayed. "But no one wants to talk about the forty years she spent sewing garments in a Yifu prison. As her value in the games declined, so did her quality of life."

"Forty years?" Carol whispered, astonished. "That's my age."

"When dignity is sacrificed for greed, people become commodities, and lives become disposable," the Samurai said, his eyes still blazing with passion.

Meihua spoke up once more, and Floyd looked at her with open affection. "She mentioned that if I hadn't found her, she would've died forgotten and alone," Floyd translated. "At the height of her fame, she lived in luxury, but that wasn't what mattered the most. What really mattered was being allowed to reunite with her family. She had friends, enjoyed herself, and experienced moments of happiness. But as she aged and couldn't fight like she used to, she got lumped into a batch deal with twenty-five other killers and ended up in a labor prison. Since then, she's just been existing, not truly living."

It was a bitter pill to swallow for Ziggy. He had more in common with Meihua than he realized. The quiet moments at Ipanema Beach had given him lots of time to think, and it was unsettling to realize they'd both had a similar epiphany.

"If there's a chance I could see my darling Jeff and our children again," Carol said wistfully, "I have to try."

"Well, we must do something," Benedict shuddered. "You all saw UltraChad. What if we end up on his team?"

"UltraChad will likely be in the Prelims," Floyd said. "You'll need to watch out for him. He's a new killer with a lot to prove, and District Taste-E Chicken has a more popular Vigilante killer they can send to the Championships if UltraChad dies."

Carol expressed her fears, her voice growing smaller with each syllable. "We'll have to watch out for everyone in there. They're all dangerous killers."

"It is the same out here," the Samurai said quietly. "But the killers are dressed in suits."

"But what happens if we snag a spot in the Championships?" Big Montana Ice asked, gripping the edge of the table as if she were itching to race into the fray. "Can we stay in DipShip?"

"It's difficult to win," Floyd said. "There will be 309 teams, including ours, in the cityscape. Technically, that gives us about a 4.2 percent chance of making it to the Championships. But making it with all our killers alive is more like a 0.01 percent chance."

"One percent?" Benedict exclaimed, his face crumpling.

"*Point* zero-one," Floyd corrected. "Bigger corporations have dozens of backups registered in each category. If they have the points but lose a few killers in the Prelims, the killers are replaceable. We don't have a killer to spare. Either all of you would have to survive, or none of you could make it to the Championships. That's why we're not really counting on a win."

"That can't be right," Carol gasped, her hand flying to her mouth. Ziggy exchanged glances with Pepper, but neither spoke. Floyd's statistics were always right. They had about as much chance of winning as a sandcastle in a tsunami.

"So, what's the plan?" Big Montana Ice said. "How do we boost our value?"

"More like, how do we stay alive?" Carol's voice quivered

Floyd looked to Ziggy for guidance. "I'm not sure," he said. "We'll have to figure it out together. Hundreds of different teams have made it through the Prelims in countless ways. The variables are endless."

All eyes turned to Ziggy, awaiting his direction. "What's the plan, Marshal Ghostshade?" Carol asked.

"I don't want to die in there," Benedict said.

Ziggy pondered for a moment, drumming his fingertips on the conference room table. "You're stepping into a bloodbath with over fifteen hundred serial killers, thousands of murderers, pedophiles, and rapists, plus at least three hundred dangerous animals. Any strategy we devise could blow to shit the moment you set foot in the cityscape."

He rose and cleared the smartboard, drawing three columns. "This column is for things we know, this one is things we can predict, and the last one is for team strengths." He turned to face his ragtag team. "Now, what do we know?"

Carol eagerly raised her hand as if Ziggy were her kindergarten teacher. "We know UltraChad will be there."

Ziggy jotted it down. "True. UltraChad will be Taste-E Chicken's Vigilante killer. Anything else?"

"He kills people by strangling them," Benedict murmured, and Ziggy nodded, eyeing. Benedict's bruised and swollen neck.

"Anything else we know?" Ziggy prodded, but no one spoke. Like Floyd said, the variables were endless. "What about predictions?"

Floyd jumped in with certainty. "We can predict that the weather will be warm," he said. "Based on the time of year in Mongaphalee, I can guess with about eighty percent accuracy that the cityscape will be sunny. Some have domes, but if it's warm outside, the dome will likely be warm too."

Ziggy scrambled to keep pace with Floyd, his hand flying across the smartboard as he wrote.

"And there's almost always a large focal-point building or structure in the cityscape," Floyd said. "Built for wealthy spectators, so they'll likely put an exciting event or some especially heinous weapons nearby."

"In their lofty golden towers, the wealthy gaze down," the Samurai murmured. "They can see the poor man's lips moving, but their ears remain closed to his cries."

The room fell into a brief silence, and when it was clear no one planned to respond, Floyd pressed on. "There might also be a handful of buildings that reflect the local architecture or theme. Most districts auction them off to fans post-games. They won't have any weapons inside, but they might be constructed with usable materials."

"Samurai, you catch all that?" Ziggy asked, and the Samurai nodded, his eyes on the growing list.

"Boomer mentioned five killer clowns on other teams," Carol said, raising her hand again. "But that could just be speculation."

Ziggy added killer clowns to the list. "What about team strengths?" he prompted.

"Benedict's corgis are a huge benefit," Carol said. "Even big animals would struggle against twenty-eight dogs."

"The Samurai is a proper wizard with weapons and armor," Benedict added. "With the right materials, we could put something together."

"The ancient one is gifted with poison," the Samurai added. "And Big Montana Ice has both size and strength."

"Pretty lady *suīrán xíngwéi xiàng gāoyáng, dàn wǒ kàn dé chū tā shì láng,*" Meihua said.

"She said the pretty one may look like a lamb, but she's a wolf," Floyd translated. "She's talking about you, Carol."

Carol looked unsure if she should feel complimented or not. "Thank you," was all she could manage.

"Now all we have to do is combine what we know and what we can predict, then use our strengths to convince the world that the DipShip killers are worth millions," Pepper said, contemplating as she gazed at the list on the board.

Ziggy glanced at her sideways. "That's all, huh?"

"What do you mean, that's all?" Floyd was indignant, sitting up in his seat. "That's actually a very difficult task, Ziggy. Maybe impossible."

Ziggy looked over the killers. Trying to summon hope was pointless. "Let's hope Boomer's a miracle worker."

Chapter 4

Blue Suede Choux

Ziggy weaved his way through the corridors of DipShip, trying to avoid motion sickness from looking too long at the gaudy, swirled carpet. It was his umpteenth visit to the conference room that week, and he was starting to wonder if he'd find more excitement staring at the wall in the lobby bathroom. Along the way, he'd been intercepted by Pepper, who'd wasted no time diving into a spirited rant about the ongoing saga of the killers.

"Carol's complaining about her bowel problems again, but she refuses to take any meds. She wants us to pay to have natural supplements shipped in from her stupid MLM district and says it's worth it since Floyd's having similar problems, and all of us are eating too much from Sweet Sally's. But there's no way Alexia will give me clearance. She thinks Carol will be dead by next week, and I can't exactly argue with her."

Ziggy nodded along, dodging the hustle and bustle of passing colleagues. Playing the role of patient listener was second nature to him now. "You're dealing with a lot," he said in response, allowing

Pepper to unload her burdens. It was easier for him to carry someone else's baggage than to unpack his own.

"People act like I'm the Constipation Whisperer or something. Here's a novel idea, Carol," Pepper threw her hands. "Stop stuffing bodies in your freezer. Maybe then you'd be home with your family instead of here making my life a living hell. I'm juggling fifty-one departments here, and the Super Serial analysts are coming tomorrow. DipShip is a mega-corporation, and I'm stuck herding a bunch of serial killers around like they're babies."

Finally reaching the conference room, Ziggy held the door open for Pepper, revealing Boomer, who was waiting for them inside. Boomer's outfit was wild—a purple tank top, fur-trimmed vest, and a plaid kilt with a daringly high slit up one leg. Ziggy smirked to himself when he realized he'd been right about the wig. Boomer's hairpiece for the day was a messy sky-blue top-knot with fringed bangs.

"Oh, you're here," Boomer said, rummaging through five massive bins on one side of the partition. "I was starting to think you'd forgotten. We need to get everyone fitted so I can have the clothes tailored in time for the interviews tomorrow."

Pepper's back stiffened, and Ziggy checked the time. They were six minutes early.

Floyd entered the room next, his hair especially molted and unruly, hinting at a morning rush. His gray shirt of the day read, "Educated Tube = Graduated Cylinder." He handed a cup of coffee to Pepper. "Black, dash of cream, no sugar, right?"

"Right," Pepper murmured, accepting the cup, her cheeks tinged with pink.

Ziggy raised an eyebrow. "Where's mine?"

Floyd settled into the seat closest to the partition. "Did you misplace your coffee, or are you asking why I didn't get you a cup as well?"

Pepper's phone buzzed, nearly startling her into dropping the coffee. "Security is bringing in the killers now, Mr. D'Chango," she told Boomer.

"About time," Boomer said, blowing a puff of air through his bangs. "There's about a million things on my plate. I've got to fit team uniforms for the interviews, finish Alexia's evening gown for the Serial Showcase, and prepare costumes for the Prelims. Serial killers first, then I'll deal with you three."

Ziggy groaned. "The Serial Showcase?" Managing a Super Serial team was bad enough, but traipsing around in a suit pretending to be proud of DipShip was not his idea of a good time.

Pepper shot him an apologetic glance. "The Serial Showcase is part of the Opening Ceremonies. DipShip is the sixth team in line to present."

Boomer peered at Ziggy through the tiny, stupid glasses still perched on the tip of his nose. "Alexia will lead the team, as well as present the corporate flag. The four of us will follow behind, and the competitors will be in their showcase cells."

"Showcase cells?" Ziggy rubbed the space between his eyes. This shit parade was getting worse by the moment.

Floyd grinned, his eyes gleaming with excitement. "The killers are contained in transparent cells for the protection of the crowd. That way, everyone gets to see them, but there's no need to panic if they decide to go on a murdering spree."

"I hope you're prepared to be blown away," Boomer said. "The uniforms are incredible. I've been up all night."

"I think I'm prepared," Floyd said, glancing at Pepper with uncertainty.

"Let me know if you need more hands," Pepper told Boomer. "The analysts are due tomorrow at nine."

Just then, the door swung wide, and DipShip's security team sprang into action, smoothly escorting the killers to their seats. Ziggy noticed there were twice as many guards as usual, and he figured it was to keep Boomer safe while he took the killers' measurements. It might also explain why none of them had chains on, including Big Montana Ice. Even with the extra muscle, the sight made Ziggy uneasy.

Once everyone was seated, Boomer took center stage, his cotton candy wig now a touch lopsided. "Your public image is absolutely crucial moving forward," he said, locking eyes with each killer as if casting them in a dramatic scene. Ziggy stifled a grin, wondering if Boomer realized he wasn't as intimidating as he thought. "Every moment of your interview with the analysts will be live-streamed, and it's my job to make sure we present DipShip in the best possible light. The kill-score given by the analysts before the Prelims plays a huge role in public perception."

Carol perked up in her chair, and Ziggy noticed she was especially make-upped and coiffed for the day despite her drab jumpsuit. "How do they decide our scores?"

But before Boomer could respond, Floyd took charge. "The analysts meet with each contestant and go over their portfolio beforehand. It's a comprehensive evaluation based on combat skills, physique, weapons usage, intelligence, the number of people they killed before their arrest—things like that."

"My score will be rubbish," Benedict said, quivering like a violin string about to snap. "I'm useless."

"There's no need to be nervous." Pepper stepped in to ease the tension. "The analysts will ask you a series of simple questions about your background and experiences. It's posted on all the Super Serial platforms."

Boomer corrected her. "Only if it's interesting or provocative. Most are just a formality."

Carol looked confused and asked, "What do you mean a formality?"

"It means the statistical chance of DipShip making it out with anyone alive is so low they don't want to bother." Floyd's blunt response seemed to suck all the air from the room.

"We're goners!" Benedict cried, flinging his torso on the table like a fairytale princess in despair. "I knew it!"

"That's not true, Benny," Carol said. "We can't give up. We have to have faith."

"She's right," Big Montana Ice said, rubbing her thick palms together. "We have the Goddess on our side. The power of Alaskan

Thunder gives me the strength of a hundred men. Amriel gave me her—"

"Forget all that nonsense," Boomer cut in sharply, snapping his fingers in the air to regain control. "This is about cementing your resale value if DipShip doesn't win. The better your public image, the more money Alexia will make when this is over."

Big Montana Ice bristled, anger flaring on her blunt features. "You think you know it all, don't you?"

"More kills, more money," Benedict said with a forlorn sigh, still sprawled partway across the table. Carol scooted her chair closer to pat his back, comforting him as if he were a small child. "That's not true. You are of infinite worth. God loves all his children." She hummed what Ziggy guessed was some kind of religious tune. Boomer grinned, observing the bizarre dynamic, and Carol glowed under the shine of his approval, unable or unwilling to see she was being mocked.

Pepper seized the moment to redirect the conversation. "That's where Mr. D'Chango comes in. He's an expert in shaping public opinion, and that plays a large part in a killer's resale value. If the public loves you, DipShip might stand a chance."

Boomer squared his shoulders. "My job is to convince viewers you're worth watching and corporations you're worth buying."

"Popularity has nothing to do with it," Big Montana Ice scoffed, her eyes locked onto Boomer. "The only way to live is to kill a motherfucker before they kill you."

"Language!" Carol griped, pushing out her lower lip. "I didn't sign up for this. I want to go home."

"We're trapped until we're dead!" Benedict cried, fat tears rolling down his cheeks onto the table.

Heat licked up Ziggy's spine. The audacity of serial killers to complain about their plight after destroying countless innocent lives was too much. "It's better than what you gave your victims," he blurted out, unable to hold back. "Or did you all suddenly forget about them?"

The room plunged into a heavy silence. Not even the Samurai spoke.

Carol was the first to speak, her hand raised tentatively, as if she were a child in a schoolroom. "Floyd, what's the longest a Super Serial contestant has stayed alive while competing in the games?"

"It's Lin Meihua," Floyd said, and every head turned to Meihua. "She's outlasted every other killer in Super Serial history."

"How did she do it?" Big Montana Ice asked.

"Tāmen xiǎng zhīdào nǐ shì zěnme huóle zhème duōnián de," Floyd continued, directing the statement toward Meihua, who nodded in acknowledgment.

"Jiézú xiān dēng," Meihua said, her voice creaking like a rusty hinge.

"The quick-footed climb first," Floyd translated in awe, smiling at Meihua as if she were a wise philosopher. "It's like saying the early bird gets the worm."

"It is better to act than be acted upon," the Samurai confirmed. "The ancient one speaks the truth."

"That settles it," Boomer said, tapping his foot against the floor in a rapid staccato. "We all agree on the importance of public image.

If that's the case, then I'd advise you all to open your ears and listen to me."

"If you're such a pro," Big Montana Ice challenged, "why the hell are you working in this shit-hole? Shouldn't you be in one of those fancy districts with the rest of the knob jobs?"

Boomer reeled, scoffing and sputtering at the insinuation, and Ziggy knew Big Montana Ice had struck a nerve. Turning on his heel, Boomer marched to his clothing bins. "Unfortunately for us all, Alexia never changed the DipShip district flag," Boomer snapped, pulling out yards of fabric and accessories. "We're stuck with lime green, magenta, black, and gold." "Like the colors in the lobby?" Ziggy asked, thinking of the monstrosity of tacky hot pink and green furniture with a massive gold-plated fountain in the center that was DipShip's lobby.

"This won't end well," Floyd echoed Ziggy's thoughts in a frantic whisper. "The lobby makes my eyes ache."

"Each of you needs to wear your uniform for tomorrow's interviews," Boomer said, ignoring the criticism with a gravity-defying eye roll. "You'll wear the same outfit in the Serial Showcase." With a theatrical flair, he produced a stack of clothing. "These are for Benedict," he announced, headed toward the partition. But before he could reach it, Big Montana Ice snarled like a rabid gazer protecting its territory.

"How many rubber ducks does it take to teach a cow to ride a bicycle?" she demanded, and when Boomer remained silent, she surged forward, slamming her fist against the partition. "Answer me!"

Pepper yelped as Ziggy rose to his feet. "Back off," he ordered Boomer as security guards grappled with Big Montana Ice.

"I need to take measurements," Boomer protested, hands on hips.

Ziggy shook his head. "You're not crossing that partition."

"The guards have it under control."

"Nobody here can activate her kill-chip," Ziggy warned. "Except Alexia, and she's not around."

"I just want to ask him a question!" Big Montana Ice rasped, straining toward Boomer as another guard joined the fray, trying to force her back into her seat. "One question!"

"You'll risk all our lives for a couple of measurements," Ziggy said, stepping in front of Boomer. "You're not crossing the partition. End of discussion."

A brief standoff took place before Boomer gave up. "Alexia will hear about this," he muttered, passing Benedict's clothes to Ziggy, who handed them to the nearest guard.

"Cut it out," Ziggy barked at Big Montana Ice on his way back to his seat. "If you're really here to defeat the demon once and for all, you'll do as the Goddess asked and wait until the moment is right." Big Montana Ice froze, processing Ziggy's words, her lips moving slightly as she whispered to herself. Ziggy knew it was a risk to play into her delusion, but he'd seen Big Montana Ice lose control more than once, and the results were deadly.

"My bad, Marshal," she said after swatting at the air for a few moments. She relaxed back into her chair. "I'm on the rag," she explained to the other killers. "All I want to do right now is eat nachos and murder. You know how it goes," she said to Carol.

"I most certainly do *not*," Carol replied, looking miffed, and Ziggy saw Pepper nodding in agreement out of the corner of his eye.

Benedict unfurled his clothing across the table—a riotous geometric pattern covered his shirt and pants, while his magenta jacket sported the blazing title "Corgi Killer." Benedict pushed his giant mole glasses closer to his face as he scrutinized the clothes.

"Corgi Killer?" he said slowly, his thin lips working their way around the words. "That's the name you chose? Oh, what a letdown this would be for Mother. She had her heart set on something with a bit more bite, you know. A title that might send shivers down the spine."

Floyd pointed out the obvious, "It's also unclear if Benedict kills corgis or uses them to kill."

Ziggy looked up at the ceiling, his mind wandering to Eugenie, Benedict's late mother, who was more of a serial killer than he was. She'd groomed him for Super Serial since he was in diapers, but when it became apparent that he was a spineless wanny, she'd trained the corgis to be killers instead. After her death, Benedict fed her to the dogs, and Mother-corgi, the oldest dog, became "Mother." All the dogs were named after their victims, but with all the sobbing and whining he did, Benedict couldn't strike fear into the heart of a mouse. Ziggy pressed his lips together, reminding himself that saying so probably wouldn't be helpful.

"That's the persona we chose," Boomer said. "It's not up to you. We're going to make everything about the dogs. They'll be outfitted with a sweater in a similar pattern to your pants, and each one will have their name embroidered on the back. That was a particular stroke of genius on my part," he added. "Imagine the looks on the families' faces when they see their loved one's name on a dog sweater. It will be a spectacle." Boomer's eyes gleamed.

"For crying out loud," Ziggy muttered. It was bad enough that Benedict's victims had to see him glorified in the name of sport, but to see his dogs bearing the name of the loved one they'd ripped to pieces was a horrific strategy. Effective in reminding the public why Benedict should be feared—but horrific.

"After you're done trying on your clothes," Boomer continued, "pop in these contact lenses." He passed a small box to a guard, then turned back to Benedict. "Those glasses have got to go—they're absolutely hideous. And we're bringing in an esthetician to address your acne."

Benedict hesitated, shuffling the small box in his hands. "Contacts?" he questioned with uncertainty.

"And the neck brace will need to come off during the interview and Opening Ceremonies," Boomer instructed. "Your bruises, however, will stay—they'll add a point of interest since everyone will want to know how you got them. We're going to play up your feud with UltraChad."

"My what?" Benedict exclaimed, slumping in his seat like a limp noodle. "Absolutely not!"

Boomer silenced him with a sharp look. "UltraChad has been giving interviews, and the public loves to hate him. If they see him as the villain and we can sell you as a worthy foe, then you get to be the hero. They'll love the idea of a weapons-grade douchebag like

UltraChad being chewed up and spit out by a pack of dogs. You'll gain support from dog lovers and older women."

Paper rustled as Pepper passed a stack to Benedict. "Here are some lines you can practice for your interview. Try to act confident." Ziggy stifled a laugh at the notion. Benedict was the biggest candy-ass wimp he'd ever known. It was like putting a lion's mane on a housecat and expecting it to win a fight with a rabid wolf.

"You're up next," Boomer said to the Samurai, passing on another tacky costume. His was identical to Benedict's, except the jacket read "Warlord of Waste" on the back.

"This pleases me," the Samurai said with a nod in Ziggy's direction, even though Ziggy had nothing to do with it. The people in the Skidmore district lived in a city at the heart of the landfill called the Soup Bowl. They called the Samurai a variety of different names, but Warlord of Waste was a good one. Although, it was strange imagining the Samurai in any color but black.

"Here's your story," Boomer said, holding both hands in the air as if he were on the stage in front of a vast audience. "You kill CEOs and executives because you envy the life they lead—a life you could never achieve. Exiled and alone, you found solace in the only place you knew you'd be accepted as an executive—Skidmore Dumping. You tried to build an empire there, bolstered by the people and fueled by their hatred for the wealthy. They made you the Warlord of Waste, and your mission is to destroy executives and take your place as supreme ruler of the corporate world."

The Samurai didn't move. He didn't even blink. He stared until Boomer wriggled like a snake on hot pavement. "You—" Boomer stammered, unaware he'd gravely insulted the Samurai. "You don't like it?"

"Who's next?" Pepper prompted.

"You'd paint me as a man who steps on the backs of his own people to stand at eye level with their persecutors?" the Samurai said with venom; the look on his face was deadly. "I would suffer death by a thousand cuts before taking part in such a disgusting lie."

Boomer sniffed. "Well, that's the story we gave to the analysts. We felt like it would make you more palatable to the public. Especially those in a lower socio-economic class. The poor represent Super Serial's largest viewership by a landslide. They can sympathize with the feeling of wanting to be one of the glitterati."

"The wealthy satiate their filthy hunger with ego and greed, while the poor satiate their hunger with bread," the Samurai said. "The only reason a poor man would want to be one of your *glitterati* is because he knows the table of the oppressor is always full. He doesn't envy the tyrant. He envies the feast."

"What will you say to the analysts, then?" Boomer asked him, exasperated by the hitch in his plan. "What reason will you give for killing all those executives?"

"The truth," the Samurai said with dark solemnity.

"And what, pray tell, is that?" Boomer snapped back, pressing his hands onto the table.

The Samurai rose, placing his own hands on the table, meeting Boomer's gaze across the partition with equal intensity. "If cutting the head off one putrid worm can save the lives of thousands"—he jabbed his thumb into his chest—"I will be the one to brandish the sword."

There was a heartbeat where Ziggy was sure the Samurai would somehow attack, and two guards positioned themselves behind him, stun batons at the ready. But he straightened, then sank into his seat, sullen but calm.

"I swear to God, I just got aroused," Boomer gushed, his hand over his heart. "That's the intensity to bring into your interview. I love it. Love the anger. Love that dominating energy. Bring it. Bring it all with you."

The Samurai's jaw clenched.

"Speaking of sexy," Boomer announced with a flourish, digging through a pile of clothes and passing them to security. "Carol, you're next."

Carol received her small pile of clothes, eyeing them with a mix of confusion and dismay. She had neon geometric jogger pants like the rest of the team, but instead of a jacket, there was a gold bikini top with the letters "MLM" on one cup, and the word "Murderer" on the other.

Carol looked like she'd seen a ghost. Her face drained of color, and her wombat eyes filled with tears. "Is this some kind of joke?" she seethed, dropping the clothes onto the table like they were on fire.

"One of our team members should appeal to the largest demographic of Super Serial viewers," Boomer said with a flick of his hand. "Males between the ages of thirty to sixty."

"I would rather die than wear this," Carol said, the words barely escaping through her clenched teeth. "What would my children think of me? What about my darling Jeff?"

"You should be grateful," Boomer told her. "Without me, you'd wind up looking like a dowdy almond mom with the sexual magnetism of a hairbrush.""I don't want s—" Carol couldn't even bring herself to say the word. "Magnetism."

Boomer laughed. "Nobody cares what you want. This is what I want and what Alexia wants. You're her property now. We also have a stylist coming in to do something with"—Boomer waved his hand in the air in front of Carol's face—"that situation."

"You mean my hair?" Carol said, fuming. "I happen to get a lot of compliments on this style, thank you very much."

"The hair, the ridiculous eyelashes. It's hideous," Boomer said, his over-plumped lip curling in derision. "Anyone complimenting you is as delusional as you are."

"Well, I'm sorry, Charlie," Carol stood, placing her hands on her hips, "but I will not be wearing that, and there's nothing you can do about it. It's degrading. We'll just have to come up with something we can both agree on."

"The alternative is that you're interviewed naked." Boomer's smirk widened. "I'm sure the analysts would love that."

Carol recoiled in horror, her eyes brimming with tears of frustration. "You—You wouldn't dare!"

"Don't try me."

"You won't get away with this," Carol whispered.

"And while we're on the subject," Boomer snapped back. "You need to give up the theatrics. This angle you're playing about being innocent is stale. I've seen it a million times over, and the public never likes it. It winds up making the killer seem desperate—like they can't come up with a better way to get attention."

"But, I *am* innocent!" Carol cried, her voice taking on a tinge of desperation.

Boomer rolled his eyes. "Case-in-point."

Benedict stood and awkwardly patted Carol's back. "It'll be okay," he told her, but she pushed him away. "I'm leaving," she said, marching for the door, which was being policed by at least a dozen guards. "I refuse to subject myself to this humiliation!"

But a guard blocked her path. "You can't leave," he said firmly. CEO's orders—all killers must be present for the duration of the meeting."

"Then I demand to see the CEO," Carol said, stamping her foot on the ground like a child. "No one should be forced to wear something so indecent."

"It was Alexia's idea," Boomer said, his tone smug. "Play along or don't. Either way, you're going to die, and if by some miracle you make it past the first ten minutes, no one will want you the way you are. You're really only here to boost the value of the real contestants."

Defeated, Carol sank to the floor, curling into a ball as tears streamed down her cheeks. "This is so unfair," she whispered.

"It'll be okay, Lil Biscuit," Big Montana Ice murmured.

"Lin Meihua," Boomer called over the table, dismissing Carol. He passed Meihua her clothes through the guard. The back of her black jacket read "The Witch."

"I told Boomer that's what people called her in her earliest Super Serial competitions," Floyd said. *"Tāmen yòu jiào nǐ nǚwū le,"* he turned to Meihua, and she smiled until her blackened teeth showed.

"I don't have any instructions for her," Boomer told Floyd with a shrug. The analysts won't consider her a threat because they'll think she's too old."

"Would you like me to tell her that?" Floyd asked Boomer, taken aback.

"I don't care what you tell her," Boomer said, and when Floyd glanced at Ziggy for direction, Ziggy shook his head. Meihua was capable of a lot more than Boomer realized. She might be an old lion, but she was still a lion.

"Last but not least," Boomer said with the pushy enthusiasm of a carnival barker, "Big Montana Ice, this one's for you." With a flourish, he pulled what looked like yards of fabric from the bin, then passed it across the partition to Big Montana Ice.

"Hell yeah," she crowed, holding up the jacket. It was black with lime green writing and read, "Alaskan Thunder." She shrugged it on over her jumpsuit. "This looks pretty damn good," she said, and Boomer looked pleased.

"You'll also be seeing a hairstylist," he added. "That mullet has to go. It's probably the least flattering hairstyle you could have. Aside from that, you need a variety of things plucked and scrubbed before the interview."

Big Montana Ice's face froze into granite. "I don't change for nobody."

"Besides that," Boomer continued, undeterred, "we need to rethink your backstory. This whole Bazgoroch thing won't fly with the press. It's nothing but a fairytale villain from a children's book."

"What did you just say?" Big Montana Ice's voice dropped to a menacing whisper, her jaw clenching. Ziggy recognized the tone. He usually heard it right before Big Montana Ice murdered someone.

Boomer backpedaled, sensing the rising tension. "I'm just saying, maybe we should opt for something more grounded in reality," he suggested. "Even in the story, Bazgoroch isn't strictly dangerous."

But Big Montana Ice wasn't having it. "Are you calling me a liar?" she demanded, her voice rising with fury. "Because Amriel blessed me. I know what I saw. You may not be able to see Bazgoroch, but I can."

Boomer sighed in frustration, throwing up his hands. "Can we maybe just tweak the details a bit?" he pleaded, clearly hoping that somehow a maniacal serial killer would be reasonable and compromise.

Big Montana Ice's eye twitched, but before she exploded into a ball of flailing fists, Ziggy intervened. "You're done," he told Boomer, stepping forward to defuse the situation before it escalated too far and someone wound up dead.

But Boomer wasn't ready to back down. "No," he said. "I'm not."

"Take the killers back to their cells," Ziggy told security, and they instantly complied, spreading through the room to secure the DipShip killers. One guard picked a still sobbing Carol up off the ground, and Big Montana Ice flayed Boomer alive with her beady eyes as she was escorted back to her cell. "I see you!" she bellowed over her shoulder. "I know who you are."

As soon as the killers departed, Boomer bristled, snapping at Ziggy. "I don't appreciate you getting between me and my clients."

Ziggy met his gaze evenly. "Your clients are vicious murderers, and one of them was about to rip your head off—literally."

Boomer scoffed. "Someone needs to tell them the truth. They need a reality check, or the public will despise them."

"You seem to be laboring under the misapprehension that these killers give a shit what the public thinks of them," Ziggy said. "They're not actors who'll perform the way you want them to. They're killers. Real killers with real murder records and real delusions."

"Well, they should give a shit," Boomer said, thrusting another stack of clothes into Ziggy's arms. "And frankly, so should you. The Corporation also receives a rating. They'll be interviewing you and Alexia as well. These interviews matter for everyone."

Ziggy recoiled in shock. "I'm being interviewed?"

Pepper whipped out her phone at the speed of light. "Is that true?" she asked Boomer. "Why wasn't I informed?"

Boomer shrugged. "Alan was supposed to tell you."

"Fucking Alan," Pepper muttered, already texting. After a tense pause she looked up, then slowly approached Ziggy as if she were preparing to dismantle a bomb. "The team leader takes part in the interviews," she said.

"Well, they can interview you or Floyd," Ziggy said, a sick panic rising in his stomach. "I won't talk to the press. Out of the question." Things were bad enough already. Hirofumi was probably already shitting a brick that Ziggy was involved in the games. He'd shit a lot more than that if Ziggy ended up all over the news.

Floyd gave Ziggy an encouraging pat on the shoulder. "It'll be fun. They'll just ask questions about the team."

Ziggy rummaged through the clothes Boomer had given him. The back of his jacket read, "Marshal DipShip." He felt like he was going to puke.

"Come on, give them a try," Pepper urged, panic in her eyes. "How bad could it be?"

Chapter 5

I Want to Hold Your Ham

Ziggy felt like a mud man with a pea brain standing in the grotesque DipShip lobby, even though he was clean and freshly shaved. The whole crew, minus Floyd, who was down with the flu, gathered to welcome the Super Serial analysts. He fumbled with the sleeves of the ridiculous neon jacket Boomer had insisted he wear, making a mental note not to scowl at Pepper, who'd somehow convinced him to put it on. Meanwhile, Alexia, ever the picture of sophistication, exuded nothing but confidence in her sleek black dress and crimson stilettos—not a hint of neon in sight. She studied her manicure while spouting orders to Pepper, who dutifully took notes on her tablet.

"We've got to do something about the ninja," Alexia said, her voice a constant stream of discontent. "How do we not know anything about him yet? Get what's his name to find something—the weird autistic guy who's always drooling over you."

"Floyd," Pepper said, a subtle irritation creeping into her voice.

"Whatever." Alexia waved it off, flipping her silky black hair over her shoulder. "We need more information. It's starting to make us look bad."

"Floyd's still not feeling well," Pepper said, "but I'll ask him for an update when he comes in later to translate for Lin Meihua's interview."

"Hopefully, the ninja turns out to be a decent fighter. He may be our best shot at bringing in a high kill-score and getting us some good press in the Prelims." Alexia leaned into Pepper as if they were best friends. "Boomer calls him 'Trash Daddy,'" she said with a snort. "I think he has a little crush on him."

Pepper's mouth gaped open. Ziggy was also at a loss for words, mostly trying not to imagine the Samurai's face if he'd heard the way Alexia was talking about him. She seemed to have forgotten that he beheaded corrupt executives, just like her.

"And what's with Carol?" she continued without waiting for a response. "She won't even consider the top Boomer made for her. She's killed people for crying out loud, but a bikini is where she draws the line? Can't you talk some sense into her? Boomer thinks she could swing the analysts in our favor; they love a sexy story. Her whole 'I'm innocent' thing is almost convincing, so she's obviously a decent actor. Why won't she just play the damn part?"

"I think a better approach might be to—" Pepper attempted to get a word in, but Alexia steamrolled over her, showing no signs of stopping.

"The giant is clearly terrifying," she continued, "but it's crucial we get her under control. We need her brutality at the Prelims, but with all the guard killings, her upkeep is getting expensive."

Ziggy marveled at Pepper's ability to listen to Alexia yammer all day without whacking her upside the head with the tablet. He couldn't hold back anymore. "That must be so hard for you. Almost as hard as it is for the kids who lost their parents. Did DipShip even pay the funeral expenses?"

Alexia shot him a withering glare, her gaze sweeping over his bald head and the tufts of arm hair poking out from his jacket cuffs. "Once I'm on the ABCD, I'll recoup all my costs and then some," she said, her tone dripping with condescension. But before he could reply, her attention snapped to a shiny black limousine pulling in front of the lobby doors. "They're here!" Alexia hissed, straightening her shoulders and plastering a smile over her sneer. The limo doors opened and five executives emerged.

"We should go out and greet them," Pepper suggested to Alexia.

"*We* are not doing anything. They came here to meet with a CEO, not a two-bit marshal and a secretary."

"Executive administrator," Ziggy stated in Floyd's honor, earning a huff from Alexia before she strutted out the door to meet the analysts. Pepper's expression went blank, but Ziggy knew her careful mask was hiding a lot of hurt. He made a show of looking down at his geographic joggers. "Boomer has a good eye," he said blithely, glancing sideways at Pepper. "It's a wonder anyone can see me standing in the lobby since I'm basically camouflaged."

Pepper frowned, but amusement twinkled in her eyes. "You look great."

"I look like I'm auditioning for a geriatric hip-hop dance crew."

"You look... very vibrant," Pepper said, her lips twitching. "Boomer said that bright colors are in style this season."

"I look like a broken kaleidoscope," he said. Pepper giggled, and Ziggy felt a small sense of accomplishment. "Speak of the devil. Where's Boomer?"

"He's with the killers, prepping them for their interviews. It's not going well. The sooner we get this over with, the better. Everyone's on edge."

"That's putting it mildly," Ziggy agreed as the doors opened again, and the analysts filed in. They looked around the lobby, each of them coming to the same realization Ziggy had when he first walked in: it looked like a backwoods brothel.

"Obviously, we'll be doing some heavy renovations," Alexia told the analysts. "We just haven't had the time with all our other projects." She stepped in front of Pepper to place her hand on Ziggy's shoulder. "This is Marshal Ziglar Ghostshade, but I'm sure he needs no introduction," she gushed, oozing false enthusiasm. It took everything in Ziggy not to shrug off her touch. "Marshal Ghostshade, this is Mr. Jomar Santos," she gestured to a portly man with a thick beard. "Mr. Santos was an executive at District Primera Iron, but now he owns a telecommunications corp in RicoAir. Is that correct?"

"That's right," Jomar said with a warm smile. "But you can call me Jomar. Nice to meet the man who brought down Red Judas."

"Ziggy," Ziggy said, shaking his hand, but Jomar's attention had already shifted back to Alexia.

"Good call on bringing in a celebrity marshal your first year in the games," Jomar said, completely entranced. "Beautiful and smart," he added, ribbing Ziggy in the side like they were fraternity brothers. "A rare combination. You're lucky to work with a woman like her."

"The luckiest," Ziggy said, with as much false congeniality as Alexia, slyly sneaking an eye roll to Pepper without anyone noticing.

"This is Ms. Dora Spiro," Alexia said, leading Ziggy to a small woman with thick eyebrows and a sleek black ponytail. "She's an associate at District Charleston-Oberfeld-Reinbeck-Ryan-Upchurch-Peters-and-Taft."

"It's a pleasure to meet you, Marshal Ghostshade," Dora said, shaking his hand. "You're a difficult man to get in touch with. I'm in the process of producing a docuseries that explores the corporate legalities surrounding Red Judas's execution, and I'd love to talk with you more about his capture," she said with careful dictation, enunciating every word.

Ziggy couldn't think of anything worse, so he was grateful he only had to grunt out a "thank you" before Alexia moved on with the introductions. He met a former criminologist with a mass of curly red hair named Stormi MacGowan. And Song Zexian was a weapon and combat expert who owned a sub-corp in Bank of Eurasia. Both couldn't make it past him without mentioning Gio's killer.

"This is Ejigu Aman Meba," Alexia pulled Ziggy to the last analyst. He was a tall man with rich, dark skin and amber eyes so piercing that Ziggy felt his mouth run dry.

"You can call me Ejigu," the man said, enveloping Ziggy's hand between his own. "I have heard a lot about you, Marshal Ghostshade," Ejigu said with a smile that crinkled the corners of his eyes, somehow making them look even more miraculous.

"Ziggy," he managed, but it came out in a gruff bark. He yanked his hand away, horrified when he realized his cheeks were flaming hot and probably bright red.

"Ejigu is the newest analyst in the group," Alexia said. "He's a former Operations Analyst for Pill Depot's Super Serial team."

"I never worked with Ziggy while he was still at Pill Depot," Ejigu said to Alexia, "but I'm honored to have met him. The marshals there still speak very highly of you," he added, and Ziggy's stomach clenched so hard he thought he might be sick. He was a different man back then. Unable to form a coherent response, he nodded, and Alexia led the analysts to her office for light refreshments before the interviews began.

Ziggy trailed behind them with Pepper, whose sideways smirk proved she hadn't missed a thing.

"Pipe it," he muttered.

"I didn't say anything," Pepper said, holding up both hands, but she was grinning ear to ear over his idiotic performance. He agonized over it in the elevator, through the upper floor lobby, and down the hallway until they reached Alexia's office, making sure to mentally slap himself before they went in—hard enough to remember that he was a seasoned criminal marshal and not a prepubescent numbskull.

The catering team, directed by Pepper, brought in a fussy charcuterie board covered in cured meats and cheeses with names Ziggy couldn't pronounce, while servers poured wine he couldn't afford. He piled some food onto a minuscule plate, parked in the corner of the office, and tried to look unapproachable. His solitude lasted a grand total of thirty seconds before Dora Spiro pounced.

"I specifically asked to analyze the DipShip team just so I could meet you," she said, sitting across from Ziggy. "My crew has been chasing your ghost for years." She waited a moment for him to reply, but he had no idea what to say, so he stuffed his mouth with cheese. "And then, out of nowhere, you materialize in DipShip, of all places," she continued, her predatory eyes roaming over Ziggy's bizarre ensemble. "You can't imagine my surprise when I heard. It's quite the enigma."

"Uh huh," Ziggy murmured, this time chewing on a small stack of cured meat and hoping she didn't bring up Hirofumi. Wondering about his disappearance would naturally lead her to wonder about the reasons behind his decision to hide in the first place.

"The public's fascination with your story is insatiable. You're the heart of the Red Judas saga, after all," Dora said, eagerly leaning in to study Ziggy. "People love a tale of vengeance, especially when it's fueled by love and loss—not to mention a devilishly handsome villain. The footage of your husband's torture left everyone wanting more, and your silence following Pill Depot's injunction only increased the fascination. Imagine the rewards if you were to break that silence. An exclusive interview could be quite lucrative."

She paused then, fidgeting in her seat, waiting for Ziggy to reply. When he didn't, she switched tactics. "You know," she said, her voice low and intimate, "I've always been curious about why you didn't sentence Judas to Super Serial. Did Hirofumi Ito really threaten you when the marshals rioted on your behalf?"

Blood rushed to his ears, and Ziggy rose to his feet. "Excuse me, I forgot to take my GlutoBlock." Dora looked crestfallen, but he didn't care. He left Alexia's office, seeking sanctuary in the nearest bathroom. He'd rather get a hemorrhoid from sitting on the toilet too long than say one more word about the monster that killed Gio. Dora talked about Judas with an almost sadistic reverence, but he didn't deserve to have his name spoken. Ziggy sat on the cool porcelain seat and buried his head in his hands.

This was another reason he'd wanted nothing to do with Super Serial. The analysts, the cameras, the probing questions—it was like being stripped-searched. Reporters swarmed like vultures after he killed Judas, hungry for even a small morsel of the story. But Ziggy never granted a single interview, no matter how tempting the compensation. Instead, he packed up and fled in the middle of the night, knowing full well that if he didn't, Hirofumi would have him killed.

Ziggy had never been the type to court danger. In his years at Pill Depot, he'd been content to toil away as a pencil-pushing marshal in corporate identity theft, far removed from the grisly underworld of crime. But fate had other plans, thrusting him into the limelight when he brought down Judas, a feat made even more astonishing by his complete lack of criminal experience. Red Judas was a celebrity. His twisted theatrics and sadistic rituals had the public hooked, live-streaming every moment from his infamous Red Room.

For years, Ziggy had immersed himself in the horrific footage of Gio's torture, desperate for any clue that might lead him to Judas. Every gasp for air, every piercing scream, and every desperate plea for death from Gio were scorched into Ziggy's mind, pushing him to the brink of sanity. For him, letting Judas live was never an option. Executing him had been as natural as breathing, and the consequences, including Hirofumi's wrath, were a price he'd been willing to pay.

That's why now, as time passed, his emergence from the shadows was gaining attention. Notoriety was infinite. The media was already rearing its ugly head, and Ziggy was forced to confront the chilling reality that he may not be able to fly under Hirofumi's radar for much longer.

The bathroom door creaked, and Ziggy sighed at the sound of Pepper's heels clacking on the tile. "Ziggy?" she called, stepping further into the restroom.

"This is the men's room," Ziggy said, dropping his voice a few cadences. "What are you, some kind of pervert?"

"Nice try," Pepper huffed. "You can't hide in here forever."

"I'm not hiding," Ziggy said, even though they both knew it wasn't true. "I just forgot to take my GlutoBlock."

There was a pause before Pepper softly asked, "What happened with Dora Spiro?"

He stood and nudged open the stall door with his foot. "Everyone talks about Red Judas," he said. "The whole damn world knows his name. I hate it. I hate that he's the one they remember. No one ever says Gio's name. His name has become 'one of Judas's victims' because in this fucked-up society, the killer is the one who gets the legacy."

"I told the analysts they couldn't ask any more questions about your past," Pepper said. "Including Red Judas."

"I'm sure Alexia loved that."

"She wasn't happy." Pepper stayed aside so he could exit the stall. "But I told her it was either that or you weren't doing the interview at all."

"It's not just the questions about Judas." He paused at the sink to wash his hands. "I'm risking my neck showing my face in public like this."

Worry flickered in Pepper's expression. "What do you mean?"

"There's more to the Red Judas story than you know," he said, drying his hands with a paper towel. A sudden wave of nerves washed over him. He'd never talked about this part of his past with anyone until now. "After Judas's execution," he began slowly, "everything was a blur. One minute, I was giving a statement to the Pill Depot marshals, and the next they were locking me in a cell."

"Not surprising considering you snubbed Hirofumi Ito." Pepper leaned back against the sink.

"Executing Red Judas put Hirofumi in a bind," Ziggy said. "Judas was able to avoid getting caught for so long because he was one of Pill Depot's top marshals. So, not only was Hirofumi embarrassed to have a serial killer working right under his nose, but he also missed the chance to redeem himself by capitalizing on Judas in Super Serial. I humiliated him, and he was ready to let me rot in a debtors' prison. He tried to pin my arrest on medical debt, but nobody bought it, and the marshals, who'd lost partners and friends to Judas, sparked a worldwide protest."

"I remember seeing the protests on the news," Pepper said. "The man who shamed the Ito enterprise. You were a media darling."

Ziggy winced. "Hirofumi tried to break up the revolt for weeks, but there were too many marshals, and none of the Pill Depot security guards would scab. Eventually, the ABCD had enough of the social pressure, and they filed an injunction against Pill Depot that forced Hirofumi to let me go. But not before he made it damn clear that if I ever showed my face again, I'd regret it."

"He threatened your life?"

"Why do you think I was so hard to find?"

"I should've guessed there was more to this than just your debt." Pepper's face scrunched up the way it always did when she was thinking hard. "You came back knowing you were risking your life?" She stared at him, her dark eyes shining.

Out of nowhere, an overwhelming burst of guilt overwhelmed him. "You asked me to come back," he said, flinching as Pepper stepped towards him.

"Why didn't you tell me?" She pulled him close and hugged him tightly before he could respond. "I would've never asked you to come back if I knew the risk."

Ziggy's eyes grew misty, and his arms held stiff at his sides, automatically lifted to hug her back. "I didn't want to be alone anymore," he murmured. Being alone was worse than being dead.

Pepper pulled back, looked him in the eyes, and gave a nod. "You aren't alone, Ziggy." He hung his head, but he knew she understood.

"Have you heard from Hirofumi since?" she asked, already back in problem-solving mode.

"No," Ziggy said. "Not yet."

Pepper's shoulders eased up as a bit of tension melted away. "You've been here for months. Everyone knows you're at DipShip. The news has been reporting it for weeks. If Hirofumi was still angry enough to try anything, he would've done it by now."

"Maybe," Ziggy said to reassure her, but he didn't really believe it.

Pepper's phone suddenly buzzed in her hand, and she glanced down at the screen. "Shit. The analysts are almost ready to start Alexia's interview, and you're scheduled right after." Pepper pinched the bridge of her nose, and Ziggy mentally prepared for the guilt trip of a lifetime.

Instead, she dropped her hands and met his eyes, searching. "If you want to call this whole thing off, we will. I can have you out the lobby door in less than six minutes. Faster if we keep a good pace and the elevator cooperates."

Ziggy's voice failed him as his throat swelled with overwhelming affection. He knew she was sincere. If he wanted to leave, even if it left her to handle the fallout alone, she'd be there for him. She genuinely cared about others, putting them before herself without thinking twice. Hirofumi might come after him at some point, or he might not, but if Pepper would sacrifice her happiness and safety for him, he could do the same for her.

"You don't owe anyone anything, Ziggy," Pepper said firmly, grasping his arm. "Me included. You're my friend and I'm with you either way."

"I know," he murmured. "I'll do the interview. It's too late to back out now. We can figure out the rest later."

"Are you sure?" Pepper asked, chewing on her lip. Her phone buzzed again.

"Alexia likes to talk, so my interview will probably be short," Ziggy said. "Besides, the analysts haven't met the DipShip killers yet. By the time they do, anything I have to say will be long forgotten."

"True," Pepper agreed reluctantly. "The media will only broadcast the juiciest parts of each interview, so just keep it simple and boring."

Ziggy snorted. "That won't be an issue. I'm nowhere near as interesting as a demon hunter or a samurai on a revenge mission."

Pepper grinned. "Not as adorable as a bunch of corgis or a dainty old lady, either."

"Maybe the same level of denial as a homicidal housewife?"

Pepper gave him a friendly slug on the shoulder and they left the bathroom together.

Chapter 6

Chips Don't Lie

Alexia sat on a black leather chair in the center of a staged area surrounded by cameras and lights. Boomer pecked around her like a wind-ruffled hen, powdering her nose and running a comb through the ends of her hair. The analysts were seated in front of a long table, and each of them had a tablet to take notes, except for Ejigu, who held a small pad of paper and a knubby pencil.

"Sixty seconds to live!" one of the dozens of production assistants called, and Ziggy and Pepper sat in folding chairs near the perimeter of the stage. Boomer rushed away, make-up case in hand, and flopped into the seat next to Pepper. His latest wig, a sleek black pompadour with a rakish curl over the forehead, crested high over his head in a greasy wave, and Ziggy was glad he wasn't stuck sitting behind him.

The camera crew gave the live signal, and Dora launched the first question at Alexia. "What made you want to include District DipShip in Super Serial?"

Alexia sat up straight in her chair, crossing her ankles with practiced precision. "The mark of any good corporation is justice. Super Serial is just a sport to some, but to me, it's a crucial part of our district's justice system. Until now, DipShip didn't have a way to execute its most heinous criminals. Participating in Super Serial is a symbol of growth. Prosecuting dangerous criminals and making DipShip safe once more is a vital part of that process."

If it hadn't been for Pepper, Ziggy would have left right then and there. He'd never seen anyone spin so much bullshit. While Alexia floated around in a bubble of privilege, shielded from the real-life consequences of risking thousands of livelihoods to play billionaire murder games, her employees struggled to put food on the table. She was painting herself as a beacon of justice, the noble protector of the people of DipShip, who she'd never once considered before risking their lives on a desperate gamble. All she really cared about was money and status. If she really wanted to protect DipShip, she could start by stepping down as CEO and letting Pepper take over.

"Why did you purchase DipShip? What sparked your interest in shipping?" Jomar continued. He leaned forward in his chair as if he were hypnotized by every word Alexia spoke. He probably was, the poor slop, but Ziggy knew he didn't stand a chance. Even among the wealthy, there was a hierarchy, and the Ito family was at the top. Jomar would need binoculars to see the social tier they were standing on.

"I was looking for an opportunity to venture out on my own," Alexia said. "My family is very successful in the corporate world, but I didn't want to have anything handed to me. Self-sufficiency is very important, and I wanted to work for it," she said, placing her hand over her heart in the most blatant display of virtue signaling Ziggy had ever seen. "DipShip had gone through some financial struggles in the past," Alexia added, "but when it became available, I felt like it was a good fit. I had the education to bring DipShip into the future, and the experience to build upon the foundation of business created in the past."

Jomar was mesmerized, basking in Alexia's radiant glow, and Ziggy noticed a few of the other analysts exchanging impressed looks.

"Is it true you leveraged the complete EBITDA value of Dip-Ship just to pay the corporate entrance fees for Super Serial?" Ejigu asked Alexia. He wasn't taking notes. He was studying Alexia as if she were a mildly interesting museum display.

Alexia swallowed. She wasn't expecting the question. Maybe she thought none of the analysts would have the guts to ask. "Is that the rumor going around?" Alexia responded with a nervous titter. Jomar joined in; his booming laugh lifted the mood in the room.

Alexia relaxed by a fraction. "The value of a corporation cannot be found in money and property but in people," she said with a cool glance in Ejigu's direction. "The people of DipShip are priceless."

If Ziggy wasn't so disgusted, he might've been impressed. She'd sidestepped the question with masterful grace. Boomer beamed from the sidelines of the interview.

"Apologies, Ms. Ito," Ejigu said, holding up one long finger. "But could you please clarify your position? Are you saying you did or did not leverage the entire value of the corporation to pay the Super Serial entrance fees?"

"I value DipShip highly," Alexia answered, this time with a curt edge to her voice. "I believe my team will be capable of success in

Super Serial, and so far, they've proven me right. We assembled a team in record time."

"Thank you for sharing," Ejigu smiled politely. "But you still haven't answered my question. Did you, or did you not leverage DipShip's book value to pay the Super Serial entrance fees?"

There was an uncomfortable pause while Alexia tried to mask her fury, blinking like she had something in her eye. She then asked Pepper to bring her some water as an obvious stall, fiddling with her mic while she waited.

Ejigu also waited. He was neither insistent nor dismissive, and didn't offer her a way to save face. Damn, if Ziggy didn't respect him for it.

Several minutes passed before Alexia finally responded. "DipShip has an excellent future ahead. I'm confident any collateral will be paid back with interest."

"So, you did leverage the company to pay the entrance fees?" Ejigu asked.

Alexia sniffed. "I suppose you could say that."

"Thank you," Ejigu said. He still hadn't written anything in his notebook. Alexia looked feral, ready to jump out of her chair and scratch his eyes out.

"What are your first impressions of your team?" Song Zexian asked as if nothing of import had happened. "How do you think they'll fare in the Preliminaries?"

Alexia smiled at Zexian with a false air of decorum. "The team we assembled is certainly interesting," she said, reverting back to her scripted answers. "Each of them has a unique set of skills that will transfer well into the Preliminaries. I'm confident DipShip can compete with the larger corporations already well-established in the games."

Stormi MacGowan held up her hand, her red hair framing her head like a fiery lion's mane. "Ms. Ito," she said, "If DipShip were to somehow succeed in Super Serial, what plans do you have for the district?"

"DipShip is forging ahead into the future stronger than ever," Alexia lied. "We've rectified years of mismanagement, boosting our profit margins and enhancing living conditions in the district by leveraging more stable sub-corps and direct leasing agreements."

Ziggy glanced at Pepper, whose expression was sour. Alexia was lucky Floyd wasn't around to point out the corrupt deals that lined her pockets, the deteriorating living conditions that kept Pepper up at night, and the overall bullshit that comprised every word she spoke.

"Even though our trajectory is already upwardly mobile," Alexia pressed on, "success in Super Serial would expedite the speed at which we can continue to make improvements."

"You're up next," Boomer sidled up to Ziggy. He was holding a makeup sponge in his hand. "We need to get you ready."

"You're out of your mind if you think I'm going to let you put makeup on me," Ziggy said. "Get lost." Boomer huffed but retreated, glaring at Ziggy like he'd canceled Christmas.

"How did you find Marshal Ghostshade?" Ejigu asked Alexia, running his fingers down the length of his pencil, "And how did you convince him to work for DipShip? It's no secret he's been removed from the public eye for many years."

Alexia looked at Ziggy sideways. He crossed his arms over his chest, waiting to see what she'd say. That she'd taken his husband's ashes to bribe him into working for her? That she had exploited him and threatened to have him thrown in a labor prison after she purchased his medical debt from Pill Depot? The options were endless.

"One of our team members managed to locate Mr. Ghostshade," Alexia said. Not a lie, but definitely vague.

"And how has your collaboration been with him so far?" Ejigu asked, and Ziggy studied Alexia's reaction, knowing how uncomfortable she'd be with the question. He was curious to see how she'd gloss over her obvious hatred for him. At least she had one thing in common with her father.

"Marshal Ghostshade has been instrumental to our success," she said, her smile never faltering. "Naturally, he understands the expectations placed upon him and the rest of his team. They each play a pivotal role in ensuring that their performance in the games aligns with DipShip's goals."

Beside Ziggy, Pepper tensed. It was a subtle threat veiled in diplomatic language, but a clear reminder that Alexia wielded the power, and anyone who failed to meet her standards would suffer the consequences. If things went poorly, Alexia would blame him, but Pepper would also be in the spotlight of her wrath. He clasped Pepper's hand for a brief moment and she gave him a hesitant smile. He'd never let that happen. She was DipShip's best chance.

"I'm sure Marshal Ghostshade can give us more information," Ejigu said, and Ziggy could have sworn he heard Alexia curse at him under her breath.

"Thank you for meeting with us, Ms. Ito," Dora said. "We're eager to see how DipShip fares in the Preliminaries."

"Of course," Alexia said, standing from her seat and stepping away from the lights. Boomer took her by the elbow, and the two retreated to a nearby corner to whisper behind their hands.

"Marshal Ghostshade," Dora said. "If you're ready, we'd like to interview you next, before we move onto DipShip's contestants."

Ziggy glanced at Pepper, who nudged him forward with her eyes. He would do it for her, so she could have a chance to fix things. He sat in the interviewing seat and faced the analysts.

"Thank you for joining us," Dora said, barely waiting for him to get comfortable. "For those of you watching online, this is famed Marshal Ziglar Ghostshade, who captured and executed Sean O'Shaughnessy—better known to the public as Red Judas. Mr. Ghostshade, how long have you been working for DipShip?" she asked.

"Twelve weeks," Ziggy responded, and the analysts murmured to each other in surprise.

"How did you manage to capture so many killers in such a short time?" Stormi said, sitting back in her seat, her eyebrows so high they disappeared into her hair.

"I didn't," Ziggy said. "I had an excellent team who worked together to make it happen. Floyd McNut, our operations analyst," he said before they could ask, "Pepper Devoux, executive administrator, and…" Ziggy's mind went blank, "Rick, I want to say? They worked tirelessly to put the team together."

Pepper beamed at Ziggy, but he noticed Alexia scowling from where she was standing with Boomer. He didn't care. Alexia didn't have shit to do with any success they'd had so far.

"You found a Centennial killer in District Motorkörper," Jomar said, whirling a gaudy jeweled ring on his finger. Now that Alexia was out of sight, he seemed to have noticed Ziggy existed. "There are a lot of rumors about what happened the night you attempted to apprehend Moritz Sauer. Care to set the record straight?"

"Moritz Sauer was a deranged psychopathic serial killer who mutilated and murdered hundreds of people," Ziggy said. "The Dip-Ship team did absolutely everything in our power to arrest him alive, but he'd prepared a trap in case he was ever caught. We were lucky to escape with our lives. The man was a coward who didn't have the guts to face up to what he'd done. He chose to die rather than give the victims of his crimes even an ounce of justice."

"Is it true that hundreds of bodies were desecrated when an explosion in a crematory ignited the gas line?" Zexian asked. "Yes, it's true," Ziggy said, clenching his fists together in his lap. "Another disgusting crime perpetrated by a disgusting man."

"Why did you decide to work for District DipShip?" Ejigu asked, a look of genuine curiosity crossing his face.

Ziggy tried not to look at his unusual golden eyes, but he wasn't successful. His mouth moved to produce an answer, but his mind went blank. Throwing Alexia under the bus would be satisfying, but he had no doubt she'd pull Pepper under with her. She could heap all the blame for her failures on Pepper's back and walk away with scarcely a scratch to her reputation.

"You're a well-known, skilled marshal." Ejigu rephrased his question. "You disappeared from the public for a long stretch of time, only to return to DipShip? You could have worked as a marshal for any district in the world."

Ziggy thought for a moment, making sure to answer with care. There was a good chance that at some point, Hirofumi would see the interview. "After my prior experiences as a marshal," Ziggy said, "I thought I was done for good. The team here at DipShip found me and made me realize I needed to stay."

"You stayed because of your team?" Ejigu asked, and Ziggy nodded. The analysts didn't need to know it was the Pepper and Floyd part of the team, not the Alexia part.

"Speaking of your team," Zexian asked, "how are you preparing your killers for the Preliminaries? Do you think they have a chance of succeeding?"

"If you qualify staying alive as a success," Ziggy said bluntly, "then, yes. They have as good a chance as any other serial killer in a battle arena full of serial killers."

"What are the team's strengths?" Jomar asked.

"Their strengths?" Ziggy repeated the words. It was a ridiculous question. "Like, what makes them good at murdering people?"

Jomar chuckled, stroking his beard to mask his obvious discomfort. "I suppose you could put it that way."

Ziggy knew what the analysts were really asking. They wanted to know what made DipShip's team a threat—or if they were simply disposable assets waiting to be eliminated. He decided to be honest. If he didn't believe in the team's chances, why would anyone else?

"Benedict was forced into Super Serial practically from birth," Ziggy began. "His mother was obsessed with the games to the point of madness. She made it her life's mission to mold him into a killer, starting from the cradle. He never stood a chance."

"Such a shame," Stormi murmured in response, and Song nodded in agreement, waiting for Ziggy to continue.

"He's good with his dogs, though," Ziggy went on. "And he genuinely loves them, which makes him an ideal competitor for the Pet Lovers category. His corgis are trained to attack on command, and they eat people alive. Given enough time, I think he would have become a Centennial killer, too."

Jomar gave a hearty chuckle. "Did you say, corgis?"

Ziggy nodded. "I thought the same thing until I saw them attack. There are twenty-eight, and they can bring down a man bigger than you in seconds. So, you asked me about Benedict's strengths. Alone, he has none. In fact, he may be the biggest coward I've ever known. But with his pack at his side, he's fierce, and that's a dangerous combination."

"It says in your team's portfolio that you've had some trouble with... Tanya Wheeler?" Dora read from her device. "Your Leo."

"She prefers to be called Big Montana Ice," Ziggy said wryly. "And yes, you could say we've had trouble. For one thing, she used to be a semi-professional weightlifter; she's tall, thick, and very muscular. When you combine her brute strength with delusions and paranoia, it can get ugly—fast. Her size alone makes her an asset to the team, but it's her total lack of remorse that makes her a real threat. If she gets it in her head that you're possessed by the demon Bazgoroch, she'll do anything in her power to kill you."

"Your Centennial competitor is an interesting case," Ejigu said. "She's more than a century old, but she has some impressive Super Serial history. Has that history benefited the team?"

Ziggy inwardly begged himself not to blush under Ejigu's gaze. "Lin Meihua has killed hundreds of people," he said, relieved when his voice came out steady. "She's responsible for the downfall of democratic governments all over the world. I once saw her murder a man in an open, ventilated room without even touching him, and I still have no idea how she did it. Only a fool would dismiss her because of her age. She has almost fifty years of experience killing and is a master of poison. Her knowledge base will be a huge advantage in the Prelims."

"I'd love to hear more about your Angry White Women competitor, Carol," Jomar said, looking at her perky, smiling photo on his tablet. "She doesn't really seem like the murdering type."

"If you ask her," Ziggy said, "she'll tell you that's because she's not. She's claimed innocence from day one, but the impressive amount of mangled bodies Marshal Edwards found stuffed in her freezer or pushing up daisies in her flower garden say otherwise."

Dora Spiro's eyes lit up, probably at the prospect of a new documentary. "It says in her portfolio that none of the bodies found on her property had fingerprints on them. Is that true? Could she be innocent?"

"That's what the report read," Ziggy confirmed, "but I wasn't the marshal who wrote it. The lack of fingerprints could just as easily have been human error or coincidence, and there was a lot of circumstantial evidence pointing to Carol. Too much to dismiss."

Stormi flipped to the Samurai's portfolio, looking confused when she found it surprisingly sparse. "I think there's been a mistake," she said, looking over her shoulder for Pepper. "My document only has one page for the Vigilante."

"No mistake," Ziggy said, signaling to Pepper that he'd handle the explanation. "The reason there's only one page is that the Samurai is still an enigma, even to us."

Zexian scanned the lone page. "It says here, he decapitates executives who were allegedly associated with the FissionCo disaster," they read, "and executives who he views as unethical or corrupt."

"I read about FissionCo in college," Ejigu murmured, his deep voice solemn. "Thousands died painful, horrific deaths from radiation poisoning."

"Well, he certainly fits the bill for a Vigilante," Jomar said, scrutinizing the Samurai's photo. "And he's a Samurai? Or, at least, he claims to be? If he is, he could be a valuable asset for the team."

"The Samurai's strength is either ingenuity because he makes his armor and weapons from trash," Ziggy explained, "or tenacity since he's hunted the executives who committed crimes against his people for more than twenty years. And that's the amount of time we can guess."

"This is an impressive team, considering you only had three months to find them all," Dora said, scrolling on her tablet, and

Ziggy suddenly realized she was right. They may not be the strongest team, but they were far from weak. Somehow he, Pepper, and Floyd had made a miracle happen. And if one miracle could happen, why not two? Maybe they could manage to keep enough killers alive to save DipShip after all.

"Thank you, Marshal Ghostshade," Zexian said. "We can't wait to meet them."

Ziggy tried not to cringe as he stepped out of the spotlight. He might've been too heavy-handed on the optimism considering what lay ahead—the analysts still had to interview the killers, and he was fairly certain Boomer was moving forward with his plan.

Chapter 7

Only God Can Fudge Me

Ziggy watched as Carol, the first of their unhinged team of weaponized killers, entered the room, escorted by Boomer, Pepper, and a trio of security guards. He had to hold back a laugh when he saw she was wearing the gold bikini but overtop a long-sleeved white t-shirt. Her trusty fanny pack of essential oils was clipped over her hip. Boomer was flushed, his face so pinched it looked like it had been sucked together with a vacuum hose, and Ziggy could only imagine the backstage wardrobe battle that must have taken place. Carol's hair, however, had a new cut, her fake eyelashes were gone, and her makeup was toned down to a soft, rosy glow. Despite all her earlier objections, Ziggy thought the makeover revealed a great deal more of her natural beauty. Boomer may have lost the bikini battle, but he was slowly winning the war.

Seated in front of the analysts, guarded on all sides, Carol arranged her wrists delicately in her lap, her posture reminiscent of a fragile origami flower.

"Could you please state your name and home district for our records?" Dora Spiro asked, her tone professional.

"My name is Carol Petersen, and I'm from the Intermountain Mining District," Carol said, batting her eyelashes. Much of the effect was gone without her fake lashes.

"It could be worse," Alexia whispered to Boomer, but Ziggy could still hear them from their seats on Pepper's other side. "At least she looks human now."

"I should've made her go naked," Boomer muttered, and Alexia giggled.

Stormi MacGowan jumped in with a direct question. "Carol, the public is calling you the Multi-Level Marketing Murderer or the MLM Murderer. What's your response to that?"

Carol tilted her head, wearing a tight smile. "I don't understand. Why would anyone call me that?"

Stormi, with a hint of derision, explained, "Your bio states you were involved in a multi-level marketing company that sells essential oils and other health products."

Carol straightened her shoulders. "We provide alternative health solutions through network marketing. MLM is a derogatory acronym created by pharmaceutical corporations to keep the public in the dark. God already gave us everything we need to heal our bodies naturally." Carol unzipped her fanny pack. "These precious gifts of the earth can reduce your body's toxic load and boost your immune system. Would you like to try some?" She extended a bottle labeled "Defensive Blend."

"God, does she ever stop?" Boomer said under his breath. The analysts exchanged glances, and Jomar couldn't suppress his laughter.

"No thank you, Carol," Dora declined, and Carol returned the bottle to her fanny pack, her unshakeable smile still pasted in place.

"Carol," Ejigu said, shifting the focus, "you were arrested and tried by DipShip Marshal Chet Edwards, who was later murdered by another serial killer in District Motorkörper. What was your impression of Marshal Edwards? Did you feel you were given a fair trial?"

"I want the world to know I am innocent," Carol declared, tears welling in her massive eyes. "I'm a good Christian woman, and I would never hurt anyone. I don't want to speak ill of the dead, but Marshal Edwards was corrupt, and the sentence he passed was false. He arrested me in front of my children. I can't imagine what they've been through. I haven't even been allowed to speak with them or my darling husband Jeff since my arrest."

Ziggy noted the desperation in her eyes as she continued to insist on her innocence. He could never quite tell if Carol was putting on a performance or not.

"Damn, she's good," Alexia quietly pouted. "If only she'd follow a script."

"At the time of your arrest, the body of Nicole Jones was found in a freezer in your basement," Song Zexian said, scrolling through Carol's bio on their tablet. "If you're innocent, as you claim, how did her body get into your freezer?"

"I don't know," Carol sniffed, a single tear running down her cheek. "I was as shocked as anyone. What happened to Nicole was a terrible thing, but I didn't kill her. I was framed."

"The bodies of Jessica Potts and Elizabeth Young were also found on your property, buried beneath your flower garden. Were you framed for those murders as well?" Zexian pressed.

"I must have been," Carol said. "But, like Job in the Bible, I will not 'despise the discipline of the Almighty.' There's a purpose to trials, even ones that seem unfair, and I pray every day to understand Heavenly Father's plan for me and my family."

"Speaking of family," Stormi said, shifting gears. "Your husband, Jeff, recently gave a statement to the press about the crimes you committed. He was with his new fiancée Becky Jones, a lovely woman. You may recognize the name on account of her being Nicole's youngest sister. They've been named Super Serial victim couple of the year." Stormi flipped over her tablet to show Carol a video of a tall, handsome man with dark hair. His arm was around a smiling woman with flowing blonde locks. "Have you seen this yet?"

Carol froze. She didn't breathe. She didn't even blink.

"This is exactly why I didn't tell her before now," Boomer whispered.

"Carol?" Stormi prompted after a few moments.

"You made a mistake," Carol said sweetly, her smile so broad and detached it looked surreal. "That's not true."

"Shit," Boomer said under his breath.

"That's not him?" Stormi asked, playing the video once more, holding her tablet forward so Carol could get a better look.

"Carol doesn't know the difference between fantasy and reality," Jeff said, tightening his hold on Becky's shoulder. "She's a sick, delusional woman caught in a web of lies, and we support her sentence to Super Serial. The families of her victims deserve closure. Even though Carol refuses to take accountability for her crimes or acknowledge the pain she's inflicted, we strive every day to forgive her because that's what our Savior Jesus Christ asked us to do."

The video ended, and Ziggy watched Carol scrunch the fabric of her jogger pants into her fists. "It's not your fault," she told Stormi, her smile faltering by a fraction, her eyes brimming with tears. "I can see how you were confused. People can make anything look real with technology. Someone must have doctored that footage to upset me."

"Looked pretty real to me," Joram said with an insufferable smirk.

As Carol struggled to maintain her composure, Ziggy did the math. Carol's arrest had been just two weeks before he'd started hunting killers for DipShip. If the video was true, that meant Jeff had gotten engaged to another woman less than four months after Carol's arrest. It was no wonder she was having a hard time accepting the truth. Carol may be a serial killer, but Jeff was a creep.

Joram tried to ask Carol another question, but Carol covered her ears with her hands and squeezed her eyes shut. The analysts exchanged frustrated glances with each other. "Are you being serious right now?" Jomar asked, rolling his eyes at Carol.

As far as Ziggy was concerned, it served them right. Why would they show Carol evidence of her husband's infidelity smack dab in the middle of her interview, then expect her to continue on answering questions like her world hadn't just exploded? Alexia looked mortified, color high in her cheeks.

"Carol?" Joram tried again, but she shut him out, humming a gospel hymn to herself and rocking in her seat.

"Abide with me, tis eventide," she whispered and Ziggy saw the dam of tears slowly chase down her cheeks, drawing delicate lines in her makeup.

After a few minutes of unproductive probing, the analysts ordered her away and asked Pepper to bring in Benedict. Carol left the room looking like a husk of herself, with a security guard on both sides.

Benedict entered the room, flanked by guards, but it was the sight of the adorable, stubby-legged corgi leading the way that took Ziggy the most off guard. The little dog strutted alongside Benedict on a short leash, dressed in a pint-sized version of the team uniform, complete with "Otto" stitched on the back. Boomer's attempt to spruce Benedict up had worked—to a degree.

The most noticeable change was in his complexion. He no longer looked like a pimply weasel; instead, his skin was fresh and glowing. Boomer had also sculpted his wispy brown hair into what was probably a fashionable faux hawk, though Ziggy thought it looked more like a squirrel pelt tacked to the top of his head. Despite the improvements, Benedict kept blinking and rubbing his eyes, obviously uncomfortable in his new contact lenses.

Watching from the sidelines, Alexia whispered to Boomer, "It's like a miracle." But as Benedict took his seat, Ziggy noticed beads of sweat dotting his brow and, upon closer inspection, realized the glowing skin was just heavy makeup. When rings began to form beneath Benedict's armpits, Ziggy silently prayed the interview would be short.

"Could you please state your name and home district for our records?" Dora asked.

"Benedict Benjamin Bork from District MingAir," Benedict wheezed, panting so heavily Ziggy wondered if he was having a panic attack. His eyes darted around, likely searching for the quickest way out, while Otto, sensing his anxiety, jumped into his lap, craning his neck to sniff at Benedict's chin.

Dora continued, "Can you tell us about your dogs, Benedict?"

"I have twenty-nine babies," he said, running his fingers through Otto's fur, a hint of relief surfacing as he spoke about his beloved corgis. "Well, twenty-nine, including Mother, but Mother was killed by UltraChad."

"What are their names?" Ejigu asked, and Benedict smiled for the first time.

"Their names are Winifred, Ivan, Amir, Shilo, Ezra, Aleera, Filipe, Darcy, Jenica, Andrew, Anna, Devon, Christian, Dakota, Gabriel, Cicily, Nora, Jude, Juraj, Sharee, Carlie, Pakpao, River, Cohen, Otto, who's here with us now, Flaviana, Cora, and, of course, my youngest baby, Ellie."

"Who trained your dogs to kill?" Jomar cut in.

"Mother did," Benedict said. "She said I was destined for Super Serial greatness, and when she thought I needed help, she took to training the dogs."

"Your mother?" Stormi MacGowan questioned, glancing at her tablet. "I don't understand. Did your mother come to DipShip with you? There's no record of that. You said she was killed by Ultra-Chad?"

Ziggy rolled his eyes. He hated this show. The analysts were prepped with a full brief of each killer's background and neuropsychological panel. They feigned ignorance, but their questions were really meant to probe out their eccentricities for the public to mock.

"Mother *was* killed by UltraChad," Benedict said with a shaky breath. His eyes filled with tears. "Bless her. All she ever wanted was to look out for me. I really miss her milkies. Having to wean early has been difficult for me. I'm absolutely gutted." Otto perked up and began licking Benedict's face and, much to Boomer's dismay, smeared his makeup.

Ejigu chimed in. "I may be able to clarify. Benedict's mother was named Eugenie Taro. After she died, her"—Ejigu cringed a little—"*essence* was consumed by Mother-corgi, the dog who was killed when Benedict was attacked. He uses the term Mother interchangeably."

"At least one of them read the brief," Pepper whispered, jostling Ziggy's elbow. She was trying to lighten his mood, but somehow it made the butterflies in his stomach feel more like a swarm of wasps.

"I see," Stormi said, fluffing her wild curls. "Speaking of UltraChad, how do you feel about facing him in the Prelims?"

Benedict's eyes darted to Boomer, and Boomer mouthed something to him from the sidelines that Ziggy couldn't make out. Benedict turned back to the analysts and smiled, but it was so stiff and forced Ziggy could barely look. "When UltraChad attacked, I didn't have my trusty canine crew by my side," Benedict said, his answer clearly memorized from a script. "Sure, they might not bark much, but these pooches have got some serious bite!" He flashed the analysts an overly enthusiastic thumbs-up, pausing for laughter that never came. "UltraChad won't know what hit him when he faces off against me and my twenty-eight 'fur-bulous' sidekicks."

"Oh God, he's gonna be a meme," Boomer breathed in horror while Alexia sat frozen, mouth agape, as if listening to a lackluster ex-boyfriend singing the world's worst karaoke love song dedicated personally to her.

"So, your mother trained the dogs?" Stormi ventured after an awkward silence.

"Mother trained most of the babies," Benedict explained slowly, this time seeming not to have an answer rehearsed. "I trained Otto, Flaviana, Cora, and baby Ellie. It was a doddle, really. I didn't have to hurt them to make them mind the way Mother did. With so many brothers and sisters, they just tagged along."

"How do the dogs know who to attack?" Zexian asked, watching Benedict scratch Otto's stomach while his stubby leg kicked in response. "Do you pick the person, or do they?"

Benedict leaned over to let Otto lick his face, laughing in delight before opening his mouth and letting Otto lick inside.

"That's nasty," Boomer whispered, his tone thick with disgust.

"I'm always on the lookout for more babies," Benedict said between a torrent of openmouthed doggy French kisses. "It's appalling how many get left and..." He trailed off as Boomer loudly cleared his throat.

"Every day, countless corgis find themselves in a 'ruff' situation," Benedict recited, snapping back to attention, his mouth opening into a forced smile. "Many of these loyal companions end up abandoned in shelters and rescue centers, never finding a 'fur-ever' home."

Boomer groaned quietly, "I told him to try out a pun," he whispered to Alexia. "Just one pun!"

"It broke my heart to see them suffer," Benedict continued woodenly, grinning so widely he looked deranged, his upper lip tucked into his teeth like a posturing chimpanzee. "And I knew I had to do something. Good thing corgis are like biscuits. You can never have just one! After I bring my new furry companion home, I begin the search for their perfect match."

"Their match?" Zexian asked, puzzled.

"Indeed," Benedict said as if in a trance. "My matching skills are so good, I could light a fire in a rainstorm!" He wiped his nose on his sleeve, soiling the jacket with the makeup dripping down his face.

"Benedict," Ejigu suddenly said, his voice firm with authority. Benedict startled, hurriedly wrapping his arms around Otto, his gaze fixed on Ejigu. "Focus on me and no one else," Ejigu said, and Benedict nodded obediently, his eyes widening. "In your own words, tell me why your corgis need a match," Ejigu asked, never looking away from Benedict.

"The babies must have a match so they can feed," Benedict murmured, his voice turning inward, almost as if he were having a conversation with himself. He seemed to retreat into his mind, leaving only an empty shell to face the analysts. "They're famished when they first come home, and they simply can't settle without their match."

"What happens when you find a match?" Ejigu asked.

"I wait until the third Thursday of the month when Mother is busy with her Super Serial fantasy league," Benedict said, his facade slowly unraveling as the killer beneath began to surface. "That's when I take the babies to the park. When their match arrives, I signal the babies that it's time to feed."

"What's the signal?"

"It's a special whistle I keep around my neck," Benedict said, still fixated on Ejigu. "When the babies hear it, they know it's time for a little snack."

"Do you have the whistle with you?" Stormi asked. "Can you show us?"

"Yes," Benedict said, rising to his feet as Otto eagerly jumped to the ground, his nubby tail wagging in excitement. A guard positioned herself in front of the analyst's table as Benedict gripped the leash in one hand and retrieved the whistle from around his neck with the other.

Otto snapped to attention the moment Benedict put it between his lips, his eyes focused intently on the guard. Benedict's cheeks puffed as he blew a pattern into the whistle, but only Otto responded to the sound. The fur along his back bristled, his lips curled back in a snarl, and he bared his teeth before viciously lunging forward, halting only by the snap of the leash.

Benedict blew the whistle again, and Otto instantly complied, returning to Benedict's side. Benedict scratched him between the ears, and the room fell into a stunned silence.

"Thank you, Benedict," Dora said after a moment. "We'll be interested to see how your dogs fare in the Prelims." She nodded to

Pepper, who signaled security to bring in the next killer. "We'll talk to Tanya Wheeler next," Dora said, but Boomer shook his head.

"Big Montana Ice ... I mean, Tanya is having a little trouble getting... settled," Boomer said with exaggerated enthusiasm. "It might be better to interview her last."

Alexia exchanged glances with Boomer, and Ziggy wondered what other drama was happening behind the scenes with the killers.

"Very well, then we'll talk to the Warlord of Waste," Dora said, and security whisked Benedict and Otto away.

The Samurai was escorted into the room. He rejected the chair facing the analysts and opted to stand instead. Even in his colorful uniform, his lithe physique and intense stare exuded an aura of coiled tension that put the guards on edge. One stood close, his hand resting on the Samurai's shoulder, with the other gripping his stun baton.

"Trash Daddy looks good enough to eat," Ziggy overheard Boomer tell Alexia. "We should forget about Carol and make him the district sex symbol."

As his words reached the Samurai's ears, his eyes ignited with contempt, and he cast a scathing look in their direction. Alexia responded with a dismissive eye roll while Boomer fanned himself with his hand. Ziggy's intuition prickled with foreboding. They were intentionally provoking and belittling a man with a track record of ruthless decapitations.

"You were arrested at the Skidmore Dumping District. Is that right?" Dora asked, scrutinizing the Samurai under her heavy brow. He didn't respond.

"What's your birth name, if you don't mind my asking?" Jomar tried next, but the Samurai stayed silent.

"Can you give us any information about yourself at all?" Stormi asked. "Why did you kill all those executives?"

The Samurai maintained his stoic silence.

"This guy's a total nut job," Jomar said under his breath after a long moment.

"A bad word whispered echoes a hundred miles," the Samurai spoke; his deep, rich voice hung heavily in the room as if he were an executioner delivering a sentence.

"So you can speak," Stormi said with a nervous chuckle. "That's a relief. I was beginning to think you wouldn't say a word."

"Words should be weighed, not counted," the Samurai replied, his eyes piercing the analysts.

"Would you please tell us about your martial arts training?" Song Zexian tried another approach. The Samurai's wild eyes licked the analysts like fire on dry bark. "Little by little, the old world crumbled," he murmured, "and not once did the king imagine that some of the pieces might fall on him."

"That's a quote from a book, is it not?" Ejigu said. "*Revolution*, by Donnelly, if I'm right. It's a historical fiction about the first French Revolution." The Samurai paused for a moment to examine Ejigu, then nodded, returning to waiting in silence.

Dora turned to Pepper with a sigh. "You can take him away. It's a complete waste of time if he won't speak."

"I apologize," Alexia said smoothly. "As you know, criminals can be impossible to work with."

"It's rare to have one who won't even speak," Dora replied, and after seeing the irritated look on Alexia's face. "Usually they're excited to be part of something as amazing as Super Serial. It gives them purpose."

Ziggy bristled. The wasps in his gut shifted to fire ants as his mind sledgehammered against the philosophy that killers had purpose and value beyond hurting others. He wondered if anyone in the room realized they were interviewing dangerous serial killers. They were talking about them like they were unruly toddlers.

"Bring in Meihua," Pepper ordered as security led the Samurai from the room.

Fifteen long minutes later, Floyd entered the room with Lin Meihua. She used her cane to shuffle across the room in painstakingly slow steps, pausing to take a long drink from a bottle of water Floyd held, bits dribbling from her wrinkly lips into the folds of her scarves. It felt like a year had passed by the time she made it to her interview chair, and Boomer looked on the brink of emotional collapse. Meihua sunk into it like she would a steaming bath.

"Hello," Floyd greeted the analysts. "I'm Floyd McNut. I will be translating today since Lin Meihua doesn't speak English." Ziggy was glad to see Floyd was feeling well enough to translate. He was slightly pale but seemed fine otherwise.

"Actually, I'll provide translation," Zexian said, their eyes on Meihua's shriveled prune face. "I was born in Yifu."

"Did you hear that Meihua?" Floyd said with a broad grin. *"Zhè wèi fēnxīshī láizì Yìfū."*

Meihua patted Floyd's arm. *"Tā néng tīng dào wǒ dehuà, dànshì nǐ míngbái de xīn. Liú zài wǒ shēnbiān hǎo bù hǎo,"* Meihua croaked, her voice like a ghost's whisper escaping from a burlap sack.

"Lin Meihua, you're the only member of the DipShip team with any Super Serial experience. Correct?" Dora questioned. "We show here that you were a contestant in the 36th through 49th Super Serial Games."

Floyd moved to translate, but Zexian spoke over him. Meihua looked at them for a moment before replying, her words halted and weak. Zexian translated for the other analysts, "She says she has been in many Super Serial games."

"Meihua, some scholars say you were instrumental in the downfall of the former Democratic Socialist Party in Central Asia. How do you respond?" Ejigu asked. Again, Zexian translated before Floyd could speak, but after a few long moments, Lin Meihua still had not responded. Her chin was tucked into her chest, and her eyes were closed.

"Is she breathing?" Dora glanced at Alexia.

"She's asleep," Floyd said, leaning over to look at Meihua. "She dozes off sometimes when she's sitting. Especially if the chair is comfortable."

Jomar laughed uproariously. "How's this old cat going to make it through the Prelims? She can't even stay awake for the interview!"

"It was a long walk up here," Floyd said, "and she's one hundred and five years old."

Jomar laughed even harder, and a security guard lifted the dozing Meihua into his arms and carried her away. There was a loud crash from somewhere down the hall, followed by a bellow that could only be from Big Montana Ice, and Boomer and Pepper exchanged hushed words on their way out, leaving Boomer looking thoroughly exasperated.

Floyd joined Ziggy. "Someone needs to tell the analysts what she did to the last person who insulted her like that," he murmured. "They're lucky she was asleep."

"No kidding," Ziggy agreed. "How are you feeling?"

"Better," Floyd said, rubbing his stomach. "Meihua gave me some tea to calm my indigestion. Now I know what it feels like to be you, Ziggy. Diarrhea is no joke."

A camera man looked back at Floyd and Ziggy and smirked. Ziggy chuckled inside. He was nervous, but it could be worse. He could also have diarrhea. "How's it going back there?" he asked Floyd.

"Not well at all," Floyd confided with a grimace. "That's part of the reason Meihua is so tired. Boomer and Big Montana Ice have been arguing for hours. Big Montana Ice found out that Boomer's middle name starts with a Z, and for some reason, it made her extremely angry. She keeps calling him a demon, but all he wants is to give her a haircut."

Ziggy looked around the room for Alexia. She was chatting with the analysts, likely trying to smooth things over in hopes of a better score. His stomach clenched with nerves. Alexia was in the room, but he had no confidence she'd trigger the insta-kill-chip even if things went wrong.

Tense anticipation hung in the air as security arrived with Big Montana Ice, who Ziggy heard screaming the entire way down the hall.

"I'm tired of being bossed around by all of you!" Big Montana Ice bellowed, ducking her head to fit in the room. "Especially that bitchy little fucktwat," she sneered, and Boomer huffed his way to his seat next to Alexia, glaring back at Big Montana Ice the whole way. "I don't mean you, Pepperoni," Big Montana Ice said as Pepper passed. "You're the only one around here worth two shits and a fuck."

The analysts collectively turned their attention to Pepper, and Alexia's eyes burned with a jealous glare. Pepper held her ground though, ignoring Alexia and motioning for Big Montana Ice to take a deep breath.

Big Montana was secured by four guards, each holding a tether attached to a restraint. There were more restraints on her ankles and wrists, along with a belly chain connecting the wrist cuffs. In an attempt to guide Big Montana Ice toward the chair near the analysts, a guard pulled on her wrist tether and said, "Come this way."

"That puny-ass seat ain't gonna hold this ripe pumpkin," she scoffed, yanking the guard holding her leg tether to the ground before kicking the chair toward the analysts, breaking off one of its legs. She glared at the panel before her. "Who do we have here? A bunch of demons in suits ready to ask me questions? Go ahead. I have questions for you, too."

"Hello, Tanya," Dora said in a cool, placating voice.

"No one calls me Tanya unless I'm riding their pole like a carousel horse, so unless you plan on taking me for a spin, call me Big Montana Ice."

Jomar laughed as Dora flushed a brilliant shade of red. "I'm sorry, Big Montana Ice," she amended.

"You have an interesting backstory," Stormi MacGowan began the questioning. "You responded to a personal ad DipShip put out requesting a serial killer join the team. What made you want to join the DipShip team?"

Big Montana Ice leaned forward slightly, and even though they were at a safe distance, all the analysts except Ejigu pressed against their chairs. "I had a vision," she said with intense solemnity.

"A vision?" Stormi probed, and Ziggy wondered if her curiosity was genuine or veiled mockery. She made a note on her tablet. "Please, tell us more."

"My truck crashed into the freezing arctic waters and I got frozen in ice. Then a spirit came along and whisked me away to another sphere. When I was in the spirit realm, Amriel, the ancient thunder goddess, granted me the power of Alaskan Thunder," Big Montana Ice said. "I became the only one who could defeat the shadow demon."

"I see," Jomar said, looking up at her staggering height. "And how will you defeat this"—he looked at his tablet—"shadow demon?"

"With the power of Alaskan Thunder," Big Montana Ice repeated, her eyes narrowing over Jomar. "I said it already. The demon can take any form, but every time I kill it, it finds a way to come back.

The only way to defeat Bazgoroch for good would be to kill it in his final form. That's why the Goddess guided me here."

"How do you see these demons?" Zexian asked. "Have you seen any since arriving at DipShip?"

A shadow crossed Big Montana Ice's face. "There's one just a few feet away, laughing at me because it thinks I can't see it. It thinks I don't know it's there."

Ziggy followed Big Montana Ice's gaze to Boomer, who was whispering into Alexia's ear.

"Do you mean, Mr. D'Chango?" Ejigu asked, his eyes darting to Boomer and then over to Ziggy.

"B. A. Z. G. O. R. O. C. H," Big Montana Ice spat out every letter like it was poison. "There's a B, two Os, and an R in Boomer. Middle name Zavier? There's your Z. D'Chango—A. G. C. and H. Baz-go-roch. The demon is here! I can see it!"

With a primal roar, Big Montana Ice lurched forward, muscles straining against the restraints as she fought to overpower the guards holding her back. With a surge of raw power, she forceful-ly twisted her wrists, the metal cuffs groaning under the pressure until they gave way with a sharp snap.

Ziggy moved instinctively, darting between the analysts and Big Montana Ice. "Stop!" he yelled, holding up his stun baton. "Stand down!"

"The demon is taking over! I'll free you, Marshal!" she bel-lowed, bringing both fists down directly on top of Ziggy's head. "Alaskan Thunder!"

Lights burst behind his eyes, and he felt a strange pop in his neck, followed by excruciating pain. He didn't recall falling to the floor, but the next thing he knew, he was face to face with Ejigu. "Marshal Ghostshade," Ejigu's brilliant eyes darted over Ziggy. His hands were on each side of his face. "Can you hear me? Ziggy?" Ziggy tried to respond, but his tongue felt glued to the roof of his mouth.

"We need back-up!" a voice screamed above the din, and the room erupted into chaos. Ziggy's mind vaguely registered a fire alarm blaring from above.

Ejigu gripped Ziggy by the armpits and hauled him behind a toppled studio light. "Stun her!" he shouted. "It… won't work. She's too—" Ziggy rasped.

"Then trigger her kill-chip!"

"I-I can't." Ziggy's stomach lurched as he spewed vomit onto the carpet. Ejigu pushed him onto his side so he wouldn't choke, patting his back forcefully. Ziggy tried to move, but the room was spinning, and his head felt like it had been flattened by a sledge-hammer. "Alexia… h-has…" he tried to tell Ejigu, but the words wouldn't come.

He watched in mute horror as Big Montana Ice threw her shoulder into the nearest guard, toppling him to the ground. She jerked one elbow back, cracking it into another guard's face. Blood droplets sprayed through the air, and after seeing how easily she dispatched the guards, he wondered if the only reason Big Montana Ice hadn't killed them before now was as a personal favor.

"Get us out of here!" Alexia shrieked, and Ziggy caught a glimpse of Pepper and Floyd ducking underneath the table. Big Montana Ice sunk her teeth into the arm of a guard who was dangling from her neck, and the guard screamed, dropping to the floor like a stone. Blood dripped from between Big Montana Ice's teeth as she spat out a sinewy hunk of muscle.

"Trigger the kill-chip!" Ejigu bellowed across the room to Alexia.

Alexia frantically scanned the room for the closest exit. "No! She's our only Leo!"

Big Montana Ice moved like a storm. Two guards managed to topple her to her knees, using the ankle tethers, but with lightning speed, she ripped one away by the hair, throwing her against the legs of another. She kicked and swung with deadly accuracy, her fists like battering rams, as guard after guard fell. They outnumbered her, but she still wrenched free from their hold, stumbling to the craft services table, where Boomer had taken cover, begging Alexia not to leave him behind.

The guard protecting Boomer attempted a tackle, but Big Montana Ice held firm and, with a bone-crunching kick to the knee, sent him sprawling across the room into a pile of filming equipment.

"Make her stop!" Boomer screamed as Big Montana Ice grabbed his ankle, laughing while she yanked him out from underneath the table. Plates and bottles clattered to the ground as she lifted Boomer into the air, grinning triumphantly, her mouth coated in blood. A guard wrapped his beefy arms around Big Montana Ice's waist, grunting as he tried to pull her down, but he was no match for her overwhelming strength. "Alaskan Thunder!" she cried, body slamming Boomer onto the carpet. The room shook with the impact, and Boomer groaned in pain as his ribs snapped.

"Take her out!" Ejigu left Ziggy, charging into the fray. "Trigger it!" he thundered at Alexia, but she shook her head, lowering her phone.

"Alexia!" Boomer choked as Big Montana Ice grabbed his arm, twisting it until it popped. She planted one heavy boot on his chest.

"Kill her!" Ejigu tried to tear Alexia's phone from her hand to trigger the kill-chip himself, but in the struggle, the phone clattered to the ground and Alexia smashed it with the heel of her stiletto.

More guards jumped onto Big Montana Ice, pawing and ripping, hitting her with stun batons. She roared against the onslaught, pushing against Boomer's chest and twisting into the security guards, wrenching her shoulders back and forth until Boomer's arm ripped free from his body with a sickening squelch. Blood spurted in gushing rivulets to the frantic staccato of Boomer's horrific screams, which drained to whimpers in moments.

Big Montana Ice held his arm above her head like a trophy, and Ejigu sprang forward, launching himself onto Big Montana Ice's back, wrapping his thick muscular arm around her neck. She fought against him, but stumbled, her strength finally waning.

"Alaskan Thunder!" She managed to choke out her war cry one more time before flipping the dismembered arm around and spearing the jagged bone shard at the end of the limb into the center of Boomer's throat. "I got you, didn't I, Bazgoroch?" she wheezed before submitting to Ejigu's headlock and slinking to the floor. Blood gurgled in Boomer's throat, and through the shuffle of bodies, Ziggy saw the last flicker of life drain from his eyes.

It took Ejigu and six more security guards to hold Big Montana Ice still while a team of medics rushed and tried to figure out how to tranquilize her.

Once she was officially unconscious, Ejigu surged to his feet, striding across the room until he was face to face with Alexia, who was drenched in everyone else's blood. "What kind of person would choose a serial killer over their friend?" he demanded, trembling with what Ziggy knew was probably a combination of fear and adrenaline.

"It's not my fault the stunning and sedation didn't work!" Alexia snapped.

"Ziggy?" Pepper's chinchilla face appeared above him, streaked with tears.

"He vomited everywhere," Floyd said, his face swimming into view next to Pepper's. "He must have a concussion and maybe a broken neck. I'll get a medic."

"Someone's coming to help," Pepper told Ziggy, placing her hand on his forehead like he had a fever. He must have been confused. Floyd was the sick one, wasn't he?

Reality blurred, and Ziggy's vision narrowed until he was staring down a long, black tunnel with no escape.

Chapter 8

Friends in Dough Places

The security protocol at Mongaphalee was bulletproof and sophisticated. It made DipShip security look like a joke by comparison. The moment the DipShip plane touched down, an impenetrable fortress of guards surrounded them, and Ziggy understood more why the Super Serial entrance fee was so expensive. Alexia, who'd traveled separately with DipShip's other important department heads and executives, was spared the thorough search and pat-down given to Ziggy, Floyd, Pepper, and the DipShip guards, even though none of them were criminals. Before the killers could set foot on the tarmac, security locked them into individual transportable cells. The shock etched on their faces at the stark contrast was almost comical, as if they'd forgotten that the rest of the world saw them for the vicious serial killers they were.

"I haven't even had a chance to water my lily and you're already boxing me in?" Big Montana Ice's voice boomed. Her wrists, ankles, neck, and waist were encased in high-tech taser cuffs that looked capable of subduing a grizzly bear. "I've got a question for you," she said, trying to engage the nearest stone-faced guard. Unfazed and disinterested, he didn't even glance her way. "Hey!" she bellowed, her blocky face mottled with patches of red. "Don't ignore me! I said I have a question for you."

"Load her in," a burly officer, almost as massive as Big Montana Ice herself, commanded, flanked by five more guards who made DipShip's standard security personnel look like someone's puny kid brother. They forced her through the door of the plane and down the stairs.

"It's the demon!" Big Montana Ice yanked on her restraints, cursing and pushing against guards with her shoulders, but it was no use. They were focused, strong, emotionless, and trained to work as a cohesive unit—trained to overpower and control murderers. "Bazgoroch followed us here!" Big Montana Ice shrieked, her desperate plea reaching Ziggy as she was loaded into a windowless cell attached to a transport vehicle. "He's everywhere! Don't let them take me!"

As the door sealed shut, her voice became muffled, her cries fading into the distance as the transport vehicle sped away. Ziggy felt a wave of relief seeing her go, grateful she'd be someone else's problem for a while. She'd given him a minor concussion as well as a herniated disk in his neck. He could barely move his head, and spent the plane trip feeling like he had a knife in the back of his neck. Which, given the circumstances, was a valid suspicion. Big Montana Ice was the GlutoBlock of their team. They paid a high price to keep her, but they'd shit their pants and die without her.

"Contestant thirty-seven B is in transport," the officer relayed into his high-tech comm device, securely fastened to his bulletproof gear. "Next!" he called out, and the Samurai was prepped in cuffs for his cell. He didn't resist and held his arms out to the guards to make it easier for them to restrain him. The cuffs and tethers looked offensive on him, like an endangered animal in a cheap cage.

Carol disembarked from the plane in silence. There was something eerie written on her face that Ziggy couldn't decipher, and he realized that she'd barely spoken since her interview with the analysts. The bombshell about her husband's swift romantic pivot had shocked her, but beneath the shock, Ziggy sensed a mess of hidden turmoil. Despite her constant proclamations of innocence, he still had to remind himself of the chilling reality that she might have dismembered her neighborhood rivals and stuffed them into chest freezers.

Lin Meihua was next off the plane, and a second security team arrived in full hazmat suits to handle her transfer. They'd left behind her poison cache at DipShip, but Mongaphalee took no chances. She shuffled along on unsteady feet, moving about as fast as a three-legged turtle. To keep pace, a guard wound up scooping Meihua into his arms and she waved to Floyd as the guard carried her down the steps. She looked like a wrinkled pile of laundry being cradled by a giant.

Benedict and his corgis were last off the plane, and since security protocol dictated each dog be kenneled separately, it took nearly an hour to label and transport each animal.

"Careful with Darcy, he's delicate! Pakpao! Winnie! Oh, my poor babies!" Benedict shouted each dog's name as they were muzzled and kenneled. His incessant sobs became so grating that a guard finally muted his cell completely.

The guard jeered, "What a pussy!" His comrade burst into laughter before they reverted back to speaking in the local language of Mongaphalee. Ziggy didn't need translation to know what they were saying. They likely could predict who was doomed in the Prelims.

During the wait, Ziggy observed several other teams' animals undergoing the same process—a mountain lion, a snarling gazer with an extra arm poking out of its chest, and what looked like two ferocious Tasmanian devils—and felt his anxiety increase. When it was finally done, Ziggy, Pepper, and Floyd barely made it to their lodgings in time to change for the Opening Ceremonies.

His formal wear looked even more ridiculous on his body than it had on the closet hanger. Ziggy pulled on the lime green suit coat with magenta trim over his black shirt, and even though there was a small moment of satisfaction over how well it was tailored, Ziggy had never worn anything so hideous. He looked like an exotic desert lizard. There was a knock on the door as he clipped on his stun baton and straightened his black tie.

He opened the door to a very confused-looking Floyd followed by—Ziggy's heart stopped—*Boomer?*

"You need to shave," Boomer snapped at Ziggy, pushing his way past Floyd into Ziggy's room. "You're too old and bald for that much stubble." He was wearing a black suit with a magenta shirt underneath a molded back brace that harnessed over his hips, rising to the chin where a thick neck ring was held in place. "And you," he pointed at Floyd. "You need to do something with that hair." Ziggy's feet were rooted to the ground as he tried to remember to breathe.

"I reacted the same way," Floyd said, patting Ziggy's shoulder. He was wearing the same lime green suit as Ziggy's, only his tie was magenta. "I never would've guessed it was possible to survive if your neck got stabbed with a bone shard from your own arm. But I suppose you learn something new every day. Once the shock wears off, you'll be fine." He leaned in to whisper in Ziggy's ear. "Don't worry, I checked his pulse. If he were a zombie, he probably wouldn't have a heartbeat."

"We thought you were dead," Ziggy told Boomer, warily closing the door behind them. "I saw Big Montana Ice crush your ribs."

"I thought so, too," Floyd said with a shrug. "Especially when they pronounced you dead and put you in a body bag."

Boomer held up a bottle of hair gel with his good hand since his other arm was resting in an elaborate sling. "Don't be ridiculous. The doctor said I'll be fine in five or six months. Your terrible fashion sense is the only thing that will kill me in this lifetime."

"F-five or six months," Ziggy repeated lamely. It was almost like Boomer's brutal death had never happened. Without Boomer's back brace and Ziggy's memory of cleaning his blood off of his arms in the shower, it would have felt like Big Montana Ice hit him so hard that he'd hallucinated the entire thing.

"Are we doing this or not?" Boomer strolled into the bathroom. "I still need to finish Alexia's makeup, and the lighting in the skybox is atrocious. Plus, this unbearable heat is making her hair limp."

Ziggy and Floyd stood in front of the mirror while Ziggy shaved, and Boomer attempted to tame Floyd's unruly shrub of wild hair. It took a minor trim and half a bottle of hair gel, but after ten minutes of struggling, Boomer managed to make Floyd's hair obey.

"I'll see you at the Ceremonies," Boomer said before rushing out the door. "Pepper will be here any minute. Don't be late."

Floyd walked out of the bathroom holding a bottle of Ziggy's cologne. "Can I use a spray or two of this?" he asked, sniffing the top of the bottle. "It smells like grapefruits and mint," he said. "And pine trees. Do you think Pepper will like this smell?"

"She'll like it," Ziggy said with a smirk, and the rapid staccato of Pepper's impatient knock sent Floyd running for the door, even though it was Ziggy's room.

"We need to hurry, or we'll be late," Pepper said the moment the door opened. She was wearing a tailored, off-shoulder magenta dress with a sleek gold belt and lime green shoes. Her dark, curly hair was pulled back at the nape and secured with a gold clasp. She looked like a golden, tropical goddess next to Ziggy and Floyd, who were a pair of clowns headed to a low-budget circus. Boomer's sense of fashion was clearly mixed—or maybe he just hated Ziggy and Floyd.

"Whoa," Floyd said, looking at Pepper with wide eyes. "You look... different." Ziggy jabbed an elbow into his ribs, and Floyd scowled, ready to protest, when he realized Ziggy had been trying to drop him a hint.

"Different in a good way?" Pepper asked, shuffling her phone between her hands.

Floyd nodded. "Seeing you like that makes me think of a perfect sunrise." Pepper's eyes lit up with surprise, and Ziggy nearly applauded. Maybe Floyd had a little more game than he realized. Floyd tugged at his collar. "This necktie is too tight, Pep. It feels like I'm wearing a silvertine devil's noose, and it's draining my hit points."

Maybe not.

"You look nice," Pepper replied. "I like your hair."

"It's crunchy," Floyd said, and Ziggy noticed the back of his neck was flushed.

"Security is waiting to take us to the stadium," Pepper said, before turning on her heel, leaving Ziggy and Floyd to follow. "We'll watch the Opening Ceremonies in DipShip's private skybox until just before the Serial Showcase," Pepper told them on their way out. "Alexia should already be in the lounge, so be careful. She can't get any hints that we're actively planning to lose tomorrow. Also, it's common for other CEOs and team leaders to visit corporate boxes, so be prepared to chitchat."

"Great," Ziggy said with heavy sarcasm. Nothing was worse than having to hobnob with slimy corporate types. Especially wearing the insane lime green getup that made him look like a radioactive stage magician.

The private car weaved through the dimly lit streets of Mongaphalee, and the city hummed, alive with anticipation. Ziggy could feel the energy in the air, a blend of excitement and bloodlust that set his nerves on edge. He was grateful for the air-conditioned space. The heat waves were visible in the distance and Ziggy's cracks and crevices weren't on great terms with heat.

"Where'd they send the rest of the team?" Floyd asked. He was sitting in the back with Pepper. Ziggy took the front seat next to the driver. "Is Meihua okay? I was worried about her. She said travel is difficult at her age. I told Alan that she needed a luxury class seat for the flight, and he laughed at me."

"Fucking Alan," Pepper muttered to herself.

Ziggy huffed. Floyd's friendship with Meihua was as strange as it was dangerous, but nothing he said would change Floyd's mind. He was convinced Meihua was a wonderful person, despite her Super Serial history, and thought of her almost as a mentor.

"Mongaphalee security took the killers from their transport cells and put them into the cells they use for the Serial Showcase," Pepper told Floyd. "They sent me a notice that they had all arrived safely."

"I don't like that they have Meihua in a cell. She's very old and feeble. If they treat her roughly, she could die."

Pepper leaned forward, her eyes glittering with a mix of determination and nerves. "There's the stadium," she said as a massive, tiered structure pulled into view. The stadium glimmered in the twilight, its exterior adorned with mesmerizing, color-shifting geographic patterns that danced in the diminishing light of the setting sun. There was a cable supported roof over the top that seemed to cover more than half the seating.

"The stadium holds over a hundred thousand people," Floyd said. He rolled down the window and stuck his head out as they joined the throng of cars headed to the Opening Ceremonies. His hair was ruined, but he was too excited to care.

The security at the stadium was as tight as ever. They were escorted through multiple checkpoints, each guarded by stern-faced personnel who scrutinized their identification with hawk-like precision.

The lime green suit felt like a neon sign, attracting more attention than Ziggy would want in a thousand lifetimes.

"I can't believe I'm actually here," Floyd said as security led them to DipShip's corporate skybox. "I've learned almost everything there is to know about Super Serial, but this is my first time seeing it in person." He shook his head a little as if he thought he might wake up from a dream.

Once inside DipShip's private viewing area, Ziggy was stunned at the level of elegance and sophistication provided to even the poorest of districts. The room dripped opulence with its sumptuous, velvety carpet, plush theater-style seating, gourmet cuisine, and a bar stocked with top-shelf liquors. Two colossal screens dominated the space, broadcasting every detail of the show. Apparently, if your district is part of Super Serial, you're considered elite, no matter the circumstances. The view of the stadium below was excellent, and Super Serial fans were shuffling into their seats like a colony of confused ants.

"Namaste, welcome to Team DipShip's luxury skybox," a host said. "Our staff is dedicated to meeting all of your needs, so please don't hesitate to ask for anything."

"Whiskey, neat," Ziggy said, and a nearby server nodded politely. Ziggy wasn't supposed to drink because he was on pain pills for his neck, but he'd need a good buzz to make it through the night.

Seated regally in the lounge, Alexia held corporate court, effortlessly captivating a group of executives who hung on to her every word. She wore a form-fitting black dress that cascaded into an extravagant train, complemented by shimmering diamond accessories.

Her presence exuded an unmistakable sense of power and sophistication that left them spellbound. Ziggy stole a quick look at his reflection in a nearby mirror and grimaced at the sight of his tacky suit. If Alexia was the queen, he was the court jester.

"DipShip has enormous potential," she said to the executives with a serene smile. "I've taken it under my wing as something of a charity case. Philanthropy is important to me."

"You've always been incredibly generous," Boomer said, seemingly oblivious to the fact that just yesterday, Alexia had stood by and done nothing while Big Montana Ice tore his arm off and murdered him with it. "DipShip doesn't deserve you."

Ziggy snorted into his cup. Truer words had never been spoken.

Alexia scowled, but it melted away as Hirofumi Ito entered the skybox, her expression shifting from dread to feigned enthusiasm in an instant. Ziggy tensed, a shiver crawling up his spine as the hairs on the back of his neck stood on end. This was the moment he'd been dreading since he returned to DipShip to help Pepper and Floyd. He watched Hirofumi out of the corner of his eye, his mind racing with the fear that today might be the day his life debt was called in. He'd hoped the ruthless CEO would consider him enough of a worm to disregard completely, but deep down, Ziggy knew that power never forgets a snub.

Despite being surrounded by hulking security guards, Hirofumi was undoubtedly the most dangerous person in the room. With just a single glance, he sent the executives surrounding Alexia and Boomer skittering out the door like frightened cockroaches trying to escape a boot. When they were gone, the largest of Hirofumi's security guards stealthily planted himself in front of the exit—a clear message, if ever there was one.

With forced respect, Alexia offered a low bow to Hirofumi. "Father, I didn't expect you. What a pleasant surprise." She shot Pepper a withering look before saying, "Had I known you were coming, I would have chosen a better location to greet you."

"There are better places than this?" Ziggy heard Floyd whisper-shout to Pepper, who looked as if she'd swallowed something bitter. She shot a quick glance at Ziggy, trying to conceal her fear, but he could see the terror reflected in her eyes, so he did his best to appear calm.

"Daughter," Hirofumi acknowledged Alexia with a stiff-backed nod. "Why would you be surprised? I'd never miss my only child's debut in Super Serial. Imagine my astonishment when I learned you'd registered your little district despite your financial standing. It's a delight to see you finally putting effort into something."

"Thank you," Alexia replied through clenched teeth as the tension in the room grew palpable. Hirofumi then turned to Boomer, extending his hand in greeting. "How are your parents?" he asked politely.

Boomer awkwardly shook Hirofumi's hand with his uninjured arm. "Fine," he managed to squeak out. Hirofumi's gaze lingered on Boomer's sling and complicated back brace, his expression shifting to condescending sympathy. "Oh, dear," he murmured. "It appears you've had some trouble during your time at DipShip."

"Not at all. A mere mishap. Our team is very efficient," Alexia lied smoothly, but her words rang hollow, and Hirofumi's skeptical expression made it clear he didn't believe her.

"But evidently not your safety protocols," he remarked, blithely flicking an invisible speck of lint from his sleeve.

Alexia's eyes flashed with rage, but she brushed off the jibe and snapped her fingers to summon a server. One swiftly approached, carrying a tray with two champagne flutes. Hirofumi took a sip, then grimaced, gingerly placing the glass back onto the tray. Alexia's shoulders drooped as she wilted under the weight of Hirofumi's prestige.

Once again, Ziggy marveled at how ordinary Hirofumi looked. If Ziggy didn't know he was the richest, most powerful man in the world, you'd think he was an everyday white-collar corporate lackey. Clad in a nondescript navy-blue suit, there were no interesting adornments or splashes of color to draw the eye. His neatly combed gray hair, with hints of white at the temples, and his unremarkable build were a stark contrast to his immense power and influence.

Glancing around the room, Hirofumi pretended to be astonished when he saw Ziggy. "Marshal Ghostshade," he said, his tone oozing false camaraderie. "We meet again. It seems congratulations are in order. Your recent success hasn't gone unnoticed."

"Mr. Ito," Ziggy nodded in respect. "It was a group effort," he continued as alarm bells blared in his head. It wasn't explicitly a threat, but Hirofumi's intention was clear—he wanted Ziggy to know that he'd been under surveillance, probably from the moment he set foot in DipShip headquarters. Hirofumi regarded him with a cool gaze, but the subtle tensing of his jaw betrayed a hidden animosity. Ziggy's fleeting hope that Hirofumi would let go of the past disappeared in an instant.

"Every victory requires cooperation," Hirofumi acknowledged, his constrained glare slowly shifting to Alexia. "But then there are always those who enjoy the victory without contributing to the work." An uncomfortable silence followed, and Alexia's face turned crimson when Ziggy didn't respond.

"Your return has created quite a stir," Hirofumi continued casually as if he weren't imagining all the ways he could have Ziggy killed for breaking their mutual agreement. "I've hardly been in a boardroom these past few weeks without your name cropping up."

"Fortunately, I don't pay much attention to the news," Ziggy grunted.

Hirofumi raised his head slightly, studying Ziggy. "But surely someone with your history understands the implications of returning to the public eye. It would be irresponsible to knowingly put unexpecting people in danger."

Ziggy's heart thundered as danger crackled through the air, making it clear no one in the skybox was safe. Least of all him. He took a quick survey of the room, scanning for an alternate escape route and finding none. Hirofumi wasn't the type to bother with an idle threat. He'd come to deliver a deliberate and poised act of violence.

Ziggy felt a soft hand on his elbow. "Mr. Ito," Pepper said with a warm smile, stepping in front of him. "Allow me to offer you some hors d'oeuvres. We have tikka and samosas, as well as an absolutely delicious gulab jamun."

"No, thank you," Hirofumi said, and Ziggy took advantage of his distraction, silently taking his seat, pretending to be captivated by what was happening below. As the crowd of executives, celebrities, and wealthy patrons settled in for the show, shielded by the floor-to-ceiling transparent, serial-killer-proof glass, Ziggy tried to quell his panic enough to think clearly. The sound of his own heartbeat pounded in his ears. He could feel Hirofumi's eyes on the back of his head.

"Father, please sit," Alexia urged, gesturing for him to join her in the front row.

Ignoring her, Hirofumi positioned himself next to Ziggy in the rear viewing seats to watch the Ceremonies. The smell of Hirofumi's cologne tickled Ziggy's nose, and his stomach turned sour as guards stationed themselves behind their chairs, making Ziggy's necktie feel like an assassin's garrote. He kept his eyes locked forward, but the suffocating shame radiating from Alexia suffused the room, and sweat trickled down his back, sticking him to the plush leather chair. Floyd settled on Ziggy's other side and Pepper next to Floyd. With no other choice, Alexia hurriedly waved for Boomer to join her in the front row, her seat directly in front of Hirofumi's scrutinizing glare.

A stage rose from the middle of the floor. Heavy rock music played, and fireworks burst into the air. The audience rose to their feet, stamping and cheering. It was the Super Serial theme song, and Ziggy hated it. It was the perfect combination of catchy and annoying, and he realized he'd probably be humming it for days.

Get ready for the ultimate fight,
In Super Serial, where fear takes flight.
This is the game where killers reign.
In this brutal battleground, only one can remain.
With every strike, with every blow,
They'll do whatever it takes to steal the show.
Super Serial, Super Serial.

Floyd, completely enraptured, mouthed along with every word as glittering light filled the air. "Wow! That was incredible!" Ziggy tried not to cringe at Floyd's enthusiasm. The Opening Ceremonies were like an opulent masquerade, except instead of masks, everyone carried a concealed weapon. There was an electric twang that sounded through the air, and an oddly familiar bassline began to play. The audience went wild, and Floyd actually squealed with delight. "It's Thunderforge Reckoning!"

Ziggy had no idea what Thunderforge Reckoning was, but when he saw guitars, drums, and unnecessary pyrotechnics, he figured it must be a popular band. Floyd sang along, his voice horribly off-key, until Pepper squeezed his hand, gently urging him to stop.

The band launched into another song, and Hirofumi scrutinized the room, his lips stretching into a calculated smile. Suddenly, he rose from his seat, a hand resting casually on Alexia's shoulder. "My dear Alexia, I've been thinking," he said as she craned her neck up to meet his eye. "You really should have a better view than this for your debut. Let's take this celebration to Pill Depot's skybox. The view is unmatched, and the drinks are exquisite."

Caught off guard, Alexia's expression flickered with uncertainty, torn between offense and gratitude at her father's unexpected offer.

"And please, bring your entire team," Hirofumi added, his gesture encompassing the room.

Floyd sprang up, his eyes wide with awe. "Seriously?" he exclaimed. "Pill Depot's skybox has the best view in the entire stadium!"

Hirofumi laughed indulgently, like a warm and loving grandfather spoiling his grandchildren with a puppy. "You certainly won't be disappointed."

"How very generous of you, Father," Alexia said, rising slowly, her gaze fixed on Hirofumi, trying to decipher his sudden shift in mood. Meanwhile, Floyd was already in motion, eagerly ushering Pepper toward the door, practically buzzing with excitement. Hirofumi's guard stepped aside, allowing them to pass, while the rest of the support staff lingered, exchanging confused glances until Hirofumi beckoned them with a welcoming wave. "Everyone means everyone."

As Ziggy moved to join them, a heavy hand descended on his shoulder, gently but firmly pushing him back into his seat. "Not yet, Marshal Ghostshade," one of Hirofumi's guards declared, his voice a low warning.

Ziggy's heart thundered, its desperate rhythm pounding against his ribcage. He'd buried the looming threat of Hirofumi Ito's revenge deep within his mind, foolishly hoping that DipShip's pitiful standing was too insignificant to warrant a backlash. He'd clearly been wrong, dead wrong. Dead.

Distracted by her father's newfound kindness, Alexia trailed behind him and a small group of guards as they headed to the exit. Ziggy turned to see Pepper, her wide eyes filled with horror, desperately trying to break through the departing crowd. He smiled at her, maybe for the last time, and prayed with his whole soul that this wouldn't be their last goodbye.

"I forgot my purse!" she called out, but the bulky guards guided her away, cutting off any chance of her return.

"What's going on, Pep?" Floyd's voice echoed down the hallway as the last server exited the skybox. Hirofumi guided Alexia through the doorway, handing her over to another set of guards. She looked back, realizing too late that Hirofumi hadn't followed. "Why are you—"

Ziggy watched as Alexia's face got smacked with a horror-filled frying pan, her polite protest fading as the guards abruptly closed the door, leaving Ziggy and Hirofumi inside.

There was a long moment of silence before Hirofumi spoke. "Please excuse my deceptive strategies," he said, gliding to the bar. "I felt our reunion warranted greater privacy."

Ziggy frantically scanned his options—six guards inside the skybox and at least four outside. He was finished. Even with a stun baton, he couldn't take down ten men, and even if he managed to, he'd just be pinned as a violent offender, a rogue gone crazy. He was a king in checkmate with no moves beyond self-sacrifice.

With all the servers gone, Hirofumi took his time selecting a bottle of scotch. The rich aroma of aged whiskey filled the room as he poured himself a glass. "Have a drink with me, Marshal Ghostshade," he said, pouring another.

Ziggy hesitated, his heart pounding as he tried to decide how he wanted to die—defiant to the end or with the taste of good scotch on his tongue. The scotch won out, and Ziggy tried to hide the wobble in his legs as he got up from his chair and moved to the bar to sit with Hirofumi, acutely aware of the guard shadowing his every move.

He raised the scotch to his lips, savoring the amber warmth that coursed down his throat. A familiar sense of finality washed over him. It had a flavor reminiscent of his near-death encounter with the Samurai in the dump but with an added layer of bitterness. Maybe it stemmed from the realization that he would die at the hands of a man consumed by power, a far cry from the Samurai, who killed to safeguard his people.

Hirofumi swirled his scotch. "I know my daughter blackmailed you into working for her. She's a foolish girl with very little talent, but she does have her mother's proclivity for manipulation."

"And her father's ruthlessness," Ziggy replied, his words flowing as smoothly as the scotch on his tongue.

Hirofumi lifted his eyebrow as if Ziggy were a mildly interesting bug he was thinking about squishing. "Ruthlessness, you say? Interesting choice of words, Marshal Ghostshade. Especially considering the extent of my generosity toward you."

"Generosity?" Ziggy scoffed, the bite of the scotch mirrored in his voice.

"Do you truly believe I couldn't have intervened and prevented Alexia from purchasing your debt?" Hirofumi asked, running his finger along the rim of his glass. "Or from paying it off when your contract concluded? Every facet of DipShip is under my control. Nothing happens there without my knowledge and permission."

"Or perhaps you lost track of my debt in your mountain of records," Ziggy said, his grip on the glass tightening as he locked eyes with Hirofumi.

"While it's true that our system failed to stop the transaction," Hirofumi said; his voice was soft, but his tone was full of fire. "Your debt serves as a constant reminder on my ledger—a symbol of the only man who dared to humiliate me and live."

A deadly tension threaded through the air. "If you could've recalled the debt from Alexia," Ziggy asked, his voice steady despite the strain, "why didn't you? I had no interest in working for DipShip. I would've preferred to stay in hiding. As we agreed."

"Alexia needed to learn a lesson in disobedience and failure," Hirofumi said, his upper lip curling at the mention of his daughter.

"And you thought it was impossible to find enough killers in time for DipShip to actually compete in the games," Ziggy added, finishing his thought.

"I'm not too proud to admit I underestimated you," Hirofumi said, polishing off his scotch. "When you tracked down Red Judas, I considered it a fluke—a determined lover who got lucky."

"You were expecting me to fail," Ziggy stated bluntly. "And for DipShip to crumble along with Alexia's ambitions."

"Your efficiency surprised me," Hirofumi acknowledged, scanning the selection of DipShip's spirits. His lips pursed with dissatisfaction as he pulled a bottle from the lineup. "But I won't make that mistake again, Marshal Ghostshade. You're much more determined than I would've predicted."

"I had a good incentive," Ziggy muttered.

"Taking your husband's ashes was a masterful move on Alexia's part," Hirofumi mused, inclining his head as he poured another drink. "Even a broken clock is right twice a day. Love can be a powerful motivator, almost as potent as hate."

He wasn't wrong. Pepper and Floyd had exposed Ziggy's grief to the warm embrace of the sun, and it was slowly evaporating, carrying away the weight of his sorrow. Even now, love for his friends had compelled Ziggy to venture into life-threatening territory.

"It's unfortunate that Alexia's one moment of intelligence led her to claim sole credit for DipShip's success," Hirofumi added with a scowl. "It only makes her look desperate and foolish."

Faint applause reached Ziggy's ears, and he turned to see the rock band had finished, and the stadium floor was being bombarded with hundreds of Mongaphalee dancers and aerialists whirling in perfect synchronization, their orange and green district colors on vibrant display. A small group of extravagantly dressed performers wheeled a giant peanut into the center of the floor. It cracked open, and dozens of dancers leaped out to perform.

"Is this all about DipShip's success?" Ziggy turned back to Hirofumi, somewhat emboldened by the potent mixture of painkillers and booze. "Alexia winning a seat on the ABCD?" If the circumstances weren't so dire, he might've laughed. "If that's the case, believe me, you have no reason to worry. DipShip's team has about as much chance of making it through the Prelims as I do of becoming Pill Depot's CEO."

Hirofumi's response was chillingly direct. "This isn't about Alexia. It's about you, Marshal Ghostshade. If DipShip makes it to the Championships, it'll be because of *your* leadership—and the public will know it."

"The public?" Ziggy was incredulous. "Why does it matter what they think?"

"Because they shouldn't be thinking at all," Hirofumi said in a lethal whisper before draining his drink in a single gulp. He paced around the bar toward the windows overlooking the teeming crowd.

"The public likes a soap opera, not me. They like the idea of love and revenge. But look at me," Ziggy gestured to himself, "Bald, overweight, and grumpy. Not a public package."

"You seem to have forgotten the thousands of marshals rallying behind you. I can still hear their chants." He clasped his hands behind his back. "They love you because you defied an emperor, and they'd still chant for you if you defied me again."

"So, what, you're jealous? That seems beneath you," Ziggy huffed.

"You're smarter than that, Mr. Ghostshade. Don't demean both of us," Hirofumi scanned the crowds below. "If they love you, then they don't fear me, and a herd of sheep can still trample a wolf."

It took every ounce of Ziggy's resolve not to laugh. Hirofumi Ito was worried about Ziggy becoming a rebel leader. Someone to rally the marshals, the only group that could hold the ABCD accountable for their long list of heinous actions and storm the Bastille. It was preposterous.

"Why not just kill me, then?" Ziggy blurted out, unable to contain his fear. He walked over to join Hirofumi at the window. "You warned me yourself. If I ever showed my face in public again, you'd end me."

Hirofumi fixed Ziggy with a piercing stare. "The only thing more dangerous than a man with the love of the people is a dead man with the love of the people."

Ziggy was stunned. "I think you're overestimating my influence."

"I wouldn't make that same mistake twice," said Hirofumi with a glance. "I don't fault you for capitalizing on a difficult situation." He continued after a moment of watching the colorful performance below. "But I expected you to return to your state of anonymity once you'd satisfied the terms of your contract with Alexia."

"That was the plan, actually," Ziggy murmured.

"Unfortunately, it's too late for that now," Hirofumi said. "The Prelims are upon us."

Ziggy shook his head. Disappearing now would have catastrophic consequences for Pepper and Floyd. Not to mention the entire district. "I won't abandon my team," he said, hating the beg in his voice. "I can't do that to them."

"I suspected as much," Hirofumi said, shifting his gaze to his guards. The hair on Ziggy's neck prickled in warning as the guards stepped in closer, surrounding them on all sides. "Even in the face of imminent death, you still refuse to submit," Hirofumi remarked with quiet menace. "I should've ended your life the day you executed Judas and the marshals stood for you. Or at least when you first entered DipShip headquarters. Yet, here you are, alive and well, ready to bask in the glow of your adoring public."

"I don't care about the public," Ziggy said. "I just want to help my friends."

"A commendable trait," Hirofumi conceded, his expression unreadable. "But it leaves me with a dilemma."

"A dilemma?" Ziggy echoed, his pulse quickening.

Hirofumi turned fully toward Ziggy, his dark eyes gleaming with a mix of ice and cunning. "Should I let you live so the public can witness your defeat in the Preliminaries, or should I eliminate you now, even if it risks another marshal uprising?"

The guards shifted on their feet, and Ziggy's mouth went dry. "W-we want the same things," he sputtered. "The district survives, but DipShip fails in the Prelims. Understand that DipShip has zero possibility of winning, with or without me."

"I don't care if DipShip wins or loses. Alexia isn't a threat. I care that the public sees you fail. I want you forgotten, and your story tarnished," Hirofumi said.

"That's already the plan," Ziggy replied, like a rabbit facing off with a wolf. "Alexia's the only one who thinks DipShip has a chance, and she's lost the support of her team. They're already sabotaging her interests in the ABCD."

Hirofumi regarded him for a long moment, assessing Ziggy with a predator's gaze. "I'll let you live," he said finally. "For now. But make no mistake, Marshal Ghostshade, if I suspect any deviation from our agreement, this time, I won't hesitate to act. The moment the Preliminaries are over, you'll disappear. Or I'll *make* you disappear."

Ziggy swallowed hard. "Understood," he said, choosing his words carefully. "I've got it under control."

"Control is a mirage," Hirofumi said with quiet malevolence, "a fragile façade worn by those who mistake it for security. People like my daughter cling to the notion of control but remain blind to the fact that it's merely crumbs left on the table by those who wield the actual power."

One of Hirofumi's security guards interrupted, stepping forward to whisper in his ear, and Hirofumi nodded, his eyes never leaving Ziggy's.

"You would do well to remember that those of us who live in the shadows where control unravels know that the illusion of control may keep a man from starving, but power is the only thing that satiates hunger."

With a curt nod, Hirofumi signaled for his guards to open the door. "Good luck tomorrow, Mr. Ghostshade," he said, disappearing into the depths of the stadium.

Chapter 9

Baking Care of Business

Ziggy stood in the humid silence, struggling to remember how to breathe. His heart pounded heavily, each beat echoing in his ears and amplifying the agonizing ache spreading from his neck. He needed to get out of there. Desperation clawed at him to flag down a taxi, return to the hotel, pack his belongings, and disappear without a trace. Hirofumi's ultimatum clung to him like dark tendrils of a malignant bacteria, infecting everyone it touched. Leaving would hurt Pepper and Floyd, but staying might hurt them even more.

He had to find a way to navigate this impossible situation: keep most of the killers alive through the Prelims, put on a show impressive enough to boost their popularity, score enough points to lift DipShip from obscurity, but not so many they inadvertently secured a spot in the Championships. He had to stay alive and pacify Hirofumi Ito while not upsetting Alexia enough to turn her fangs on him, too. It felt like juggling chainsaws while running from a tiger and rocking a baby to sleep. Something was bound to fall, and he hoped to heaven it wouldn't fall on his friends.

His mind raced as he tried to formulate a strategy. He needed to give Alexia just enough information to placate her, but not so much that she figured out their sabotage. Pepper and Floyd, of course, would be in a panic. Pepper knew all about Ziggy's past with Hirofumi, so she'd already be expecting the worst, and Floyd was a lot more intuitive than people gave him credit for. Luckily, their plan to lose the Prelims aligned perfectly with Hirofumi's demands—not to mention it was the most likely outcome. But once it was done, he'd have to disappear. That was the part he dreaded the most.

The prospect of facing solitude again, relying on custard-filled maple bars and vodka for comfort, felt like a fate worse than death. The very thought was a lump of hot coal on parched leaves, igniting into a pent-up rage. He loathed Hirofumi Ito with every fiber of his being. Alexia, too. All he'd done was ensure Gio received the justice he deserved, but in return, they'd taken everything—his life, his career, and even Gio's ashes. He had nothing left except his friends, and now Hirofumi was trying to take them, too. And he felt powerless.

He stared down at the crowd of wealthy spectators, who were applauding a massive troupe of Mongaphalee dancers as they moved in intricate synchronization. Hirofumi had said that power was the only thing that satiated hunger, but those weren't the words that resonated in Ziggy's soul. Instead, he recalled the words of the Samurai: *The wealthy satiate their filthy hunger with ego and greed, while the poor satiate their hunger with bread.*

No one wanted Hirofumi's power. Not really. They wanted the comfort he enjoyed at their expense. *The only reason a poor man would want to be one of your glitterati is because he knows the table of the oppressor is always full. He doesn't envy the tyrant. He envies the feast.* Hirofumi was afraid of the poor because he didn't understand them. His insatiable hunger for power led him to believe that everyone else was driven by the same motives. In reality, thoughts about power were a luxury most people couldn't afford when they were struggling just to put food on the table.

Ziggy clenched his fists. Maybe Hirofumi was right to be afraid. He easily devoured all the big fish, asserting his dominance as the leviathan of the corporate ocean, but it was the millions of tiny water parasites burrowing into his skin that would ultimately eat him alive. A mob, a union, a collective.

The doors to the skybox were flung open, and Pepper rushed in, followed by Floyd.

"Ziggy!" Pepper cried, flinging her arms around his shoulders. "You're okay," she said, her voice thick with tears. "I thought—"

"I told you he wasn't dead," Floyd said, following closely behind. He gave Ziggy a quick once-over. "She thought Hirofumi was going to kill you even though we could see you sitting at the bar from the Pill Depot skybox. Didn't you see us waving at you after you moved in front of the window?"

"Alexia will be here any minute with some of the DipShip shareholders and department heads," Pepper said, releasing him from her embrace. "She's furious and has tons of questions. What are we going to do? What did Hirofumi want with you?"

"Later," Ziggy murmured as Alexia stormed through the skybox doors with Boomer hot on her heels. A gaggle of confused executives followed, visibly relaxing when they noted Hirofumi's absence.

"That smug, self-righteous bastard!" Alexia exploded the moment the door closed behind them. "How dare he treat me that way!" she seethed, her words dripping with venom. "Like I'm still a child running some dirty sub-corp!"

Pepper quickly took Alexia by the arm and in a hushed voice, cautioned, "Remember, there are shareholders here." She forced a sunny smile. "Boomer? Could you do me a favor and get Alexia a well-earned drink?"

Ever the loyal toady, Boomer took charge, using his good arm to guide Alexia away from the window to a more secluded part of the skybox. Pepper shooed the executives over to their seats in front of the window to watch the show. Alexia's chest heaved as she paced back and forth, her designer heels sinking into the plush carpet with each step.

"I've busted my ass to show him what I'm capable of, and he can't even give me an ounce of respect! Shutting me out of my own skybox. The nerve!" she ranted.

"You've worked so hard," Boomer said emphatically, his expression mirroring Alexia's indignant glare.

"They're interviewing the cityscape designers, and then it'll be time for the Pedo-Trials!" Floyd's attention shifted to the show happening below, and he drifted toward the viewing seats.

Pepper tried to diffuse the tension, offering Alexia a bottle of water. "Stay in your game, not his play," she said, but Alexia brushed past her, swatting the bottle from her hand.

"Nothing I do is ever good enough!" she shouted, her petulant fury rising with every word. She pounded her fists against a nearby end table, then picked up a vase of flowers and hurled it against the wall. "I'm not just some pawn in his game! I'm his daughter! This company is mine!"

None of the executives seemed the least bit surprised by her outburst. Maybe it was their stiff poker faces or the whiskey and pill combination still coursing through his veins, but Ziggy couldn't help it—he laughed. Here was a grown woman throwing a tantrum because her rich father was rude to her. Her lackeys acted like it was just another day in the office while she stomped around, tossing vases and swatting champagne flutes from their hands. Hirofumi had just threatened Ziggy's life and forced him into hiding for a second time; he should be the one having a tantrum. And it was absolutely hilarious. He wheezed and gasped for air as if he'd run a mile, tears streaming down his cheeks.

Alexia whirled around, strands of hair whipping in her face. "What the fuck are you laughing at?" she demanded, a muscle ticking in her jaw.

Ziggy's laughter doubled, dulling his usual Alexia filter. "You're pitching a fit because a person with more power and more money treated you like shit. Sound familiar? Now you know how the rest of us feel."

Boomer gasped in melodramatic shock and that made Ziggy laugh even harder. The entire situation just tickled his fractured spirit.

"I'm nothing like him," Alexia spat, marching across the skybox to confront Ziggy, murder in her eyes. "What did he want from you, anyway? He had no reason to kick me out without explaining.

Especially to talk to you. You're nothing but a fat nobody without a dime to his name."

Ziggy's laughter slowly faded, replaced by a newfound sense of freedom. He stood his ground, not breaking eye contact as they squared off. "Well, this fat nobody has had about enough of you and your pathetic family drama. It's nothing but entitled bullshit the whole way down."

Alexia's eyes widened with shock. "You son of a bitch! How dare you speak to me that way!"

"Well, someone has to!" Ziggy threw up his hands. "You're surrounded by ass-licking ego-strokers who don't have the balls to tell you when you're wrong. Look at them!" He gestured to the executives, and as if to punctuate his point, not one so much as turned in their seat. They stared ahead, fixated on the performance unfolding below, desperate to avoid interacting with Alexia.

"Don't you see what you've done?" Ziggy continued. "You've risked thousands of jobs and ruined countless lives, all to impress a man who can't be impressed. He doesn't respect you, Alexia, and he never will."

A flicker of devastation crossed her face, quickly replaced by white-hot fury. "Tell me what my father wanted from you, or I'll have you thrown out onto the street right here and now!"

"You want to know?" Ziggy's voice shook with rage. "Fine. He thinks you're a joke. Your gamble for the ABCD is a joke. The only thing that could've been worth something was DipShip, but you gambled it away on a worthless Super Serial team. He's trying to minimize the fallout when you fail because he knows you'll go running back to Papa Ito for money when you bomb here at the Prelims. What do you think the public will say when DipShip collapses because of your recklessness? Thousands of people jobless and displaced? They'll hate you, and they'll curse the Ito family name."

It was the truth. Half of it, at least.

Alexia reeled, and Ziggy was disgusted to realize she'd thought nowhere beyond the tip of her own snooty nose. "Well, none of that will happen if we win!"

Pepper stepped forward, trying to diffuse the situation. "I think we've all had a little too much celebration today. Why don't we all cool down and watch the performance?"

"Yeah!" shouted Floyd, the only one actually interested in watching the ceremonies. "Some of us are trying to enjoy the show."

"She needs to hear it," he told Pepper firmly before turning back to Alexia. "You don't get it," he said quietly. "We're not going to win. And everyone can see it but you."

Alexia's arms clenched tightly across her chest, and she spared a glance at the executives, still pretending not to watch her tantrum. "I expect results. If I didn't push everyone to succeed, nothing would get done." She eyed her executives, looking for weakness and doubt in their faces.

Ziggy shook his head. "All I've seen you do is bitch and moan about how our killers aren't good enough. You've helped Boomer with some costumes and sweet-talked your shareholders, but honestly, all you've done is waste money on unimportant things and hold back where it actually counts. You would've failed already if it weren't for Pepper and Floyd busting their asses."

"I was the one who put Pepper in a position of authority and allowed her to hire you back. She has the freedom to use resources as necessary. That's my leadership!"

"You can't even get her title right," Ziggy retorted before lobbing a finger at Boomer. "Plus, a leader wouldn't let her friends get their arms ripped off."

Boomer winced as he swiveled on his bar stool, pointedly averting his gaze away from the argument.

Ziggy's face flushed with heat as he barked, "You're delusional if you think we can win. You sound like a three-year-old who's never heard the word 'no.' Things don't just happen because you want them to. DipShip would be better off if we focused on keeping the killers alive and selling them after the Prelims. Getting a seat on the ABCD is a pipedream. Cut your losses and start damage control for the disaster you've already created like any half-decent CEO would."

"That's not true," Alexia hissed. "We have a decent enough team. Good enough to qualify for the Championships, at least!"

"Good enough?" Ziggy said with a scoff. "Those aren't exactly winning words. It takes resources and loyalty to win. You may be able to scrounge up the money to play with the big kids, but it'll never be enough to buy loyalty."

"You're bringing everyone down!" Alexia cried. "The rest of us are committed. Pepper believes in my bid for the ABCD. She believes we can win. All the executives do!"

Pepper bit her lip when Alexia turned toward her. "Pepper?" she prompted. "Tell him he's just getting cold feet because my father got into his head."

The silence was deafening. "Alexia, the chances of winning are low," Pepper finally said, her eyes trained on the floor. "We'll do everything we can, but we should be realistic."

"How low are the odds of winning the Prelims, Floyd?" Ziggy shouted over his shoulder.

"Extremely low," Floyd called back. Maybe he'd been listening more than Ziggy thought. "Especially with no backup killers. There's a greater probability of a single shark devouring each member of the ABCD on different days of the same month."

"It makes sense to have a backup plan for the district," Pepper added carefully. "We've got a lot of people depending on us."

"You said the exact same thing when I entered Super Serial," Alexia fired back, her eyes narrowing in on Pepper. "You told me it was impossible to get a team in time, but look at us now."

"We got lucky," Pepper said, her brows furrowed. "You're jeopardizing the future of DipShip, and the livelihoods of everyone in the district, for a long shot. The consequences will be devastating when we lose."

"*If* we lose," Alexia corrected, looking around the skybox for a potential ally. No one would meet her eye, and her jaw dropped in disbelief. "Wait a minute," she said slowly. "Do any of you think we can win?" With a fiery glare, she burned holes into the backs of the executives' heads. Not a word of encouragement. Not even from Boomer.

"Why the fuck did I hire all of you, then?" she raged, veins pulsing in her temples. "We've proven we can beat the odds, so why not do it again?"

"Odds don't work like that," Floyd said, still watching the performance and bouncing his fists to the music.

"Let's all take a moment to calm down," Pepper said, stepping in front of Alexia and holding up her hands in a gesture of peace. "This is a big paradigm shift, and we really need to consider backup contingencies for DipShip. The Prelims are tomorrow, and we have to work together. The goal should be for DipShip to survive."

"So that's it?" Alexia said bitterly, pushing Pepper's hands away. "You're not even going to try?"

"Why should we?" Ziggy spat out, shaking his head. "We gain nothing by helping you, and if we sacrifice the lives of our killers by trying, we lose everything. You're the only one who wouldn't suffer in the long run. You're not entitled to our loyalty or our help, Alexia, and you sure as shit haven't earned it."

Alexia froze, her face contorted in a mixture of fury and shock. No one spoke. The executives remained motionless, resembling business casual mannequins in their seats. Even the servers were still. The only one who moved was Floyd, swaying to the music in his seat and mostly unaware of the severity of the argument at hand. Alexia's lips squeezed together, and Ziggy could see her mental gears spinning.

Then, her expression shifted, and a terrifying glint flickered in her eyes. "You're right," she said, her voice surprisingly calm. "I haven't earned your loyalty." She turned to Boomer. "Bring me a piece of paper and a pen," she commanded.

Boomer looked bewildered but moved to the bar, rummaging through the drawers until he found a small notebook with a pen attached. He handed it to Alexia, and she slapped it onto the countertop, reading aloud as she wrote.

"I, Alexia Ito, hereby swear that if DipShip's team wins the 117th Super Serial Championships. I will make Pepper Devoux CEO of District DipShip." With a flourish, she signed her name at the bottom of the page.

"There," she said smugly, crossing the room and pushing the notebook into Pepper's hands. "Now we'll all have the incentive to win. I get a seat on the ABCD, Pepper gets to run DipShip and create her fantasy workplace of fairness and equality, and you guys get to keep your jobs. Sign it."

"You're making the secretary the CEO? That's not fair," an executive with a sleek ponytail and glasses complained.

"Shut up, Janet," Alexia barked. "She's an executive administrator." Janet slumped in her chair and downed her champagne.

Pepper looked like she'd seen Joe's ghost drift through the room. Her mouth gaped open in astonishment as she looked at Ziggy, who couldn't properly gauge his own expression of shock thanks to his heavy-handed self-medication. Floyd left the performance and stood by Pepper, placing his hand on her lower back. "Pep?" he asked. "Are you all right? Your face looks the same as it did when you watched the footage of Benedict's arrest."

Floyd's touch seemed to sharpen Pepper's focus. "Alexia, this is a huge gamble," Pepper said. "If we lose, DipShip..." she paused, swallowing hard as she considered. Her eyes strayed to the contract and then to Ziggy. It was everything she'd ever wanted, and even with next-to-impossible chances and his potential doom, Ziggy could see she was torn. He wondered what she'd say if she knew winning meant handing his dismembered head to Hirofumi on a silver platter.

"We won't lose," Alexia said, her eyes boring into Pepper. "And this way, we both get what we want. It's a win-win."

Earlier, Hirofumi said Alexia had a talent for manipulation, and this was yet another example. She could sniff out weakness like a bloodhound on a wounded rabbit, and she was good at using those weaknesses to get what she wanted. Pepper wanted DipShip to survive and Alexia wanted to win Super Serial. It would be a win-win for them. If it weren't for the fact that winning was impossible.

Pepper deliberated, and Ziggy wondered what was going through her mind. As she reached for the pen, he felt a bizarre mix of emotion flood through his veins. In some ways, it hurt to see her waffle with the pen in her hand. The selfish part of him wanted her to choose his safety without a second thought. The pragmatist knew Pepper had the potential to make a big impact running DipShip. In a few years, DipShip could be a sanctuary for thousands of people. Who was he to stand in the way? The skeptic knew it was all manipulation and wanted to slap the pen away from Pepper to teach Alexia a hard lesson in loss. DipShip was just Pepper's version of Gio's ashes.

"It gives us a reason to try," Pepper murmured to Ziggy and Floyd. "But not an obligation. And if it doesn't work out, we can still sell the surviving killers. Right?" She looked at them both.

"Technically, both are possible," Floyd said, holding up a finger. "We could both win and sell the killers at the end of the competition."

"That's the spirit!" chimed Alexia.

"It's your call," Ziggy said, his heart in his throat. "I'll be with you either way."

He was humble enough to admit he was scared she'd sign the paper. He'd once made a deal with the same devil, so he knew how trapped she must be feeling. What he didn't know was if he was afraid for his life or afraid of the turmoil he'd have to face choosing between his life or Pepper's dream. Not to mention the future of everyone in the district. But maybe he was fear-mongering. The odds of that choice ever having to be made were ridiculously small. Impossible. Practically non-existent.

"Go ahead." Floyd encouraged Pepper with a pat on the shoulder. "I wouldn't get your hopes up, but it could be fun to try."

"Sign it," Alexia urged, her nostrils flaring as if sensing a kill.

"Then can we celebrate?" Boomer asked from the bar. "Because I can't take any more of this drama. The tension here's worse than a pillow fight at a high school slumber party."

"You're missing the good stuff!" an executive called.

As Pepper's signature graced the makeshift contract, everyone but Janet cheered.

Boomer popped another bottle of champagne and sprayed it into the crowd of goons who eagerly opened their mouths to lap up Pepper's dream like piglets at the teat. Floyd swept Pepper into a bear hug, and she laughed.

"Congratulations, future CEO," Ziggy said with a smile.

"It'll be okay, Ziggy," she said. "Everything will work out if we stick together."

And Ziggy's guts shifted from "uncomfortably terrified" to "comfortably horrified." Which was a marked improvement.

Chapter 10

Pie of the Tiger

With the contract in place, Alexia downed a flute of champagne, quickly followed by another, visibly relaxing as she and Boomer returned to their bitchy chatter about socialites and CEOs who periodically dropped into DipShip's skybox.

As the conversation flowed, Boomer traded an empty champagne bottle for a full one and struggled to lift it to his lips, brace, sling, and all. Alexia giggled, her cheeks tinged with pink. "Did you see Tatyana Kuznetsov's dress?"

Boomer burped, abandoning the bottle on the table. "It looked like she put it in a blender!" The room filled with their laughter, and Ziggy did his best to tune it out.

"The Pedo-Trials are starting," Floyd said, watching every moment with the rapt attention of an expert. "I was afraid we'd miss it."

"The Pedo-Trials?" Pepper asked. "I don't know a lot about Super Serial beyond administration. My mother never allowed us to watch it, and now I'm too busy. Is this something they do every year?"

"You haven't watched it before?" Floyd's eyes sparkled with anticipation, and Ziggy knew he was about to drop a load of information. "The Pedo-Trials have been part of the Opening Ceremonies for the past sixty-eight competitions. It's not my favorite part of Super Serial, but people get excited because they bring in last year's Championship winners. It's live streamed for a fee, but tickets to the stadium sell out years in advance. They save the worst pedophiles for the Pedo-Trials instead of sending them to Super Serial, where there's still a chance of survival."

Floyd pointed at a massive swirling tube slide being lowered from the top of the stadium. It snaked down to the center of the track. "That's what they call the 'Piggle-Chute.' There's a platform at the top where they take the pedophiles. They coat the slide in a lubricative substance before pushing them down."

Pepper recoiled. "What for?"

"One of the serial killers from last year's championships will be waiting at the bottom for them," Floyd explained, his grin widening as he peered down at the growing crowd. "But, that's the exciting part. We don't know which killer it will be. Their fans have to vote for them. After they introduce the pedophile, the public votes. The killer who receives the most votes gets the pleasure of murdering the pedophile in any way they choose."

"Their fans vote to watch them kill someone?" Pepper said, her expression a mix of horror and disgust.

Ziggy understood the feeling. The Pedo-Trials were grotesque. Not because the pedophiles were being harmed—they were getting what they deserved as far as he was concerned—but because the whole thing felt more like satiating bloodlust than meeting the demands of justice.

Floyd shrugged. "It's not always the fans who vote. Sometimes the victims will raise money and rally support for the killers, so they can see the pedophile punished the way they want.

Ziggy had stood in those shoes, and didn't blame the families of the victims for using the only path to vengeance they had—but he wished he could tell them that it wouldn't fill the hole that loss created in your soul. Some crimes were so heinous that no amount of suffering could ever pay for what was taken. And no amount of revenge or justice could ever aid in healing personal grief. Ziggy had learned that healing was a personal choice.

The anticipation in the stadium reached a fever pitch, and Alexia and Boomer rushed back to their seats. "I love this part," Boomer said.

An announcer's voice boomed, commanding the attention of the chanting crowd. "This man deserves no name," he declared, as a picture of an ordinary-looking man with short hair and a wide face appeared on the screens. "He's an anonymous wormy pig and nothing more. This pig is responsible for the rape and murder of at least six victims, each under the age of six. He recorded and distributed his disgusting crimes until he was apprehended by Corporate Marshal Jone Nadruku, and sentenced to die in the Pedo-Trials."

The audience cheered, and the smug, handsome face of Marshal Nadruku was highlighted across the screen. He stood from his seat and waved to the crowd, but his face was somber. Marshals that worked on homicide and sexual violence cases all had a similar haunted look. They'd seen too much depravity to find any joy in society's glamorized version of justice. This was spectacle and money, nothing more.

"Six beautiful, innocent children were defiled, tortured and destroyed because of this inhuman scum," the announcer continued, and the cameras shifted, landing on the victim's section of the arena.

"They always have a victim's section at the Opening Ceremonies," Floyd told Pepper. "Families of the victims can pay to see justice done in person."

The lights illuminated a group of grief-stricken parents. Most of their grief was distorted by anger, but some held pictures of their lost children against their hearts. One woman stood frozen, her expression a mask of blank sorrow. It was gutting. Ziggy couldn't bear to look. He wore that face for years. Sometimes he still saw it in the mirror when he shaved in the morning.

The screens lit up with a video montage of the victims blowing out candles on their birthday cakes, playing with kittens and riding bicycles. The video then shifted to new footage of parents and families sobbing, pleading for the safe return of their children. Then they showed the crime scene photos and every horrific piece of evidence gathered in the case. By the time it was over, even Ziggy was ready to see the bastard sail down the chute.

Tears streaked down Pepper's face. "He's a monster," she whispered. Floyd offered her a tissue before passing them on to Alexia and Boomer. "The Pedo-Trials can be very emotional," he said.

The scene shifted to the top of the Piggle-Chute, where security guards stood at the mouth of the slide, gripping the arms of the pedophile.

"What should we do with our disgusting little pig?" the announcer's voice echoed, igniting a chant from the crowd. "Kill the Pig! Kill the Pig!"

Floyd, ever prepared, donned noise-canceling headphones. "Plug your ears!" he said as an earsplitting drumroll sounded, followed by a gong crash that felt like it vibrated to the back of Ziggy's skull.

"Send him down!" the announcer commanded, and the audience roared as squealing sounds filled the air. Ziggy watched as a black shadow inside the chute flew downward like a marble in a toy marble run, shooting out the bottom with a thump. The pedophile screamed as he hit the floor, rolling along the ground as forcefully as if he'd jumped from a moving vehicle.

"Who should be the executioner of this inhuman scum?" the announcer roared, igniting a frenzy in the crowd. Banners waved, signs declared allegiance, and the entire stadium pulsed with chaotic energy.

The pedophile crawled along the ground. He was wearing only a pair of thin underwear. Blood dripped from his scalp, and his back was scraped from his trip down the chute. "Please," he begged. "Don't do this!"

"Spectators here in the stadium and our viewers at home, it's time to place your votes," the announcer declared, and a countdown appeared on the monitor. Ziggy sighed, reaching for his whiskey. Floyd had his phone out and was on the Super Serial app.

"I hope they pick Tiger Scorpion," he said, clicking on the image of the ferocious tiger-man. "The best Super Serials always begin with him."

"I'm voting for the Dominator," Boomer said, tapping to vote for a large, hairy man with rippling abs. "Tiger Scorpion is so two years ago."

As the timer ran out, a crash of the gong signaled the pedophile's fate. He was curled into a ball on the ground.

"The public has spoken. The executioner will be…" the announcer paused, letting the anticipation build. "…Tiger Scorpion!"

Heavy metal music blared, neon lights flashed, and Tiger Scorpion entered the arena, emerging through a cloud of red smoke and glittering flames. Ziggy had seen footage of him online, but it was nothing compared to seeing him in person. Tiger Scorpion, a veteran of the Pill Depot Super Serial team, somehow managed to look more terrifying every year.

Floyd pressed against the glass, breathless. "Can you see him, Pep? That's him. That's Tiger Scorpion! I knew he'd be chosen first. He was discovered in District YupoDeep when he was in a ship-breaking prison yard. That's why he's so big and strong. He's incredible. I can't believe it's him!"

Tiger Scorpion walked slowly toward the pathetic man on the ground, his rippling muscles firm and primed, glistening in the lights of the arena. He was covered in thick tattooed stripes, and his face had been modified to make him look like a snarling tiger. He was bare-chested and wearing only a pair of black, sparkling shorts that landed at the knee and a flowing cloak made from tiger pelts.

"That's the Stinger!" Floyd cried, practically shaking with excitement. "It's right there! He made that from salvaged ship parts!"

Tiger Scorpion held his infamous scorpion whip in his hand, a gleaming, silver monstrosity of connected segments with a sharpened stinger at the end. The Stinger was coated in poison that paralyzed the victim.

Tiger Scorpion stopped when the pedophile was at his feet, and the music swelled as he let out a terrifying, inhuman roar. Ziggy had never heard a sound like that in all his life. He wasn't even sure how it was possible. Tiger Scorpion's teeth had been sharpened into lethal points. Floyd squealed with delight, his hands flapping in the air.

The pedophile peed himself, screaming and covering his ears with his hands. "Have mercy!" the man sobbed. "Please, I'll do anything!"

Alexia and Boomer burst into laughter, and the audience booed and hissed, only falling quiet when Tiger Scorpion held his scorpion-tail weapon aloft.

"You'll receive the same mercy you gave your victims," he said, his deep voice dripping with menace. "None. As for the pain," he added, his strange golden cat eyes narrowed into slits, "you'll get it all back tenfold!" The scorpion tail descended with a sickening crack, the needle point stinger piercing the pedophile's spine.

Alexia, Boomer, and what felt like the rest of the stadium groaned and gasped. The man writhed in agony, the audience reveling in his suffering. It took less than a minute for him to fall silent. Tiger Scorpion dropped the Stinger and kicked the man onto his back. The immobilizing poison had done its work, rendering the pedophile a petrified husk.

"The poison immobilizes the victim," Floyd explained to Pepper, who had long since turned away. "He can't move, but believe me, he can feel everything."

"It's time!" Tiger Scorpion roared, raising his hands in triumph. His fingernails were thick, curved claws so sharp Ziggy wondered how he managed to wipe his ass without turning his cheeks into a spiral-cut ham.

The fog thickened, and the rhythmic thump of a beating heart resonated through the stadium to spectacular effect. A spotlight illuminated Tiger Scorpion from above, and for a moment, he actually looked like a tiger ready to pounce on its prey.

"Here it comes!" Floyd said, sounding like he was being choked with excitement. His face was smashed against the window.

There was a flash of light as Tiger Scorpion ripped at the man's chest, tearing open his skin and wrenching his claws under the man's rib cage. Blood sprayed everywhere, coating Tiger Scorpion's arms and torso, and he grabbed at the exposed ribs, bracing a foot against the flayed man's torso before wrenching them free.

He turned to the victim's section with a feral sneer. "He took your heart, and now you shall have his!" he cried, reaching into the man's chest cavity with a powerful thrust and ripping his heart from his body.

The crowd screamed, some in joy and some in fear. Ziggy couldn't look away. Pepper ran for the nearest wastebasket, her hand over her mouth. The heart pulsated in Tiger Scorpion's thick fist, and then, before Ziggy even had a chance to collect himself, Tiger Scorpion sank his teeth into the still-quivering muscle, ripping off a piece and swallowing it whole. Blood dripped down his chin, and he blew spatter into the air, laughing as he circled the body. He gathered up a mouthful of meaty phlegm and spit on the pedophile before marching across the arena to the victim's section.

Separated only by a thin barrier of glass, Tiger Scorpion flaunted the shredded heart before the families whose lives had been shattered. Most of them just stared at the scene with dead, glassy eyes while the rest of the stadium cheered. The stark memory of the moment when Ziggy pulled the trigger on Red Judas crashed into the front of his mind. He was sure he'd looked just the same, his eyes dead and glassy, realizing that death did nothing to ease the pain of loss. His vision blurred and for a moment, he grappled with the darkness of trying to merge justice and this sadistic spectacle.

"Bring in the next piglet!" the announcer called.

Chapter 11

Livin' on Eclair

After the Pedo-Trials were over, Ziggy was left with some mild nausea and a feeling of detached numbness reminiscent of a Sweet Sally's and vodka hangover. His brain had been through a town square flogging, and the dread of his encounter with Hirofumi Ito was raw and mangled in his thoughts. He needed to tell Pepper and Floyd, but shame had quickly built barriers to keep outsiders from accessing his fear.

Mongaphalee security loaded the team into a passenger transport cart and drove them through a complicated system of tunnels to an expansive underground area where they queued up for the Serial Showcase. The sound of the crowd reverberated from above them as carts and cars zipped by in an intricate dance of organization that reminded Ziggy of a beehive.

The DipShip flag, a gaudy black shipping container against a field of hot pink and lime green stripes, was attached to the back of Alexia's glossy, black convertible. Whoever designed it obviously intended for it to look graphic and modern, but it more resembled neon vomit with a turd planted in the center. At least Alexia looked like a beauty queen, poised to steal the spotlight for the evening—which Ziggy preferred. Let her be the face of this shit show.

Squashed between Pepper and Floyd on the bench back seat of the following vehicle, Ziggy's nerves frayed at the thought of countless eyes fixed on him. His interview with the analysts had been live, but at least he hadn't been face-to-face with the audience. Private and removed, the stadium skybox gave him a view of the crowd but no feeling of engagement with it. But here, with thousands upon thousands of people gathered, the reality that he couldn't hide any longer bore down on him. Ziggy had avoided his grief for three years, and being forced to talk about it had flayed him open, exposing his most sensitive parts. The Serial Showcase felt like being thrown into the dirt so vultures could pick away at what was left.

Boomer, who was driving their car, turned awkwardly in his back brace, scowling at the DipShip killers trailing behind them in their parade cells. "Someone should tell her we can't hear her," he said, pursing his lips as he glared at Big Montana Ice.

Ziggy turned, gesturing to his ears in an attempt to convey Boomer's message, but there was no point. Big Montana Ice, first in the lineup of killers, was foaming at the mouth, screaming at Boomer as she flailed in her cell, kicking and pounding on the transparent walls. The moment she'd spotted him alive and mostly well, she'd come unglued, her fury so intense it had burst a blood vessel in her eye.

"At least Benedict's happy." Floyd nodded toward Benedict, who was squashed into his cell with all twenty-eight of his corgis. He'd been so overjoyed to see them he'd burst into tears. Ziggy could see the dogs barking, but the sound was trapped inside. Their stubby paws and lolling tongues pressed against the glass, leaving marks along the surface. Benedict sat on the ground with his legs crossed, rubbing the dogs' tummies and giving them scratches behind the ears. One dog lapped at Benedict's open mouth with stomach-turning enthusiasm.

"Why do they prevent the killers from speaking?" Pepper asked.

"Some of them are quite loud," Floyd explained. "If they were all yelling at once, no one could hear their kill-point values announced, which is the entire point of the Showcase."

Pepper glanced across the parade at the trail of killers. "I know we can't hear them, but why can't they hear us?"

"The cells are soundproof in both directions." Floyd glanced pointedly at Big Montana Ice, who'd braced her tree-trunk legs against the wall of her cell, trying to push it open. "It heightens the drama. The only time the killers are allowed to speak is when they drive past the victim's section. Some of the victims confront the killers, which makes for a bigger spectacle, but it depends on what the host district is going for."

"Carol's husband is in the victim's section with his new fiancée and all six of their kids," Pepper said, and Ziggy grimaced. Ever since her interview with the analysts, something had changed in Carol. She stood in her cell, adorned in her gold MLM bikini, this time without the undershirt, hair and makeup styled to Boomer's liking. Her back was ramrod straight as she stared out of her cell with a distant look on her face.

"Should we try to warn her?" Pepper asked.

Ziggy shook his head. "It won't make any difference. At least this way, her kids can see her one last time before…" his voice trailed off, the unspoken reality hanging heavy in the air.

"Before she competes in the Prelims, where she's statistically likely to die?" Floyd finished.

Ziggy sighed. "For fuck's sake, Floyd."

"I was only finishing your thought," Floyd said. "It's not like Carol or her kids can hear us."

The line of vehicles inched forward, and Ziggy was relieved that DipShip was in sixth place. At least the nightmare wouldn't drag on all night. His stomach grumbled, ready to prove him wrong. The back of his neck was burning where his disc had been injured, and the muted roar of the bloodthirsty crowd above them made his ears ring.

"DipShip will enter the stadium next," a passing Mongaphalee employee told Pepper, and she took a deep breath. "This is it. Cross your fingers for good scores."

"Sometimes bad scores are better since they shield the competitors from being an instant target," Floyd said.

"Good for protection, but bad for resale," Pepper said. "Everyone ready?"

Ziggy stole a glance at the Samurai, who was in a midair split with his feet on two walls, and Lin Meihua, who was fast asleep, curled into a ball at the bottom of her cell. Her scrunched face looked like an old baseball mitt from far away. Big Montana Ice was still screaming, and Benedict appeared to be singing to his dogs. Carol remained frozen in place, her eyes glassy.

"As ready as we'll ever be," Ziggy said, just as another transport vehicle descended into the tunnel from the stadium above, and Tiger Scorpion passed by in his cell, snarling like an actual caged tiger, his mouth still stained with blood.

"It's Tiger Scorpion!" Floyd exclaimed, gripping Ziggy's arm so hard he could feel the bite of his nails, which should've been impossible on account of Floyd's nails being perpetually chewed to nubs. "Ziggy, look! I've never seen him up close before. Did you see the Stinger? He made that himself. It's a surprisingly complex weapon. I can't believe this is happening!" Floyd gushed like a schoolgirl with a crush.

"Would you let go of my arm already?" Ziggy muttered, wrenching himself free, his elbow accidentally barreling into Pepper's side.

"Knock it off, you two," she snapped like they were naughty children.

"Pepper, look!" Floyd pointed across Ziggy's body like he wasn't there. "It's Tiger Scorpion! Do you see him? He's right there!"

"I see him, Floyd," Pepper replied wearily. "I've seen him a hundred times tonight."

"Well, sure, Pep," Floyd went on, bouncing in his seat. "Everyone gets to see him on screens and posters, but no one gets up close like this. No one! We're so lucky!"

Ziggy had to bite his tongue. Only in the corporatocracy would you call running into a serial killer, "lucky." And it wasn't like Floyd was the only one with a killer crush. They were about to enter a stadium full of people who fawned over the worst members of society as if they'd done something worthy of admiration.

The DipShip procession entered the stadium, driving up onto the tarmac track that surrounded the outer rim of the arena. The moment Alexia was visible, the DipShip flag unfurled and the crowd screamed so loudly Floyd had to cram on his headphones.

"Sixth to take the track is District DipShip!" a disembodied male voice echoed through the stadium. "District DipShip—a shipping company on the Western coast of North America, offers a diverse fleet of tugs and barges, freight forwarding, and personalized supply chain solutions. DipShip's broad portfolio includes transportation, e-commerce, customs brokerage, and international business services. DipShip—where prices dip so you can ship!"

It was a ridiculous corporate summary, but Pepper's eyes sparkled with awe as she took in the overwhelming sights of the stadium, and Ziggy realized she'd probably been the one who'd written it. He might not think much of DipShip, but he thought a lot of Pepper. He attempted to rearrange his face into something less cynical.

"I recognize those voices!" Floyd exclaimed. "That's Chuckles and Jovy! Chuck Romero and Jovy Johnson, the Super Serial commentators for the past seven years. Make sure to look for them in the booth by the victim's section."

"This marks DipShip's inaugural entry into the games," Chuckles observed as their procession crawled along the track. "CEO Alexia Ito, daughter of Pill Depot pharmaceutical tycoon Hirofumi Ito, is also the youngest CEO with a team in Super Serial."

"The analysts have described her as, quote, 'scrappy and cunning.' An apt description of someone making bold moves like this," Jovy added, and Alexia waved to the crowd like a rodeo queen.

"I'm intrigued to see how that translates into DipShip's performance. She's clearly a risk-taker," Chuckles said.

"She'd have to be with a flag like that!" Jovy quipped, "What an eyesore!"

"Following Alexia is DipShip Marshal Ziglar Ghostshade, Publicist Boomer D'Chango, and two of the team's operations analysts," Chuckles said, eliciting a cheer from the crowd that caught Ziggy off guard.

"You may remember that Ziglar Ghostshade was the marshal who executed Red Judas, one of the most notorious serial killers of all time."

Ziggy steeled his expression. He'd known it was coming but hated it all the same.

"It's said Marshal Ghostshade pursued Judas after the infamous killer tortured and killed his husband, Giovanni Neves," Chuckles said, and Ziggy's heart stopped for a beat at the sound of Gio's name."That's quite the romantic tale," Jovy added. "How do you think Ms. Ito pulled it off? Marshal Ghostshade hasn't taken a case in years."

"She must have a few tricks up her sleeve, considering the public's reaction when he started hunting killers again," Chuckles speculated.

"The analysts have awarded DipShip an overall score of three." Jovy announced, prompting a dramatic gasp from Chuckles. "That might very well be the lowest score of the night. Let's hope Ms. Ito has a few surprises in store because in a game like Super Serial, that score's a death sentence."

"Speaking of surprises, here come the DipShip Serial killers."

"The first killer in the DipShip lineup is their Leo. This buxom beauty is called Alaskan Thunder, and boy does she look like she can pack a punch!" Chuckles exclaimed, his voice filled with intrigue.

"She's a trucker for a small sub-corp called Fizzbuzz," Jovy chimed in, "and, from what I've heard, quite the trouble-maker."

"Is that right?" Chuckles bantered. "Well, I'm interested to see what all that trouble looks like in the Preliminaries. I'm told this giant of a woman kills with her bare hands."

"If you don't answer a riddle correctly, she kills you for being a demon!" Jovy laughed like it was a joke, and not the awful truth.

"I can't wait to see this colossus unleashed in the cityscape tomorrow. She's an absolute juggernaut, and it seems the analysts agree. She's been given a whopping score of eighty-three!" Jovy announced, her words met with thunderous applause. Phones were whipped out, capturing every moment of the spectacle as Big Montana Ice continued to rage in her cell.

"Eighty-three is a fantastic score!" Floyd exclaimed. "Only nine percent of competitors score above and eighty."

"Let's see what she has to say now that she's reached the victim's section," Chuckles suggested, but Big Montana Ice wasn't looking at the crowd. Several victims stepped forward to give gut-wrenching impact statements, but she was oblivious to their presence, unable to take her eyes off Boomer. When her microphone was unmuted, she unleashed a torrent of insults and threats, all directed at him.

"I'll slap you in the dick with a cactus!" she bellowed, and the entire audience burst into peals of startled laughter. "I see the stab wound on your neck, you demon son-of-a-bitch! You can't fool me! I'll rip off your face and shove it up your asshole!"

"Oh my," Jovy said, laughing nervously. She continued to speak, but she was drowned out by Big Montana Ice, who hadn't let up long enough to draw breath.

"I'll peel your teeth in half!" she screamed, dragging her fingernails down her face. "Alaskan Thunder!" She ran at the wall of the cell, slamming into it so hard she reverberated back, cracking her head on the opposite wall. Blood dripped down her face. "I see you, Bazgoroch! The goddess blessed me! I'm gonna pull your spine out your asshole and whip your mother with it! If you think—" The sound cut off abruptly, and the crowd roared in response.

"I don't know about you, Jovy, but I can't wait to see what that kind of rage looks like in the Preliminaries," Chuckles said as Big Montana Ice soundlessly banged her fist against the wall.

"So dramatic," Boomer tsked to himself from the driver's seat.

"This young chap is called the Corgi Killer," Chuckles said as Benedict's cell was brought front and center. "The Corgi Killer hails from District MingAir and is registered in the Pet Lovers category. Don't try and count the corgis, there are twenty-eight! The Corgi Killer named the dogs after his victims, and as you can see, each dog has the name of a victim embroidered on the back of its sweater. Isn't that adorable?"

"I think it's cute," Jovy said, "but I'm hearing a hailstorm of dissent from the victim's section of the crowd."

"You're right, Jovy. This crowd is furious. They don't seem to appreciate the namesake sweaters at all!" It was the understatement of the century. As Benedict passed by the victims' section, dozens of people screamed in outrage.

It turned out Chuckles was a short, middle-aged man with a full head of brown hair and a smug smile that matched his voice perfectly. He'd left his booth and was standing next to a woman with strawberry blonde hair and a distinct snaggle tooth. Ziggy recognized her. It was Avery Jean, the woman who was with Benedict's last victim before she was killed.

Ziggy knew the moment Benedict's microphone switched on because there was a maelstrom of barking from inside his cell.

"This is my closest mate, Ellie Templeton," Avery said, holding up a picture of Ellie laughing at a pub, drink in hand. "She was a gentle soul, her heart brimmin' with love. She worked as a nurse, and every week, she'd volunteer to help disabled veterans. I ain't come across another like her since, and now she's gone!" Avery burst into tears.

Benedict stumbled to his feet before reaching down and picking up one of the smaller corgis. It was red and white, and wearing a hot pink sweater with the word "Ellie" embroidered on the back. "Don't cry," Benedict said, his giant glasses slipping down his nose. "She hasn't gone. She's right here with us, and I'm looking after her. We love each other."

Avery's eyes flashed, and she stared at Benedict with a raw anger Ziggy knew too well. It's the way he'd felt when he'd executed Red Judas. Avery's chest swelled with fury, but her voice was cold. "That's not my Ellie, and I curse you for sayin' it. Mark my words, Benedict Bork. Me and all those whose lives you've shattered will be tunin' in, waitin' for your death and the deaths of every one of your bloody mutts. We're countin' on it being slow and agonizing, and when you're gone from this world, we'll be celebratin' whilst we spit on your grave."

Benedict's jaw fell slack as if he couldn't fathom why anyone would be upset with him, and the crowd buzzed in outraged unity. Ellie-corgi squirmed in his arms, and by the time Benedict finally blinked, his microphone was muted.

"If you're wondering," Jovy said, as the attention shifted to Carol, "the Super Serial analysts gave the Corgi Killer a score of forty-seven points. We'll see how he and his dogs hold up against Taste-E Chicken Vigilante, UltraChad. Word is he's got a personal beef with the Corgi Killer."

"I get why they want Benedict to die," Floyd told Ziggy over the noise of the crowd, "but the corgis didn't do anything. They were trained to obey their master. It's not their fault they ate all those people. Some of them are still puppies."

"Forty-seven?" Pepper said with a wince, and Boomer looked over his shoulder at her.

"It would've been worse without me," he said.

"This next killer falls under the Angry White Women category," Jovy said, descending from the booth to stand next to Chuckles. Jovy adjusted her wavy brown hair as Carol's husband, Jeff, and his fiancée moved to the front row with a passel of kids. "Her name is Carol Petersen, hailing all the way from the Intermountain Mining District. They call her the MLM Murderer because apparently, she's not just a murderer—she also sells essential oils!"

Ziggy couldn't stop watching the disaster unfold anymore than he could look away from a helicopter crash. Carol's dazed expression vanished in an instant, replaced by an uncomfortable blend of sweetness and menace. A shiver raced down his spine.

"She's smiling," Floyd noted. "But I don't think she's happy."

"Carol was awarded a kill-score of twenty-nine by the Super Serial analysts," Chuckles reported, and Pepper groaned. "Not exactly a high mark."

"Tonight we're graced with the presence of Super Serial's couple of the year," Jovy exclaimed. "Let's give a warm welcome to Carol's soon-to-be ex-husband Jeff, his lovely fiancée Becky, and their six children."

Carol's mic must have been activated because she cleared her throat, and Ziggy could swear the entire stadium went silent.

"Yes, Carol?" Jovy responded, struggling to stifle her amusement. "Is there something you'd like to add?"

"I apologize if I'm speaking out of turn, Ms. Jovy," Carol began, her voice polite but firm. "But you seem to have made a mistake."

"A mistake?" Jovy said, her voice dripping with mockery.

"You mentioned 'Carol's husband Jeff, Becky, and their six children.'" Carol clarified, her voice filling the eerie still of the stadium. "I'm sure it was unintentional, but those six children belong to Jeff and me."

The crowd tittered as Jeff stepped forward, his gaze icy as he addressed Carol, "Not anymore," he declared, looking at Carol like he would a chewed up piece of gum stuck to the bottom of his shoe. "These are my children," he continued, his arm encircling

Becky's waist. "Mine and Becky's. You're dead to us. I only brought them here because Becky thought they deserved the chance to say goodbye."

Becky's voice, soft and flinty, followed. "I should hate you for what you did to Nicole, but I can't because when I look at the beautiful children you gave Jeff, I'm actually grateful. While you'll receive no mercy on earth, we'll continue to pray that the Lord has mercy on your eternal soul."

Ziggy expected Carol's collapse—perhaps tears or even screams—but instead, he watched riveted as she straightened her shoulders, meeting Jeff's glare head-on. "For nothing is secret, that shall not be made manifest; neither anything hid, that shall not be known," she quoted, her words landing like a punch.

Jeff recoiled, eyes wide. "How dare you spout scripture at me? Priestcraft! Murderer!"

"Shots fired!" Chuckles quipped, eliciting laughter from the crowd.

"I am your eternal companion," Carol said, crossing her arms in defiance. "And those are our children. I carried them, nurtured them, and held them in my arms. I am their mother, and will protect them until my last breath. And no one, not Becky, not even you, can take that from me."

"Silence her," Jeff hissed at Jovy. "Can't you see she's upsetting them?"

Ziggy looked at the children. Four of them were racked with sobs, and the youngest, who couldn't have been more than four, reached her arms toward Carol. "Mommy!" she cried, and the oldest daughter swept her up into her arms, quiet tears streaming down her face. The eldest boy didn't cry, but his expression was devastating, his resemblance to Carol striking. He exchanged glances with his father, who nodded resolutely.

"Goodbye, Mom," the boy choked out.

"I love you, Mommy!" a young boy with blond hair shouted.

"I'll miss you so much, Mom!"

"There's not much time," Carol cut in, her voice thick with tears. "Rykker, Makaylee, Bridger, Brakken, Laykyn and Oaklee—listen to me. Don't be afraid. This is *not* goodbye."

"Don't go, Mommy!" a young boy shouted in panic.

"I'll find a way back to you. Whatever it takes, I promise." Carol pressed her hand against the glass. "I love you all so—" Her cell went silent.

Jeff scowled, glaring at Carol before he and Becky ushered the kids away. A knot formed in Ziggy's stomach. Jeff was wrong to subject his children to that, regardless of what Carol had done.

"That was brutal," Pepper said, echoing Ziggy's thoughts.

"Poor Carol," Floyd murmured.

"Moving on to our next competitor," Chuckles interjected smoothly, his voice cutting through the heavy emotional tension like a knife. "This sinister-looking individual is called the Warlord of Waste, District DipShip's Vigilante killer. He was captured in the Skidmore Dumping District, but his origins are a mystery."

"Does this killer ever smile? I don't think so!" Jovy chimed in.

"The Warlord of Waste is responsible for the deaths of dozens of executives all over the Corporatocracy."

"I heard he made a sword from a pizza cutter and sliced their heads clean off!" Jovy exclaimed in exaggerated shock.

"I'm eager to see if he delivers any of that remarkable ingenuity at the Prelims tomorrow. He looks like quite the formidable foe," Chuckles said.

"The victims' section isn't especially large for this mysterious killer," Jovy observed before gesturing toward a large group of spectators in the stadium, "but his supporters have shown up in spades! There's got to be hundreds, and would you believe it? They're all dressed like ninjas."

"Perhaps it's the impressive kill-score the analysts gave him—a ninety-two!" Chuckles speculated, and Pepper released a breath. Boomer turned around again to shoot her an excited grin.

"It's unbelievable how many people don't know the difference between a ninja and a samurai," Floyd said, rolling his eyes. "Samurai generally use katanas, while ninjas have a plethora of weaponry like shuriken, more commonly known as throwing stars, nunchaku, ninjato—"

As Floyd continued his ninja weapons seminar, Ziggy scanned the crowd, wondering if any of the Samurai's supporters came from the Soup Bowl, a patchwork settlement nestled deep in the heart of the Skidmore landfill. The residents of the Soup Bowl loved the Samurai and revered him as a vengeance-exacting warrior for justice. He looked out for the people there, and in turn, they protected his anonymity. But with so few resources, how did so many of them make it all the way to Mongaphalee? The crowd of samurai supporters stamped their feet and cheered, seeming to make more noise than the rest of the stadium as the Samurai passed by in his cell.

The Samurai's cell took center stage, and Chuckles stood next to a woman with sleek, dark hair, wearing an expensive-looking dress. "I'm here with Katherine Watson, widow to the late William Watson, Senior Vice President of Operations at Skidmore Dumping. William Watson was brutally murdered and decapitated by the Warlord of Waste earlier this year. Mrs. Watson, do you have anything to say to the man who killed your husband?"

Katherine sniffed before glaring at the Samurai with tears in her eyes. "William was a wonderful husband and father. We loved each other in ways someone like you can't even fathom. He deserved so much more. You robbed my children of their father and their future. You took everything from me, and I'll never forgive you!" she cried, balling her hands into fists.

The crowd of samurai supporters began to protest, but the Samurai held up his hand to silence them. "Your husband did deserve more," he replied in a tone so cold it sent chills down Ziggy's spine. "He deserved to *suffer*." The word hissed through the stadium. "He deserved to scream in agony while fire licked the flesh from his bones—which was the fate of thousands of innocent people who died when he ordered their homes be burned."

Mrs. Watson gasped in outrage, her hand flying to her chest. "You—You're a liar!"

"He deserved to suffocate under the mountain of trash he dumped on families who refused to leave the property they owned by right," the Samurai continued with venom. "They were buried alive at his command! He deserved more pain than you can fathom. Open your eyes to the—"

The Samurai was abruptly silenced and the stadium erupted into a bizarre combination of angry dissent from the victims and passionate support from the armor-clad warriors as Chuckles quickly escorted the sobbing Mrs. Watson away.

If Hirofumi saw Ziggy as a threat and a public idol, there was no need to guess what his opinion of the Samurai might be. Not only did he have a loyal following in Skidmore, but it seemed he also had a dedicated following in Mongaphalee. As Ziggy watched the crowd, he couldn't help but think that Hirofumi would see the Samurai's actions as an extension of the philosophical threat Ziggy posed to the Ito empire. After all, Ziggy was the one responsible for bringing the Samurai into the world of Super Serial.

Jovy's eyes darted nervously before jumping into action, her voice barely rising above the commotion. "If you look closely, you may recognize DipShip's Centennial killer," she announced, practically yelling. "Dubbed The Witch, she comes from District Yifu."

"My word, she looks like she's a hundred years old!" Chuckles remarked returning to the booth as if nothing unusual had occurred. Ziggy cringed. Maybe it hadn't. With so many teams to interview and an ever-rotating victims' section, there were sure to be many emotional moments. "That certainly brings a new spin to the Centennial category.""A hundred and five years old, to be precise, and fast asleep in her cell," Jovy said with a giggle. "Apparently, she's a master with poisons, but it doesn't look like she'll be able to prove it anytime soon.""We can only hope she gets her hands on some poisons for the Prelims because I can't imagine she's able to run, let alone walk, anymore," Chuckles said, his amusement carrying into the unsettled crowd.

"The Witch was purchased by DipShip at a labor auction, thanks to the astute eye of Operations Analyst Floyd McNut, who recognized her on the auction roster and purchased her debt," Jovy explained.

"Well, that's a stroke of luck," Chuckles added, and Floyd gripped Pepper's hand at the mention of his name on Jovy's lips.

"This might be the best day of my life," he whispered, eyes wide with wonder.

"Centennial killers are notoriously difficult to find," Jovy continued, "and I don't imagine that stroke of luck will carry through the Prelims."

Both announcers shared a laugh. "I can't imagine an elderly woman posing much of a threat at a hundred and five years old," Chuckles remarked.

"Not unless she dies first, then comes back to haunt the other players."

"It seems the analysts agree," Chuckles lamented, feigning regret. "They've awarded her a kill-score of fifteen."

"That's it for District DipShip," Jovy said as their procession moved along. "Tomorrow should be a very interesting day for this newcomer team."

As the DipShip convoy reached the end of the tarmac, Ziggy felt like a dirty dishrag left to rot in the sun. The throbbing ache in his head, courtesy of Big Montana Ice, pounded like a mallet against his skull, and he could feel Pepper's watchful eye hovering over him like a protective mother hawk, suggesting he looked as bad as he felt.

As soon as their caravan pulled back into the underground waiting area and Alexia vanished to the safety of the DipShip private box, Pepper sought out security and arranged for a car to take Ziggy back to the hotel. He was so grateful he nearly kissed her, and as he stepped from his seat, he felt Floyd's hand on his elbow.

"You're wobbling," Floyd said with concern, "and I didn't see you drink more than two alcohols, so that must mean you need more rest. Rest is important for concussion recovery. Too much stimulation can increase stress on the brain, leading to headaches and nausea."

"I had no idea," Ziggy said mulishly, exhausted to the core.

"Really?" Floyd replied. "Because it's common knowledge, Ziggy."

"You're looking worse for the wear, Marshal Ghostshade," a familiar voice cut through the haze. It was Marshal Imelda Diaz, the lead marshal for District Taste-E Chicken. Their team was preparing to enter the stadium, just as DipShip was exiting.

"You could say that," Ziggy muttered. It was hard not to dislike Marshal Diaz, even though she didn't deserve it, given the way they'd snatched DipShip's first Vigilante, UltraChad, right from under their noses and nearly cost Ziggy his freedom. If they hadn't found the Samurai, he would have lost everything.

"If it's any consolation," Marshal Diaz said, jutting her thumb at the Taste-E Chicken serial killers, "UltraChad is the biggest prick walking the planet. The best day of my life will be when someone ends his. Hell, I plan on inviting you to the party."

Despite himself, Ziggy couldn't help but crack a smile at her bluntness as he watched UltraChad pass by in his cell. Like all the killers, Ziggy couldn't hear him, but he read lips well enough to know that UltraChad was busy spewing a toilet sludge stew of slurs and threats. UltraChad pressed himself against the wall of his box, banging on it with his fists as he passed Benedict.

Benedict burst into panicked tears as he watched him go by, and UltraChad leered, running his thumb across his throat in slow motion. Ziggy wondered if it would be Benedict's last night alive. He'd already gotten lucky once when Marshal Diaz intervened, but UltraChad clearly wanted him dead.

As Ziggy's gaze shifted to the DipShip killers being escorted to the holding facility where they'd await the start of the Preliminaries, he pondered their fate. According to Floyd, there was only a two percent chance that all the killers would survive to the end, and it was strange to think they held the future of DipShip in their murderous hands.

Super Serial violated the dignity and sanctity of human life, and part of Ziggy hated how much it bastardized justice. But he couldn't shake the images of the devastated victims from his mind and a primal part of him wanted to see the killers hurt. It was the medieval drive to hurt those who hurt you. Having experienced the profound sorrow of losing Gio, he understood firsthand the agony of that loss.

Some crimes were so atrocious they warranted atrocious punishment. He wondered if it mattered how that sentence was carried out. Was it all justice in the end? Did it matter how they were punished, so long as they were punished? In his gut he knew it mattered, but violence was one hell of a bandaid on a broken heart.

Chapter 12

Marshmallow Ledbetter

Team DipShip's control room was a cramped space, barely large enough for the three of them to fit side by side without bumping into each other. Ziggy found himself in the center, sandwiched between Pepper on his right and Floyd on his left. The walls, painted a sickly shade of green, peeled in patches, revealing the dingy gray concrete underneath. Ziggy highly doubted the larger corporations with dozens of analysts, were shoved into dank spaces like these. It was a visual representation of their low expectations, a reality he was accustomed to. It didn't exactly inspire confidence. No one expected them to be in the room for long.

Floyd wrinkled his nose. "It smells like stale coffee and old electronics in here." But Ziggy's last concern was the smell. In front of them, a U-shaped desk took up the entire wall. On the desk were nine monitors—three in front of him and three on each side.

"Why so many?" Pepper asked, gesturing toward the screens.

"The monitors can shift in and out of different vantage points using the drones in the cityscape," Floyd explained. "Five monitors are to watch the killers. We're linked to their body cams, biometrics, and endocrine data. With the other four, we can toggle between a 3D virtual map of the cityscape, a mobile aerial view, and special event cameras.

Ziggy's head spun when Floyd showed him how to use his fingers to type commands, toggle between vantage points, zoom in on the cityscape, and mute the control room so they could talk without the killers listening in. He felt like he'd been transformed into a raven, free to soar high or dive low, seeing each structure from a literal bird's-eye view. Except a raven was likely smarter and better equipped for what was to come.

"Five minutes to access," Pepper said, signaling the beginning of the thirty-minute window of time when analysts had access to the cityscape before the Preliminaries began.

"We need as much information as we can get, as quickly as we can get it," Ziggy said. "Floyd, the minute we have access, switch to the aerial view. We need to mark the map so we can steer clear of the riskiest locations. Pepper, head into the 3D virtual map and scout the surroundings on a street level. Keep your eyes peeled for traps, choke points, and anything the Samurai can make into a weapon. I'll look for landmarks and special events. We need to find locations where there might be above-average kills or opportunities for spectacle and interest."

"There's usually a kick-off event," Floyd added. "So keep your eye out for a venue with enough space to hold all the teams plus some fodder."

"Fodder?" Pepper asked.

"Cannon fodder," Floyd explained. "It's the colloquial term for the criminals in the arena who aren't serial killers."

"That's awful," Pepper said, sucking air through her teeth.

"If you think that's bad," Floyd said wryly, "you're in for a rude awakening."

A countdown appeared on the monitors, and Ziggy found himself struggling to remember how to breathe. His heart raced with anticipation, dread tightening in his chest like a vice. Suddenly, Pepper's touch on his forearm broke through the haze of anxiety. Her chinchilla eyes, usually so sharp and focused, were now brimming with genuine concern.

"I shouldn't have put so much pressure on you to come back," she said, her voice quivering with emotion. "I knew how difficult it would be. It was selfish of me. I can only guess what happened in the skybox with Hirofumi, but if you don't want to do this, you don't have to. I mean it, Ziggy. Just because I need you doesn't mean you don't have a choice. You're my friend first. Before anything else."

Ziggy felt a lump form in his throat at Pepper's words. Her sincerity washed over him like a gentle tide, erasing the fear Hirofumi had planted in his heart. He hadn't found a moment to tell her about Hirofumi's threat to his life if he didn't force DipShip to lose, but it didn't matter. He'd stick by his friends through this nightmare, no matter what.

"We can't dismantle the system," Ziggy reminded her. "But we sure as shit can rip off a few pieces of scrap and build something decent in DipShip." He met Pepper's gaze with a weak smile. "I'm here because I want to be. Whatever happens, we're in this together."

Floyd nodded in agreement. "Even if we fail, DipShip is no worse off than before we started. In fact, it's arguably better off, even if we only keep one killer alive."

The countdown ended with a loud beep piercing through the air, and the monitors flickered to life, illuminating the control room with the vibrant colors of the Mongaphalee Jubilee. Ziggy's eyes widened as he scrolled over the sprawling cityscape, feeling like a mouse in a maze of neon cheese.

"It's an enclosed dome approximately half a mile in diameter," Floyd said, his nose nearly touching the monitor. "It's arranged a bit like a donut with six distinctive border sections surrounding a common center and two tracks running along the outer perimeter. A wider track that looks maybe"—he squinted—"two hundred or so feet wide, and a narrower track on the inside that's maybe a quarter of that size. And look there! The middle looks like it could be... a Ferris wheel?"

"I don't even know where to begin," Pepper admitted, tiny beads of sweat forming on her brow. "It's... it's just so massive."

Ziggy zoomed in closer, taking in the colorful chaos of booths, food trucks, amphitheaters, and flashing amusement rides. "It's a fair," he said, and Floyd laughed with glee.

"It's the Mongaphalee Jubilee!" Floyd exclaimed, highlighting a section of the map. "Our guess on the theme was spot-on! And look at those mini-domes scattered around."

"I see them," Pepper said, leaning in closer to study Ziggy's monitor, "but what in the world are they for?"

Floyd grinned, shooting Pepper a sly glance. "Notice the stripes on those domes?" He was giving her a clue, Ziggy realized. His weird version of flirting.

"Circus tents!" Pepper gasped, the pieces clicking into place. "Dozens of them."

Floyd darted around the map, zooming in on a larger tent on the upper west end of the cityscape. "Check out the banners!" he said as if Ziggy and Pepper couldn't see it clearly. "There's one on each tent."

"Debting Zoo?" Pepper read the thick, blocky lettering.

"It's a play on words," Ziggy explained grimly. "Like Petting Zoo."

"That's not good," Pepper said. "Do you think they're holding the pets there?"

"It's a strong possibility," Floyd said, marking the area with a fluorescent green digital flag. "Good thinking, Pep."

"Everyone get on the cityscape map," Ziggy ordered. "We need to get the names off all those banners."

"I found the one on the outside track!" Floyd exclaimed moments later, zooming in on what looked like a walled-in race track. "Pervy Derby." He marked the map with another green flag. "Demolition derby, anyone?"

"Depending on what it looks like, the Pervy Derby could be a good way to rack up points quickly," Ziggy said. "Killing a whole bunch at once makes for a good spectacle, but we'll have to play it by ear."

"Just remember," Floyd said. "If we're thinking that, other teams are thinking it, too."

"There's an enclosed purple tent in the lower west quadrant," Pepper added. "Scary-Go-Round. What could it be?"

"It's probably some kind of Merry-Go-Round," Floyd hypothesized. "But...scary."

"Put a red tag on it," Ziggy said, tamping his exasperation. "If we can't make a good guess, we should steer clear."

□"Got it," Pepper said.

"I found another one!" Floyd announced. "Straight south. 'Con'Cessions. Food booths, by the looks of it."

"I'm guessing that's their way of forcing teams to interact if the games run long and they need food and water," Ziggy theorized, and Floyd marked the area with an orange flag.

"I'm not sure about this," he said. "We may have no choice, but we have to be careful—the food provided in a lot of past cityscapes was poisoned." His nose scrunched up. "Or used to make poison."

"That might be good for Meihua," Ziggy suggested.

Floyd put a note on one of the booths. "This one's a bit of an outlier," he explained. "If we send the team there, this might be the safest option."

Ziggy leaned in to read the placard on the outside of the booth. "Funnel Fakes. Sounds... appetizing."

"Rapist-No-Escapist." Pepper's fingers hovered over a tent with pink stripes. "It's a large tent in the northeast quadrant."

"Could it be a maze?" Ziggy wondered, his mind racing through possibilities.

"Whatever it is, it likely uses rapists as the fodder," Floyd said. "They're also worth more points on average."

"I'll mark it with an orange flag," Pepper said with a wince. "If we need more points, we may have to send them there."

Ziggy's fingers darted across the landscape, his eyes scanning for anything significant. Eventually, he spotted a red, warehouse-style building slightly north of the Debting Zoo. "Here's one," he announced. "It's called the No Inhibition Exhibition."

"It's common for carnivals and fairs to have galleries with arts and crafts," Pepper said. "That could explain why they used the word 'exhibition.'"

"I think we should red-flag that area," Floyd said. "It reminds me of an event in Super Serial seventy-one where the kill score was based on public opinion."

"Red flag," Ziggy agreed. The thought of DipShip getting a positive vote from the public was about as likely as Boomer marrying Big Montana Ice.

"This tent is huge," Floyd remarked after a few minutes of scrolling. "It takes up almost the entire southeastern quadrant. It's called the Despair Fair."

"Those have got to be carnival games," Ziggy said. "Another play on words. That section is sometimes called a Funfair."

"I get it now!" Floyd exclaimed. "That's clever."

"This must be what they meant by earning tokens," Pepper said. "I'll bet if you win a carnival game, you get a token."

"That's the only way to get weapons," Floyd said. "It's a green flag, and the sooner we can get the team there, the better. It's highly unlikely we can win without good weapons, especially if we can't get to Benedict's dogs."

"Is there any way to see inside the tents?" Ziggy asked Floyd, attempting to scroll in but finding only thick plastic walls. "We can guess it's full of carnival games, but the games could be anything."

"I doubt we'll be able to see inside until the start time," Floyd said.

"That just leaves the inner track." Pepper's voice was tinged with anxiety.

"I already found it," Ziggy said, zooming in on the smaller track running the perimeter of the dome on the inside of the Pervy Derby. His stomach turned when he read the banner. "Pedo-Stampedo."

"I'll bet that's a rodeo," Floyd said, chuckling as if he'd never been more relaxed. "I was wondering if that would crop up. We're going to want to avoid that area if possible." He marked the map with a red flag. "Pedophiles are worth more points, and teams with more seasoned competitors will go there first."

Ziggy navigated through the cityscape, scanning their notes on the map. "The largest areas are the Rapist-No-Escapist, the Despair Fair, the Pedo-Stampedo, and maybe the Pervy Derby track," he said. "That means opposing teams will be spread out in a larger area. Those areas might have a better chance of avoiding other killers directly."

"That's true," Floyd replied, scrolling to the center of the map, "but those areas tend to have more fodder, which is problematic for a different reason. Statistical analysis tells us that getting our hands on a good weapon, or Benedict's dogs, will improve our odds the most.

That means if the Debting Zoo isn't close, we send the team to the Despair Fair first, so that they can win tokens."

"Where do they get weapons?" Ziggy pondered aloud. "Is there a place to redeem tokens that we missed?"

"Right here," Floyd said, zooming in on the central structure of the cityscape. "I called it! It's a Ferris wheel. Well, more of an observation wheel, really."

Despite his disdain for all things Super Serial, Ziggy was hard-pressed not to be dazzled by the colossal, sparkling Ferris wheel slowly rotating in the center of the arena. "They get their weapons there?" he asked, eyeing the spacious gondolas adorned with colorful lights.

"Not there," Floyd corrected, pointing to a smaller wheel nearby. "Here. It looks like a prize wheel. You must have to turn in a token to spin it. The banner says, 'Wheel of Misfortune.'"

"We're down to ten minutes," Pepper said, just as her phone blared a high-pitched song. "It's Alexia." She accepted the call. "Good afternoon, Ms. Ito." A pause. "You're where?" Another pause. "Yes, we've seen it. We're strategizing now." Pepper's eyebrows shot up in disbelief. "We didn't know that yet. Is it confirmed?" Another pause. "I see. So it's entirely based on chance? I understand. I'll be in contact after they get their first token."

Pepper ended the call, looking slightly dazed. "Alexia's in the Ferris wheel with Boomer and Hirofumi."

"That makes sense," Ziggy said.

"That doesn't make sense," Floyd said simultaneously.

"There are hundreds of gondolas on the Ferris wheel that were auctioned off to the highest bidder to watch the games up close," Pepper said. "Apparently, the people in the gondolas get to decide what prizes are on the Wheel of Misfortune."

"Why is Hirofumi with them?" Floyd asked. "His team won last year, so none of them are in the Prelims."

"She didn't say." Pepper shrugged. "Curiosity, maybe?"

"He's probably the one who paid for the gondola," Ziggy said, but he knew the real reason. Hirofumi was there to make sure Ziggy kept his word. He was there as a reminder and a warning.

"How do the CEOs influence the prize wheel?" he asked. The landscape of the Prelims was coming together, and the more they learned, the more impossible it seemed they could keep any of their team alive.

"The Wheel of Misfortune has different types of weapons and armor, but the quality is chosen by whoever's gondola is at the bottom position when the prize wheel is spun," Pepper said. "The more they pay, the better the weapon."

"Shit."

"Exactly," Pepper agreed, shaking her head. "Let's hope at least one of those CEOs feels generous."

Ziggy muttered, "Or is at least trying not to piss off Alexia."

"It actually adds an interesting layer to the games," Floyd said. "In a way, the CEOs have to strategize too. They have business contracts and relationships together. If you short a strong team after they spin the wheel, the odds of another CEO doing the same to your team skyrocket."

"Plus, there's the chance that your own CEO ends up in the bottom gondola, which would be a huge win," Pepper said, and Floyd snorted.

"Unless your CEO is broke."

"Our focus needs to be on getting as many tokens as possible," Ziggy said. "Five shitty weapons are better than nothing."

"I agree," Pepper said, but her brow furrowed. "What about Benedict's dogs?" she asked. "They're weapons, too."

"It may be worth it to go to the Debting Zoo and get them, but it will depend on timing and where the killers come into the arena," Floyd reasoned. "We need to figure out where they are in the arena before we make any moves."

Suddenly, an alarm blared. The countdown clock hit one minute, and each killer's body cams and health stats popped up on their monitor.

"Can you hear me?" Ziggy checked the audio. "Team DipShip, do you copy?"

"I can hear you, Marshal Ghostshade." Carol's lilting voice rang in his ears.

"I am here," the Samurai confirmed.

"It's dark as fuck down here," grumbled Big Montana Ice. "But I can hear you loud and clear. I've got Granny strapped to my back. Boomer made her a carrier, and she's swaddled up like a sweet little death baby."

"*Wǒ bèi bǎng zài jùrén de bèi shàng,*" chuckled Lin Meihua, her voice a faint glimmer in the darkness.

"She can hear us," Floyd confirmed. He chuckled. "Her health stats are surprisingly good, and her dopamine level is high. She's excited."

"It's too dark to see anything," Ziggy said, but he could hear Benedict sniffling.

"Do you know where my babies are?" he asked with a broken sob. "I haven't seen them since last night."

"We think they're in the Debting Zoo," Floyd said. "But it's impossible to know for sure."

"The what?" Carol exclaimed.

"The zoo? Oh, no!" Benedict's anguished cry rang out.

"We'll find them," Ziggy told Benedict. "Remember, you're supposed to be a dog-loving hero, so act like it. Get your head on straight before someone chops it off your neck. Listen up," he snapped, his words sharp and urgent as the countdown ticked down its final seconds. "The cityscape is a massive, domed fairground. There are two tracks around the perimeter and six quadrants, each with different carnival-themed events. We don't know how you'll enter or where."

"The most likely locations are the Despair Fair, the Rapist-No-Escapist, and the Pedo-Stampedo," Floyd said. "Those events have the biggest venues, and Super Serial always kicks off with a huge spectacle."

"The what?" Carol repeated in dismay.

Crackling circus music began playing through the shoddy speakers in the control room. The hairs on the back of Ziggy's neck stood up. "It's time," he said. "Focus. Watch each other's backs."

"Heavenly Father, protect me in my time of need—" Carol began to pray, and Big Montana Ice whooped, "Let's crack some skulls!" as streams of light filtered into the holding room, and it rose into the unknown.

The Super Serial Preliminaries had begun.

Chapter 13

Live and Let Fry

Ziggy was momentarily blinded by the flood of light illuminating the monitors and scrambled to regain his bearings as Team DipShip landed at the edge of a muddy arena. Their small platform was on an incline, surrounded by other teams rising around them in every direction.

"Ladies and gentlemen, boys and girls, serial killers of all ages!" boomed an enthusiastic ringmaster's voice over a carnival jingle. "Welcome to the first special event of the Mongaphalee Jubilee!" A deafening drumroll followed, leaving Ziggy's ears ringing. "The Rapist-No-Escapist!"

"The Rapist-No-Escapist arena is in the northeastern quadrant of the cityscape," Pepper told Ziggy, pinpointing the event on the map.

"Our inside arena view is up," Floyd said. "It looks like an oval about five hundred feet in diameter. It looks like Team DipShip is in the southern section of the building, close to the floor."

"In the center of the arena are thousands of filthy convicted rapists," the ringmaster continued. "We've tagged every deplorable with a confession detailing their crime. Your task: locate the revolting human filth with a surprise hidden inside. But beware, these pigs are slippery!"

"It's a greased pig contest!" Floyd exclaimed with mounting excitement. "This is going to be a blast."

"Hell yeah!" Big Montana Ice hooted, shadowboxing the air. "Let's catch some piggies!"

Pepper choked in horror. "A surprise hidden inside? As in, inside the rapist?"

Roaming spotlights swept through the air, illuminating the center of the floor to expose a densely packed pen containing thousands of half-naked rapists. Their white loincloths were saturated and stained, magnifying their humiliation rather than masking it. Sweat and grease were visible on their bodies even from the monitors, evidence of the sweltering heat and humidity of the arena. Ziggy's morals and wish to help Pepper clashed like oil and water. This wasn't a greased pig contest. It was a human slaughter.

"No team can move to the next event until the task is complete," the ringmaster instructed with a flourish. "Rapist-No-Escapist is proudly sponsored by District SteelForge. SteelForge, the finest steel erections since 2058."

A low horn sounded, followed by the energetic picking of a banjo, and the arena erupted into chaos like a spark igniting a gas line. The walls of the pen retracted into the floor, and the rapists scattered, screaming as they ran for their lives.

"Move!" the Samurai shouted as a stampede of killers charged into the mud, their wild hoots and menacing laughter reverberating through the air. Benedict yelped in terror, and Carol screamed, but they swiftly followed the Samurai onto the muddy floor.

A rapist darted past with the chilling words "I raped my ex-wife" printed across his chest. Big Montana Ice made a grab for him, but he wriggled from her arms like a fish off the hook, scrambling back into the fray.

"Those fuckers are covered in lube!" Big Montana Ice shouted, rubbing her goopy arms on her pants, and Ziggy noticed the team's costumes for the first time. Each killer wore a fusion of clothing that blended their individual killing style with Boomer's flamboyant fashion sense. He was relieved to see DipShip's battle costumes were more utilitarian than their interview outfits and likely wouldn't be a hindrance.

All around them, murderers slammed into the rapists like a cavalry charge. The crunch of bone and gurgle of blood made Ziggy's stomach clench. Bodies slipped and churned in the mud like angry lovers. A bruised and bloodied rapist flew across the mud as if he were on a twisted slip and slide, barreling into Benedict's legs, sending him sprawling to the ground.

"Help!" Benedict squealed, and the Samurai yanked him to his feet, pulling him away from the rapist.

"Gotcha!" Big Montana Ice shouted with glee as she jumped in the air, mercilessly crushing the rapist under her thick, steel-toed work boots. Meihua tightly gripped the carrier's edge to avoid being jostled out as Big Montana Ice grunted with every blow, her boots squelching in the gruesome mess of tissue and bone.

Ziggy saw a score appear at the corner of his monitor—seven. DipShip also appeared on a scoreboard in the arena that ticked and shifted constantly as teams racked up points. District BeefBoys, a massive cattle ranching operation, was at the top of the leaderboard.

"Congratulations on your first kill," Floyd said cheerily. "Good job everyone!"

"I feel better," Big Montana Ice said, breathing hard. "I needed to get some of that sexual tension out."

"There should be something hidden inside of them," Ziggy said, cringing at the puddle of rapist squished into the mud. He could just make out the edge of the words "tortured him" inked across the rapist's upper chest, and his mouth dried out like a salty cracker topped with desert sand.

"What do you mean hidden inside?" Carol's voice trembled. "Like in the body?"

"I'll search," the Samurai said, crouching to sift through the gore. "Keep watch," he ordered Big Montana Ice, who nodded, crouching as she leered at anyone who ventured too close.

Scrolling over the arena map, Pepper said, "I'll try to figure out what we're supposed to be looking for." Even though her voice was steady, the color had drained from her face.

"We're all dead!" Benedict whimpered, swiping at the thick mud on his dark green tracksuit. Following his disastrous interview, Boomer made some changes and opted for a trendy dog walker look. But the oppressive Mongaphalee heat had already ruined Benedict's faux hawk, and sweat cascaded down his face, fogging his glasses, which were kept in place by a brown leather strap.

"My best calculation is that there are at least two thousand rapists in the arena," Floyd said, scrolling so fast his screen looked like a blur.

"Not for long," Ziggy said, struggling to keep from gagging as the Samurai lifted the rapist's splintered rib cage and shoved his hand underneath.

"If there are more rapists than killers, that probably means there's not a 'surprise' in every single one," Pepper said.

"It also means there's a good chance a few lucky ones will make it out alive," Floyd added. "If there's hope, the rapists will probably fight back. They outnumber the killers and could band together."

"Back up, motherfucker!" Big Montana Ice bellowed as a killer in a black trench coat inched toward them, his eyes darting over Big Montana Ice's massive form.

"Carol, watch your back. Benedict, open your damn eyes and focus," Ziggy ordered, zeroing in on the space surrounding the team. "Trench Coat is probably not alone."

"I searched thoroughly and found nothing in the body," the Samurai said, blood covering his hands and the front of his ornamental vest Boomer had made to look like armor. He was also wearing a kabuto-style helmet that looked like it came from a child's Halloween costume.

"A few teams have pulled something out of the rapists' stomachs," Pepper said, flustered, "but I couldn't see what it was."

"Samurai," Ziggy said, noticing a bare-chested man with a horned Minotaur headpiece moving in DipShip's direction. "On your left."

"I see him," the Samurai said, eyes narrowing.

"Don't engage unless you have no choice," Floyd said. "The helmets and armor are just for show because of the rules, but he's still a threat; his kill-score is seventy-one. Attacking this early in the competition hardly ever works because the top killers are still fresh."

"I'm fresher than all these pecker-heads," Big Montana Ice said as the team rushed around the perimeter of the mud pit. She turned to face the Minotaur, skipping backward on her heels. "Stop being a tease and ask me on a date already," she taunted him with a vicious smile.

The Minotaur flexed his thick muscles and growled, "The only date you're gonna get is a death date!" He charged at her but ended up on the ground when a massive pack of rapists fleeing from two teams of killers bowled him over. The rapists stumbled and collided with each other, their cries filling the air as the killers attacked, while the Minotaur, struggling to rise to his feet, had his head trampled into the mud.

Moments later, when the stampede had moved on, a trailing man in a pristine suit hopped across the dead, keeping his leather toe-capped shoes clean as he balanced on the Minotaur's unmoving body. He glanced at the DipShip team. "Can you believe this mess?" he called as if they were engaging in casual banter, and Carol let out a strangled sound.

"Don't go anywhere near that guy!" Floyd shouted, his voice so loud through the mic the entire team winced. "Don't even look at him. That's Big Money Bill. He'll order a hit on anyone who crosses him in the Prelims."

"There's a group of rapists banding together at the west side of the arena," Pepper said. "We should avoid that area. They're building a wall with dead bodies."

"I see it," Ziggy said, watching two rapists dragging the pulverized body of a murderer across the mud.

Benedict's whimpers filled the control room, his grip on the band at the back of Carol's sporty black tank top tightening as three rapists ran by, their mud-covered bodies vanishing into the crush. Even though it still said "MLM Murderer" across the chest, Ziggy was glad to see Carol's costume was at least more practical than the gold bikini.

"Go there!" Lin Meihua suddenly shouted from her perch atop Big Montana Ice, pointing out an injured rapist who was hobbling by, trying to disappear in the commotion. The marking across his chest read, "I raped a woman out jogging." The Samurai sprinted forward, sliding in the mud. His boot slammed into the rapist's legs, sending him crashing to the ground.

"I can't die like this! Please!" he begged as the Samurai bounded to his feet, but a passing competitor got there first, grabbing the rapist by his matted hair. The killer was a bald, muscular man in a leather motorcycle vest. His eyebrows were shaved, replaced with tattoos that read 'PAIN' and 'AGONY.' With relentless force, he kicked at the rapist's stomach until a torrent of vomit and blood spewed from his mouth.

"Finders keepers, motherfucker!" the tattooed murderer yelled at the Samurai as his four teammates closed in to dig at the rapist's body. There was a loud crack and a louder scream as the killers stomped on the rapist's ribcage, popping bone shards from the skin.

With the agility of a viper, the Samurai tensed his muscles, poised to strike, but then he retreated slowly back toward the team, murmuring, "He will win who knows when to fight and when to flee."

"That sounds like Sun Tzu," Floyd noted. "Sun Tzu was the minister to King Helü—"

"Floyd!" Ziggy barked as the tattooed killer let out a chilling laugh, snapping a protruding rib. "There's a prize inside," he snarled before plunging the jagged bone into the man's stomach, carving through flesh and muscle until he was wrist deep. After a moment of struggle, he wrenched his arm free, pulling out an object dripping in entrails. "It's car keys!" he shouted triumphantly to his teammate.

"Suck my big floppy udder, you thieving son-of-a-bitch! That was our kill!" Big Montana Ice roared, flipping the tattooed murderer the bird with both hands as he bolted away with his team.

"Of course, they're car keys," Pepper said with an irritated huff. "I'm such an idiot. They must be for the Pervy Derby."

Floyd leaned into his monitor. "You're probably right, but I'll see if I can locate the exit point to see where it leads."

"Did you say derby?" Benedict's voice was thick with horror. "Are you taking the piss? Like banger racing?"

"Hear that, everyone?" Ziggy said, zooming out to widen his view. "Those keys are your ticket out of here and into the next event."

"Roughly one in five rapists will have keys inside them," Floyd said. "Odds are you'll have to kill more than a few. Watch for injured outliers or move in slowly and try to catch one as they pass."

"Benedict just collapsed. His adrenaline and cortisol levels are skyrocketing," Pepper said, her voice tense. "I think he's having a panic attack."

Big Montana Ice stared into the battle with a wild look in her eyes. "Who's the lucky fuck-burglar holding my keys?" she said, cracking her knuckles.

"Stay with the team," Ziggy ordered before she did anything rash. "Benedict!" he barked, but got no response in the din. He switched tactics. "Carol!" he called out. "Do something to calm Benedict. He can barely stand, and Meihua can't battle in hand-to-hand conflict. You're all dead if you don't make a move."

Carol frantically unzipped her fanny pack, pulling out a bottle of patchouli oil. "Here, Benny Bear," she coaxed, waving the bottle under his nose. Ziggy watched in disbelief as the oil acted like smelling salts, and Benedict jolted to his feet.

"Team OmniFood!" a beefy killer wearing only a pineapple print jockstrap ran past Big Montana Ice's body cam. His thick ropes of chest hair glistened as he lunged toward a scrawny, naked rapist branded with the words "I raped two of my math students." He grabbed hold and, with a mighty wrench, twisted the man's neck until even Ziggy heard the snap. In one strong movement, he lifted the lifeless rapist over his shoulder, giving his buttock a playful slap before turning to wink at Carol and Big Montana Ice. "See you in the cityscape, ladies," he said before darting away, the limp rapist flapping against his muscular back.

Big Montana Ice's jaw dropped open in awe. "This is the best day of my life."

"This is the worst day of my life," Carol groaned at the same time.

"Jinx! You owe me a beer, Lil Biscuit!" Big Montana said, swatting Carol on the back, nearly knocking her to the ground. Another group of rapists ran by, and Big Montana Ice stamped her foot, shouting, "We can't just stand here! All the good ones will be taken!"

"It's up to you and the Samurai to keep the team safe," Ziggy said. "If a rapist gets close, go for it and grab them, but otherwise, play it safe and stick together."

"Fuck that noise," Big Montana Ice growled. "We gotta get in the game! Alaskan Thunder!" she shouted, barreling into the action.

At the sight of her thundering approach, terrified rapists and killers scattered like cockroaches and praying mantises. The Samurai followed, keeping pace at her side, shielding her and Meihua from attacks as she lunged for anything that moved.

She snatched a tiny, gothic-looking killer in a vampire cape by her neck and began repeatedly punching her in the head with her thick fist. When the killer went limp, Big Montana Ice dropped her to the mud like a wet towel.

"*Jiāyóu! Jiāyóu!* Good job, big lady," Meihua said as their kill point total notched up—fifty-eight. She patted Big Montana's head like she was a favored niece.

"That was the Raven," Floyd said. "She was only worth fifty-one points. Probably because of her size."

Big Montana Ice was indignant. "The big ones with more points are harder to kill!"

"That wasn't a criticism," Floyd said, mystified at her hostility, when Benedict let out a sudden blood-curdling scream.

"Help us!" he cried, and Ziggy's heart leaped into his throat when he saw a group of rapists closing in on Benedict and Carol.

"Samurai!" Ziggy said, and the Samurai raced back to help, dodging and weaving through the pandemonium, leaving Big Montana Ice and Meihua behind to fend for themselves.

The sight of Benedict's cowering form made the rapist with "I kidnapped and trafficked young men" written across her chest burst into laughter. "Look at this sook," she said with a snort. "He's more pathetic than a barbie with no snags." She made a grab for Benedict, but Carol surged forward with surprising speed, landing a solid kick to her shins.

"You will not touch him!" she shrieked. "Shame on you, kangaroo!" But before the rapist could retaliate, the Samurai emerged. With lightning-quick reflexes born from years of training, he delivered a precise strike to the solar plexus of the nearest rapist, causing them to double over, gasping for breath. A second tried to flank the Samurai from the side, but he anticipated the move, spinning on his heel, landing a roundhouse kick that caught the rapist squarely in the chest. The force sent him tumbling to the ground as a third rapist lunged forward with a wild, desperate swing. The Samurai ducked under the attack, sweeping his leg in a low arc, knocking him off balance.

Before any of the rapists could right themselves, the Samurai closed the distance between them, landing a series of rapid strikes to the base of each one's skull. The kill point total increased rapidly as they slumped to the ground—sixty-five. Seventy-two. Seventy-nine.

"Holy Mother Mary on a tricycle," Ziggy murmured. He'd seen the Samurai in action before, but this was on a whole new level. The Samurai was barely out of breath.

The woman who'd attempted to attack first slipped in the mud as she tried to escape, sobbing and pleading as the Samurai gripped her by the ankle. With two swift kicks to the head, she joined her fellow rapists in death, her body coated in mud. The kill point total ticked up—eighty-six.

Floyd laughed with delight, slapping his knee. "That's one of the coolest things I've ever seen in Super Serial! The fans are going to love it."

"Search their bodies for keys," Ziggy ordered, startled when the kill point total suddenly increased to ninety-three.

"Big Montana Ice got one, too," Pepper explained, and Ziggy toggled viewpoints to Big Montana Ice, who was holding an already dead man by his short brown hair, punching his face into a pulp.

"You're mine, Bazgoroch!" she roared, gripping the man's broken jaw with three fingers. "Bye-bye, little fucklet!" She yanked it free with a pop. She gripped his slimy esophagus and wrenched it free from his body, stomach and all. "No keys in this one," she panted, and Pepper dry heaved, turning to another monitor, only to see the Samurai working with Carol to open the bodies without weapons.

"What about a piece of bone?" Carol suggested over the din. "Like Big Montana Ice did to Boomer?"

"Floyd, what's the easiest bone in the body to remove?" Ziggy asked, and Floyd's face pinched.

"Probably the clavicle," he said after a moment. "If you break it in the right spots, it should push through the skin. Luckily, they killed enough rapists that they don't have to get it on the first try," he added with a grin, and the Samurai went to work, stomping and pulling at the rapists' shoulders and arms to break a bone free.

"There's a team approaching with eyes on your bodies," Pepper said as the Samurai used his combat boot to rip out a sinewy bone shard. He placed it in Carol's shaking hand before rising to his feet.

"Big Montana Ice," Ziggy ordered, his pulse pounding. "You and Meihua get back to the team. We need you now!"

"Coming!" Big Montana Ice said as she ran past a killer, the sound of bones crunching filling the air as a nearby killer tore a rapist's arms from his body. Another let out a piercing wail as a fur-clad murderer with razor-sharp fangs and talons bit and clawed into her abdomen, eating her alive with the ferocity of a grizzly hunting a doe. The killer howled like a blood frenzied wolf.

"It's District BrewHaha," Floyd said. "They look like they're down a few killers and probably think we are, too, since they can't see Big Montana Ice or Meihua."

"The keys should be in the center of the body cavity," Pepper told Carol. "Benedict! Help her!"

Carol kneeled before jabbing the bone shard through the rapist's belly button. Blood dribbled from the wound. "Our soul waits for the Lord; he is our help and our shield," Carol said to herself as Benedict pulled both flaps of the wound open, his arms straining with the effort.

"Fuck, fuck, fuckity fuck!" Benedict grunted, nearly losing his grip.

"Language!" Carol hissed as she gingerly felt around inside. Her face fell. "Nothing," she said, and the Samurai prepared to defend the team, quickly surveying the scene as he dropped into a protective stance.

"That girl in front of you is a street fighter called Club Rat," Floyd said as a woman with a high ponytail and odd orange-tinted skin slowly approached, sizing up the Samurai. "The other two sneaking up from the sides are Captain Cutthroat and Slaughterhouse."

Carol frantically sliced into another body. "Pull Benny!" she said, and Benedict grasped the rapist's stomach on both sides.

"Give us the keys and we'll let you go," Club Rat said in a lilting accent. She gestured toward Carol and Benedict. "And we'll take the points for those two while we're at it."

"To engage an enemy is to invite death," the Samurai said to the rival killers, his tone ominous.

Club Rat laughed. "It's three to one, *ya ghabi*. There's no use fighting to save them. They're already dead."

"You're the one who's already dead!" Big Montana Ice bellowed as she burst onto the scene.

Chapter 14

Cake My Breath Away

Kill-Score: 93

Big Montana Ice's giant ham fist swung in an arch before it connected with Club Rat's ear, denting her skull. Club Rat's body flopped to the ground, one eye bulging from its socket. Their kill-score reached 159, and Captain Cutthroat and Slaughterhouse took one look at Big Montana Ice and bolted, abandoning their fallen comrade without even looking back.

"That bitch had a hard head!" Big Montana Ice flexed her hand, the knuckles red and raw.

"This body didn't have keys in it either!" Carol exclaimed, soaked to her elbows in blood. She was on the verge of tears when Big Montana Ice took the collarbone shard from her, pushing Benedict to the side and jabbing it through the rapist's hairy belly button.

"Let me do the rest," she said, poking a single finger through the opening. Blood spilled out, but she jammed another finger in, wrenching and tearing until the skin gave way. She pawed through the bloody organs, like a raccoon rummaging through a trash can after a Taco Tuesday feast.

Floyd laughed. "I've seen you poke your finger into Boston creams like that, Ziggy."

"For fuck's sake." Ziggy scowled. "Is nothing sacred anymore?"

Big Montana gave the last of the Samurai's kills the same treatment before standing up and wiping her bloody hands on the hem of her sleeveless T-shirt, which featured a lone wolf howling at the moon. "No keys in either of them," Big Montana Ice said, her nostrils flaring. "Something tells me Bazgoroch is behind this."

"We need a new strategy," Ziggy said, his mind racing. "Big Montana Ice is the most intimidating, so she needs to stay with Benedict and Carol to discourage anyone from attacking. Samurai, can you chase a rapist or two in her direction? Try picking a weaker one from the herd."

"It will be done," the Samurai said, retreating a distance away.

"We just need one," Pepper said, scrolling over the arena, eyes fixed on the area surrounding the Samurai. Moments later, the Samurai took off after a middle-aged rapist with the words "I raped my roommate" across her chest. She screamed when she saw him coming, darting in DipShip's direction.

"There's one on the way," Pepper said, and Big Montana Ice was ready, grabbing the rapist by the wrist as she passed, yanking her to the ground. The woman screamed and donkey-kicked backward, causing Big Montana Ice to slip, barely catching herself on one knee before she crushed Lin Meihua.

"*Aiya! Xiǎoxīn, xiǎoxīn,*" Meihua grunted, her chunky orthopedic shoes grazing the mud, and Big Montana surged to her feet, gulping in air.

"Damn, those rapers are slippery," she said as the Samurai skidded beside her, gliding to a stop in the mud. "And not just the demons. Even the human ones are running. Why do they do that if they know they're gonna die anyway?" Big Montana complained, watching rapists dart through the arena in zig-zag patterns, dodging other killers.

"Clinging to life is the last vestige of humanity," the Samurai said, turning when he heard Carol cry out. The image on her monitor flipped, and Ziggy caught a glimpse of a rapist's thick fist punching Benedict's tear-soaked face before Carol hit the dirt, landing so hard the camera bounced. She groaned as two more rapists twisted her to her back, pinning her arms and legs.

"One more cunt before the end," a low voice hissed. Ziggy watched in mute horror as a greasy, bearded rapist sat on top of Carol and began tearing at her clothes. She bucked her hips, flailing desperately as she tried to escape. Benedict screamed as blood gushed from his nose. "Help!"

"Do something, you coward!" Ziggy yelled to Benedict, who howled like a whipped puppy, crying for his corgi pack as he slinked away, leaving Carol to the gang of rapists.

"Bazgoroch!" Big Montana Ice thundered, and the Samurai roared, charging forward at an inhuman speed. His camera dipped as he flew through the air, kicking the nearest rapist to the ground, freeing one of Carol's arms. Carol seized the opportunity and shoved her open palm up and into the nose of the pawing predator—a move straight out of a women's self-defense class. His head snapped back, but the pain only seemed to fuel him, and he surged forward with renewed fervor. He pulled his elbow back, ready to deliver a devastating punch, but Big Montana Ice got there in time, grabbing his arm and ripping him off Carol. She slammed her fist into his face before planting her steel-toed boot into his crotch with a powerful kick. His eyes rolled back into his head.

"Zhēnshi kěxí wǒ méiyǒu dú," a red-faced Meihua spat on his hunched over form. *"Yīnwèi nǐ shìtú qiángjiān wǒ de* friend, *suǒyǐ nǐ de sǐ yīnggāi shì huǎnmàn ér tòngkǔ de."*

With a yelp, the third rapist tried to escape, but the Samurai swiftly struck his throat with rigid fingers. He wheezed as his windpipe collapsed, and his mouth gaped open as he tried to crawl away, but his efforts were in vain. The Samurai dug his knee into the inscription on the rapist's back, "stalked and raped nine women," and leaned forward, grabbing the rapist's hair and jerking back his head.

Placing his lips against the ear of the struggling rapist, the Samurai whispered, "All things are dry and brittle in death," before slamming his fist into the man's neck twice in quick succession. It bulged like a balloon and the rapist's mouth opened and closed like a drowning fish as a line of blood dribbled from his nose.

Big Montana Ice helped Carol to her feet. "Now for this slimy little crotch warlock," she snarled, flipping the rapist over like a rotten log in tall grass. His limp body splayed out like a bloated frog.

"Big lady, kill bad guy," Meihua crooned, patting Big Montana on the shoulder.

"Let me ask you a question," she said, looming over him, and Lin Meihua unexpectedly cackled with glee. "What do leaves smell like after a squirrel party?"

"Guh-uh-kuh—" The rapist choked out foamy blood.

"Nope," Big Montana Ice said, and her boot came down on his face, stomping him into oblivion. She moved like a battering ram, only stopping the bloody assault when she was too out of breath to continue. The rapist was spread out like a stray cat squished on the road by a passing semi-truck. Pepper had long since turned away, her face buried in her hands.

"Please have keys," Ziggy said as their kill point total increased—180.

"I'll look." Carol's weak voice chimed in. She was shaking, covered in a gooey mix of mud and blood, but she walked over to the mass of scarlet porridge, head held high. With no fear or hesitation, she retrieved a set of keys from the rapist's abdominal cavity, her hands now stained with blood. She tucked the keys into her pocket, then woodenly unzipped her gore-covered fanny pack, extracting a bottle of lemon oil. She poured three drops into her palm, then vigorously rubbed her hands together before wiping them on the legs of her yoga pants. "Lemon oil will sanitize your hands without harmful chemicals," she recited in an eerie, detached voice.

"You know what?" Big Montana Ice said, putting her enormous arm around Carol, who, surprisingly, didn't resist. "I think we'll be okay, Lil Biscuit. I'm not so sure he was the demon, after all. He caved in pretty easily. My bad." She swiped at the sweat dripping down her face, then suddenly, her eyes narrowed. "That one could be, though," she said, slogging toward the third rapist who was attempting to crawl away after the Samurai's brutal takedown. She kicked him in the face until he fell still.

"There's only one way out of the arena," Floyd said as their kill-score moved to 187. "It's an exit on the east side of the tent. They're funneling teams into the Pervy Derby."

"Head for the exit, stay together, and watch each other's backs," Ziggy said, and the killers picked their way across the corpse-strewn arena toward the exit, led by Big Montana Ice with Carol and Benedict in the middle, and the Samurai bringing up the rear. Meihua, still strapped to Big Montana Ice, pointed at potential dangers as they navigated the terrifying terrain.

"Bad guy!" she shouted when any killers got too close.

Fortunately, the Samurai's intimidating presence, the team's blood-spattered and gory appearance, and Big Montana Ice's massive size made potential attackers hesitate, even though she carried an old lady on her back.

"Pepper, look!" Floyd exclaimed, his eyes wide with astonishment as he held up his phone. "DipShip is blowing up on social media. Our kills are already trending. They keep showing the Samurai's attack in slow motion."

"What about me?" Big Montana Ice demanded, breathing heavily. "I'm way stronger than he is, and twice as good-looking."

"It's not about strength or looks," Floyd answered. "Plenty of killers are strong, and even more are attractive. It's about showmanship."

Pepper glanced at Ziggy, and they shared a look of resignation. Floyd's obsession with Super Serial was one of those things they both had to hide in the dark corners of their minds. But it wasn't the time for personal grievances. Everyone had their vices—his was donuts,

Floyd's was Super Serial, and Pepper's was caring too much about people who didn't care about her. But at the moment, Ziggy was happy to admit he was grateful for Floyd's fixation on the games.

"Chuckles and Jovy just reported that ninety-four teams have already made it through to the Pervy Derby," Floyd said, absorbed in his phone. "Excluding District TerraFluer. They technically made it through Rapist-No-Escapist, but most of their team was electrocuted when they tried to bypass the walls on the walkway between events."

"Electric walls," the Samurai panted as he ran, listening to the exchange. "Noted."

From the corner of the monitor, Ziggy saw a murderer in a red armored bikini costume rush Big Montana Ice with a jagged bone shard.

"Bad guy!" Meihua warned, and he heard a thud as Big Montana Ice swung her hammer fist, knocking aside the woman as if she were nothing more than a tether ball. She lay unmoving on the ground, and DipShip's kill-score notched up to 245. Ziggy's heart was in his throat by the time DipShip made it to the exit.

The exit was a row of bulletproof ticket booths, each with an attached turnstile. Inside each booth stood an animatronic clown. "It looks like you present your keys to the animatronic in the booth," Floyd said, "and the turnstile should let you pass."

"This way!" Big Montana Ice hollered, leading the team to the nearest vacant ticket booth. As they approached, they noticed the lifeless body of a beautiful killer with long red hair and a flower crown slumped against the turnstile. Her eyes were charred craters, smoke curling from the hollow sockets.

"I guess we know what happens if you try to pass without a key," Pepper said with a grimace.

"That's the Botanist Lobotomist from District TerraFluer," Floyd gasped. "What a shame. She was rated a sixty-five. I can't believe she's out this early."

The adrenaline of every killer spiked as they approached the booth, the eerie animatronic clown's painted grin seeming to widen as they drew nearer. Its eyes, two soulless voids, bored into them with an unsettling intensity. "I hate clowns," Benedict whispered.

"I dated a clown once," Big Montana Ice whispered. "Nice hands, but a crooked weiner."

The team exchanged uneasy glances, and Carol hesitated for a moment before tentatively holding out the keys toward the clown, her movements slow and deliberate. The clown's mechanical hand jerked forward, snatching the keys with a metallic clank. Benedict shrieked, and its eyes flickered momentarily, scanning the keys before dropping them back into Carol's waiting palm.

"Congratulations," an uncanny voice crackled from some-where inside the clown. "Your keys belong to vehicle number forty-one." The turnstile lurched into motion to the tune of "Entrance of the Gladiators," its gears grinding as it rotated like a music box winding down. Team DipShip stepped forward, and each turn of the mechanism felt like an eternity as they passed through one by one.

"Stay alert," Ziggy said when the entire team had landed on the other side. Down the line, another team was emerging from the booths, but they only glared before hurrying down the walkway.

"They're less likely to attack without weapons," Floyd said. "They'll take the opportunity if they get it, but the real fun doesn't start until the weapons come out."

"Can't wait," Ziggy muttered.

"Me neither," Floyd replied with a grin, and Pepper rolled her eyes. Ziggy zoomed in on the walkway as the DipShip killers crept forward. It was about three hundred feet long with towering electric fences on both sides, crackling with lethal energy.

"Don't let anyone get too close," Ziggy warned, his stomach churning. "If any of you so much as lay a toenail on that fence, you're dead."

"That's... right," Pepper said, sitting forward. "In that case, maybe we should give a few of our rivals an electric execution, courtesy of team DipShip."

"Well, fuck me, Pepperoni," Big Montana Ice said, her wiry eyebrows lifting in surprise. "You're a spicy little hotpot, ain't you?"

Then, like a disturbing déjà vu, a commotion erupted ahead. A team of killers launched an attack on another team, filling the air with screams and curses. With a violent shove, one killer sent a lethal-looking gray-haired woman crashing into the fence. There was a shower of sparks, and her mouth opened in horror, spewing smoldering gray smoke. She was stuck there like a mouse in a glue trap, cooking from the inside out, whatever scream she'd been about to scrum stuck in her throat by the deadly current.

Without hesitation, a brawl ensued, fists flying and bodies colliding as the two teams clashed in a frenzy of violence. Two men locked in combat, arms entangled, met their collective electric doom as they pulled each other into the fence.

"Who gets those points?" Ziggy asked.

"Whoever dies second," Floyd said, using the monitor to scan the walkway ahead. "That's why they monitor their vitals so closely."

"Stay put," Ziggy said to the team as a man in a purple cape lifted a small woman in a crisp black dress off the ground. He flung her into the fence like a discus, only to be pulled backward by that same cape to his own shocking death, his head erupting with a loud pop, bursting into flame.

Realizing her teammates were dead, the lone survivor of one team, a blonde woman in a pink bodysuit, made a break for it, sprinting back down the walkway toward DipShip. "Help!" she screamed, waving her arms. "My marshal says you can have whatever you want!" The three remaining killers chased after her, their faces twisted into malicious grins.

"I think that's Barbie Cude," Floyd said. "The Angry White Women killer from District NeuroGenixx."

Big Montana Ice stepped forward, a look of genuine compassion crossing her ruddy face. "You've got a deal!" she called encouragingly, waving her pancake hand. "We'll help you. Hurry!" Carol and Benedict exchanged bewildered glances.

A look of immense relief crossed Barbie's face. "Thank you," she cried breathlessly as she arrived. "My marshal said that—"

Big Montana Ice grabbed Barbie by the front of her jumpsuit and threw her into the fence. Sparks popped into the air, and Barbie let out a half-scream before her muscles seized from head to toe. Her jumpsuit melted against her skin, and thick red branches of burned flesh sizzled up her neck as she was torched from the inside out. Their kill-score rose to 312.

"Barbie Cude," Big Montana Ice said with a wink in her voice, "has been barbecued."

Floyd gasped in awe. "That'll go viral in minutes," he said, and Big Montana Ice grinned with self-satisfaction, cracking her knuckles. She turned to the three killers who'd just lost out on their prey. "Who's next?" she said with a snarl, and the Samurai quietly flanked Big Montana Ice, sinking into his attack stance.

"Oh, hell no!" one killer hissed, turning on his heel. "She's huge. I'm outta here."

"You're not going nowhere," Big Montana Ice said, and when the killers ran for it, she thundered after them, racing toward the large red tent at the opposite end of the walkway.

"There's no one ahead of us, but two teams are coming from behind," Floyd said, watching the walkway from above.

"Follow her," Ziggy ordered the team. "You're too exposed."

The killers darted to the end of the walkway as fast as they could, bursting through the open tent flap on the opposite side of the electric fence. Ziggy was unsurprised to see they were in a crude parking garage. It was halfway empty, but each spot was marked with a number ranging from one to 309.

"Cowards!" Big Montana Ice wheezed when she realized she'd lost sight of her targets. "Fucking shit jugglers!"

Carol looked too exhausted to scold her for swearing. "The electronic clown said we got forty-one," she said, breathing hard. The team ran along the rows of vehicles. As they passed, Ziggy noticed that some of them were formidable monster trucks and jeeps with massive tires and plated body work. But it was clear that at least half the vehicles existed purely for spectacle.

"This is going to be hysterical!" Floyd laughed, slapping his knee. "Look at the giant hotdog car! And the one next to it looks like a cement truck."

"That's an Austin Westminster," Benedict said as they passed an old-fashioned sedan. Ziggy saw a graffiti-painted Chevy Impala on his monitor. There was even a stall with a tractor parked in it. Every vehicle was covered in sponsorships and ads.

"Please, let it be anything but a hotdog car," Pepper murmured, begging the universe for mercy, but as team DipShip made their way to stall forty-one, Ziggy came to the sinking realization that the hotdog car would have been a blessing.

Vehicle number forty-one was an ice cream truck.

Chapter 15

Jesus Take the Veal

Kill-Score:312

Ziggy's heart plummeted as he laid eyes on the ice cream truck, complete with a whimsical spinning cone on top. It was wrapped in a cheerful pink and yellow striped print with a massive "WhimsiCream" logo on the hood. The large, rounded service window framed by a delicate candy-striped awning looked like a darling girl dressed for church in the middle of a medieval biker bar full of roaring engines and crunching metal. Ziggy clenched his teeth as an off-tune music box melody blared from the exterior speakers. Even the truck was laughing at them for bringing a popsicle stick to a sword fight.

"It could be worse," Floyd said with a chuckle, his eyes already glued to the event camera view that had just popped up. "District Vanguard & Vanguard got stuck in a golf cart, and GazPro's in a turn-of-the-century tank. The crowd loved it until they realized how slow it was."

"I'm driving," Big Montana Ice announced to the group. "Get in." She reached behind her to loosen the strap of Meihua's carrier. "Sorry, Granny, but someone's gotta steer this rig, and I drove a

FizzBuzz freightliner for fifteen years. I'm the best there is. You're on your own for a while." She crouched to help Meihua slide off her back.

As Big Montana Ice took her position in the driver's seat, the Samurai inspected the outside of the truck, his eyes landing on the sliding door at the back. He gave it a firm tug, and the door rolled up, revealing the heavy-duty interior—stainless steel walls and a cold plate freezer bolted to one side. "An inconvenience is an unrecognized opportunity," he murmured.

"Who's sitting bitch?" Big Montana Ice hooted, her head inches from the roof. "Granny can't see over the dash, and I need someone to navigate. Samurai?"

But the Samurai shook his head. "A battle with vehicles may require great balance and coordination. My abilities are better used elsewhere."

Carol drew a shaky breath, closing her eyes for a moment before reluctantly climbing into the passenger seat.

"Hell, yeah! Alaskan Thunder and her sidekick, Lil Biscuit!" Big Montana Ice said with a mischievous grin.

"Heavens to Betsy," Carol said under her breath.

Benedict helped Meihua to the truck and the Samurai lifted her in, pulling Benedict up behind her before rolling down the door.

"Carol, keep an eye out," Ziggy said. "Teams are still coming into the garage. The rest of you secure yourselves as best you can. Meihua's safety is a priority. Any spare seat belts? Anything to anchor her down?"

"There's nothing back here but the bloody fridge!" Benedict exclaimed, running his hands along the seams in the wall. The Samurai scanned the cramped confines of the truck, pressing against the sides, searching for hooks or holds.

"Dog Boy, go in," Meihua grunted, gesturing toward the freezer. She shuffled over, rapping her knuckles against its side. *"Bīngqílín hěn ruǎn, rúguǒ chēhuò kěyǐ bǎohù wǒmen."*

"She suggested putting her in the freezer with Benedict," Floyd translated, his skepticism clear. "She said the ice cream will act as a buffer."

"What ice cream?" Ziggy asked. The Samurai cracked open the freezer, and Ziggy jaw dropped at the sight of the frozen treasures packed inside—an arsenal of ice cream cones and popsicles.

"Will we both fit? It looks a bit snug," Benedict asked. The stress, and his normally sweaty nature made him look like he'd jumped in a pool.

"Ask Carol," Big Montana Ice said, grinning over her shoulder at them. "She knows all about fitting bodies in freezers."

Pepper snorted, and Carol crossed her arms over her chest. "Oh, fimble famble!" she said with a huff.

"Theoretically, it could work," Floyd said, rubbing his chin. "If they're snug enough, the cones and wrappers would absorb some of the impact. The freezer is stainless steel and solid as a rock. Even in the event of a direct hit, they'd be better off in there than strapped to the side of the truck."

"Won't they freeze?" Ziggy asked, still struggling to wrap his head around the idea of cramming an elderly woman and a scaredy-cat into a freezer.

"Tǐwēn," Meihua said.

Floyd shrugged. "Body heat."

"Someone's coming," Carol said, her adrenaline spiking. "A team of five. They must be looking for their vehicle."

"I see them," Pepper said. "Three men and two women."

"That's District ConcuMine," Floyd said, toggling vantage points. "A mining corporation. Until last year, they were part of the ABCD. Another district won their spot and they spent a fortune on the Blackbird Butcher hoping to get it back. We'd better get going. They're out for blood."

"Get them in the freezer," Ziggy's voice cracked with urgency as the team scrambled to coordinate their defenses. "Carol, give Big Montana Ice the keys, then get back there and help the Samurai."

"Here you go," Carol said, turning over the bloody keys to Big Montana Ice before darting towards the back of the truck. She and the Samurai worked in frantic unison, pulling armfuls of ice cream from the freezer to make room for Benedict and Meihua. Big Montana Ice started the truck, revving the engine as an announcement rang through their radio.

"Welcome to the second special event of the Mongaphalee Jubilee!" The ringmaster's voice boomed through the garage. "The Pervy Derby!"

"Shit, that's loud!" Pepper said.

"Turn it down!" Carol scolded, practically forcing Benedict into the freezer.

The Samurai lifted Meihua over the waist-high freezer lip, and Benedict wrapped his arms around her as she settled in. "Good Dog Boy," she said, snuggling into Benedict's sweaty chest.

"I'm trying," Big Montana Ice said, spinning dials and jabbing furiously at the radio buttons. "Nothing's working!"

"On the track above are thousands of perverts," the announcement continued. "They may be dressed like clowns, but their crimes are no laughing matter. Your task: Clobber some clowns! Use your Pervy Derby vehicle to gain a hundred points and rid the world of twenty offenders. Teams will not have access to the general cityscape until the task is complete."

Pepper looked confused. "Twenty offenders worth a hundred points? That's five points apiece, not seven. Perverts are sex offenders, too, right?"

"Correct," Floyd said. "But their crimes were non-violent or didn't happen in a serial pattern, so they're not worth as many points. Plus, it makes the games more fun!"

The Samurai tossed armfuls of ice cream cone packages over Benedict and Meihua. "Quickly!" he ordered. "Cover them."

"We need to tuck them in tight," Carol's voice was muffled as she leaned so far into the freezer that her feet were off the ground. "Put more on the sides!"

"Your Pervy Derby vehicle is proudly sponsored by WhimsiCream," the ringmaster's voice continued, the garish logo on the truck's hood looming ominously over their fate. "Whimsi-Cream—We won't stop 'til you're creamin'!"

"Pipe it, everyone!" Ziggy barked, his attention drawn to movement at the far corner of Big Montana Ice's monitor. A clattering sound, followed by scraping near the back of the truck, sent a chill through Ziggy's body. The Samurai froze, his arms full of popsicles, as the back door to the truck flew open.

"Drive!" he bellowed, and Big Montana Ice slammed her foot down on the gas pedal. The engine roared to life as the ice cream truck lurched forward. With an explosion of energy, the Samurai bombarded the ConcuMine killers with popsicles, throwing them like knives, and leaving them stunned in a cloud of exhaust.

"Right turn ahead!" Floyd's voice rang out. "You're close to the derby entrance."

In the midst of the chaos, Carol scrambled to secure the freezer, her hands shaking as she struggled with the latch. But just when Ziggy thought they were in the clear, a sudden jolt rocked the truck, sending Carol hurtling across the cabin towards the open door. Acting on instinct, the Samurai lunged forward, catching her in his arms and pulling them both to the floor.

"What was that?" Pepper squealed, her hand at her throat as she surveyed the monitors.

"Speed bump?" Floyd guessed. "But that wouldn't make sense in a parking garage. I wonder—" He gasped as their monitors lit up and their kill-score recalculated—393.

"Guess it wasn't a speed bump," Ziggy said, and that's when he noticed the severed arm slapping the ground with each rotation of the wheel, fabric and tendons tangled somewhere in the bolts and axle. Big Montana Ice let out a triumphant whoop, her fist pumping in the air.

"Told you I was the best," she crowed as the Samurai bounded to his feet, slamming the sliding door shut with a resounding clank.

"Don't forget the latch!" Ziggy said as the ice cream truck careened around a sharp left turn, barreling up an incline toward the derby track. The Samurai quickly secured the door as Carol fought to get back into the passenger seat, yanking the seatbelt over her hips. The truck ascended, veering sharply to the left as Big Montana Ice squirreled onto the asphalt track.

"What can you see?" Ziggy asked. The roar of engines filled his ears as his brain tried to make sense of the madness surrounding them on every side.

"Watch out!" Carol cried, pointing ahead, and Big Montana Ice swerved, narrowly avoiding a toppled forklift, its forks coated in blood. The track was a maelstrom of destruction and death. Vehicles careened wildly in all directions, their engines roaring and tires squealing as an army of clowns weaved through the pandemonium. Car and body parts littered the ground in equal numbers, and Ziggy's chest tightened to the point of pain.

"The track goes all the way around the cityscape and is about 150 feet in width," Floyd said, zooming in from their aerial view. "About the same as a seven-lane freeway."

"Some places on the track have bumps and hills," Pepper said, using their map street view to scout ahead. "There are also dirt patches and muddy areas where lots of teams are getting stuck."

"Hang on!" Big Montana Ice warned, veering hard to one side. Pepper jumped, and Carol screamed when a loud thwack rang through the control room, and a clown in an orange yarn wig flew through the air like a rag doll in a hurricane.

Big Montana Ice hooted. "One perv down, nineteen to go!"

"Nice hit!" Floyd said, shooting Ziggy a thumbs up as their kill-score moved to 331.

"We've got trouble ahead," Pepper said, her eyes glued to the monitor. "Looks like a group of clowns is trying to set up a barricade. They're hiding behind that wall of wreckage."

Big Montana Ice's grip tightened on the wheel as she spotted the makeshift barricade looming ahead. "Fucking gropers. Demons, for sure. Huddled together like rats. Hold on tight, kids!" she warned, her voice wild with excitement. "We're gonna plow right through them."

"Are you insane?" Carol shrieked. Big Montana Ice laughed maniacally as the Samurai braced his hands on the walls as the ice cream truck sped toward the barricade. Debris exploded in all directions as it tore through the makeshift obstacle like a wrecking ball. Clowns scattered, and when the windshield cracked, blood dripping down the glass, Ziggy watched the kill-score recalculate in rapid succession—403, 408, 413, and 418.

"Twenty points!" Floyd exclaimed.

"Only four?" Big Montana Ice complained, spritzing the washer fluid and turning on the wipers to wash the blood away. The window turned a foamy pink, and when it cleared, she jerked the wheel hard to avoid a pickup truck with fighting killers and clowns in the back.

Moments later, the truck hit a bump, and bodies flew in all directions like confetti.

"Are you okay in there?" Floyd asked Benedict and Meihua. *"Nǐ hái hǎo ma?"*

Ziggy couldn't see much more than wrappers through their body cams, but their vitals were good despite Benedict's frequent adrenaline spikes. "What the bloody hell was that?" Benedict cried, his voice muffled by the freezer's icy walls.

"Just splatting some pervos," Big Montana Ice said, whistling cheerfully along with the ice cream truck's music as they blew past a hulking killer hunched in a tiny red micro-car with plastic eyelashes on the headlights. The front tires were flat, and there were clowns everywhere, trying to tip the car over. The sight was unsettling, but only because both parties were so desperate to survive, and the likelihood was that, in the end, none of them would.

"There's a Hummer headed your way, and they're moving fast," Pepper said, watching the aerial view.

Big Montana Ice's response came back thick with bravado. "Looks like someone wants to play chicken!" she whooped, her foot pressing the gas pedal to the floor. Carol scrambled, whispering a prayer and frantically digging through her fanny pack.

Ziggy's heart skipped a beat as he watched the disaster unfold. "Disengage," he ordered, struggling to keep his voice steady. "If you hit head-on, it'll kill you all."

"No can do, Marshal," Big Montana Ice muttered, her voice barely audible over the roar of the engine. "One of us is a bitch-ass pussy, and it sure as shit ain't me."

"You shouldn't purposefully collide," Floyd said with alarm. "The Hummer has a much sturdier frame and was built to be crash-resistant. Our truck is for urban mobility. The kinetic energy won't disperse well!"

"This is unwise," the Samurai said, his grip tightening on the headrests as he struggled to maintain his balance. Big Montana Ice only responded with a snarl, her hands gripping the wheel tighter.

"Turn away!" Pepper cried, rising to her feet as if she could somehow run onto the track and prevent the crash.

"Big Montana Ice," Ziggy barked, trying to get through to the behemoth driver. He could hear the roar of the Hummer's engine as it barreled toward them. "Tanya!"

"You're all chickenshit!" she yelled. "Alaskan Thund—"

At the last second, Carol's hand whipped out, jerking the wheel and sending the ice cream truck careening across the track. The Hummer thundered by, missing them by inches. The Samurai was thrown into the ceiling of the van, crashing to the ground as the truck spun and shuddered to a stop, stuck in a puddle of sludge.

"You"—Carol's voice was trembling with adrenaline as she rounded on Big Montana Ice—"buffoon! You almost got us killed!" But Big Montana Ice seemed unfazed, focused on pressing the gas pedal, only to find the wheels spinning uselessly in the mud.

"Ziggy," Pepper said, eyes squinting as she focused on the monitor. "Something's wrong."

"We could've died back there, and you don't even care!" Carol ranted at Big Montana Ice. "I have six children to think about!"

Big Montana Ice rolled her eyes. "Get your panties out of a twist. We're fine."

"Thanks to me!"

"Ziggy!" Pepper screamed, and Ziggy snapped to attention. Her fingers trembled as she pointed to the screen. The Hummer smashed into the tiny red micro-car and sent a mist of red into the air. It spun around, engines roaring. "The Hummer circled back. They're coming for us!"

Chapter 16

Stuck on Stew

Kill-Score: 418

The Hummer's engine roared as it accelerated. "Everyone out!" Ziggy ordered. The team might not last long on foot, but at least they'd be alive to try. The Samurai sprang into action. He flung the freezer door open and grabbed Meihua, lifting her out as if she weighed nothing. Ice cream cones and popsicles flew through the air as he ripped open the sliding door, leaping into the mud.

"Run Benny!" Carol screamed, launching herself from the passenger seat. Benedict hurled his body from the freezer, landing on the ground in a heap.

"Fuck!" Big Montana Ice swore, jerking open the door as Ziggy watched the Hummer draw closer. The sallow-faced driver grinned as he closed in. Everyone braced for impact, but the moment before the imminent collision, a massive garbage truck appeared out of nowhere, smashing into the Hummer's side and sending it hurtling through the air, along with the killer who clearly wasn't wearing a seatbelt.

"Holy shitballs!" Ziggy cried, unable to contain his shock. Pepper gasped in shock while Floyd just laughed. The Hummer crashed to the ground with a crunch, and after a moment, when no one emerged from the wreckage, Floyd said, "Classic Super Serial. I wonder how many points that was worth?"

"Jesus, Floyd," Pepper said, sinking back into her seat.

"Sorry?"

The garbage truck veered and hissed as it stopped along the edge of the mud pit. A girl with pigtails and a pink jacket poked her head out the window. "If you were any closer, I'd crush you with my garbage compactor. Guess it's your lucky day." She revved the truck back to life and headed the opposite direction.

"That girl couldn't have been more than twelve years old," Carol gasped.

"Actually, that's Killer Pop," Floyd said. "She's thirty-six."

"Is everyone okay?" Ziggy asked the team.

"Benedict's bleeding. He must have gotten cut falling out of the freezer," Carol reported. "But helichrysum oil will help with that." She turned to Big Montana Ice, who was knee-deep in mud. "I'm sorry for swearing at you earlier. It was a tense situation."

"When did she swear?" Floyd whispered to Pepper, who sighed.

Big Montana Ice's eyes narrowed, and for a moment, Ziggy feared she might decide Carol was the demon. Instead she said, "If you're really sorry, you'll watch my back while I pop a squat. I've got a cigar sitting at the tip of my lips. Girl stuff. You get it."

Even with dirt caking her face, Ziggy saw Carol flush as Big Montana Ice trudged a few feet away and pulled down her pants to squat in the mud.

"What do we do now?" Carol asked over the din, nervously eyeing a Range Rover as it blew through the mud. Ahead of them, also stuck, was a team pushing the back of a hearse, complete with a sponsored coffin bolted to the top. A lanky man in a cowboy hat stuck his naked butt out of the Range Rover's window as they passed the hearse, laughing as he mooned the frustrated murderers.

"You're going to have to work together to push it out," Ziggy said, suppressing his mounting panic at the team's vulnerable position. At any moment, a bigger, more vicious vehicle could blast through the mud and flatten them all.

"You're in the first twenty feet of the mud pit. It covers the width of the track for about two hundred feet," Floyd said. "There are eleven other teams stuck so far. Since the truck is already pointed in the direction we came from, we should backtrack that way once we get it unstuck."

"You'll drive," the Samurai told Carol, not releasing his hold on Meihua. "Meihua will sit in the passenger seat, and the three of us will push."

"I'll push when I'm done pushing," Big Montana Ice grunted, still squatting. "All this excitement's got me more turd locked than a swollen cork in a bottle of cheap champagne." She snorted at her own joke.

"You mean me?" Benedict sniffed, his glasses now smudged and cracked. "Are you mad? I can't push."

"The man who says he can and the man who says he can't are both correct," the Samurai said before placing Meihua gently in the passenger seat and buckling her seatbelt. She smiled and slurped on a red popsicle she'd pocketed from the freezer. Carol climbed in on the driver's side, and Ziggy counted every second of the agonizing minute it took her to move the seat forward enough to see over the dash.

"Someone's coming," the Samurai murmured, and Ziggy's eyes flicked to the corner of his monitor, catching the movement. "It's the clowns. They're camouflaged in mud."

"They must be after the truck," Floyd said. "On foot, their chances of survival are slim."

"You're about to be ambushed," Ziggy warned the team as Pepper and Floyd frantically adjusted their viewpoints on the monitor. "Carol, lock the doors. Meihua, duck down and hide if you can. Samurai, you and Big Montana Ice defend the team and get that truck out of the mud. Benedict, open the back and get in. Move!"

Floyd translated as fast as he could for Meihua, and the team jumped into action, their movements fueled by a burst of frantic energy. Carol swiftly locked the doors, and Meihua ducked down, slinking into the space between the seat and the dash. Mud-coated and disoriented, Benedict managed to pry the door open, scrambling into the van, while the Samurai began to push with all his might, his muscles straining against the weight.

"Move! Move! Move!" Carol gripped the steering wheel, her knuckles turning white as she twisted, flooring the gas.

"Slow and steady!" Floyd cried. "If you go too fast, you'll never get traction!"

Big Montana Ice was hurriedly zipping her fly when the first muddy clown attacked, slurping out of the mud and jumping on her from behind. She roared like a bear when the clown stabbed a jagged piece of metal through her shoulder blade.

Clowns swarmed from all sides, rising from the mud to rush the team with the unleashed ferocity of people with nothing to lose and little to gain. Carol screamed as a mud-covered man with filthy pink pom-poms on his shirt swung at her window with a broken muffler, the glass cracking under the force of the blow. But the Samurai was ready, swiftly moving away from the bumper to kick the attacker's feet from underneath him. He circled around the truck, quickly dropping four more clowns into the mud.

"I counted twelve attackers, but there could be more not showing up on the feed," Floyd said, speaking so quickly the words slurred. "Plus, another group of five are keeping watch behind the stack of tires near the edge of the mud pit."

"The hearse is also getting attacked!" Pepper cried.

"I'm going down!" Big Montana Ice bellowed when a second clown with oversized shoes took a flying leap and latched onto her mullet, dragging her off balance. Three more clowns pounced, holding jagged pieces of glass wrapped in torn upholstery, and the Samurai sprinted to her aid. The clown with the muffler pulled himself out of the mud and took another swing at the window. The tempered glass splintered and buckled under the force, falling away in a crunchy sheet of ruin.

Wild with panic, Carol threw the van into reverse, then drive, over and over again, twisting the wheel. "I can't get any traction!" she screamed, and the muffler clown launched himself through the window, attempting to wrap his thick hands around Carol's throat.

Suddenly, the man lurched backward, falling into the mud, clutching his face. He screamed, and that's when Ziggy noticed the popsicle stick jutting out from his eye.

"Bad guy," Meihua said with venom. "*Dāng dúyào shā sǐ tā hòu, jiāng tā fàng zài lúntāi xià, ránhòu nǐ jiù yǒu qiānyǐnlì cóng níjiāng zhōng pá chūlái.*"

Floyd looked at Meihua, his eyes glowing with unabashed devotion. "She said to wait for the poison to kill him, then put him under the tires for traction so you can get out of the mud pit." Moments later, the man was convulsing in the mud, scarlet popsicle juice running from his mouth like blood. He fell slack as the life left his eyes, and Meihua pointed at the freezer.

"Dog Boy, help! Bad guy too big!" Meihua cried, pointing at Benedict, who pointed at himself, confused.

"Benedict," Floyd clarified as fast as he could. "Help Carol move the body under the tire."

"What?" Benedict sounded like he'd been crying again, and Ziggy went off. "Get your ass out!" he shouted, and Benedict crawled out of the freezer, joining Carol in the mud to move the dead muffler clown.

"More incoming!" the Samurai yelled to Big Montana Ice as a red-nosed clown lunged at him with a glass shard, the whites of her eyes stark against the viscous muck. But the Samurai evaded the clumsy attack, grabbing the clown's outstretched arm and twisting it with controlled force until she screamed. With a swift kick to the knee, she went crashing to the ground, landing on the glass shard and slitting her own throat.

Still on her feet, Big Montana Ice had wrestled a scrap of jagged metal from a clown and was swinging with so much savagery that a pile of four bloody, dead clowns had fallen at her feet. Another went sailing through the air as her fist met his jaw with bone-crushing force.

"Push harder," Carol shrieked at Benedict.

"I told you I hated clowns!" Benedict grunted, his scrawny arms shaking as he and Carol jammed the clown corpse in front of the back tire.

"Let's go!" Carol cried when they were through, and she and Benedict moved as fast as they could through the sticky mud back to the truck. Her foot hit the gas the minute the door shut, and the wheels spun in the mud for a moment until the back tire found purchase against the dead clown and broke free. With a sudden jolt, the van lurched forward, nearly sending Benedict tumbling out the back door. In a blur of motion, they tore away from danger, leaving Big Montana Ice and the Samurai behind in a splatter of mud.

"The five clown reinforcements are headed their way," Floyd said. "They'll be outnumbered ten to two. Even with their skills, they might not be able to hold them all off."

"It's not ten to two," Carol said, her jaw clenching. She pulled the wheel hard, and the brakes squealed as she turned the truck around. "It's ten to five—and we've got an ice cream truck." She slammed her foot on the gas. "On our way, stingray!" Meihua crawled back into her seat and buckled her seatbelt. Benedict opened the freezer and barreled back inside, head first.

"She's coming back!" Ziggy shouted to Big Montana Ice and the Samurai. "Hang on!"

Still focused on the battle, the Samurai grunted as two clowns attacked, executing a seamless pivot, extending his leg in a powerful arch to deliver a forceful blow to each clown's chest. Big Montana Ice was bleeding down her back, struggling to stay on her feet as three clowns jumped on top of her, punching her sides, determined to pull her down.

"What's Carol thinking?" Pepper hissed, muting the control room as she watched the battle unfold. "None of them can fight. Especially Meihua. And we all know Carol wouldn't go back for..." But the truck suddenly veered to one side, driving along the edge of the mud pit. Pepper's jaw dropped.

"Hold on!" Carol hollered seconds before plowing directly into the five clowns headed to join the fight. Bodies catapulted through the air, the sickening thud of impact reverberating through the truck. The windshield cracked again under the force of the collision, but Carol turned the truck around, her eyes locked on their attackers. One clown had miraculously survived and was desperately trying to hobble away, but Carol hit her again, the body thumping under the truck, jostling Meihua so hard Ziggy swore he heard her teeth rattle.

The bloodshed seemed to have revived Big Montana Ice, who shook off the clowns like a dog after a bath. Her renewed ferocity, coupled with the fact that their friends were dead, sent the surviving clowns running for cover. All but one got away—the one who'd tried to rip off Big Montana Ice's mullet. She held her aloft by her long, thick, lime-green hair.

"Please," the woman managed to choke before Big Montana Ice wrapped her meaty fist in her hair and ripped it from her scalp. The woman screamed as she fell to the ground, clutching her head, but Big Montana Ice was already on her, shoving the mass of muddy hair down the woman's throat until she choked on it. Her face turned a sickly shade of purple, and this time, when the monitors in the control room lit up, Ziggy was expecting it. Kill-score—483.

Big Montana Ice spat on the body. "That'll teach you to interrupt a good shit! My ass is gonna be covered in toot butter because of you!"

The truck came to a stop at the edge of the mud pit, and Carol staggered out, doubled over at the waist. "She's gonna hurl," Big Montana Ice said, making her way to the truck, and Carol obliged, puking all over her filthy cross-trainers.

"It's for my kids. I have to survive," Carol choked, spitting out vomit. "I'll be God's avenging angel on the wicked."

"Good job, everyone!" Floyd's chipper voice cut through the tension, and nausea roiled Ziggy's stomach. Calling any of this a "good job" was akin to congratulating a group of bloodthirsty Vikings for successfully plundering and burning a village to the ground.

"Get back in the truck," he ordered the team as a steamroller crawled by, followed by a battered 1955 Chevy pickup with shattered windows and a dump truck with a bed full of dead clowns. "Everyone's still alive. Get out of there before that changes."

"Nǐ hái hǎo ma? Nǐ shòushāngle ma?" Floyd said to Meihua, who was sitting calmly in the front seat eating a blue popsicle.

"Bù yánzhòng, méi wèntí," she said between slurps. The blue juice had dyed her lips.

"What if they're poisonous?" Benedict asked, eyeing the popsicle as he peeked his head out of the freezer.

"I don't give two shits if they are," Big Montana Ice said, nudging Carol aside to brush glass shards off the seat. "I'm dying of thirst. Hand one over, Benny Boy." Benedict produced a popsicle, but before she could put it in her mouth, Meihua slapped it out of her hand.

"Hóngsè, fěnsè, lánsè dōu bùnéng chī de," she said sternly, wagging her wrinkled finger in Big Montana Ice's face. *"Zhǐyǒu zǐsè hé lǜsè méiyǒu dú."*

"Only the purples and greens are safe," Floyd translated, and Big Montana Ice groaned. "Those are the shittiest flavors! How come she gets to eat a blue?"

"Meihua is immune to most poisons," Floyd said. "I wouldn't risk it if I were you." Big Montana Ice grudgingly tore open a purple popsicle with her teeth.

"The team in the hearse didn't survive," Pepper said grimly, watching the scene from above. "The clowns killed them all and pushed the hearse out on the other side of the pit. Now they're piling inside."

Floyd toggled to the aerial view. "Hey, Pep," he said with a grin. "How many clowns do you think will fit?"

"Seriously, Floyd!" Pepper exclaimed, but Ziggy saw her lips twitch.

"Where's the Samurai?" Carol asked, and Ziggy toggled to his bodycam to find him rapidly filtering through scattered wreckage. His nimble fingers snapped things together, bending them around and pounding them on the dirt. He set his project aside for a moment before ripping apart the mechanical ice cream cone that had fallen off the top of the truck, using the rainbow shoelaces from a dead clown to tie the pieces together. He even used part of the worthless helmet from his battle costume. His work was interrupted by the sound of screeching tires and a blaring police siren. They were out of time, and other teams were headed their way from both directions.

"Let's go," Big Montana Ice said, urging a still-woozy Carol into the back. The Samurai emerged with an armful of scraps and a gnarly homemade weapon that looked like a cross between a scythe and a sword, with a curved blade and a rainbow wrapped handle. He wordlessly climbed in after Carol, who sat in the small space between the freezer and the back of the front seat.

They beelined back in the direction they'd come, tires squealing as the air from the broken windows ruffled their grime-caked hair. "How many pervs left to go?" Big Montana Ice asked, watching clowns darting in every direction. "I'm exhaustipated." The truck lurched as they drove over a detached limb.

"Exhaustipated?" Floyd's eyebrows shot up. "What does that mean?"

"Don't encourage her," Carol said.

"Too tired to give a shit."

"Twelve pervert clowns left to go," Ziggy said as the police siren drew nearer. "We're more than halfway there, so take some deep breaths and, for fuck's sake, think twice before playing chicken with another Hummer."

"There's a police car headed straight towards you with a Ferrari and an ATV chasing," Floyd reported, scrutinizing the aerial view, "also a bulldozer coming through the mud behind you, and what looks like a big wreck ahead on the right side of the track. It's hard to see through the smoke."

"What do we do?" Pepper asked, trying to scroll through the sooty air. "I can't tell if the track is blocked."

"Slow down and stay on the left side of the track as close to the wall as possible and away from the wreckage. Let's hope we miss any passing teams," Ziggy said.

The police car radio chirped as it neared, and a malevolent laugh rang through the air over the noise of the siren. "I see you behind those tires, you fat little cockroach. Run, run, little butter hogs!" it jeered at the clowns as they scattered in fear.

"Got one!" Big Montana Ice swerved, and when a bloody clown thumped over the dash, ripping off the bumper, Ziggy began to worry the truck wouldn't make it much further. He caught a glimpse of the police car as it tore past. Two killers were sitting in the trunk, dragging bruised and bloody clowns behind them.

"Switch to the right side of the track and head toward the wreck," Ziggy said, an idea taking shape. "Clowns will be fleeing in your direction and will try to hide in the wreckage."

"Good idea," Pepper said.

"There's a limo coming toward you," Floyd told the team, "but it's not moving very fast. Looks like it's blown a tire. You should be able to go around them without too much trouble." The Samurai positioned himself between the seats, his eyes narrowing as the limo approached.

"Go around them on the left and stay close," he growled to Big Montana Ice before moving to the back of the truck and climbing out of the shattered service window. He crouched on the window ledge, gripping the jagged frame, his patchwork scythe firmly grasped in his opposite hand, the curved blade dipping low.

Floyd figured out his intentions first and let out a whoop of excitement. "Get as close as you can!" he cried to Big Montana Ice, and when she swerved left to pass the limo, Ziggy's gut clenched. A killer with bushy blond hair and sunglasses stood out of the sunroof, laughing and pumping his fists. If it weren't for the sunglasses, Ziggy might've seen his eyes widen in horror as the ice cream truck of death appeared through the smoke.

"Look away," Ziggy ordered Pepper just as the Samurai lunged out, the scythe slicing cleanly through the killer's neck, decapitating him in a single, sharp blow. The head bounced down the track like a bloody tumbleweed, and the monitors flashed their new kill-score—552.

"Holy mother of fucks!" Big Montana Ice yelled.

"Awesome!" Floyd pumped his fist, cheering as the Samurai ducked back into the van. "That's going to make the highlight reel!"

"You were right," Pepper told Ziggy. "There are loads of clowns fleeing in our direction. The only problem is we can't get by the wreckage on the track. We either wait like sitting ducks, or turn around and go back through the mud." As the ice cream truck neared the site of the wreck, Ziggy wondered if he'd led the team to their doom. It was a scene of violent pandemonium.

A school bus lay upside down, smoke and flames billowing through the air as injured clowns struggled to crawl away. Atop the wreckage sat a massive monster truck with the word 'Chomobile' emblazoned across the side, its driver screaming as flames engulfed the cab and burned him alive. Darting in between the throngs of runners was the Vanguard & Vanguard golf cart, its killers stabbing anyone they could reach with jagged pieces of metal. A front-end loader barreled into the fray, its bucket full of injured, screaming clowns. Beat-up cars and dented trucks screeched over the track, trying to run over anything that moved. The wreckage pile grew by the second as teams smashed into the school bus blockage.

"Drive further away and circle the outskirts," Ziggy instructed the team, torn between his need to keep them alive and his need to get enough points to make an escape. "Floyd, watch for possible threats. Pepper and I will look for easy hits on the street view monitor where the smoke isn't as bad. I don't want anyone getting out of the truck. You'll get swarmed again."

Ziggy's eyes raked over the gruesome scene, searching for easy targets like a wolf stalking an injured sheep on the edge of a flock. Pepper was doing the same, zooming in and out on the monitor.

"The Gazpro tank just arrived," Floyd said, "but they're not too close. And there goes an old ambulance. I'll keep an eye on that motorhome to the west. It's a little too close for comfort."

"There!" Pepper cried, pointing at a man near the truck, stumbling and dazed, his skin mostly burned away and his curly clown wig still on fire. "Just ahead," she said, and Big Montana Ice rushed in the direction of the man. He went down with a sickening crunch, and as their kill-score rose to 557, Ziggy felt nothing but a hollow sense of emptiness.

"The front-end loader's headed our way," Floyd said. "But do whatever you can to avoid it since it probably weighs at least fifteen tons. We'd be squashed."

"Look at the tank. It's already stuck. High-centered on a crushed car," Pepper pointed out, drawing Ziggy's attention to its tracks turning uselessly in the air. "Maybe there's a way we could breach it."

"Too late for that," Floyd said with a delighted chuckle. "The loader will beat us to the punch."

Sure enough, the loader surged across the track, its tires rolling smoothly over the dirt as it rumbled toward the stranded tank. Then, with a sudden jolt that sent all three killers in the cab reeling, the loader careened over a loose tire, a jumble of bodies spilling over the sides of the bucket, scattering across the ground like discarded toys. The loader pressed on, hurtling toward the tank at a surprising speed, its now-empty bucket serving as a makeshift battering ram. In a display of brute force, the loader reached the tank and used the edge of its bucket to tear the top clean off, exposing the killers crouched inside.

"Holy guacamole!" Carol gasped, watching the scene unfold through the open service window. Ziggy's focus wasn't on the loader but the bodies that littered the ground in its wake. A bloody hand reached up, clawing at the air, and Ziggy's heart lurched as he realized not all the people in the bucket had been dead.

"Look at the bodies," Ziggy said, hating himself as the idea tumbled out. "Some of them are still alive. If we finish them off, then—"

"We could get out of here!" Pepper cried. "Big Montana Ice, go!"

The ice cream truck took off with a squeal, rushing toward the fallen bodies, and thumping over them in quick succession. Ziggy watched as the kill-score climbed—562, 567, 572, 577, and 582.

The weight of every kill bore down on his mind as they continued rolling over the dead. It was just like taking GlutoBlock to avoid shitting himself—using a system he hated to prevent something he hated even more. "Again," he said, his voice strained. The truck thundered over more maimed pervert clowns, jostling everyone inside as the kill-score recalculated—607. "One more," he uttered. "We just need one more."

"You got it, Marshal." Big Montana Ice maneuvered the truck back over the bodies, each impact hitting like a punch to Ziggy's gut. And then, with an ominous thud, the final blow was delivered, and the kill-score ticked up to 612.

"That's twenty," Pepper whispered. "We did it."

There was a breath of silence before the radio rang out with what Ziggy was sure might be the most beautiful sound in the world. "Congratulations team DipShip! You have completed your task in the Pervy Derby. Please proceed to the toll booth at the northernmost point of the track, where you will be allowed to enter the Mongaphalee Jubilee cityscape. Brace yourselves for the sights, sounds, and screams that await you in this cursed carnival!"

Chapter 17

I Want to Bake Free

Kill-Score: 612

After a few close calls on the Pervy Derby track, and another spin through the creepy clown turntable, team DipShip finally entered the cityscape. Ziggy's hopeful respite from being corralled into any more mandatory events was swiftly crushed by the overwhelming sounds of horror on the team's camera feeds. The immaculate venue, filled with vibrant flowers, lush foliage, and bright colors, was paradoxically teeming with thousands of dangerous serial killers and criminals. The Super Serial jingle had been transformed into a lilting carnival melody that reverberated through the air via loudspeakers, masterfully accented by predatory howls and the screams of dying prey.

With Meihua securely strapped to Big Montana Ice's back, the team ventured onto the paved walkway winding through the cityscape, seemingly connected to every violent event.

"First things first, find cover and stay quiet," Ziggy told the team. "When we have a decent plan, we can tackle questions."

Guiding the team off the main path, the Samurai murmured, "This way," and they huddled together behind a tall leafy hedge. Big

Montana Ice dropped to one knee, but had to lie on her stomach when they realized her head was still visible above the leaves. Meihua dozed off in the prone position and was snoring softly.

Ziggy's mind was buzzing with strategies, and he wanted to give as much information as possible before plunging back into the adrenaline-fueled nightmare of minute-to-minute survival. "The entire cityscape revolves around the Ferris Wheel," he said.

"Wowzer Bowser!" Carol exclaimed, her gaze fixed on the glittering observation wheel. "Is there an event there? I've never ridden a Ferris wheel that big. Maybe I'll get a chance."

If Ziggy had any hair, he would've pulled it out. Carol was acting like Dorothy entering the colorful Land of Oz instead of a convicted serial killer being dumped in a murder competition. "No, Carol," he said abruptly. "You can't stop killing people to take a little spin on the Ferris wheel. What oil have you been sniffing? A denial blend?"

Floyd turned in his chair. "Technically, there aren't any rules prohibiting her from riding the Ferris wheel."

Ziggy rubbed the achy spot between his eyes, fighting back the post-concussion fatigue. "Am I the only one who cares if this team survives?"

"You're just grumpy because they gave us salad for lunch," Floyd said.

Pepper gave them both a stern look. "Bring it down a notch, you two. Sorry Carol," she said. "Everyone's a little on edge after the derby."

"Thank you, Pepper," Carol said with a sniff, and Ziggy could feel her glare at him all the way from the control room.

"Salad isn't a meal," Ziggy muttered to himself, attempting to shake off the sluggishness that came from his unsatisfying, rabbit-food lunch.

"Only spectators are allowed on the Ferris wheel," Pepper said, giving Ziggy a chance to collect himself. "Gondolas were auctioned off to the highest bidders before the games."

"Spectators for Super Serial?" Carol was astonished. "Who in their righteous mind would want to watch this?"

"Approximately two and a half billion people, according to analysts," Floyd chimed in. "And with this spectacular venue, this year's viewership is expected to break records. Mongaphalee has really outdone itself."

Pepper added, "Alexia mentioned that the spectators in the gondolas can interact with the killers by making picks on a prize wheel called 'The Wheel of Misfortune.'"

"A prize wheel?" Big Montana Ice's interest perked up, rising to her elbows. "I could sure as fuck use a prize right now. I'd blow every last one of those fat cats for a steak." She ran her hands through her hair, attempting to dislodge some of the dried mud and blood.

"*Shénme dōngxī,*" Meihua snorted, jolted from her sleep.

"Correct," Floyd said. "The Wheel of Misfortune is at the base of the Ferris wheel. You use tokens to spin it and win various items—weapons, armor, advantages, you name it. But the catch is that the people in the gondolas decide what you get."

"What about guns?" Big Montana Ice asked eagerly. "Are firearms on the wheel? Imagine if we got our hands on a machine gun and just lit this place the fuck up. We'd qualify for the Championships in no time."

"Guns were banned after the 41st Super Serial Games, for that exact reason," Floyd said. "With guns in the mix, the games ended too quickly and sponsors lost money."

"There are three constants in this world," the Samurai muttered, "gravity, gluttony, and greed."

"It wasn't all about money. The public didn't like it either," Floyd said. "They thought getting shot in the head was too easy a death for serial killers."

"Silence," the Samurai hissed suddenly, and everyone tensed as a strange slapping sound filled the air, growing louder by the moment. Screams and gurgling, followed by cackling and honking erupted from a side path only a dozen yards away. Feathers bloomed into the mid-day sun as a pair of massive geese flapped onto the path in pursuit of a lone man covered in tribal tattoos. Stumbling, the man's eyes widened in terror, a chilling scream escaping his throat, as the vicious geese pounced, mercilessly ripping into his flesh. Blood splattered onto the concrete as a gray-haired woman wearing a farm dress emerged from the shadows.

With a burst of excitement, Floyd shouted into the mic, "That's Mother Goose! Her trained geese, Georgie and Porgie, have razors attached to their feet and threaded through their feathers."

A thin, gangly man with huge buck teeth joined Mother Goose on the pathway. "That's the last of 'em," he said. "You're one bad bitch." Mother Goose cackled before calling her geese back to her side, their gray and white feathers now stained with blood.

"That guy's called the Pickler," Floyd said. "He's got a rating of seventy-three and is famous for pickling and eating his victims."

"Should we blast 'em?" Big Montana asked in a careful whisper.

"You'll be too vulnerable out in the open. Only engage if you're certain we can win," Ziggy said, relieved when Mother Goose and the Pickler retreated into the shadows.

"There are loads of places to hide," Pepper said. "We have to be extremely careful."

"Wait," Carol cut in, holding up her hand before pulling out a bottle of essential oil from her fanny pack. "Before things get too topsy-turvy, everyone should have a drop of this. It will ward off fear and anxiety."

Big Montana Ice snorted. "I'm not afraid of anything."

"I'll take some," Benedict whimpered, and Carol placed a few drops of oil onto each of his outstretched palms. They shook as he tried to rub them together. "I'm terrified of birds."

"We have a few options for strategy," Floyd said, his brow furrowed in thought. "One option is going directly to the Despair Fair and try to win tokens playing carnival games so we can get weapons. That strategy prioritizes speed and we are likely to engage other teams quickly. High risk, high reward."

"*Better* weapons," Carol said, stowing the oil bottle in the fanny pack and pulling out a small dagger made from bent metal and glass with a piece of pipe wrapped in an electrical cord for the handle. "The Samurai already made us some."

"True," Floyd acknowledged. "We're better off than most coming out of the derby. But those weapons may not last long."

"These weapons are indeed makeshift and temporary," said the Samurai. "I was rushed in the craftsmanship."

Using the cityscape monitor, Ziggy looked over Meihua's small hubcap shield, Big Montana Ice's metal rod spear, and Benedict's upholstery and seat belt chest plate. The Samurai was still holding his sickle. They were better than nothing, but Floyd was right about their durability.

"The Debting Zoo is much closer than the Despair Fair," Pepper said. "Getting Benedict's dogs could be a bigger boon for the team than weapons."

"Oh, please!" Benedict pleaded desperately, the pants of his tracksuit tie-dyed from mud, popsicle drips, and ice cream smudges. "Please, can we save the babies? I promise they'll do a splendid job of it!"

"With the Debting Zoo so near the Pervy Derby exit, other teams will probably go there too to retrieve their pets," Ziggy said, watching closely as another team entered the cityscape from the Derby. "It may be a safer option to go somewhere else first."

"Unless most of the marshals thought the same thing," Pepper countered.

"Statistically speaking," Floyd said, his finger in the air, "most teams will prioritize locations where they're most likely to get weapons. Which means they'll be after tokens."

"The problem is, we don't know what to expect in the Debting Zoo," Ziggy said. "Well, besides debtors. And probably animals."

"I say we go for the dogs," Carol reasoned, keeping her voice low. "We don't know what it's going to take to get tokens, but we do know the prize in the Debting Zoo is probably Benedict's dogs. Besides, it would make him so happy."

Ziggy couldn't deny it was a solid argument. "Samurai, Big Montana Ice, Meihua?" he asked, purposefully overlooking Benedict's desperate, longing expression. "What do you think?"

Big Montana Ice winced as she stretched her thick neck, revealing the beginnings of mottled bruises on her face and arms. "I'm with sexy Jesus housewife," she declared. "Let's get the ass-kicking pooches. An extra handful of bitches might be nice if we get attacked again."

Floyd translated the situation to Meihua, whose rumpled-tissue face pinched before she said, "Dog Boy with no dog is just boy."

"We're a strong chain with a weak link," the Samurai said, crossing his muscular arms. "The corgis will restore strength to our most vulnerable team member."

"Since everyone's on board, looks like we're going to the Debting Zoo!" Floyd exclaimed. "Good thing I've studied which Pet Lovers would be most likely to make it this far into the competition, and what their pets might be."

"Move slowly and stick to the shadows," Ziggy cautioned, his nerves already frayed at the thought of what might be waiting for them. "The last thing we need is to make it easier for criminals and killers to murder us. Not to mention their pets."

"Head southwest," Floyd directed, pouring over the cityscape map. "There's a paved path that leads directly there, but I think we should approach the tent from the north side instead. We're less likely to encounter rival teams."

The team had just set off when the ringmaster's voice rang through the cityscape. "Attention, Super Serial contestants! It's our pleasure to inform you that District CoreCorps and District JestWrite have both qualified for the Super Serial Championships!"

"Two teams already?" Pepper said, worry creeping into her voice.

Ziggy was surprised, but Floyd wasn't. "The Derby's ratio of killer to fodder likely skewed things in favor of teams with better vehicles," he said as if it should have been obvious to everyone.

"Did you hear that, team?" Pepper said. "Two teams have already qualified for the Championships. That means there are eleven spots left."

"Don't worry, Pepperoni," Big Montana Ice said as the team darted from a row of marble clown statues to a pyramid of straw bales, midway to the Debting Zoo. "There's still plenty of time to put on a good show."

"There's a man charging toward you on a buffalo," Floyd warned, almost casually, spurring Ziggy to zoom in on the team from above. The sight was surreal—a man dressed in leather hides atop a colossal wooly buffalo thundered toward them. His chaps clung to his muscular thighs as he whooped victoriously, brandishing a crowbar. Carol's blonde bouffant stood out from the stack, and Ziggy could see the rider was charging for her.

"Buffalo is the colloquial term used for the species bison-bison," Floyd added, but Ziggy gestured to silence him.

"Carol's the only one in his line of sight," Ziggy said. "He doesn't seem to realize she's not alone."

Big Montana Ice cracked her knuckles, but the Samurai stepped forward, holding his sickle. "I'll do it."

"Don't jump out until you know you can hit him," Ziggy warned. "Carol, wait for my signal, then get out of the way."

"I'm supposed to stand here and wait to be murdered until you say so?" Carol muttered under her breath, as the buffalo's galloping approach reached a deafening crescendo.

"Hold," Ziggy ordered, and Pepper sucked in a panicked breath. "Now!" he cried when the bison was only feet away. Swift as a flash, the Samurai catapulted himself off the straw bales, soaring diagonally toward the bison, and unleashed a skillful swing of his sickle. There was a loud crack as it sliced into the killer's chest, and Ziggy felt a pang in his stomach when he realized the sickle had splintered into pieces. Blood sprayed into the straw, and the man tumbled backwards off the buffalo.

With a short, rattling grunt, the buffalo smashed through the side of the straw pyramid, narrowly missing team DipShip. It tossed its head and galloped away, leaving its rider behind.

The Samurai's jaw clenched as he picked up the broken and bent pieces of metal.

"That's what I was afraid of. Can you fix it?" Floyd asked, and the Samurai examined the pieces before shaking his head.

"Fall seven times, stand up eight," he said, dropping them back onto the ground. "I'll find a way to make another."

"Take the spear. I like my boots better," Big Montana Ice said, thrusting the spear into the Samurai's hands. Brushing past him, she approached the buffalo rider, who had part of the sickle's blade lodged in his chest. He glared up at her. "I won't beg," he spat the words out as blood dribbled from his mouth. "I'm the last of my team and there's no point."

"Good," Big Montana Ice said before leaping into the air and stomping, his chest cavity collapsing under her massive boots. Meihua winced against the impact, the man's breathing stuttering as blood ran from his nose. Carol pinched her eyes shut, and Benedict buried his face in a nearby straw bale. Big Montana Ice adjusted her tank top, smearing gore on the howling neon-orange wolf, then wiped guts off her boots in the scattered straw.

"That could've been worse," Ziggy breathed. "Good teamwork."

Floyd was scouting the path ahead. "From your positions, you should be able to see the front entrance of the—"

"He's not dead," Pepper said, her voice shaky. She was right. Their kill-score hadn't budged. The man let out a sickening, wet gurgle.

A shadow crossed Big Montana Ice's face. "He's the demon!" she said with a yelp. "Why didn't I see it before? Alaskan Thunder!" she cried, jumping into the air and dual stomping the man's head. His skull popped like a water balloon.

"*Hǎo lìhai,*" Meihua laughed, smiling like a bizarre toddler.

"The kill-score finally ticked up sixty points—672. Big Montana Ice was breathing hard, and tightened Meihua's carrier. "Sorry Floyd," she panted, her voice strained. "What were you saying?"

Floyd cast a quick glance at Ziggy before responding, "I was saying you should be able to see the front entrance of the No Inhibition Exhibition."

"Forget about seeing it," Benedict whimpered, his voice muffled by the straw. "We can hear it."

Ziggy heard it, too. Screaming, grinding, and wailing blended in a soup of gnashing animals, cursing murderers, and carnival jingles.

"Benny, if you don't take your face out of that straw, you're sure to get a rash, and I'm all out of frankincense oil," Carol chided gently, tugging on his shoulder.

"What's the No Inhibition Exhibition?" the Samurai asked.

"We don't know," Ziggy said. "And we don't have any good guesses, so we should steer clear." Gut-wrenching screams and cries floated from the warehouse-style building.

"I can wager a good guess," Big Montana Ice chimed in with a chuckle. "That racket sounds like torture."

"It does," Ziggy agreed. "But the torture of who? The killers or the criminals?"

Understanding dawned on Big Montana Ice's blunt face. "Don't worry, Marshal. We'll steer clear, like you said."

"Once you pass by the No Inhibition Exhibition you should see the tent for the Debting Zoo," Floyd said. "It's an orange tent with one solid wall, and it looks like you can get in through either the north or south, but most of the teams seem to be entering from the south."

"There's a line of porta-potties on the northern border," Pepper said. "They look pretty vacant. They could hide behind them until the north entrance is clear."

Carol sighed with relief. "Oh, thank heavens. Nature has been calling for some time now. I need to refresh myself."

Big Montana Ice snickered. "Is that your way of saying you gotta squeege?"

"*Wǒmen yào qù nǎlǐ?*" Meihua asked Floyd.

"*Nǐmen dōuhuì qù dòngwùyuán zhàngpéng pángbiān de cè-suǒ,*" he responded.

"No," Meihua said with breathy alarm. "Bad guys in toilet."

"Ah, that's right," Floyd said. "Killers sometimes hide in the tanks."

"What?" Carol's face fell. "How disgusting! Where am I supposed to..." she trailed off.

"Piss?" Big Montana Ice finished the sentence with a smirk. "Whizz? Take a leak?" She lobbed her thumb at a nearby tree. "Try over there, your majesty."

Carol glared at her before rushing behind the tree.

"Hiding in the tanks is actually an excellent strategy," Floyd said once Carol had returned, and the killers were darting across the path toward the porta-potties. "In Super Serial eighty-eight, team CybrCoPlus got into the Championships that way. They'd wait for the killer to sit and then sever their femoral artery."

"What about that buffalo?" Benedict asked, surveying their surroundings. "What if it comes back?"

"It ran toward the Ferris wheel and stopped to eat some grass," Pepper said. "I think we're okay for now."

Ziggy scanned the cityscape through every monitor as sweat ran down his brow. Killers and animals lurked in the distance, too far away to make out details, but too close for comfort. It was a miracle they hadn't come across more than the few they already had. Hell, it was a miracle they were all still alive.

The team approached the massive orange-striped tent that housed the Debting Zoo and the sounds of death morphed to the bleating and bellowing of animals from inside.

"Can anyone hear the dogs?" Pepper asked when the team was hidden behind the toilets. "It would be easier if we knew their exact location."

"They allowed me to bring my whistle with me," Benedict started, but the Samurai immediately halted him with a sharp hand gesture.

"Quiet," he rasped, pointing through the crack in the space between porta-potties where a massive Komodo dragon prowled, its scaled hide glinting in the light.

"Komodo dragons are extremely dangerous," Floyd said. "Their bites are venomous, and they're aggressive when provoked. Stay as still and quiet as you can, and it should wander away."

"Is there any benefit to killing it?" Pepper asked. "Even for show?"

Floyd shook his head. "It's not worth the risk. And if you want to score points you have to kill the Pet Lover. Not just their pet."

The team fell silent, and after what felt like an eternity, the sound of rustling foliage signaled the Komodo dragon's departure.

"I wonder where the owner is," said Ziggy.

"Dead, probably," responded Floyd.

"I hope so," said Pepper.

"Blow your whistle," Ziggy told Benedict when the danger had passed. "Let's see if we can hear what side of the tent the dogs are on."

Benedict practically ripped the whistle from the thin cord dangling from his neck. He piped a high-pitched tune, and the distant symphony of dogs barking in response was unmistakable.

Unable to stop himself, Benedict ran around the porta-potties toward the tent, his arms spread open wide.

"Stop, Benedict," Ziggy commanded. "It's not safe."

"My babies!" he cried, snotty, noisy tears running down his cheeks as he bolted for the tent.

"Cover him!" Ziggy ordered, and the rest of the team rushed to catch up, the Samurai last, diligently scanning the area for more giant reptiles. Benedict entered the tent first, followed by Big Montana Ice and Meihua, then Carol and the Samurai. The view from inside the Debting Zoo flashed onto their monitors, but Floyd was checking in on the games from his phone, simultaneously analyzing the media coverage.

"Most of the coverage right now is at the Scary-Go-Round. It's a fast-moving Merry-Go-Round surrounded by walls of spikes." Pepper flinched when she looked down at the screen. "It spins for three minutes every time Chuckles and Jovy can convince the viewers to pay fifty thousand dollars," Floyd said with a grin. "If the killers survive the spin, they can attack the fodder on the carousel. They're the ones painted like carousel horses."

"I need your eyes in the Zoo," Ziggy said gruffly, and Floyd tucked his phone away so he and Pepper could return to their surveillance.

"That looks like a trapeze," Pepper noted, studying the structures in one corner. "And...a tightrope? There are nets over there that look like an obstacle course."

"There appears to be a row of a dozen or so oversized cannons along the edge of the center ring and a wall of targets on the other," Floyd said, looking puzzled. "You must have to hit the target to win your animal, but I don't see any cast iron balls or ammunition."

Bile burned up Ziggy's throat when he saw the dead bodies piled beneath the targets. "The debtors are the ammunition," he said, and Pepper sucked in a breath.

"Almost all of them are taken," Big Montana Ice pointed out, and Ziggy turned his attention to the cannons. They were surrounded by teams of killers, some preparing to shoot and others on guard duty. They jeered and shouted at each other, but so far, nothing had escalated into a brawl.

"It's surprising none of them are attacking," Pepper said.

"Easy violence is a distraction from dangerous violence," the Samurai replied.

"It's a powder keg," Ziggy said. "We need to get the dogs and get out before something explodes."

"The closest team is District Green Royale," Floyd told the group. "I'm not surprised to see them here. Their Pet Lover has a genetically modified polar bear."

"A polar bear?" Big Montana Ice looked surprisingly wary. "Forget it. Those bastards are bigger than me and twice as mean. We're leaving before that thing gets loose and rips off our faces."

"I thought you weren't afraid of anything," Carol said with a huff.

"If we hurry, we can get to Benedict's dogs first and leave before they get the bear." Pepper said. "Where are the dogs?"

"Look up," Floyd said, and Ziggy scrolled to the top of the tent where hundreds of cages were suspended by a complicated system of chains. Each cage was marked with a number.

"Babies?" Benedict yelled, and from a large cage in the corner above the trapeze, the dogs erupted into desperate barks and howls. "I see them!" Benedict pointed to a cage. "Number 06669. Daddy's coming!" He took off, but the Samurai grabbed him around the waist, yanking him back.

"Fire in the hole!" Green Royale ducked to the ground with their hands over their ears, and the cannon went off with an ear-drum-rattling boom. Benedict yelped as the Samurai pulled him to the floor, and Ziggy watched in horror as a woman sailed through the air from the depths of the cannon, slamming into the wall of bullseyes on the opposite side. She hit just underneath the target with a vomit-inducing crack, her body seeming to jellify as it compressed into itself, rebounding and dropping to the ground in a heap of bloody limbs. The Green Royale team groaned in disappointment.

Carol murmured, "That poor soul."

"What happens if you hit the target?" Big Montana Ice asked. "I'll bet two tits and an ass I can get it on the first try."

"There's an information button on the wall near the entrance," the Samurai said, circling back. He pushed the button, and the ringmaster's voice echoed from a speaker above.

"Welcome to the Debting Zoo! In this event, Pet Lovers can put their aim to the test and win back their animal companion through the Debt Blasters. On the west perimeter of the center ring are thirteen cannons. Your task: Use the cannons to hit a bullseye! To load the cannon with our special ammunition, type any sequence of four numbers into the pin pad located on the left side of the cannon. When you've nailed the bullseye, an alarm will sound, and your team will have thirty seconds to use the same pin pad to enter the five-digit code associated with your chosen pet. This pet will then be lowered to the ground and released from its cage for your use."

Ziggy was devastated by the horror. The "special ammunition" was debtors—people desperate enough to risk their lives in hopes of clearing their debt, praying their four-digit number wouldn't be arbitrarily selected. It was a sin against the poor, an atrocity that reduced the value of human lives to mere coins. Acid burned in his throat as he realized they were about to send someone careening into a brick wall.

His eyes involuntarily drifted to the Samurai's feed. The blank eyes on the screen didn't betray the spikes in adrenaline and cortisol Ziggy could see on the monitor. It could be his people behind those four-digit lottery tickets, their fates dependent on the whims of a serial killer. Ziggy felt sick as more debtors fired from smoking cannons, crunching into the wall. A siren sounded, and a team at the far end of the tent celebrated hitting the bullseye.

"Hello? Can you hear me?" a voice called from a small cage above. "I'm in here by mistake. My cage number is 02442. Whoever just won, I'd really appreciate it if you could let me out or find someone who can."

"Is… there a person in there?" Pepper asked, her mouth dropping open. She zoomed in on the cage to see a scruffy, middle-aged man wearing a fluffy, blue fox costume, complete with a white-tipped tail.

"I'm not really an animal," the man tried again, his voice growing hoarse, pleading with the winning killers. "SeaCrown Sugartail is my fursona. My human name is Russell. My wife is my owner, and she's in District TheraTreat."

"You're safer in the cage, my foxy friend," one of the winning killers shouted in a heavy accent. Laughter broke out. "Besides," he added as another cage dropped to the ground, "this fiery beauty needs her friends."

A red-haired woman cried out with joy, racing forward to open the cage door, and ten giant otters streamed out, smothering her in nuzzles. The team moved toward the exit, but the otters broke off, nipping and growling at a rotund man who'd strayed too far from his cannon. The otters nearly ripped the man's calf off before his teammates came to his rescue. Tension peaked in the tent as uneasy teams raced to be the first to release their deadly animal companions.

"I get to shoot first!" Big Montana Ice said, rushing to the nearest, and last unoccupied cannon and punching four numbers into the pin pad. "I chose 7777," she announced as the cannon whirred to life. "It's the number for the Goddess." From the floor underneath the killers, Ziggy heard a system of clunks and clicks as the cannon was loaded.

"Κύριε δείξε έλεος," a panicked squeal carried from inside the cannon. *"Πατέρα μας, που είσαι στους ουρανούς, αγιασμένο το όνομά σου."* Ziggy's chest tightened to the point of pain when he realized the debtor inside must be praying. Big Montana Ice yanked on the handles, aiming the cannon. A button on the top where the fuse would be flashed green.

"έλα η βασιλεία σου, γενηθήτω το θέλημά σου, όπως και στον ουρανό, στη—" the voice abruptly cut off as the cannon fired, and a debtor with long dark hair flew out, her body slamming to the left of the bullseye with a sickening thwack before she flopped to the ground, blood spatter dripping from the wall.

"What language was that?" Floyd asked, and Pepper shrugged, her face in her hands. "It's all Greek to me."

Big Montana Ice howled with fury, inciting raucous animal noises from above. "Let me do it again! This shit's rigged."

"No!" Ziggy said. They needed someone with better aim, or they'd be wasting lives just to appease Big Montana Ice's ego—lives of people like him. "Green Royale is watching us," he lied. "I'm not sure if I imagined it, but I think one of them had a red tint to his eyes. We need you to stand guard in case it's Bazgoroch."

She took the bait. "Which one?" she demanded, glaring at the Green Royale team, who'd missed the target for a third time.

"I can't be sure," Ziggy said, feeling Pepper's eyes on him. "You'd better watch them all."

"You fire it then," she said, turning the cannon over to Carol and standing guard with her eyes on Green Royale, who glanced back at her with growing alarm.

"I don't want to do it!" Carol protested. "Where's the Samurai?" she asked, and Ziggy realized he'd stealthily snuck past Green Royale to study the various circus tasks in the ring at the opposite end of the tent. He pushed the button on the nearest wall.

"Congratulations!" the ringmaster's voice announced. "You've discovered a bonus token event. Your task: complete one of three death-defying feats to collect three tokens. And keep your eye out for the sponsored prize on the other side. You may find it's worth its weight in points."

"Three tokens and a sponsored kill?" Floyd exclaimed with a squeal of delight. "If one of you does that, we could leave with the dogs, enough tokens to get some good weapons, and at least thirty more points!"

"That would be a serious advantage," Ziggy agreed.

"That's easier said than done," Pepper remarked, watching the Samurai's monitor. All three events were at least twenty feet above ground over a pit of nasty-looking spikes. Opposite the pit sat a quivering criminal dressed in the outfit chosen by their sponsor: a hideous metallic purple bodysuit with "ErectaCare" splattered across the chest and back. Ziggy tried not to imagine himself sitting on a platform in an erectile dysfunction-sponsored bodysuit, waiting for someone to end his misery—but it was difficult.

Team Green Royale stopped firing their cannon to study the feats and whisper about how lucky they were to have found a way to get tokens so fast. After a moment, one of the killers from Green Royale, a fit young man wearing a camouflage jacket and pants, climbed the nearest pole that led to an overhead obstacle course of nets and ropes.

"Don't do it if you're not sure," Ziggy told the Samurai, observing the ladder next to him leading to the tightrope. "We can survive without tokens, but we can't survive without you."

The Samurai secured the spear against his back and began to climb, racing against the GreenRoyale killer.

"There's another team coming in from the south entrance," Pepper said as a group of four killers darted into the tent. One of them was covered in angry red burns.

"Fucking UltraChad," he said, sinking to his knees. "Who the fuck would give him a flamethrower?" His teammates surrounded him, and Ziggy made note of the way Green Royale looked at the new arrivals—sizing them up.

"There aren't any cannon's left," Pepper said. "We don't have much time before this place ignites."

Two more sirens blared as two cages were lowered from the ceiling. A camel bolted free, running wild in the tent, and yipping laughter filled the air as a hyena was released. The hyena's owner, a dark-skinned man in a blue robe, called it over by rattling a black chain. However, as soon as the beast saw the robed man's teammates, it pounced. A bald woman in faux silver armor screamed as it crunched her face.

"Media coverage is shifting to the Zoo," Floyd said. "Pepper's right."

"Get out of there," Ziggy said, and Carol nodded, determined as she typed four numbers into the pin pad—0615. "The month and date Jeff and I were married," she said with quiet venom. The cannon whirred as it was loaded and Carol pulled on the handles, her eyes squinting as she studied the target.

"Oh, God! Oh, God! Oh, God!" the person inside sobbed. *Boom!* Carol fired, and Ziggy knew the moment the body left the cannon that she'd succeeded.

Benedict clapped his hands as a gray-haired human missile smacked dead center on the bullseye. "You did it!" he cried with joy. "Rescue the babies! Their number is 06669."

"Not yet!" Pepper broke in, bursting from her seat. "Look!" she zoomed in on the north entrance. "There's a second team sneaking in behind you to attack. They have a sword!"

"That's District HappyChompers," Floyd said, his eyes wide with horror. He zoomed in on the cages closest to DipShip. "They're one of the highest-rated teams this year. The dogs are too far away! Type in 00199!"

"No!" Benedict screamed, bursting into tears as Carol punched in the code. There was a short rattling sound as a cage lowered directly above them, landing smack-dab between DipShip and HappyChompers, who were just feet away from attacking.

"Whatever you do, don't run!" Floyd ordered as a massive silverback gorilla burst from the cage. "Get down!" he cried, and DipShip obeyed, hitting the dirt. Even Big Montana Ice shrank to the ground, curled into a ball with Meihua curved against her back.

HappyChompers was overwhelmed with panic. A man in an orange wrestling singlet screamed before the entire team attempted to flee in the direction they came. The angry gorilla bared its teeth, snarling as it pounced on the closest attacker. Its powerful jaws clamped down while its sharp claws shredded through flesh and bone until only pieces were left to hit the ground. His teammate turned around, brandishing the sword, but the gorilla was on him so fast there wasn't time to swing. Pounding his head with both fists, the silverback grunted, only stopping when the man was more pulp than man.

Floyd was still rattling off instructions. "If it approaches you, don't look it in the eye. Don't show your teeth, and don't scream or cry. Make yourselves as small as possible."

Ziggy's eyes darted to the Samurai's monitor. He was at the top of the tower, ready to cross the tightrope. "Samurai…"

Killers fled from the tent, and the gorilla chased them with astonishing speed, bolting past the DipShip team as if they were part of the scenery. The hyena was busy feasting, and the ostrich had long fled the tent.

"I see it," the Samurai said quietly, lowering himself to the platform and tucking into a ball. The Green Royale camouflaged killer was halfway across the obstacle course, red-faced and terrified as he clung to the net above the spikes. His teammates had fled the tent, leaving him to fend for himself, and for a moment, Ziggy thought the gorilla would follow them out. Instead, it darted back inside, and within moments, was running circles around the ring where the feats were, beating its chest in challenge.

"What's it doing?" Ziggy asked Floyd as he watched the chaos unfold.

Floyd snorted. "I'm not a gorilla expert, Ziggy," he said, his eyes fixed on the screen.

The gorilla's huff reverberated through the tent, and Ziggy's pulse raced as the massive creature stood and pounded its chest, its primal roars shooting a bolt of fear down his spine. The noise from the animals above seemed to agitate it more, and Ziggy could feel the tension peak as its rage grew.

With a sudden burst of fury, the gorilla grabbed hold of a nearby pole and shook it violently. Pepper gasped as they watched the camouflaged killer clinging to the net above, his grip slipping with each jostle. As the shaking continued, the man's feet came loose and he dangled precariously over the spikes. He sobbed as he swung, trying to kick his feet back up. In a desperate attempt to save himself, he reached for the next section of the net, but lost his grip, falling to the spikes below, impaling himself in more places than Ziggy could count.

Just then, an unsuspecting team rushed into the Debting Zoo at the south entrance, their laughter and high-fives quickly turning to terror as they caught sight of the charging gorilla. Ziggy felt a surge of adrenaline as they fled from the tent, the silverback hot on their heels.

None of the DipShip killers moved, staying frozen in place in case it came back. But after a minute of silence, Ziggy ordered his team into action. "Carol, load that cannon and get the dogs. Benedict, get ready to receive them because we're leaving as soon as possible. Big Montana Ice, Meihua, you're on gorilla watch. Samurai," Ziggy took a deep breath. "Cross the tightrope and get us those tokens."

Carol's face blanched as she loaded and aimed the cannon, ignoring the cries from the unlucky debtor inside whose number, 4444, had been chosen by Meihua. With a deafening blast, the cannon fired, once again with deadly accuracy. Sobbing, Benedict plugged in the code and released his dogs in a joyous, fluffy cloud of fur and wagging tongues.

"Why didn't we get the points for HappyChompers?" Pepper asked Floyd, muting the control room. "We're the ones who released the gorilla."

"You only get the points if it's your animal," Floyd explained. "Otherwise, it would be impossible to know where to draw the line between calculated decision and an animal's indiscriminate killing."

Meanwhile, the Samurai began his slow and deliberate journey across the tightrope, his movements deliberate and precise. He teetered for a moment on the last stretch when screams erupted outside the tent—probably from a gorilla attack—and Pepper had to bite her knuckle to keep herself from reacting. With a final leap, the Samurai reached the safety of the opposite platform, his breath coming in ragged gasps as he stared down at the sponsored pedophile tied up and waiting for him like a homicidal present. The pedophile's lips worked around his gag, but his words were clear. "Make it quick," he said, and the Samurai obliged, collecting their tokens before throwing him onto the spikes below. Their kill-score rose to 722.

The Samurai descended from the tower, crouching for a moment to scratch Amir, Benedict's wheelchair-bound dog, behind the ears. He looked as tired as Ziggy felt, and Ziggy wondered whether his stoic demeanor in the face of such relentless violence stemmed from a survival instinct or the quiet decay of his belief in humanity.

"Let's go, before the hyena gets bored of its meal," said the Samurai. The hyena had gorged itself on human flesh before settling down for a post-meal nap.

Fortunately, team DipShip received a much-needed boost of optimism from the surge in points and the possibility of new weapons from the tokens.

Unfortunately, in Super Serial, optimism was a fragile currency.

Chapter 18

I Still Haven't Found What I'm Cooking For

Kill-Score: 722

The gorilla rampage had temporarily evacuated the Debting Zoo, giving team DipShip a chance to formulate a plan. They huddled near the outer perimeter inside a whimsical sound garden. As the sun crept lower in the sky, Ziggy noted that hours of killing had passed, with hours, maybe days to go.

"The first thing we need to do," Pepper said, "is distribute the tokens. That way, even if you get separated, or someone tries to steal it, we'll still have options."

Floyd looked at Pepper with a noticeable spark of affection in his expression. "Excellent idea," he said, and the Samurai passed out the tokens.

Carol, of course, placed hers in her fanny pack while Big Montana Ice passed hers to Meihua, who deftly concealed it in the dark layers of the costume Boomer had given her to both look mysterious and stay warm. Benedict zipped his token into the tiny sweater pocket of his smallest corgi, Ellie's, bright purple sweater.

"Why not keep one for yourself?" Floyd asked the Samurai, watching Ellie, who was still a puppy, chase her tail. "Just in case."

"I'm worth the most points," the Samurai answered. "Which means I'm the most susceptible to being killed."

Ziggy seriously doubted that but chose to keep quiet. If anything, the Samurai was the least likely to be killed. Benedict had his dogs but was useless without them. Carol had turned out to be braver than he'd expected, but she was unskilled in combat. Meihua could die at any moment because of her age, and Big Montana Ice was impulsive and reckless.

"The gorilla rampage is trending." Floyd smiled as he watched the footage from his phone. "But it climbed a tree somewhere near the No Inhibition Exhibition, so now they're replaying the Samurai's tightrope walk. Great job everyone!" He turned to Ziggy. "This is going better than I'd hoped."

"We need to keep moving," Ziggy said. "Now that we have the tokens, we can either spin the Wheel of Misfortune for weapons or try a different event."

With no hesitation, Big Montana Ice said, "Weapons. The team we saw in the Zoo got burnt to a crisp by a flamethrower. Imagine how badass that must've looked."

"But we have the babies now," Benedict said confidently. With his blood-thirsty corgis surrounding him, he seemed completely different

"The dogs help," Carol said, her brow furrowed in thought, "but if we're trying to improve resale value, we may need something more sensational."

Floyd listened as Meihua spoke. *"Yǒu wǔqì zǒngshì gèng hǎo."*

"Meihua says it's always better to have weapons, and I agree," Floyd said. "Statistically, teams with fewer weapons don't survive as long. Plus, we already have the tokens. May as well put them to use."

"Samurai?" Ziggy asked, and the Samurai looked at the scrappy spear in his hand.

"What is a weapon to one who cannot wield it?" he murmured, and Ziggy understood his meaning. What good is a sword to Meihua, who couldn't hold its weight? How would Carol use a set of nunchucks? The wheel was exposed, and it was a risk.

Pepper zoomed in on the prize wheel, its circumference stretching at least six feet. Its surface was covered in a kaleidoscope of vibrant triangles. "There are twelve segments that seem to repeat at random on the wheel," she said. "Blades, explosives, projectiles, fire, chemicals, armor, stealth, stun, blunt objects, poison. There's also one segment that reads, 'food and water,' and another that says, 'viewer's choice.'"

"It looks like some weapons are practical," Ziggy said, more for the Samurai than the rest of the killers. "Anyone can use them."

"I'll support the majority," the Samurai said after a moment, and Big Montana Ice clapped him on the back.

"Thank the Goddess," she said. "And don't worry. I'll take anything you don't want. My hands are deadly weapons, but they're even more deadly when I'm holding a couple knives and a chainsaw."

"It's good to have tokens, but they're worthless if you don't make it to the wheel alive," Ziggy said. "You'll be exposed, so you'll have to work together. This could make or break us."

"Head east toward the Ferris wheel," Floyd said, scrolling ahead of the team on the aerial view. "And I'd run if I were you. The gorilla is gone, but the murder buffalo is grazing nearby, and Chuckles and Jovy reported that team QuirkWorkInc released their Siberian tiger from the Debting Zoo and they're ambushing people from the trees."

"My ass is dragging like a baby diaper in a motel hot tub," Big Montana Ice groaned but begrudgingly picked up her pace.

Ziggy surveyed the area, but it looked like the majority of the violence was concentrated elsewhere in the cityscape. The team was out in the open, moving through a wide patch of short grass off the main asphalt drive. He was uneasy with the lack of cover, but at least there was no risk of a tiger springing out from the bushes.

"Mongaphalee probably created open space between the events and the Ferris wheel to heighten the suspense for the viewers," Floyd said. "The spectators can see the killers coming from their gondolas, and with no hiding spots, you know there's gonna be some epic clashes."

"So far, so good," Benedict puffed to himself, and Ziggy could see the dogs running beside him like a swarm of fuzzy, earth-bound bees, overjoyed to frolic in the open. One of them stopped to lift a leg on a sprawled corpse in the grass.

A looming shadow passed overhead, casting a dim pall over the team. "What was that?" Carol's panicked cry rang through the control room.

"It's just a bird," Big Montana Ice reassured, her breaths heavy with exertion. "Calm your tits."

"A bird?" Carol's eyes widened in horror. "I've never seen a bird that big. It's coming straight for us!"

"It's an eagle!" the Samurai called. "It must belong to a Pet Lover."

Ziggy's pulse quickened with a sense of helplessness. He swapped to the aerial view but could only watch as the colossal raptor banked and descended on the team, its massive wingspan blotting out the artificial sun. It swooped with terrifying speed, and the dogs sensed its attack, barking and jumping as it approached.

"My babies!" Benedict screamed. The bird dive bombed and plucked one of the smaller corgis out of the pack with its massive talons. It screeched at the team, a strange crown of feathers ruffled on its head, before flapping its gray wings. The corgi yelped in distress as it was carried away.

"Otto!" Benedict sobbed. He tried to run after it but tripped over a bloody torso in the grass, falling to his knees. "My poor baby Otto!" Benedict collapsed in despair as Otto's yelps grew distant, then abruptly stopped. "No!" Benedict cried, curling into a ball on the ground, his dogs surrounding him like a stubby fur shield.

"You need to move. You're vulnerable there. Look at all the bodies!" Ziggy ordered. "Lower your voice, get up, and get out of there."

"He was only a puppy!" Benedict continued to sob, his cries increasing in volume.

"Another team is approaching from the west," Pepper said urgently. "There are only three of them, but they're running fast." The opposing team had likely just collected weapons from the wheel and was ready to use them on team DipShip.

"Listen to me, Benedict," Ziggy tried again as the rest of the team caught up. "An eagle is nothing in comparison to three serial killers with weapons. If you don't want the rest of your dogs to die, then you need to get up!" His words seemed to spur Benedict into action, and he scrambled to his feet, his survival instincts kicking in.

"It's District SynApex," Floyd said, sparking a momentary flicker of recognition in Ziggy's mind. "I remember because SynApex's Centennial is the man in the long red cloak—the Carolina Reaper. The one with the red hair and face tattoo holding...a flail? I'm trying to remember the two other killers, but I can't. The one in the white robes holding that canvas bag looks familiar."

Ziggy barely had time to process the significance of the canvas bag before SynApex attacked. The Reaper, his fiery mane billowing behind him, charged forward with surprising agility for his muscular frame, his flail poised to strike. It screamed through the air, aimed at Big Montana Ice's torso, but she stepped out of reach just in time. Using a circular swing, the Reaper attempted to sustain the velocity of the studded ball and decapitate Big Montana Ice.

"Alaskan Thunder!" she let out a primal scream, kicking the Reaper in the chest before he could complete the flail's arch. He sprawled to the ground, the handle flying from his grip.

Meanwhile, the third killer, a woman dressed in a zebra-striped shirt and pants, made her move for the Samurai. His trained instincts kicked in as he rolled aside, evading her lunge and retaliating with a precise jab of his spear, plunging it into her leg. She screamed and fell hard on the ground, clutching her thigh. The Samurai jerked the spear free and pulled it back, preparing to deliver a death blow, when the man in the white robes unexpectedly hurled his canvas bag into the midst of the battle, setting free a nest of writhing, hissing snakes. The Samurai bellowed, hurriedly dancing away from the viper's strike zone.

"That's right!" Floyd said, smacking his forehead. "Now, I remember! The man in the white robes is Serpentore, the SynApex Pet Lover. Those snakes are venomous, by the way, and bred to be extremely aggressive."

"No shit, Floyd!" Ziggy snapped as panic took over the Dip-Ship team. Snakes slithered from the bag, and Carol sprinted for the dogs, diving into the center of Benedict's protective circle of fluff. The corgis barked wildly, snapping at the snakes, keen to protect their master.

"Oh, fuck!" the Reaper cursed when Big Montana Ice beat him to the flail. He scrambled to his feet, attempting to flee, but just when Ziggy thought he'd get away, the Samurai chucked his spear like a javelin, slamming it into the Reaper's back. It sliced through his chest, and he staggered forward, taking a few more steps before collapsing to the ground. The kill-score lit up—*790*.

Seeing the Reaper dead, Serpentore quickly tried to escape, but stumbled over his white robes and fell to the grass in a heap, his snakes slithering around him.

"I'm gonna tenderize you like a discount ribeye steak," Big Montana growled, whipping the flail through the air. The situation devolved into madness as Serpentore screamed, triggering Big Montana Ice to unleash her wrath upon the snakes, stomping indiscriminately, crushing anything that moved under her heavy steel-toed boots. "Die, you wormy little poison fuckers!" she bellowed, and the snakes hissed, attempting to wriggle away as Big Montana unleashed a flurry of strikes, whipping at the vipers anywhere she could reach. One reared up, striking her boot, but the snake's fangs couldn't penetrate the leather,and she smashed its head with deadly force.

Serpentore had barely risen to his hands and knees when Big Montana Ice brought the flail down on his back. His spine collapsed inward, buckling him into a bizarre yoga pose. He wailed, paralyzed, but not dead, as Big Montana Ice unleashed a barrage of swings, denting the man's body until he resembled a ruined clump of bloody clay.

"This spiky thing kicks ass!" Big Montana Ice crooned as she ripped the spike-ball free and gave it a little kiss. The kill-score rose to *854.*

At the same the Samurai kicked the zebra-clad woman's chin so hard her neck nearly snapped. She fell backwards, right into the midst of the venomous vipers, whimpering as several struck, sinking their fangs into her side. Avoiding the snakes, the Samurai skirted the perimeter of the area and retrieved his spear from the Reaper's chest. He jabbed the spear at the snakes as they slithered toward him, watching the zebra-lady out of the corner of his eye. She rose to her feet, but Ziggy could see her lower jaw and one of her hands was swelling fast and turning purple. Her breathing was shallow, her neck muscles so taut they looked like they might snap.

Benedict's corgis barked ferociously, savagely attacking the snakes, a few yelping as they were bitten. It was excruciating to watch, but caused enough distraction to give Big Montana Ice the opportunity she needed to crush the bulk of the vipers.

In moments, the ground was littered with the lifeless bodies of the snakes, the survivors long since slithering away to safety. Benedict's voice was hoarse from screaming for his corgis, and his whistle's shrill notes pierced into the eerie silence. Even Carol patted her knees, enthusiastically encouraging the dogs to give up their snake chase and come back to Benedict's side.

Pepper counted the fluffy bodies lying on the ground, her jaw clenching as she realized the extent of the casualties. Two were panting hard, and one was still. "At least three dogs were bitten," she told Ziggy. "I don't know which ones."

"Devon!" Benedict wailed, tears streaming down his cheeks. "Cicily, my sweet girl And Shilo? Not Shilo. Oh, God!"

Big Montana Ice snorted before spitting in the grass. Meihua patted her shoulder to signal she wanted to be let down. "Stay close," Big Montana Ice told her, releasing her from her sling and crouching so she could climb down.

Meihua leaned in closely, observing Big Montana Ice's legs. *"Wǒ zhèng zài jiǎnchá shìfǒu bèi shé yǎoshāng le."*

"She wants to check you for snake bites," Floyd relayed, and Big Montana Ice patted Meihua's head as if she were a child.

"Isn't she sweet?" she said, pursing her lips. "She's worried about me. Lucky for you, Granny, I got my boots on."

Meihua then leaned down and plucked up a few vipers. She pulled a small knife out, cut the heads off, and stowed them in her robes.

"The sun is waning," the Samurai broke in, never taking his eyes off the zebra woman, who was moaning and tearing at her face, her hands shaking violently. "We must take her life before the venom does."

"Help!" the zebra-clad woman called weakly into the distant trees. "P-please, Facundo..." her voice trailed off.

"I can do it," Big Montana Ice said, swinging the weapon still in her hand. "I'm still breaking in this spike whip ball thing."

Floyd sighed. "It's called a spiked ball-and-chain flail. Despite how it looks, it's not medieval. It's actually from the Victorian age and probably existed more as art than a practical weapon."

"I want to do it," Benedict suddenly broke in, his voice thick with tears and fury. "The babies must have their justice." He walked slowly toward the zebra woman, who'd slumped to the ground. The corgis inched around him, growling low in their throats. Benedict held up his whistle, glaring down at the woman with a sneer so chilling, for once, he looked every bit the serial killer he was. "Dinner time, babies," he sang, blowing a tune on his whistle that made Ziggy's only remaining hairs stand on end.

The dogs pounced, ripping into the woman like a succulent steak. Biting and snarling, they tore her flesh from her body while she writhed in agony, her screams eventually fading to weak moans. Blood coated the corgis, staining their fur as they licked their maws, chewing through thick bits of muscle and flesh to get to the soft interior of torn guts. Horrified, Ziggy watched as they swiftly eviscerated her body. His mind rejected reality, and the passing minutes dragged on like never-ending hours.

Pepper averted her gaze, focusing on the kill-score, waiting for it to change, signaling the end of the gruesome torture. It wasn't the first time they'd seen Benedict's dogs tear someone apart, but it was the first time they'd done nothing but wait for it to be over. Pepper choked on a ragged breath when the monitor finally lit up, and the kill-score changed—*911*.

"It's done," Ziggy told Benedict. "Call off the dogs and get to the wheel before something else happens. We created a ruckus and there are probably already other teams headed our way. Get Meihua off her feet and get back to the asphalt. There could still be snakes in the grass."

"That's one way to put it," Pepper muttered, and Floyd snorted in response.

"Good one, Pep."

Ziggy watched his team dive into the melee, dreading the next part of the shit show. Maybe it was the pack of blood-stained corgis or the angry giantess swinging a flail above her head, but no one approached as they closed in on the Wheel of Misfortune.

The ringmaster's voice suddenly boomed over the cityscape. "Attention, Super Serial contestants! It's our pleasure to inform you that District OmniFood, District ValueMart, District ExportAlt, and District ZenithConsortium have qualified for the Super Serial Championships!"

"Seven spots left," Pepper murmured, and even Floyd noticed her shoulders droop.

He patted her back. "We're at the weapons wheel," he said. "And all our killers are alive. We're doing better than most."

"Thanks for the pep talk," Pepper said with a wan smile, and Floyd glanced at Ziggy, confused.

"It wasn't a pep talk," he said. "Statistically, we're doing better than the majority of teams."

"It may not have been your intent, but I still appreciate your words. It was encouraging to hear," Pepper said, and Floyd looked flustered, fussing with his monitor and keyboard.

Under the close supervision of the control room, the team snuck behind a whimsical head-in-the-hole peep board that featured a line of circus animals on a train. Big Montana Ice crouched down to stick her head out of the hole surrounded by a glorious lion's mane, and Floyd couldn't help but snicker at the sight.

"That thing is ginormous," Big Montana Ice said, craning her neck to look at the Ferris wheel. The Samurai's serious face peeked through the lion tamer's hole, making him look like he was wearing a sparkly suit and holding a cartoon whip. The entire peep board wobbled as Benedict attempted to herd his dogs in closer.

"There are bodies strewn around the base of the wheel," the Samurai noted quietly. "We must exercise patience. Someone could be lurking, waiting to strike."

Ziggy could see what the Samurai meant. Dotting the ground around the Ferris wheel were a handful of corpses, stiff with death. "Stay put team," he said. "Let us do some recon before heading for the wheel. If anyone approaches, use the dogs."

Ziggy scanned the area around the Ferris wheel, watching for any signs of movement.

"I counted, and there are two hundred gondolas in total," Pepper said, using the aerial map to watch it slowly turn.

"I see Alexia and Boomer in gondola 155!" Floyd exclaimed. "Look right there! They're watching us through the window."

Ziggy saw Big Montana Ice's eye twitch as she looked up at Boomer in the gondolas. "He thinks I can't see him in the shadows," she muttered to herself through the lion's head, her voice laced with suspicion. "He's plotting to destroy us all."

"Two killers are approaching from the southwest," Pepper said, her monitor still on the aerial view. "I think they're running for the weapons wheel."

"Duck down," Ziggy ordered the team. "Benedict, get your whistle ready in case we need the dogs."

"That looks like Ms. Maniac and Momus Necator from District TechnaLots," Floyd said. "Looks like they don't have any weapons or an animal, so they're probably not as much of a threat on their way to the wheel as they will be when they leave."

Ziggy zoomed in to see two killers sprinting toward the Ferris wheel. One wore a chintzy apron covered in blood spatter, and the other a Greek toga with a gold sash. They had just reached the edge of the Ferris wheel when the Ms. Maniac cried out, face-planting onto the ground, an arrow embedded in the back of her neck. She prodded the arrow tip poking out from her esophagus and went limp.

Ziggy winced as the killer moaned, her body twitching. "I guess that explains the bodies. Where's the shooter?" he asked Pepper and Floyd.

Momus dropped to his knees to dig through Ms. Maniac's pockets, eventually producing a gold token. When another arrow landed just inches away, he quickly dove to the side. "Shit!" he cursed, giving one final glance at his fallen comrade before sprinting back in the direction they'd come.

Pepper took a sharp breath. "Is she dead? Maybe we ought to—" Thunk. Another arrow sunk into the Ms. Maniac's spine. "Never mind."

"It's District CareWare," Floyd said, squinting as he zoomed in on a line of antique tractors. "It looks like they've won an archery set and a pair of binoculars. They're hiding behind the tractor display and firing on anyone trying to use the wheel." He zoomed in further, focusing on a woman with intricately braided stark white hair that went all the way to her knees. "I see," he murmured. "That makes sense. That's Skadi. She's named after a hunting goddess from Norse mythology. No wonder she can shoot so well."

"Why do none of the bodies have arrows in them?" Pepper asked.

"They probably wait until the coast is clear and then go collect them," Floyd said. "It doesn't look like they have many."

A variety of possibilities raced through Ziggy's mind. "Turn the peep board toward CareWare and use it as a shield," he said. "It may deter them from firing if they can't get a clear enough shot."

Pepper nodded, adding a warning. "Just watch out for the head holes, especially with the dogs."

Big Montana Ice shook the frame holding the board in place. "Piece of cake. We can get this off here easy. I'll lift from this side, and the Samurai and Carol can handle the other. Benny, keep the dogs out from under our feet."

With their plan in motion, the team crept slowly toward the metal platform that held the prize wheel. "CareWare's watching us," Floyd reported, "but Skadi is shaking her head. She may not want to risk any more arrows with the board in the way. Great idea, Ziggy."

"Get in, then get out. The quicker, the better," Ziggy said, and Big Montana Ice left Carol to prop up her side of the board as she stepped forward. Meihua produced the token from the ball of fabric surrounding her and handed it to Big Montana Ice, who slipped it into the coin slot at the base of the wheel, twisting the handle until it clicked.

The ringmaster's voice boomed out, "Congratulations on winning a token! This token allows you one spin on the Wheel of Misfortune! Spin the wheel by pulling a handle all the way down, then releasing your grip. The lighted arrow at the top of the wheel will indicate what prize you've won when the wheel comes to a stop. May misfortune smile upon you!"

Big Montana Ice grasped the highest handle she could reach, grunting as she yanked it to the ground. Meihua stretched her head away like an old turtle to avoid getting struck, and the wheel whirred in a riot of colors. The anticipation thickened as it slowed, and the Ferris wheel rolled to a stop, landing on gondola eighty-four. Big Montana Ice let out a whoop when the Wheel of Misfortune settled on "Fire."

"Fuck yeah! Let's light some shit up!" she pumped her fist, and the people in the gondolas snickered, applauding her demented enthusiasm.

"Gondola eighty-four is sponsored by Mr. Blair Blizzard, CEO of District ConcuMine!" The ringmaster announced, and a bulky man in a cowboy hat with a long gray beard leered down at them.

"This could be a problem," Floyd said. "Do you think they're still mad we ran over their killer?"

Ziggy rubbed his temples. "Yeah, Floyd, I think there's a good chance."

"Of all the districts," Pepper sighed. "What are the chances?"

"One in two hundred," Floyd replied automatically.

"District ConcuMine is located in the northwestern region of North America," the ringmaster said enthusiastically. "Their number one export is—you guessed it—copper!"

Ziggy watched as ConcuMine made their choice on the computer screen in the gondola. Ziggy could see them laughing when they were through, and Ziggy braced himself for a bad outcome.

"District ConcuMine has made their selection," the ringmaster said. "Team DipShip has been rewarded with"—the ringmaster's voice was drowned out by a pattering drum roll—"a spark-wheel lighter and a can of hairspray!"

"The fuck?" Big Montana Ice snapped as the metal box next to the prize wheel slowly opened. She reached in, pulling out the pathetic items they'd risked their lives to get, then slowly lifted her head, glaring at the people in the gondola. "I see you in there, Bazgoroch," she shouted at Blair Blizzard, her face flushing an ugly purple color. "And when I get the chance, I'll put my fist in your dick box! I'll fuck you with sandpaper and piss on the wounds!"

Even though he couldn't hear them, Ziggy could see the District ConcuMine gondola was roaring in response. When the Ferris wheel began to move again, Big Montana Ice wound up a wad of phlegm and hocked a loogie on their window.

"Please insert your next token," the ringmaster said, prompting Carol to step out from the safety of the peep board. After inserting her token, she stood on her tiptoes to reach the highest handle she could. When she spun the wheel, it barely made one rotation before landing on "Poison." The Ferris wheel stopped, this time landing on gondola 121.

"Gondola 121 is sponsored by Mrs. Bamidele Abebe, CFO of District Malitel!" The ringmaster announced, and Mrs. Abebe, a statuesque woman with brilliant white teeth, moved to the gondola window. She waved, and Carol politely waved back, turning pink when she realized the wave was meant for the cameras and not her. "District Malitel is located in the western region of the African continent and offers global telecommunication solutions and digital technology for corporations large and small!" the ringmaster said with a flourish.

"She'll help us," Pepper said, breathing a sigh of relief. "We give them a massive discount on shipping IT infrastructure."

Ziggy hoped she was right. Abebe paused before making her selection, and Ziggy realized she was talking with someone on the phone. After a moment, she ended the call, frowning before she tapped the computer screen.

The ringmaster said, "District Malitel has made their selection! Team DipShip has been rewarded with"—the campy drumroll was back—"a mystery poison!"

Carol looked uneasy as the metal box next to the prize wheel opened again, but she removed the small amber bottle and held it up to the light. "It looks like an essential oil," she said with delight, but when she attempted to unscrew the lid, Meihua barked at her.

"Bèndàn, nǐ xiǎng sǐ ma?" she said, holding out her delicate, veiny hand. *"Jiāo gěi wǒ."*

"She said to give it to her," Floyd translated. Carol huffed with irritation but obediently placed the bottle in Meihua's hand.

"Maybe it's something decent?" Pepper said, wringing her hands. "Meihua can do a lot, even with a simple poison."

"Please insert your next token," the ringmaster said. "If you have no more tokens, please step away from the Wheel of Fortune to make room for the subsequent competitors."

"Screw you!" Big Montana shouted at the hidden ringmaster. "We got tokens to spare."

Ziggy's patience was hanging by a hair-string by the time Benedict retrieved his token from Ellie's pocket. Benedict struggled to spin the wheel, and his sweaty hands slipped off the handle. When he went to wipe them on his pants, they came away covered in dog hair, which made him sneeze violently. There was the sound of an explosion in the distance, followed by crashing metal and screams. If he didn't hurry his ass up, Ziggy might reach through the monitor and choke him.

Eventually, he managed to give the wheel a weak spin, and by the time it came to a stop on "Blade," the Ferris wheel had spun back to the single digit gondolas, landing on Gondola four. The Samurai's eyes perked up.

"Gondola number four is sponsored by District NeuroGenixx CEO, Dr. Rohan Desai," the ringmaster's voice echoed through the air.

Ziggy's stomach knotted. "Why does that district name sound familiar?"

"Because we barbecued Barbie Cude," Floyd said with a wince.

"Shit."

"Pretty much."

"NeuroGenixx is located on the southern part of the continent of Asia and is the industry leader in innovative neurological research and solutions," the ringmaster continued, and Ziggy closely observed Dr. Desai, who had a smirk playing on his lips. He made his selection and the drumroll seemed to mock them as the metal box beside the prize wheel opened once more, revealing a single metal kebab skewer.

The control room was silent as Benedict retrieved the pitiful prize, the look of disappointment on his face mirroring Ziggy's. It was clear that the privileged upper crust in the gondolas were intentionally awarding them with useless garbage as a form of petty revenge for their kills—or Alexia had a lot more enemies than he realized.

"The king may build his castle high, but the sweat of the peasants holds up the walls," the Samurai said when the Ferris wheel began to move, the faces of the elite blurring as they passed.

Big Montana Ice was less eloquent. "All you richies can go fuck yourselves with a barbed lemon!" she hollered, clenching her fists.

"There's another team headed your way," Pepper cut in, her monitor scrolling over the open area around the prize wheel. "It doesn't look like they have a weapon, but one has a pet on a leash that looks like a giant cat. They'll be there any minute."

"If it's a mountain lion, that means it's likely District Summit-Seeker," Floyd said, his tone stressed. "CareWare is preparing to fire on them, but they don't see District Chomputere sneaking up on them from behind with a machete. This could be bad. We need to get out of before we're caught in the crossfire."

"I don't care where we go, but I have to get off my feet for a minute." Big Montana Ice hunched over, still holding up the bulk of the peep board, the flail drooping in her grip. "My gams are on fire, and Granny's too pooped to poop."

Ziggy tried to subdue his panic. If it weren't for her gentle snoring, he'd think Meihua was dead. She was slumped against Big Montana Ice's back like a rag doll in a sack.

"We need to find water," Carol said, her throat sounding raw. "I'm weak from dehydration."

"Con-Cessions is the closest," Floyd suggested, looming over the pre-marked flags on the map. "We can send them to the booth on the outskirts we talked about earlier. It's our safest bet."

Chapter 19

Take It Cheesy

Kill-Score: 911

As the golden orb of the simulated sun descended, casting its last fiery hues on the cityscape, a sense of foreboding settled like a shadowy shroud. Amid the labyrinth of booths, tents, and winding pathways, the carnival lights flickered to life, illuminating the surroundings in a kaleidoscope of vibrant colors. It was a festive façade—a distraction, concealing the sinister darkness where murderers stalked, waiting for the opportunity to strike. Ziggy's anxiety gnawed at him like a relentless garbage gazer.

It was impossible to predict what would come next, and uncertainty hung thick in the control room. Every shadow held the threat of an ambush. Every sound jolted his senses, signaling an attack. The daylight was nerve-wracking. The darkness was paralyzing.

"It would be better to rest now while it's still early," Floyd said. "Most of the teams are still pushing for points in the events, and it may be easier to get by without drawing attention."

Ziggy consulted his cityscape map. "It might be safer to follow the south perimeter to the Con-Cessions instead of trying to get through the direct pathway. If we cut past the Scary-Go-Round, we may have a better chance of avoiding confrontation until we're ready."

"There's nothing too exciting happening there right now, anyway," Floyd said. "Most of the targets are dead, and the live coverage has moved on."

"I'll lead the way," the Samurai volunteered, his gaze sharp as he scanned their surroundings. Following Floyd's direction, the team stealthily made their way to a concessions stand at the edge of the dome near the Scary-Go-Round. The stand, trimmed in flashing red and yellow lights, was about twenty feet long. Signs covered in swirling, golden funnel cakes hung from the eaves and crowded every surface of the exterior. Above the service window, a blocky, lettered sign read, "Funnel Fakes." To Ziggy, it looked like a death trap, but there was no better choice.

After checking for intruders, the Samurai ushered the team inside, including all twenty-four of Benedict's remaining corgis, then locked the door behind them using the kebab skewer as a pick. He then jammed the skewer into the seal of the service window, effectively locking it shut, as well.

"Don't cover the service window," Ziggy said. "It would look too obvious to someone on the outside. If you sit on the ground, you'll be mostly hidden."

Carol gasped as she turned the sink handles, and water gushed out from the faucet. "Can I drink it?" she asked, and when no one responded immediately, Floyd jumped in.

"The vast majority of the time, the water in Super Serial is potable. The host district knows that killers can't fight to their potential without it. Food is another story. That's not usually worth the risk. In Super Serial ninety-six, the cityscape didn't—"

Carol didn't wait for the rest, quickly dipping her head under the faucet to gulp down water as fast as she could. Several long minutes passed, and she moved aside to let Benedict have a turn, before scrubbing her arms and face in the smaller handwashing sink.

"No soap!" Floyd cried when Carol began searching for some around the sink. "Super Serial 103 was muddy like this one, and the host district made all the soap caustic. The killers who used it got horrible chemical burns."

Carol went for her oils instead. When she was satisfied, she leaned against the wall with a sigh, sliding to the floor. She unzipped her fanny pack, took out a bottle of peppermint oil, stuck it under her nose, took a deep breath, then opened her mouth and put a drop on her tongue. She glanced longingly at the rotating carousel of oversized funnel cakes in the corner.

"Don't even think about it," Ziggy said. "They called this booth Funnel *Fakes* for a reason."

While the Samurai used the sink, Benedict scavenged a couple of bowls from a cupboard and put out water for his dogs. Pepper paled at the sight of blood running from their muzzles as they drank. Big Montana Ice unstrapped the now awake Meihua, then groaned, her back cracking audibly as she tried to stretch in the cramped space. Her head grazed the stand's roof, her scraggly hair brushing against the metal.

After everyone had water and a moment to catch their breath, Big Montana Ice tossed the lighter and can of hairspray onto the floor in the center of their haphazard circle. "Absolute horse shit," she growled. "Three tokens and fuck-all to show for it."

Floyd muted the control room. "It doesn't make any sense," he said, his frustration bubbling over. "I get that they were mad at us for killing their competitors, but you'd think they'd be more careful about not getting on Alexia's bad side. "Eventually the games will be over and it'll be business as usual."

Pepper frowned, turning in her chair to look at Ziggy. "I know we haven't talked about your conversation with Hirofumi in the skybox, but could this have something to do with him?"

Ziggy blanched, too afraid to confess that Hirofumi was most certainly blacklisting them. She didn't know yet that they had to lose. She was practical enough to realize it was unlikely they'd win, but she'd already allowed herself to hope. There was no point in dashing that hope when their team was struggling just to survive.

"Anything's possible," he said cryptically, already knowing Pepper would see right through him.

"Anything's possible?" Pepper said, her nostrils flaring. "Then I suppose it's possible Hirofumi had something to do with the weapons we were given."

Ziggy swallowed. "It's possible."

"And that means it's possible he could be intentionally sabotaging our team in order to seek petty revenge?"

"But that would be cheating," Floyd said in a huff.

Ziggy gave a little nod, lips pressed together. He could be honest without being an open book.

Pepper sighed. "That's what I was afraid of."

"Which means we need a new strategy," Floyd said, unmuting the control room. "Sorry, guys, but there's no point in fighting for tokens if this is the result. The focus should be on spectacle and direct kills."

"What do you suggest?" the Samurai asked, and Ziggy was relieved the topic had veered away from Hirofumi.

"The Pedo-Stampedo is the fastest way to earn points," Floyd said. "Pedophiles are worth double the points. And we should avoid hand-to-hand combat since most teams probably have weapons by now. The Samurai has the spear, and we have the flail, but it's not easy to kill a human with it in a single blow."

Big Montana Ice snorted. "Speak for yourself."

"We need something more interesting or flashy that can rake in multiple kills at once," Floyd said.

"Maybe we could steal a weapon from another team," Ziggy suggested.

Pepper crossed her arms over her chest. "So we can't win tokens or engage in combat, but now we have to steal a heavily guarded weapon from another team of killers?"

"Are you mad at me?" Floyd asked, caught off guard. "Your face looks frustrated. All I'm doing is presenting the options. That's my job."

"But you aren't presenting options," Pepper countered, her brows furrowed. "You're just listing all the things we can't do."

Floyd froze, and Ziggy could see his mind processing. "You're right," he said after a moment. "Sorry, Pep. I'll shift the focus to things we can accomplish with what we have."

Pepper uncrossed her arms, slightly mollified. "I shouldn't have snapped at you," she said. "I'm tired."

"The problem is that we don't have much," Benedict whimpered. "Except the babies, and look what's happened to them. Four gone." Tears filled his eyes, and Carol handed him a napkin.

"Benedict's right," Carol said, absently scratching a corgi behind its ears. "Unless you can make something good from a lighter, hairspray, a mystery poison, and a kebab skewer, we're in trouble."

"Floyd, ask Meihua if she can identify the poison," Ziggy said. "Maybe it wasn't as bad as we think." Deep down, he knew he was grasping at straws, but a chance in hell was better than no chance at all.

"Nǐ zhīdào nà shì shénme dú ma?" Floyd asked Meihua, who produced the bottle from her layers of fabrics. She toddled over to the service window, inspecting the bottle under the flashing lights outside. Unsatisfied with whatever she saw, she held the bottle outward in her hand, then rolled it between her fingers. She pressed it to her wrist and held it there for a long moment before slowly opening the cap. She sniffed the contents, then surprisingly, ripped a hair from her head and dipped it inside. Ziggy held his breath.

"Zhè shì yǐ èr chún," Meihua told Floyd when she was through.

"It's ethylene glycol," Floyd translated for the group, cringing at Pepper's hopeful expression.

"Is that good?" she asked. "What does it mean?"

"It's antifreeze," Floyd explained. "Technically, a poison if ingested, but not a very useful one in this case."

"Well, shit," Big Montana Ice said, shaking her head. "This situation's a bitch prick and a half, isn't it?"

"Language!" Carol hissed, and Ziggy knew she must be feeling better if her self-righteousness had returned.

"What are we going to do?" Benedict sniffled, dabbing at his eyes. "I can't bear to lose anyone else." He pulled a dog close and let it lick his face, his eyes rolled back in ecstasy.

Ziggy muted the control room. "I have to get it out of my system," he said, choking on a gag. "That is fucking disgusting." He shuddered before unmuting.

Meihua raised both her hands to silence the team. *"Wǒ yǒu gè zhǔyì,"* she said firmly. *"Xiǎomèng, wǒ zuì qīn'ài de, qǐng kuài diǎn fānyì."*

Floyd sat up straighter in his seat. "Listen everyone," he said. "Meihua has an idea and said I need to translate it quickly because there's no time to waste." Meihua began speaking, her words cracking and weak, leaving Ziggy struggling to pick up more than a few consonants and vowels.

Floyd listened intently. "She wants to make a weapon and needs everyone's help. She asks that you complete your task as quickly as possible and says she promises to explain when you return," Floyd relayed the instructions. "The Samurai must find a large pipe or cylinder. At least twenty-five centimeters in diameter with one end tamped shut."

"It will be done," the Samurai said before slipping out of the booth and vanishing into the shadows. Meihua watched him go before turning her attention to Benedict.

"Dog Boy," Floyd translated, then shook his head. "Sorry, Benedict. She says you must remove the sweaters from your dogs. We need the fabric." Benedict looked bewildered but snuggled his dogs closer and began the lengthy process of removing their tiny embroidered sweaters.

"Carol," Floyd said as Meihua turned in her direction. "Meihua wants to know if you have horseradish or balsam fir oil in your collection." He paused to listen to Meihua, then asked several clarifying questions before continuing. "She said cypress oil could also work, but the translation may not be exact."

Carol's expression was so surprised Ziggy almost laughed. He supposed it was rare that anyone asked Carol for an essential oil without her first shoving it down their throat. "Of course!" she gushed, digging through her trusty fanny pack. "I have both balsam fir and cypress." She handed the bottles to Meihua, who inspected them closely.

"What about me?" Big Montana Ice asked with an annoyed sniff. "Do I get a job, or am I supposed to just sit on my thumb and spin?" Meihua's milky eyes narrowed as if she somehow understood Big Montana's words.

"Floyd?" Ziggy prompted when Floyd reeled mid-translation. His mouth popped open as Meihua continued speaking.

"Funny thing," Floyd began. "I-I think I may have misheard her," he said, his expression growing alarmed. He glanced frantically at Ziggy before correcting himself. "No, I heard correctly the first time. She wants Big Montana Ice to go out and collect some... heads."

"Heads?" Ziggy, Pepper, and Big Montana Ice all said at the same time.

"Yes, human heads," Floyd said, his voice tinged with skepticism. "She said the heads of corpses will work fine, but try to pick ones that are mostly intact if you can."

Big Montana Ice grinned wickedly. "I'll be back," she said before thundering out into the night, flail in hand.

As the team watched her go, Meihua produced two of Serpentore's vipers' heads, gingerly placing them on the counter next to Carol's oils and the bottle of antifreeze. Then, without warning, she opened her mouth and yanked out one of her back molars. Ziggy watched in astonishment as she cracked it open, revealing a thin white powder within.

"I make bad, bad poison," she said with a smile, her teeth coated in blood.

Floyd turned to Ziggy, his mouth gaping open, and Pepper's voice wavered with panic. "Poison? I don't understand what all this is for. What weapon is this supposed to make?"

Floyd listened to Meihua with an earnest expression, asking a few questions and receiving answers in return. "We're going to build a cannon," Floyd announced. "We'll take it into the Pedo-Stampedo, wait for the stampede to pass, follow behind them, and get all our points at once."

Ziggy was dumbfounded. "Let me get this straight," he said. "You want to build a cannon and shoot it into the Pedo-Stampedo? What will you use as..." He froze as the reality dawned on him.

"Not the heads," Pepper whispered as the color drained from her face.

Meihua spoke again, her voice sounding like the squeaky battle cry of a mouse. "She wants to coat the heads in poison so when they break apart, they could hit anyone in range. A direct hit will kill one, but the poison can kill dozens," Floyd translated, his excitement growing.

"You have no idea how cool this is going to be," he exclaimed with awe. "A move like this will put DipShip in the Super Serial Hall of Legends!"

Chapter 20

Banana Split Open and Melt

Kill-Score: 911

They were weaponizing human heads. It felt like being trapped in a fever dream, yet here he was, watching from the control room as Meihua mixed a deadly poison to slather onto actual human remains. His stomach churned. It was immoral. It was the desecration of a corpse. But none of that mattered when the games provided absolution, all in the name of profit and entertainment. A great evil for a greater good.

Meihua swirled the mixture in the bowl, looking for something Ziggy would probably never understand. He didn't even want to think about the implications of how immediately she'd come up with the plan. Floyd, however, didn't seem the least bit disturbed, digging into his dinner while monitoring the Samurai as he crept through the darkness. Pepper's face was bloodless; her dinner pushed aside as she watched Big Montana Ice rip heads off of slain bodies, holding them aloft by their hair.

Meihua muttered as she stirred, blending a noxious green sludge in a large metal bowl. Her milky eyes watered, and Ziggy wondered if it was from the smell or the fumes.

A light tap on the door interrupted them, and the Samurai returned with what looked like a massive metal pipe. He placed it on the counter with a resounding thud.

"Where did you get that?" Ziggy asked, his curiosity piqued. "I haven't seen anything like it in the entire cityscape."

The Samurai's face remained unreadable. "Antique tractor."

"The smokestack," Floyd said. "Genius idea."

Suddenly, the ringmaster's voice rang out over the cityscape. "Attention, Super Serial contestants! It is our pleasure to inform you that District CareWare and District Pawsitronix have qualified for the Super Serial Championships! Congratulations to our newest finalists."

"Five spots left," Pepper said, closing her eyes and pinching the bridge of her nose. "And going fast."

"There's still time to make an impression," Ziggy reminded her, trying to buoy her spirit. "We can save the district."

"Open up," Big Montana Ice cooed from outside the door. "My hands are full." The Samurai obliged, and she pushed her way inside. "Got 'em!" she declared triumphantly, holding up eight severed heads—six in one hand, gripped by their hair, and two in the other, held by their eye sockets. She plopped them on the counter next to the smokestack, their faces frozen and stiff, their lifeless eyes staring into the void.

Pepper couldn't suppress a shudder. "I can't believe we're doing this."

"It's Super Serial," Floyd reminded her. "We came here to make a mark, and this is a great opportunity to put on a show. Plus, we could get a ton of points. Maybe even enough to win."

"I've just finished," Benedict said, placing a pile of dog sweaters on the counter. "What's our next move, then?"

"I'll ask," Floyd said, communicating with Meihua, who gave instructions. "She wants to know if the end of the pipe is tamped shut."

The Samurai nodded in confirmation. "It was already capped when I pulled it off."

"That's convenient," Floyd said, surprised. "They must have capped the stack to prevent moisture from getting in since it's really more of a decoration than a tractor."

Floyd relayed the message, and Meihua spoke again. "The end of the pipe needs a pinhole near the cap," Floyd translated, and the Samurai swiftly pulled the kebab skewer from the window track.

"Big Montana Ice," Floyd continued, "Meihua says you're the only one strong enough to carry the cannon and keep it in place while it fires."

"Damn straight," she said smugly, flexing her biceps.

"She's asking if the three of us in the control room can figure out the logistics of where and when to enter and exit the Stampedo," Floyd said, turning to Ziggy. "I told her we could. Is that alright?"

"Of course," Ziggy said. The truth was, he was relieved Meihua had come through with a plan. Most of Ziggy's ideas had revolved around weapons, but that clearly wasn't panning out.

Pepper scrolled over the Pedo-Stampedo. "It's a track about twenty-five feet in width that runs along the inner perimeter of the Pervy Derby. It's slightly below the Derby, but there are thick transparent walls on both sides that are too high for the pedos to climb over."

"If it circles the arena just inside the Pervy Derby track. It should be a loop a little over a mile long," Floyd said.

Ziggy was also looking over the map. As he surveyed the brightly lit track, he felt a pang of frustration. He'd been counting on the cover of darkness to execute their attack unnoticed, but Mongaphalee had prioritized the view of the spectators in the gondolas, ensuring that every murdery moment was easy to see.

"The stampede begins and ends from the southeast between the Con-Cessions and the Despair Fair," he said. "There are three access points where the killers can enter the Stampedo from the cityscape. The first is about three hundred yards after the starting point, the second is between the Rapist-No-Escapist and the No Inhibition Exhibition, and the third is on the western edge of the track near the Scary-Go-Round."

"What's the Pedo-Stampedo, exactly?" Carol asked, her face pinched with disgust. "It sounds awful!"

"It's a stampede but with pedophiles," Floyd replied, rolling his eyes to Ziggy behind Carol's back like the answer should be obvious to anyone.

Pepper's nose wrinkled as she watched the event from their aerial view. "At the starting point, there's a narrow, boxy covering over the track meant to look like a cattle chute. I can't see inside very well, but once the buzzer goes off, the stampede begins, and thousands of pedophiles flood the track. They're painted up like cows, horses, and sheep," Pepper added with a frown. "Of course."

"Their goal is to get back into the chute at the end of the loop," Floyd said. "If they make it, they're safe. At least until they cycle back through and have to stampede again."

Big Montana Ice scoffed. "We should've gone there first. That doesn't seem hard. All you've gotta do is chase down some chomos."

"I'd agree if the killers were only there to get pedophiles," Ziggy said. "The problem is that they're also hunting other killers who think going into the Stampedo is an easy way to rack up points. The exits and entrances will be especially dangerous since there's a limited window of time where killers can get on or off the track. We're not only vulnerable to anyone with a ranged weapon but also risking confrontations with other killers who probably have weapons by now."

"It's not just running," Pepper said, leaning in to see the track more closely. "It's more like an obstacle course with hurdles, sand pits, walls to climb, tires to run through, and an A-frame cargo nets. My God," she murmured as she zoomed in. "There are dead bodies and animals everywhere. Imagine a fun run, but in hell."

"They've timed the entrances and exits to open right before the stampede arrives," Ziggy said, keeping a close eye on the event. "I'm guessing a lot of those bodies were trampled by the herd."

"The path to glory is fraught with danger," the Samurai said. "But the reward of victory outweighs the risk of defeat."

"High risk, high reward," Ziggy agreed.

"It was probably easier to get points initially," Floyd said. "But now the pedophiles still alive are the ones who can consistently outrun or outsmart the killers. That's why Meihua's plan is so ingenious," he added, smiling at the sight of her on the monitor as if she were a movie star. "There's a good chance a lot of teams have given up on the Stampedo. That lowers our risk significantly."

"Floyd's right," Pepper said, looking at her tablet's Super Serial live coverage. "They're not even covering the Stampedo right now. Most of the attention is on the Despair Fair. Team QuirkWork is playing Whack-a-Molester, and the commentators love it."

"We'll get ahead of the stampede and fire back into the herd when they least expect it," Ziggy said.

"How many shots can we take before we become the hunted instead of the hunters?" the Samurai asked.

"That's impossible to predict," Floyd said. "There are too many variables."

"We need to find the entrance and exit with the fewest obstacles in between," Ziggy said, and Pepper and Floyd got to work. "We get in, launch the cannon into the stampede as many times as we can, then break for the nearest exit."

"What about the babies?" Benedict asked. "It may be difficult to get them all through the entrance before it shuts again, wouldn't it?"

The telltale throb of a monster headache niggled at the backs of Ziggy's eyes as he tried to think through the plan from start to finish. "You're right," he told Benedict. "We can't take the dogs into the Stampedo. They'll bolt at the sound of the cannon."

"We get to stay here?" Benedict squeaked with relief.

"We need you posted near the exit. We'll find a place for you to hide," Ziggy said. "You and the dogs will add a layer of protection from killers trying to get in while we're trying to get out."

Benedict sucked in a tortured breath at the idea. "By myself?" he whimpered, his mud-crusted eyes welling with tears.

"Not by yourself," Pepper said. "You'll have the babies with you to keep you safe."

"True." Benedict sniffed, and Ziggy shot Pepper a grateful thumbs up.

The killers set to work assembling the makeshift cannon. The Samurai managed to puncture a tiny hole in the side of the smokestack using the spear, but his palms formed blisters from the effort. Meihua, her hands and arms protected by plastic wrap and corgi sweaters, explained the firing procedure while meticulously coating each head with the poison before carefully wrapping them in Benedict's dogs' sweaters. Benedict kept watch as the rest of the team practiced the motions of loading and firing the cannon.

Big Montana Ice would hold the pipe aloft while Carol, the smallest of the team, tucked into the mouth of the cannon with the can of hairspray. "Spray long enough to saturate the base," Floyd relayed for Meihua, who was holding the lighter. "One you've sprayed, get out of the way as quickly as possible and tuck one of the dog sweaters midway into the pipe. The Samurai will immediately load a head into the hole, and after Big Montana Ice has the cannon on her shoulder, Meihua will place the lighter near the pinhole and fire it."

Meihua snapped to catch Floyd's attention again, and he translated, "Meihua says to grip the pipe tightly because the poison is also an accelerant."

Ziggy timed their efforts while the team did a few dry runs. "The longest it's taken was twenty-four seconds," he said. "The fastest you've done it is sixteen seconds."

"Bùyào pèng dú tóu," Meihua looked at each of the killers. "No touch or death." She made a choking sound and crossed her eyes.

"Don't touch the heads directly," Floyd reiterated the warning for the group. "Meihua says once they're done curing, contact with the poison will kill you. Wrap your hands and arms in plastic wrap before leaving."

"I found a spot for Benedict to hide with the corgis," Pepper told Ziggy and Floyd, marking the area so they could find it on their maps. "It's near the second entrance behind the No Inhibition Exhibition." She zoomed in on the monitor to reveal a giant statue of a golden Mongaphalee peanut. "All the dogs should be able to hide behind it."

"That means we need to go in through the east entrance," Ziggy said. "There aren't as many obstacles between there and the start of the Stampede, anyway."

Suddenly, the ringmaster's voice boomed through the air. Pepper groaned. "Attention, Super Serial contestants!" the ringmaster announced. "It's our pleasure to inform you that District Sale-SailCharter has qualified for the Super Serial Championships!"

"Four spots left," Pepper said quietly, and Floyd, once again, muted the control room.

"Think about it, Pep," he said, turning in his chair to pat her shoulder. "This plan will either get us enough points to qualify for the Championships or create such a huge sensation that the killers' resale values will skyrocket. The fans are going to love this!"

Pepper nodded slowly, placing her hand on top of Floyd's. "The audience is probably hyped to see the cannon go off."

"That's the spirit!" Floyd said, beaming as he turned back to his monitor.

"It's time to go," Ziggy told the killers, unmuting the room. The cannon was ready, a gross amalgamation of steel, poison, and death. They gathered around it, looking at one another with grim determination.

"We've come too far to fail now," the Samurai said with steely resolve. He held up a thick pair of tongs he'd found next to the funnel cake stand. "If we work together, we can do this." He handed the tongs to Meihua.

Meihua was focused, her hands steady as she loaded the heads into the lumpy bag Carol had made with the dog sweaters. The Samurai hefted the bag over his shoulder, and Meihua climbed back into the sling on Big Montana Ice's back. Since they needed their hands free to load the cannon, they reluctantly left the spear and Meihua's shield behind. Big Montana Ice point blank refused to sacrifice the flail, and she tucked it into the side straps of Meihua's carrier. Carol made them all pray together before she and Benedict picked up the pipe, and the team left the temporary safety of Funnel Fakes.

"Go northeast," Ziggy said. "There's a thicket of bushes outside the Rapist-no-Escapist arena near the Stampedo entrance. We'll hide behind it and wait for a good opportunity."

Outside, the cityscape buzzed with activity. Lilting carnival music floated through the air, punctuated by the tortured screams of criminals and killers in the Despair Fair. Mini battles raged in the open spaces and Ziggy saw more than one team slinking in the shadows, headed for different events. He was grateful for the noise, knowing it masked some of their movements as they crept through the dark. He knew it was impossible for them not to draw attention to themselves because of the corgis. They followed Benedict obediently, but ninety-four stubby legs and a doggy-sized wheelchair were hard to miss.

There was a moment of panic when a frantic killer, covered in bruises and bloody scratches, darted past, but luckily he was much more focused on the murderous kangaroo hot on his tail. As they sprinted to the thicket, they passed a duo of killers. The pair hesitated for a moment, but after seeing Benedict's blood-covered dogs, they must have decided an attack wasn't worth it, because they veered in the opposite direction.

The Samurai led the charge to their hiding spot, pausing behind various structures and attractions to make certain they weren't being followed or walking into an ambush. Long minutes later, after hiding from a grizzled killer with a wolf-dog and sprinting away from a woman swinging a mace, the team made it to their destination, sweaty, but unharmed.

Ziggy did his best to make sense of the horrible sounds from the Stampedo as he monitored the entrance. A loud buzzer pierced the air, signaling the start of the stampede, and he counted the seconds until the first entrance slid open. "About one minute," he said.

"There's another team headed through," Floyd said.

Sure enough, a group of four killers sprinted toward the entrance. One lanky man brandished a chainsaw, while the woman beside him carried a hatchet, and their two other teammates gripped serrated knives, the bloody blades shining in the carnival lights.

"Excellent timing," Floyd said, watching them slip through the sliding doors. "Now we can see how long it takes for the stampede to go by."

"Thirty seconds," Ziggy reported a few moments later as the front of the stampede passed by the now-closed entrance.

Hundreds of pedophiles raced by. It was one of the most bizarre things Ziggy had ever seen. Sweaty, exhausted bodies inked in whimsical animal patterns moved together in a chaotic crush of limbs and panic. Their faces blurred into one another as they tramped forward on the track. Pedophiles were universally condemned, even by serial killers. Their blatant humiliation pricked at Ziggy's sense of humanity; he couldn't deny they deserved it. It was both revolting and reluctantly gratifying to watch the stampede go by.

"Let's see," Floyd said, his eyebrows furrowed. "If the estimated distance between the start of the Stampedo and the first entrance is about three hundred yards, and the average human can run seven miles per hour, which is roughly two hundred and five yards per minute, it should take the stampede approximately one minute and forty-six seconds to pass the first entrance after the buzzer sounds. So, if the killers are allowed to enter the track thirty seconds ahead of the stampede, for DipShip to have enough time to load the cannon and fire it at the pedos, they would need to gain at least twenty yards, meaning they would need to increase their speed to seven point five miles per hour for the plan to work. Barring any obstacles, of course."

"Did anyone catch that?" Big Montana Ice whispered after a long moment. "Because I have no idea what the fuckity fuck he just said."

Floyd opened his mouth to clarify, but Ziggy stepped in. "He said you need to run faster than the stampede so you'll have enough time to load the cannon."

"I'm pretty sure that's not what he said." Big Montana Ice muttered, cracking her knuckles, and Pepper snickered at the frustrated look on Floyd's face.

"Not everyone speaks Floyd McNut," she said with a smile.

Suddenly, the ringmaster's voice echoed like a badly timed nightmare. "Attention, Super Serial contestants!" the ringmaster said with enthusiasm. "It's our pleasure to inform you that District Gene-O Dynamics and District WriteRightEd have both qualified for the Super Serial Championships!"

"Two spots left," Pepper whispered, her cheeks drooping with fatigue.

The news went off like a bomb, and desperation blanketed the cityscape like a vengeful cloud. The sound of violence and recklessness in the cityscape seemed almost audible to him. "We're running out of time," Ziggy said. "There's the buzzer for the stampede. We need to make a move."

Floyd started the timer on his phone. "I don't see any other teams coming, but in one minute and sixteen seconds, we've got to be at the entrance, ready to go."

"Pepper," Ziggy said. "Stick with Benedict. Do whatever it takes to get him to the golden peanut safely. Send him around the west side of the Rapist-No-Escapist. Otherwise, you'll run into the electric fence."

"Okay, Benedict," Pepper said. "Are you ready to go?"

"Carol, quickly!" Benedict cried, holding out his hand. "Give me the bravery oil." Carol swiftly rifled through her fanny pack before handing it over, and Benedict popped the cap, pulled out the stopper, and downed the entire contents in one swallow.

"Oh Benny," Carol said with a frown when he handed her the empty bottle. "That's going to make your tummy feel crummy."

Xióngxīn bàodǎn, Meihua whispered.

"That's one minute," Floyd announced, and team DipShip, minus Benedict, bolted for the doors, reaching them only seconds before they slid open. As they stepped onto the track, Ziggy's event monitor lit up, and the scene was so horrific his brain could barely process what he was seeing. Severed limbs and cattle-painted bodies were scattered across the ground, blood spatter staining the green rubber of the track. Screams rent the air, and Ziggy could hear the stampede at their heels as the team took off running. He scrolled ahead on the track.

"There's an obstacle just ahead," he warned, his heart in his throat. "It looks like a block of hurdles."

"Good thing I ran hurdles in high school," Carol said, breathing hard.

"Hang on tight, Granny!" Big Montana Ice bellowed, one beefy arm wrapped around the smokestack. Ziggy clenched his teeth and prayed they wouldn't lose any of their poisoned heads as he watched the Samurai gripping the dog-sweater bag with both hands, soaring over the hurdles. Big Montana Ice didn't jump the hurdles, but stepped over the top of them, and Meihua held onto her shoulders as she barreled forward. Carol showed surprising agility as she jumped but tripped over a headless body at the last hurdle and crashed to the ground, skinning her face and hands against the track.

"Get up!" Floyd cried. "The stampede is gaining on you. You'll be trampled!"

The Samurai yanked Carol to her feet, then snaked his plastic-wrap-covered arm around her waist to support her as they ran. Floyd frantically monitored the distance between the team and the Stampede, doing math in his head that Ziggy couldn't fathom.

"Faster!" Floyd's panic was obvious as he nervously flicked his fingers against his controls.

"Oh, shit! There's a wall coming up," Ziggy said, zooming in so fast his fingers squeaked on the controls. "It's about ten feet tall. There are ropes to climb it, but the team of killers that went in ahead of us is waiting on the other side!"

Floyd sucked in a fast breath before yelling, "Stop in front of the wall. Then load that cannon as quickly as you can!" His face paled as he watched the army of pedophiles blast over the hurdles. "I think I cut it too close," he told Ziggy, his voice hitching in fear. "They have less than seventeen seconds to fire the cannon, and they only loaded it that fast once."

The killers skittered to a stop in front of the wall, the stampede approaching so fast from behind them Ziggy could see their body-cams vibrating.

Big Montana Ice tipped the pipe so Carol could reach inside with the hairspray. Ziggy heard the hiss of the aerosol can over the screams and cries of terrified pedos, and moments later, Carol slid out of the mouth of the pipe, swiftly pushing one of the dog sweaters in after her. The Samurai, using the tongs, carefully loaded a severed head into the cannon.

Big Montana Ice hoisted the pipe onto her shoulder. "Fuck it up, Granny," she grunted, and Meihua smiled as the lighter flickered to life. She'd barely touched the flame to the pinhole when the cannon erupted, the resounding boom so loud Ziggy's ears rang just from hearing it through their mics.

The poisoned head flew from the cannon with devastating force, hurtling into the pedophiles like a bowling ball into pins. Ziggy hadn't even blinked before it hammered into the herd like a battering ram, exploding on contact, raining poisonous, gray-matter-soaked bone shrapnel through the crowd. Big Montana Ice nearly squashed Meihua as she hit the wall on the recoil but righted herself before lowering the cannon to the ground so they could load it again.

Pandemonium was unleashed as poison-coated body chunks collided with a terrifying hiss, as a noxious cloud erupted, choking the herd. With nowhere to run or hide, the pedophiles bolted erratically across the track, some making a desperate attempt to surge ahead while others made a frantic effort to retreat. Bodies dropped like flies, collapsing in violent tremors, pink foam spilling from their mouths, noses, and ears. The killers waiting on the opposite side of the wall fled in fear, sprinting down the track toward the exit.

Ziggy didn't waste a second. "Fire again!" he bellowed, surging to his feet. The team burst into action, re-loading the cannon. This time, Ziggy was prepared for the boom, and the next head slammed into the track at the front of the stampede, bouncing over the sea of bodies before splattering into pieces.

The depraved pedos grabbed their throats as foam curdled from their mouths. A man fell into violent tremors, tripping and pulling others down with him. A woman cried tears of blood. When the third head barreled into the Stampedo, Ziggy glanced at the kill-score, rising so rapidly it made his head spin. He didn't know if he could fully grasp the magnitude of death at this level.

"That's enough. Get to the exit!" Floyd commanded, and Ziggy realized that even though pedos were dying in droves, the bulk of the stampede was still too great and would overwhelm and crush them if they didn't move.

"Get over the wall!" the Samurai yelled to the team, and he slung the sweater bag of heads over his shoulder before climbing to the top with astounding speed. He slowly stood, balancing on the precipice of the wall.

Carol grabbed the rope but cried out, jerking her hands away. They were covered in scrapes from falling at the hurdles, and she couldn't grip the rough manila.

Big Montana Ice shot-putted the cannon pipe over the wall. "I got you, Lil Biscuit!" she bellowed, grabbing Carol and plastering her to her chest. "You better hold on tight, Spider Monkey," she said with a grin, and Carol let out a broken sob before clinging to Big Montana Ice's middle. Big Montana Ice grunted as she hauled both Carol and Meihua up and over the wall, landing with a heavy thud on the heap of bodies beneath it.

"Āiyo! Jìdé wǒ yǐjīng lǎole!" Meihua shouted as she jounced in her carrier, and Big Montana Ice set Carol back on the ground. The Samurai's eyes narrowed as the pedos approached. He bent his knees slightly, twirling the sweater bag above his head.

"What are you doing?" Floyd cried. "They're coming!"

"The exit door will close if we don't outpace the herd by thirty seconds," the Samurai said, his wrists twisting as he spun the bag so fast it looked like a helicopter blade. With a grunt, he let go of one end of the fabric, slingshotting the remaining poisoned heads into the herd. The heads exploded like a shotgun blast, bursting and breaking, spraying sinew and bone in every direction. A shockwave of death jolted through the stampede and the front lines crumbled.

The Samurai jumped to the ground. "That should gift us additional time. Let's go."

"Leave the cannon," Ziggy ordered. "The heads are gone. Run!"

"Alaskan Thunder's 'bout to haul some fucking ass!" Big Montana Ice roared as she raced forward, and team DipShip flew down the track, gliding over fallen corpses and dodging jellied blood puddles as they tore toward the exit.

Benedict's dog whistle rang in Ziggy's ears as Pepper's voice drifted into focus. "Duck down and keep the corgis close," she instructed, and Ziggy was relieved to see that Benedict had arrived at the golden peanut statue in one piece.

Pepper zoomed in to study the area surrounding the statue. "What *is* that?" she murmured, toggling to night mode. She gasped. "You're being attacked!"

"What?" Benedict cried when a feather-cloaked killer with a pair of aggressive ostriches emerged from the shadows. The ostriches hissed as they charged toward him, their thick-beaked mouths open wide, ready to bite. Immobilized with fear, Benedict screamed as his corgis lunged toward the massive birds.

"The killer has a leash pole!" Pepper yelled. "Get out of there and let the dogs take care of it! Move!"

The corgis moved like a cohesive unit, barking fiercely and dodging around their muscled legs to deliver swift bites. The ostriches recoiled from the onslaught, their hisses turning to startled squawks as the dogs darted and dodged with coordinated precision, herding them away from their cowardly master—who still hadn't moved. He made a pathetic attempt to call them back, but his whistle only sputtered as snot ran from his nose.

Taking advantage of the distraction caused by his ostriches, the feather-cloaked killer closed in on Benedict, his movements fluid and predatory as he circled his prey.

"Your little puppies will be fun to kill one-by-one, after I'm through popping your eyes from your skull," the feathered killer said in a lush accent.

"No! No! No!" Benedict moaned, slinking against the peanut statue. The ostrich killer looped the leash pole over Benedict's neck and cinched it tight. His whistle fell from his bulging lips.

"Fight back!" Ziggy shouted at him, but to no avail. Time slowed as Ziggy turned back to the Stampedo. Everything was down to the wire, and his eyes darted back and forth between the sprinting killers and Benedict's fading life.

"The door is closing!" Floyd yelled to the killers in the Stampedo. They were feet from the exit. "Hurry! Hurry!" He held his breath.

DipShip burst through the opening, so close to missing the exit that the door pinched the fabric at the back of the Samurai's decorative chest plate. He tore it free as Carol hunched over, her hands on her knees as she gulped in huge lungfuls of air. Sweat poured down Big Montana Ice's face, and she squinted when it dripped into her eyes.

"Get to Benedict!" Pepper screamed as the ostrich killer yanked Benedict to the ground.

The Samurai got there first and drop-kicked the killer to the ground in one smooth motion. Before the man could even draw breath, the Samurai seized a slender branch from the ground, bounded to his feet, and mercilessly drove it into his left eye. The ostrich man howled and dropped the leash pole, but the Samurai was already on him, delivering a rapid punch combo to his brainstem. The bird man collapsed. Death in an instant.

Big Montana Ice loosened the leash around Benedict's neck and he sputtered and coughed as he sucked in oxygen. "I'm getting sick and tired of this," she said, glaring down at him. "I turn my back for one minute, and you're getting choked again. And not in a sexy way."

"Benny!" Carol cried, dropping to her knees to embrace him.

Benedict gasped. "My babies!" His hand shook as he put the end of the whistle into his mouth, finally able to blow it again.

There was a terrifying moment where Ziggy worried they'd lost all the dogs, but a minute later, they heard the first yip, and the dogs came running back to Benedict's side, licking their feather coated maws. There was a disgusting reunion of panting and slurps before Big Montana spoke.

"Well?" she rasped, still out of breath. "What's the damage? How many of those fuckers did we take out?"

As the adrenaline rush subsided, Ziggy realized he'd forgotten to check their kill-score. "It's 1667," he said, blinking as his mind tried to catch up to reality.

"That's 108 pedophiles!" Floyd let out a startled laugh. He whipped out his phone, rapidly scrolling through fan forums and live streams. "Can you believe it? DipShip is absolutely everywhere. We even have our own trending hashtag. It's '#theheadc annonisheadcanon.'" He looked confused for a moment before breaking into a massive shit-eating grin. "Oh, that's clever. I get it now."

"We're nearly there," Ziggy told Pepper, but as hope gleamed in her eyes, dread consumed his heart. *The chances are still too l ow.* He reminded himself that this was the best-case scenario. A colossal spectacle, but without a win.

Suddenly, a burst of fire lit up the darkness, billowing smoke through the air. A figure stepped through the haze, and Ziggy froze, hot panic blazing through every pore on his body.

"You've gotta be fucking kidding me," UltraChad said when he spotted team DipShip huddled behind the statue. He laughed, and the sound was so chilling Pepper burst into tears.

Chapter 21

Girl on Fryer

Kill-Score: 1667

The rest of the Taste-E Chicken killers emerged from the smoke and shadows, flanking UltraChad on both sides. "This is bad," Floyd said.

"That him?" A shirtless man with a torn kilt and a grizzled beard pointed at Benedict, who was shaking so violently he looked like he was having a seizure. "The pure wee wimp that gave ye the slip?" He flexed his muscles, accentuating his rough tattoos.

"That's him," UltraChad confirmed, squeezing the trigger on his flamethrower. The fiery blast illuminated his overfilled, too-tight skin, giving him the bizarre appearance of a man wearing a mask of his own face.

"UltraChad is their Vigilante, but I only recognize two of the others," Ziggy told Floyd, frantically trying to recall killer profiles.

"The big guy in the chef's coat is Gogi-Gui, the Cannibal—their Centennial," Floyd said. The chef grinned and Ziggy noticed his teeth were stained red and filed to points. "The one with the bald head and beard is Bear Knuckle, their Leo—a former streetfighter."

"I hate that douche nozzle," muttered Big Montana Ice, glaring at UltraChad. She reached out her thick hand, and Meihua wordlessly handed her the flail. "Knew he was the demon the first time I laid eyes on him."

"Keep your composure and listen," Ziggy said. "All the other paths of retreat are blocked except the one that leads to the Ferris wheel. As soon as you get an opening, run in that direction."

The Samurai, partially hidden by the peanut statue, crouched down, assuming a battle-ready position—his eyes never leaving the Taste-E Chicken team.

"You thought you could hide from me, didn't you?" UltraChad taunted Benedict, flexing his boxy muscles. "Miserable fucking uggo. Blackpill coward. I told you to lay down and rot. They should have let me kill you the first time. Would've done the world a favor."

"Don't listen to him, Benny! You're a good man!" Carol protested courageously, but Benedict's bladder betrayed him, and he soaked his pants.

UltraChad's piercing gaze roamed salaciously over Carol's entire figure, his upper lip curling into a snarl as he assessed her. "When I get my hands on you, the first thing I'm gonna do is rip out your heart because it's pumping inside you, and I'm not."

Ziggy had seen Carol scandalized by Big Montana Ice more times than he could count, but he'd never seen her more furious than she was at that moment. Her face flushed an unholy shade of red, and the corgis, gathered at Benedict's feet, snarled at UltraChad, the fur on the back of their necks standing straight up as if they'd understood the insult.

The Samurai moved quietly to Benedict's side. "On my signal," he murmured, "you and Carol make a run for it."

UltraChad moved forward, holding the flamethrower in front of him, ready. "You were too weak to kill yourself when you had the chance," he said, his stretched-out lips wobbling like two plump leeches. "So I'll do it for you. Swallow the Blackpill, Benedict."

"Go!" the Samurai shouted as UltraChad surged forward, his flamethrower spitting out a stream of fire. Benedict grabbed Carol's hand and fled, screaming at his corgis to follow him as the flamethrower whipped through the air.

In a sudden move, the Samurai leaped, launching himself off the statue's base as he turned in the air, twisting above the flames. With a powerful kick, his foot slammed into the side of UltraChad's face, splitting his overstuffed skin and sending him crashing to the ground.

"That was a perfect tornado kick!" Floyd exclaimed in awe, and the Samurai rolled as he landed, swiftly regaining his footing. Bear Knuckle charged into the fray. Fists flying, Bear Knuckle landed a furious blow to the Samurai's head, causing him to stumble and drop to his knees. Bear Knuckle pulled back his elbow to strike again, but bellowed when Big Montana Ice sunk the flail into his back with a heavy thud.

"Stop them!" UltraChad's roar rang out through the chaos as he grappled to his feet, the weight of the flamethrower tank throwing him off balance. Two Taste-E Chicken killers bolted after Benedict and Carol, who raced toward the Ferris wheel.

"I need to know who those two killers are!" Pepper sprang into action, swapping to the aerial view on night mode, her cheeks still wet with tears. "Who's after them?"

"The woman with the long whip-braid goes by Horse Whisperer. She's their Angry White Women killer," Floyd said, his foot tapping against the ground in a panicked staccato. "The man in the white suit is the Beekeeper."

"Behind you!" Ziggy shouted as Big Montana Ice wrenched the flail free from Bear Knuckle's back and the Samurai struggled to his feet. The Cannibal barreled his thick shoulder into Big Montana Ice's side, the flail flying from her grip as she hit the ground hard, Meihua pinned beneath her.

"No!" Floyd choked when Meihua let out a strangled cry of pain, and the Samurai bolted for the flail, grabbing it just in time. The Cannibal jumped back, forced to retreat as the Samurai whirled the flail through the air.

"Run!" the Samurai bellowed, but it was too late. Big Montana Ice barely had time to cover her face with her hands before UltraChad hit her with the flamethrower.

Ziggy cried out in shock as searing hot flames billowed over her and Meihua for agonizing seconds. The Samurai whipped the flail at UltraChad, the weapon spinning through the air, embedding itself in his chest.

He crumpled to the ground, the flamethrower extinguishing as he fell. The Samurai wasted no time rushing to Big Montana Ice's side. "Roll!" he commanded, and when Big Montana Ice turned on her side, the Samurai yanked Meihua from the carrier, tearing off the layers of fabric still on fire, and smothering the flames in her hair.

"Fuck!" UltraChad screamed, spitting out a fine mist of blood, and the Cannibal rushed to his aid. Bear Knuckle groaned, blood dripping down his back, while Big Montana Ice writhed on the ground, attempting to put out the flames.

"Climb on," the Samurai said, bending down for Meihua, and she clung to his back like a baby orangutan. The Samurai turned to Big Montana Ice, frantically dousing the last of the flames. "We must leave," he barked, pulling her to her feet before she even had a chance to blink.

Pepper gasped. Big Montana Ice was covered in blistering burns. Her hands and arms, which took the most damage, were charred and peeling, and most of the hair on the top of her head had been seared away. Her legs and chest were mostly spared because of her denim and leather, but one side of her face looked like raw hamburger. Ziggy could hear it sizzling through her mic.

"Something around here stinks," she said, making a face, "Like burnt assholes." Pepper choked out something between a hysterical laugh and a sob.

"Horse Whisperer and the Beekeeper are gaining on Benedict and Carol," Floyd cut in. "They're almost to the wheel."

"We're on our way," the Samurai said, hiking Meihua up higher on his back before breaking into a run. Big Montana Ice winced but started a slow jog behind the Samurai.

"Ready the dogs," Ziggy told Benedict, whose hands trembled so violently he could barely hold his whistle.

"Hurry!" Carol cried, glancing over her shoulder before picking up speed.

"How does Horse Whisperer keep her braid so long?" Pepper asked, zooming in on the frantic chase.

"It's extended with hair from her dead horse's mane," Floyd explained matter-of-factly. "Her land was invaded by a band of men who slaughtered all her horses after she refused to marry their leader. Well, all her horses but one. She exacted revenge by riding in and killing them all."

"Is she dangerous?" Ziggy asked, watching Carol pick up speed..

"Well, yeah," Floyd said, looking at him like he was from another planet. "She's a serial killer, Ziggy."

"Jesus, Floyd, I meant, what threat does she pose if she catches up to Carol and Benedict?" Ziggy repressed the urge to smack Floyd upside the head.

"Aside from being skilled in hand-to-hand combat, she's extremely volatile and hates men," Floyd explained. "Oh, and she sometimes sews knives into the end of her braid. It's about twelve-feet-long. The braid, not the blade."

"You probably should have led with that, Floyd."

"What about the Beekeeper?" Pepper asked.

"He's Taste-E Chicken's Pet Lover," Floyd said as the man turned from Carol and Benedict to face the swarming corgis. "That canister he's towing holds a colony of Africanized honey bees. He uses the spray gun attached to his belt to douse his victims with pheromones, which triggers an attack. My guess is that's how they plan to neutralize Benedict's dogs."

"My babies!" Benedict cried out in distress.

"African bees?" Big Montana Ice moaned like she was half-dead.

"Actually, they were bred in South America," Floyd said.

"That's weird," Big Montana mumbled, stumbling forward. Ziggy saw her biometrics rapidly dumping adrenaline.

"UltraChad is on the move," Floyd warned the team. "He's headed your way with Bear Knuckle and the Cannibal."

Amid the chaos, the ringmaster's voice resonated through the arena. "Attention, Super Serial competitors!" the ringmaster chimed, eerily pleasant. "It's our pleasure to inform you that District Wheely-Good Motors has just qualified for the Super Serial Championships! Only one spot in the Championship remains. Best of luck to all our remaining competitors."

Resolve flared in Pepper's eyes as she processed the announcement. "There's only one spot left," she said, "and we're 333 points from qualifying. We could face Taste-E Chicken and win so long as we don't lose any killers."

"What do you want to do?" Ziggy asked the question, even though he already had a good idea of the answer. Everything Pepper had done up to this point was to save DipShip. No hastily written contract on a scrap of paper would change that. They'd fought a good fight, but everyone knew their killers were exhausted and outmatched.

"I want to save the lives of our killers," Pepper said, swallowing hard, "and make it to the end without losing anyone. We already got what we came here for. DipShip's a sensation. Everyone loves the killers. I could sell them tomorrow for a fortune."

"Without question," Floyd said.

Pepper chuckled, adding, "And at this point, I probably won't need to. We're famous enough to make all sorts of brand deals. We can keep them at DipShip if they want to stay. I know they're serial killers, but…"

"But they're *our* serial killers," Ziggy suggested.

"Exactly."

"You'd be giving up your shot at CEO," Ziggy reminded her, but she shook her head and his heart rate leveled. It was a decision that happened to save his life, but that didn't mean it wasn't the right call.

"Floyd said there was less than a point zero one chance that could happen. If we fight to win now, we could walk away with nothing. Who cares about the title? We need to do what's best for the district."

"Ziggy and I are with you no matter what," Floyd said. "But for the record, I think this is the right choice."

"They're almost here!" Carol's shriek interrupted as the lights of the Ferris wheel illuminated her face. "I think I can see them. What do we do?"

"Get behind Benedict," Ziggy ordered, snapping back into the games. "It'll be hard for them to see you in the dark. Wait until they're close enough, then send in the dogs. Hold them off as long as you can. Help is on the way."

Pepper's phone rang suddenly, startling her with its loud, campy ring. Ziggy knew without asking that it was Alexia. "Don't answer," he barked, but Pepper hesitated.

"What if she knows something? Maybe she can see what's happening from her gondola."

"It's dark out there," Ziggy said. "What could she possibly see that we can't?"

"Well, actually," Floyd said, "there have been significant advancements in night vision technology over the past decade. During the—"

"Hello, Ms. Ito." Pepper's voice interrupted as she answered, her expression transforming from anxious to aghast as she listened to the call. "What do you mean?"

Ziggy watched the Beekeeper, who'd paused on the pathway to uncap his canister. "I think he's planning to mark the dogs," he said, trying, and failing, to tune out Pepper's conversation.

"Marshal Ghostshade?" she continued into the phone. "He's busy at the moment. Taste-E Chicken is about to launch an attack."

"Stay at least ten feet away from Horse Whisperer at all times," Ziggy ordered Benedict and Carol, feeling a pang of guilt for what he was about to say next. "Leave the dogs if you have to flee. If it's your lives or theirs, leave them behind."

"No!" Benedict sobbed as Horse Whisperer and the Beekeeper closed the gap.

Pepper set the phone on the desk in front of Ziggy. "She wants to be on speakerphone," Pepper said, and Ziggy scowled.

"We don't have time for this!"

"Marshal Ghostshade!" Alexia's voice intruded into the control room like the irritating squawk of a magpie. "District Taste-E Chicken only needs fifty more points to qualify for the Championships. DipShip is the next closest district in terms of points, and none of the other teams are even close. It's us or them, and I want it to be us."

"Taste-E Chicken could get fifty points scratching their asses," Ziggy said. "Let it go."

"But we're so close!" Alexia said with an annoying pout in her voice. "Imagine if DipShip won. All those people who laughed at me for buying it would have to eat their words."

Benedict blew his whistle, and the corgis attacked as the Bee-keeper unleashed a torrent of pheromones, misting over their fur. "I can hear the bees coming already!" Carol cried as Horse Whisperer whipped her hair, striking one of Benedict's dogs in the side with the blade at the end. It yelped, tearing away into the night.

"Alexia, DipShip's in an excellent position," Pepper said. "We've outperformed expectations, but we're just too far behind Taste-E Chicken to catch up. Let's focus on keeping our killers alive."

"Winning will keep them alive!" Alexia griped. "If you don't take a chance, you're not cut out to be a CEO, Pepper."

Pepper's nostrils flared. "People are depending on us. It's not worth risking losing DipShip on a Hail Mary."

"Fuck DipShip!" Alexia snapped. "Who gives a shit about some Podunk shipping corporation? It was a means to an end, and that end is me getting a seat on the ABCD."

A spark ignited in Pepper's brown eyes. "We're talking about thousands of jobs, lives. Lives of people you should care about."

"Well, I don't. Besides, I'm in charge here, Pepper, not you. Don't forget I sign your paychecks. If I tell you I want to win, you win!"

Ziggy had heard enough. "What do you want to do, Pepper?"

"Where are you guys?" Carol screamed, and the Samurai grunted as he picked up speed. Ziggy noticed the tension in his jaw and wondered how much of Alexia's tirade he'd heard. Pepper's speakerphone was clear enough.

"Pepper?" Ziggy prompted again.

"Why are you asking Pepper? She's a secretary!" Alexia was losing her temper. "You work for me, Marshal Ghostshade. If I tell you to—"

Pepper disconnected the call, staring in dazed disbelief at the phone in her hand. It instantly began ringing again, but Pepper powered it off.

"Executive administrator," she said, straightening her spine before returning to her seat. "Let's get our killers out of there."

Chapter 22

The Dinner Takes it All

Kill-Score: 1667

Ziggy switched to the aerial view to search for the team in the growing light of the artificial dawn. "They're close," he told Pepper. "We need to use the dogs to scatter Taste-E Chicken so we can regroup and flee."

"Circle the outskirts of the Despair Fair to avoid the dogs," Pepper said to Carol and Benedict. "We can't risk any of you getting stung, and they're covered in pheromones."

"Why are some of the corgis covered in more bees?" Ziggy asked Floyd, who was surveying the frantic scene with grim focus. Corgis rolled and darted erratically, desperate to escape the swarm.

"I'm not sure," he said. "The bees have been genetically modified to respond to the pheromones, but it's possible they were spread onto too many moving targets simultaneously, and the bees are confused."

"I'm not complaining," Ziggy muttered under his breath as more than a dozen corgis surrounded Horse Whisperer. She was a good fighter, and her hair whip sliced deep wounds in some of the dogs, but she was still overwhelmed by their sheer numbers and they'd worn her down. When she tried to swing her braid in a wide arc, a corgi latched onto her arm and she couldn't gain the momentum to use it properly.

"Help!" she cried to the Beekeeper, who was sheltered from the swarm in his bee-suit. He ran to her aid, but the closer he got, the more the bees he attracted, and Horse Whisperer was soon fighting off both dogs and bees. Ziggy knew it was over when two corgis latched onto her braid, and the pack pulled her to the ground. The noise from the swarm drowned out her desperate screams and the dump of bee venom into her system caused her throat to swell, cutting off her airway. The kill-score rose to 1732.

The dog pack dissolved into chaos. While some of the pack continued their relentless assault on Horse Whisperer, the remaining corgis either turned their attention to the Beekeeper or frantically ran in circles, trying to escape the swarm of insects. The Beekeeper cursed in frustration, swinging his container wildly as he tried to fend off the chasing canines.

Carol and Benedict huddled together at the bottom of the Ferris wheel, swatting away stray bees with desperate swipes. They both shouted in relief when they saw their reinforcements arrive. But their cries of relief turned into horrified gasps as they took in the sight of Big Montana Ice, her skin a ruin of burns.

"When things settle down, I'll give you an oil for that," Carol said weakly as the Samurai set Meihua down, gently guiding her to Carol's arms.

"Meihua is also hurt, but I can't understand what she says."

"*Nǐ shòushāngle ma?*" Floyd immediately asked, and Meihua replied, but her voice was scarcely more than a whisper. "*Wǒ de shǒubì duànle.*"

"She's hurt," Floyd said, shifting his focus to Meihua as if she were his own grandmother. "She thinks her arm is broken."

"Most of the Taste-E Chicken killers are distracted," Ziggy interjected, feeling his panic rise. "Keep running. Head toward Con-Cessions."

"Get out of there while you have the chance," Pepper cried, but it was too late.

"You putrid, little fucks!" UltraChad bellowed as he came upon the scene, followed by Bear Knuckle and the Cannibal, both breathing hard. Bees were everywhere, and dogs covered in bees were everywhere, yelping and nipping at their skin, trying to escape the stings. A pack of six uninjured corgis formed a circle around the Beekeeper, snarling as they readied for attack.

"Kill the dogs!" the Beekeeper screamed to UltraChad as he desperately kicked and stumbled away from the deadly ring of encroaching, furry death. UltraChad ignited his flamethrower.

"No!" The roar of the flames drowned out Benedict's anguished plea, and the Beekeeper dropped to the ground for cover. "Come, babies!" Benedict blew his whistle in panic, and although some of the dogs obeyed, two hesitated, and UltraChad roasted them alive, laughing at Benedict's devastated sobs.

"We'll never outrun UltraChad," Ziggy said. "He won't stop until Benedict's dead."

UltraChad's entire chest was covered in thick, sticky blood from the flail, and half his face appeared to be leaking off his skull above his bruised and swelling jaw-strap chin. He looked like a wax figure melting in the firelight. They needed to get the team out of there, but UltraChad's obsession with killing Benedict was making it impossible to gain ground. It was only a matter of time before one of them was killed.

Big Montana Ice's snarl reverberated through the control room when she saw Bear Knuckle. He lunged toward the DipShip team. "Back fer mair, are ye?" he taunted.

"I'll always be back for more, Bazgoroch," Big Montana Ice replied, running forward to meet him in battle. "Alaskan Thunder!" Ziggy watched the giants collide and knew Big Montana Ice had to be running on pure endorphins because her adrenaline was maxed.

UltraChad unleashed a torrent of flames upon a bee-covered corgi as it darted by. "Swallow the Blackpill, Benedict!" he yelled over the crackling of the fire. Smoke from the weapon and the burning bodies billowed through the air, and after a moment, Ziggy noticed the hum of the bees dissipating. The Beekeeper noticed it too.

"They're fleeing from the smoke, you idiot!" he screamed at UltraChad, who didn't even glance in his direction. His intense gaze remained locked on Benedict, who was hysterically crying on the ground, his head buried between his knees.

"Samurai," Ziggy said. "Keep UltraChad and the Beekeeper together. The bees hate the flamethrower smoke."

"Good thinking," Floyd agreed. "We can't manage both a flamethrower and a swarm."

"Pakpao, Cora, Ezra, Filipe... Sharee and Flaviana are gone!" Benedict wailed, his voice raw with anguish. "Winifred! You're covered in stingers. My darling girl! There's Cohen and Aleera. Where's Christian? Has anyone seen Christian?" Benedict finally spotted him, munching through a flap of Horse Whisperer's cheek. "Christian, come back!"

UltraChad surged forward, his eyes bloodshot from the smoke, but the Samurai intercepted him, dodging the flames as he attempted to draw UltraChad away from Benedict.

"A fool may be known by three things," the Samurai said, swiftly crouching to avoid the fire. "Anger without cause." He rolled to one side before bounding back to his feet. "Speech without profit." Back arching, he leaped into the air, narrowly avoiding the flames. "And choice without consequence."

"Fuck off, you fugly Beta!" UltraChad roared in frustration. He blew an arch of fire, chasing the Samurai, but nearly collided with the Beekeeper.

"Benedict, help!" Carol screamed when the Cannibal lunged forward with a swiftness and speed Ziggy couldn't believe, considering his size. Carol pulled Meihua to the ground as he swung the stolen flail he must have gotten from UltraChad.

"Babies! Get him!" Benedict's command was swift. He blew his whistle, and the dogs abandoned the Beekeeper for the Cannibal, their instincts to protect their master finally overpowering the chaos of a feeding frenzy. The Cannibal danced away, whipping at the dogs.

Nearby, Big Montana Ice grappled with Bear Knuckle, her arms locked around his torso. "Fuck you to hell, Bazgoroch!" she bellowed, and Bear Knuckle grunted as he tried to pull away, landing a punch to the wounded side of her face, forcing her arms to slacken. She screamed in pain, surging forward, burying her head in his stomach, knocking them both to the ground.

Carol's concerned voice brought Ziggy's attention back to the unfolding drama. Carol was trying to hold back Meihua, but the old woman was swatting Carol away with her good arm. "She's saying something, but I don't understand," Carol said as Meihua shuffled closer to the fray.

"Wǒ huì shāle nàgè yǎngfēng rén," Meihua rasped, clutching her injured arm.

Floyd's expression darkened as he translated her words. "She says she's going to kill the Beekeeper."

Pepper recoiled in horror. "What? No! There are too many bees. She'll be stung to death. Carol, stop her!"

"She can't get stung to death," Floyd tried to reassure them. "She's immune to bee venom."

Ziggy wracked his brain for solutions as he scrolled through the cityscape, searching for the Beekeeper. After a moment, Ziggy spotted him slowly creeping his way through the clouds of bees. "He's headed toward the Cannibal with his pheromone gun."

"Maybe Meihua's right," Floyd fretted, watching the Samurai dodge the flamethrower, sweat pouring down his face. "If the Beekeeper and the Cannibal kill the corgis, then Benedict, Carol, and Meihua are toast. The dogs are their only defense."

"I don't like it either, but if someone killed the Beekeeper, it would be easier for them to escape," Pepper said, chewing on the inside of her cheek. "We could sic the dogs on UltraChad and make a run for it."

"Take her to the Beekeeper," Ziggy ordered Carol. "And fast." Carol's massive eyes widened with fear as she helped Meihua to her feet, hiking her onto her back. She carried Meihua with the strength of a mother lugging their noncompliant children to a fun event and stealthily headed for the outskirts of the bee swarm so Meihua could sneak up on the Beekeeper.

Ziggy turned back to the heart-pounding showdown between the Samurai and UltraChad, the dawn light over the Ferris wheel casting strange shadows on the ground. The Samurai moved with a fluidity that seemed to defy the laws of physics, weaving through the torrents of fire from the flamethrower. UltraChad, fueled by fury and arrogance, aimed haphazardly, sending bursts of flames through the air that licked at the Samurai's shadow but never managed to catch him.

"Let's hope this works," said Ziggy, affirming the plan. "The Samurai could probably kill UltraChad, but he can't reach him as long as he has the flamethrower, and Big Montana Ice is the only one who could hold off Bear Knuckle."

"If we free up the dogs, we might have a chance," Floyd said, his eyes sparkling with excitement. This was the crescendo he'd been waiting for.

"Answer the question!" Big Montana Ice's fierce yell jolted Ziggy as she charged at Bear Knuckle, her half-burned mullet streaming behind her like a battle banner. Bear Knuckle met her charge with a guttural roar, his kilt swirling around his legs, his fists like battering rams.

"Ye're aff yer heid, ye daft moonhowler!" Bear Knuckle's voice thundered, his head colliding with Big Montana Ice's nose in a bone-crushing headbutt. But Big Montana Ice gained the upper hand by grabbing a fistful of Bear Knuckle's beard and yanking it free. With a bellow of pain, Bear Knuckle stumbled backward, only to retaliate with a savage uppercut that landed on Big Montana Ice's jaw with staggering force.

Amid the chaos, Benedict's sobs pierced the air as his corgis encircled the Cannibal, who gnashed his bloody teeth at them, swinging wildly with the flail. The weapon had already bashed in the heads of several attacking dogs, their motionless bodies lying nearby, so close to the fallen Horse Whisperer's blonde braid they were nearly touching.

Ziggy watched as the Beekeeper crept up to the ferocious corgis, pheromone gun in hand. Pepper's cry broke in. "There's Meihua! I lost sight of her in the bees, but she's right behind him!"

Meihua moved behind the Beekeeper like an ancient specter, the furious swarm of bees swirling around her like a phantasmal mist. She walked slowly, step by step, inching her way toward the Beekeeper. Moment's later her approach caught his attention, and he jumped in surprise.

"I can't watch," Floyd said, turning away from the monitor for the first time since the Preliminaries started. But Meihua didn't pull out a weapon or a vial like Ziggy expected. Her lips moved, the words swallowed in the discordant hum of the bees. She wasn't even within arms reach of the Beekeeper when he staggered. Frantically, he clawed at his mesh hood, struggling for breath until he collapsed to the ground. Pink foam spewed from his mouth as he convulsed, his gurgling muffled behind his mask. The kill-score rose to 1780.

Meihua limped back to where Carol waited on the edge of the Ferris wheel battlefield. *"Wǒ lèile,"* she uttered before her eyes rolled back in her head. Carol caught her before she hit the ground.

"Benedict, get out of there!" Ziggy bellowed when he noticed the Cannibal had broken free from the dogs and was looming over their defenseless master, cradling the injured Amir in his protective embrace.

The Cannibal lifted the flail over his head and grinned. "I'll bet you taste better than a tit-latched baby," he sneered, but before the flail could crash down, he was engulfed in a billowing cloud of flames. The Cannibal's wretched shrieks filled the air as Ziggy toggled through camera angles until he found the Samurai's tenuous hold on UltraChad's flamethrower. He kept the nozzle pointed at the now roasted Cannibal while the two struggled for dominance as fire hissed through the air.

Benedict screamed, scrambling backward and grappling for his remaining dogs, the blaze so close his hair was singed. Some dogs followed his retreat, but most darted away, barking and howling with terror at the flame. Gogi-Gui's chef's hat billowed smoke like a steam locomotive as he violently hit the ground and the kill-score rose to 1840.

Pepper and Ziggy looked at each other. "Stay the course," Pepper said firmly, but Ziggy heard the hope come back to her voice. Floyd was bouncing out of his seat, jumping up and down. "I can't believe it! We're so close!"

A point zero one chance, Ziggy reminded himself, taking a ragged breath.

UltraChad's scream of frustration pulled Ziggy's attention back to the battle where the Samurai twisted under UltraChad's arm and jerked the hose connected to the flamethrower's tanks. UltraChad fell backward with a cry of surprise, the flamethrower slipping from his grasp.

"Get back here!" Big Montana Ice shouted.

Everyone watched as Bear Knuckle appeared through the smoke, coming to UltraChad's rescue and tackling the Samurai to the ground. UltraChad kicked and rocked like an upturned turtle as he struggled to stand under the weight of the fuel tanks, but he unhooked the fuel pack and wriggled free, giving up as soon as Big Montana Ice appeared.

Big Montana Ice's face was swollen and dripping with blood as she yelled, "I'm gonna donkey punch your taint!" And UltraChad made a break for it, bolting through the smoke and debris.

"He's leaving! This is our chance to run!" Pepper cried as he sprinted past the Ferris wheel. Big Montana Ice spat out blood and at least one tooth before she turned her fury on Bear Knuckle, pummeling kicks and stomps from her boots, allowing the Samurai to tear free from his grasp.

The Samurai whipped his head around as he surged to his feet, his eyes scanning the area for a quick escape. He suddenly froze—his gaze shifting to Gondola 155 as it gracefully sailed past the base of the Ferris wheel. Alexia was standing at the window with Hirofumi. Arms crossed over his chest, Hirofumi glared at the Samurai as they wafted past.

Ziggy's heart raced as he watched the Samurai pivot on his heel, sprinting back towards the fight between Big Montana Ice and Bear Knuckle. "Help her take him down," Ziggy urged. "Then get the rest of the team out of there!" But the Samurai ignored him and ran past the brawl, hefting the flamethrower over his shoulder in one smooth motion.

Ziggy's breath whooshed out of his lungs as relief flooded through him. It was a good plan. With the flamethrower in hand, the Samurai could kill Bear Knuckle and better protect the team in one blow.

"I don't know what to do!" Floyd's attention was drawn to a frantic Carol as she softly patted Meihua's cheeks. "She won't wake up!"

"*Nǐ néng tīng dào wǒ ma?*" Floyd asked her, his voice trembling with worry. "*Méihuā, nǐ hái hǎo ma?*"

"She's breathing but unresponsive," Carol said.

"Her health stats aren't critical," Floyd said, "but they're not good either."

"I'll check my oils," Carol said, already sifting through her fanny pack. "I might have something."

The fight between Big Montana Ice and Bear Knuckle intensified, the air thick with grunts and the sound of fists meeting flesh. "Got ye!" Bear Knuckle yelled before grabbing her boot and yanking her down, her head slamming against the ground. She groaned as she tried to rise, but he was on her too fast, his fists pounding into her with the force of a sledgehammer.

"Samurai!" Ziggy barked as he bypassed the brawl again, running to where Horse Whisperer lay on the ground, stiff in death. With a quick blast from the flamethrower, he lit her hair on fire at the roots, only to stomp out the flames moments later.

"What's he doing?" Floyd asked, his facial expression somewhere between intrigued and horrified as the Samurai drug Horse Whisperer's severed braid to the pile of burned flesh that used to be the Cannibal. Puddles of blood, muscle, and fat saturated the ground, and the Samurai lifted the braided hair, soaking it in the melted fat before dropping the flamethrower and unscrewing one of the fuel tanks. There was a hiss as he opened the valve on the canister, and to Ziggy's surprise, he began dousing the hair in fuel.

"I have no idea what you're making," Ziggy said, panic lighting in his gut. "But you need to help Big Montana with Bear Knuckle or she will die. UltraChad's gone. Whatever you're planning won't be worth it. Let him go. Get somewhere safe and we'll ride this out."

But the Samurai ignored him, and when the canister emptied, he wound the braid around his arm, unhooked the second tank, lifted it into his arms, and ran after UltraChad.

Or at least that's what Ziggy thought. Right up until the Samurai leaped onto the Ferris wheel platform and latched onto one of the gondolas. He whipped off his belt, using it to tie the fuel canister to his chest.

A life for a life, was the only thing Ziggy's scattered mind could produce. He was going after Alexia.

Pepper sprang to her feet, zooming in on the clash between Big Montana Ice and Bear Knuckle. "Benedict," she yelled at the trembling ball of coward and dogs still shivering on the ground. "Big Montana Ice is dying. Sic your dogs on Bear Knuckle!"

Benedict sniffed but obeyed, dragging himself to his feet and shoving the whistle between his quivering lips. The now bee free corgis growled, their hackles raised, as he piped a tune. Then, with a whispered command, "Dinner time," they surged forward, a furry avalanche descending on Bear Knuckle, who roared in defiance as he tried to fend them off. Big Montana dropped to the ground.

Floyd was now checking both Meihua and Big Montana Ice's health stats. "Her heart rate is dropping!" he said brokenly.

"Which one?" Pepper cried in dismay. "Both?"

By the time Ziggy turned his attention back to the Ferris wheel, the Samurai was weaving through the labyrinth of metal and gears within the wheel, and the spectators in the gondolas began screaming in fright. He stopped when he reached the platform at the center of the wheel, watching the gondolas pass until he found the one with Alexia inside. Ziggy watched as he began his climb up the spoke of the wheel.

He kept his focus on the Samurai as Bear Knuckle kicked and thrashed against the onslaught of corgis, his strength waning. He was no match for the ferocious fluff balls coming at him from all sides. Suddenly, the lower half of one of Ziggy's monitors was enveloped by a fine mist, drawing his attention back to Bear Knuckle and the dogs.

Pepper was the first to realize the source. "The pheromone gun!" she cried in disbelief, and Ziggy realized that he'd been too fixated on the Samurai. While Pepper and Floyd were preoccupied with Meihua and Big Montana Ice, UltraChad managed to gain the upper hand unnoticed. A smirk played on his puffy lips as he blasted Bear Knuckle and the dogs with the Beekeeper's gun until it ran dry, then tossed it aside. A low hum built as the bees surged to life once more, swarming around their prey.

"Ye lavvy-heided wankstain!" Bear Knuckle's roar rose above the buzzing of the bees. "Dinny leave me here tae die like a dug!"

A loud thump reverberated through the control room, drawing every eye to the Samurai as he leaped onto the roof of DipShip's gondola. He unfurled the sticky braid with swift dexterity, his nimble fingers working quickly as he wrapped it along a grooved section of the gondola's roof.

Floyd's eyes nearly bugged out of his skull. "It's a wick!" he exclaimed. "He's going to blow open the emergency hatch!"

"What do you mean? Oh, my God!" Pepper yanked out her phone, nearly hyperventilating as she waited for it to power on. "I have to warn her!"

Benedict's panicked screaming filled the control room as Ultra-Chad closed in, but he didn't run. Instead, he desperately tried to call the corgis back for protection. But his efforts were in vain as the dogs howled and whimpered, covered by the relentless bee swarm, their agonized cries filling the control room.

"She's not answering!" Pepper's hands shook violently as she tried again to call Alexia. "I was mad at her, but I don't want her to die!"

"What do we do?" Floyd asked Ziggy, all semblance of composure gone. "If he attacks her, she'll trigger his kill-chip for sure."

"There's nothing we can do," Ziggy said. The Samurai's actions might not make sense to Pepper and Floyd, but Ziggy knew how badly he wanted Alexia dead. He'd voluntarily joined the team just to get close to her, knowing he was risking his life. There was no stopping him now.

The fuel canister hissed as the Samurai twisted it open, his hands working swiftly to prime the makeshift explosive, snapping off the top and hurriedly funneling the tip of the braid inside. Ziggy's gut wrenched as Pepper cried, "Don't do this!" But her plea fell on deaf ears as the Samurai ignited the fuse with a flick of the lighter, then sprinted across the roof, leaping through the air and landing hard on the gondola just below.

With a deafening roar, the canister detonated, tearing the escape hatch open and spewing fire through the air. Pepper's horrified scream rattled Ziggy's eardrums, her trembling hands gripping the edge of the desk as her legs threatened to give way beneath her. The wealthy spectators, watching from their gondolas, panicked in fear, descending into frantic madness as they pulled out their cellphones to call for aid.

Benedict's strangled cries for help rose above the din as UltraChad tackled him to the ground, wrapping his hands around Benedict's neck.

"You'll never ascend," UltraChad growled in a guttural rasp, tightening his grip. "But I'll deliver you. I'll give you the Blackpill if it's the last thing I do." Benedict thrashed and clawed at his arm, but it was no use. His face turned a brilliant shade of purple.

"The Samurai's going back!" Pepper choked, and the Ferris wheel ground to a halt as he clambered his way back up to Gondola 155, where Alexia was trapped. There was a struggle as he reached through the ruined metal, his muscles straining with effort. A tortured scream rocked the air as he emerged, yanking Boomer through the opening by his arm.

"Trash Daddy, please!" Boomer begged, but the words had barely left his lips when the Samurai seized him by his collar and pitched him over the edge. His screams faded into the distance as he plummeted to the ground below, his colorful scarves billowing behind him like butterfly wings.

Pepper slumped back into her seat. "We're going to lose them all," she whispered, her voice choked with defeat.

"Wait, Pepper!" Floyd whirled in his chair, jolting her attention back to the fight on the ground. "Look!" he exclaimed, his finger trembling as he pointed to the monitor. Ziggy gasped as Carol emerged from the shadows, the Samurai's makeshift dagger in her hand.

"She's going to kill him," Floyd whispered as Carol lunged forward, sinking the dagger into UltraChad's neck, right at the base of his skull. She used both arms to pull the knife down his spine, screaming as blood spilled from the wound.

UltraChad went limp. It wasn't like the other deaths they'd seen, where life drained slowly, and they waited in agony for the final moment. With UltraChad, it was done in an instant. Gone like a fart in the wind. His muscles slackened, and Benedict wrenched free from his grasp, collapsing to the ground. He sucked in a desperate, rattling breath that was barely audible over the sound of Carol's screams. She was on top of UltraChad, stabbing his torso with the dagger over and over again.

"You. Horrible. Man!" she punctuated every word with a stab. Blood spattered through the air, spilling onto the grass. She dragged the knife across his throat, slitting it open from ear to ear, and the kill-score rose—1913.

"Babies!" Benedict rasped as he gazed around at the devastation. Tears streamed down his face as he blew his whistle and the corgis that hadn't been consumed by bees came running. Nearby, Bear Knuckle, bitten, stung and mangled beyond recognition, attempted to crawl away, his tortured breaths rattling in his chest, a few dogs still gnawing at his limbs while bees assailed them.

Ziggy opened his mouth to direct his team, but Alexia's scream rang out from inside the gondola before he could, making his heart clench with fear. He looked up in time to see the Samurai freeze, in a sudden, electrifying moment, his limbs stiffening as if struck by a bolt of lightning.

"She triggered his kill-chip," Pepper gasped as the Samurai went limp, tumbling from the gondola, hurtling through the air before landing—directly on top of Bear Knuckle. The giant man's spine crunched, and the dogs scattered.

There was a moment of stunned silence before the kill-score flashed on the screen—2003 points. Pepper choked back a sob, burying her face in her hands.

Watching her heart break crushed Ziggy's heart, too. Enough points to qualify, but not enough killers alive for it to matter. It was the worst-case scenario.

Ziggy tried to comfort her. "We still have Benedict," he said gently, his voice cracking on the last word. "And Carol." He paused for a moment to watch Carol, who'd abandoned the knife and was clawing at UltraChad, ripping out handfuls of his hair and digging her fingers into this eye socket until his eye popped out. She tore it from his face, the retaining septum snapping like an overstretched rubber band, and threw it as hard as she could. Strange keening noises erupted from her throat and Ziggy couldn't tell if she was laughing or crying.

"I can't believe he's still alive," Floyd said over Ziggy's shoulder.

"Are you kidding, Floyd?" Ziggy couldn't take it anymore. "He's covered in hundreds of stab wounds and had his throat cut! He's dead!"

Floyd looked confused for a moment before chuckling. "You thought I was talking about UltraChad." He switched Ziggy's screen to the Samurai's health stats. "See here? Most of his stats are critical, but he's breathing."

"What?" Pepper choked, looking up.

"The Samurai," Floyd said with a smile. "He's alive."

"Now's not the time for a joke, Floyd." Pepper was so upset her body trembled from head to toe.

In shock, Ziggy found his voice as he gazed at the screen. "It's not a joke, Pep. He survived the fall."

Pepper shot up in her seat, frantically toggling to the Samurai's health monitor. Then to his bodycam, and she sat in silence listening for the sound of his breathing. It was raspy and weak, but it was there. "Alexia didn't kill him," she said with a gasp. "She must have stunned him, instead."

"Big Montana Ice is wounded and unconscious, but she's alive, too," Floyd added, changing screens. "She'll need immediate medical treatment for her burns and may have some internal bleeding."

Pepper's voice shook. "And Meihua?"

"Alive," Floyd said, zooming in to show Pepper where she lay on the ground, moaning and clutching her arm. "Exhausted and hurt, but alive."

Pepper blinked. "That's everyone." She flipped through the killers' health stats again. "Benedict, Carol, Meihua, Big Montana Ice, the Samurai," she murmured as she counted. She looked at Ziggy and Floyd. "That's everyone, right?"

Floyd beamed. "That's everyone!"

"Attention, Super Serial competitors!" the ringmaster's voice rang through the cityscape. "We'd like to congratulate District DipShip, our thirteenth and final team to qualify for the Super Serial Championships! Thank you to all our participants. We hope you enjoyed the Mongaphalee Jubilee!" There was a beat of silence before every killer in the cityscape suddenly collapsed, their automatic sedation mechanisms taking hold.

"Holy shit," Ziggy breathed, dread and shock warring in his chest.

Pepper looked on the verge of fainting as she uttered, "We won."

"We did it!" Floyd cried, jumping up and down, pumping his fists. "DipShip is going to the Championships!"

Chapter 23

Baguette Down On It

Ziggy went numb, his eyes vacant as he stared at the screen, consumed by a hollow emptiness. DipShip had just secured the final qualification slot in the Prelims, and the sedated killers slumped to the ground, creating piles of bodies—some dead, some unconscious. Ziggy longed to join the slumbering. It would be a welcome change to sleep through the worst of the hullabaloo, only waking up when it was over. Even though it was only the beginning, a dark part of him knew it was the beginning of the end.

Pepper's voice cut through the haze as she shouted into her phone, "Get medics to our killers now! We should be prioritized as a qualifying team!"

Operations teams swarmed the cityscape like worker bees, tending to the wounded, and securing murderers in their protected cells. They prioritized the corporate assets, with utmost care, as if they were fragile and precious, leaving the deplorables and lesser criminals for later.

Surrounded by armored guards, sleek medics carefully placed the Samurai's limp body onto a gurney before swiftly loading him into one of the many ambulances racing toward the hospital. Another team tended to Carol, who had collapsed on UltraChad's chest, her face dripping with blood. It took six medics and a handful of armored guards to lift Big Montana Ice onto a stretcher, which nearly buckled under her weight. Veterinarians checked each of Benedict's corgis, gently placing them into kennels, while another medic struggled to get an IV drip into Meihua's diminished veins.

Pepper's voice drifted into focus. "I never let myself hope we'd win," she said, her eyes shimmering with unshed tears. "It was such a long shot. It would've been a miracle if any of them had made it out alive. I know it wasn't the plan, but maybe it's for the best. Maybe we really could win the Championship."

"I don't think anyone saw DipShip coming," Floyd replied, grinning ear to ear. "The scores the analysts gave the killers were far too low, especially now that we've seen them in action. I need to run some numbers, but DipShip could actually be competitive in the Championship if they can keep up the same level of ingenuity."

Ziggy barely registered the voices around him. His eyes were glued to the screens, toggling through different vantage points as medics pulled killer after killer from the cityscape, leaving criminals and debtors to bleed out on the ground. He imagined himself among the fallen, dying and alone, and squeezed his eyes shut, trying to banish the image.

Pepper's hand on his arm made him jump. "Ziggy? Are you okay?" Her face was full of concern.

He shook his head, but before he could respond, Mongaphalee security stormed into the control room.

"Marshal Ghostshade," a beefy officer said. "We need to take your team to the recovery hospital. Two of your competitors are in critical condition, and your CEO is also being treated there. She requested your immediate presence."

"I'll call her right now," Pepper said, panic flooding her voice.

Ziggy stood, shaking with adrenaline, gripping the edge of the desk until he felt steady. "Point zero one percent," he murmured. "Those were the chances. Point zero one percent."

"A point zero one percent chance isn't the same as having no chance at all," Floyd said as they were escorted from the room.

"What happens if one of our killers dies?" Ziggy asked. There was still time. If one of them died, DipShip would lose their spot, and maybe Hirofumi would consider letting him live long enough to disappear.

Floyd frowned. "It depends. Some teams have more than one killer per category, but since we don't, I imagine we'd forfeit, and the Championship slot would go to another team. However, the rules are quite complex. Depending on the manner of death, there are specific addendums to consider. Before introducing any alternates, the body must undergo an examination by a qualified Super Serial physician. Depending on the coroner's evaluation, a district can substitute different levels of alternates." Floyd trailed off when he noticed Ziggy wasn't paying attention.

Misinterpreting Ziggy's question and subsequent silence as worry for their team, Floyd placed a hand on his shoulder. "It'll be okay. Our killers are strong. Especially the Samurai."

That was what worried Ziggy. They were strong, and DipShip had a knack for defying the odds. At this point, they were a statistical anomaly.

Pepper's conversation with Alexia grew louder and more urgent as Mongaphalee security guided them through a series of hallways, finally arriving at the lobby of the control room building.

"I'm so glad you're okay!" she exclaimed, the color high in her cheeks. "Poor Boomer... Yes, we'll be there soon. I don't know," she added. "I'll have to ask Floyd. He knows the rules better than I do."

"Ask me what?" Floyd questioned as they approached the main entrance.

"Alexia wants to know what happens if one of the killers dies," Pepper said as she ended the call.

"It's complicated," Floyd began again, but Pepper shook her head, shushing him.

"What's the point of asking questions if you don't actually want to know the answer?" Floyd muttered, miffed.

Several marshals from another qualifying team exited, and the Mongaphalee guard leading their escort held out his hand, pausing the team. The overwhelming clamor of reporters, journalists, and flashing cameras that awaited them outside made Ziggy's knees feel like jelly. In a few moments, his face would be everywhere—if it wasn't already.

"It looks like we have to pass through a media gauntlet to get to the hospital," Pepper said. "Let's give the other team a moment before we go through."

"That's District ValueMart," Floyd whispered-yelled in excitement. "Their Centennial is Home Skillet, and the analysts said she could be the next Thunderclap. I can't believe we're in the same boat as them. We should go talk to them and make friends!"

"Now's not the time," Pepper hissed behind her hand. "No more discussion until we're alone. And no one says anything to the press. We'll do nothing until we know the status of the killers."

"Follow me," the Mongaphalee guard commanded. Security flanked them on all sides, guiding them out of the building. Shouts and camera flashes hit Ziggy like a flash grenade.

"Marshal Ghostshade!" a reporter called out. "Any comment on why the Samurai attacked the DipShip gondola? Who was he after?"

"Over here, Marshal Ghostshade!" another yelled over the guards.

"Give us a smile, Marshal!" The overlapping shouts and flashing lights overwhelmed Ziggy, disorienting him. Relief washed over him when they finally reached the unmarked SUV waiting for them.

"Have you spoken to DipShip's CEO? Can anyone confirm if Alexia and Hirofumi Ito survived the explosion?" an enthusiastic reporter shouted as they climbed into the back seat. "Who will take over as CEO if they're dead?"

If only the universe would be so kind. He should've been more forthcoming with Pepper and Floyd. The bitter taste of irony filled his mouth. He'd spent so long having nothing to live for, wishing he could die. Now, just when Pepper and Floyd had pulled him from his despair, he was afraid the life he wanted would be taken from him. He needed to prepare his friends for his inevitable funeral. He hoped they could forgive him.

Security closed the door behind them, but a sharp knock on the window startled them. The undeterred reporter pressed her face against the glass. "Can you make a statement about the Samurai's attack? Are the rumors about his death true? Does DipShip have any replacement killers?"

The SUV pulled away, leaving the bellowing reporters behind on the curb. "There are more waiting at the recovery hospital," the guard warned them as the driver navigated the crowded Mongaphalee streets.

"Land sakes alive," Ziggy muttered. It felt like a malicious force was intent on keeping him right under Hirofumi's nose. Staring out the window at the blur of passing vehicles, he wondered when Hirofumi would make his move. Maybe he was already waiting with Alexia at the hospital. Despite the scorching heat of Mongaphalee, an icy chill ran up Ziggy's spine.

"Do you think it's true?" Pepper asked softly. "Is the Samurai dead?"

"If it were confirmed, the news would be reporting on it," Floyd said, eyes glued to his phone's Super Serial news feed. "Right now, it's just speculation. Some sources are even saying Big Montana Ice might be the one who's died."

"I guess we'll find out soon," Pepper replied as the SUV rolled to a stop in front of a large building. "We're here."

A chaotic media circus had taken over the entrance, with reporters, cameras, microphones, and blinding lights everywhere. "Are the press allowed inside?" Ziggy asked, his voice cracking with strain.

"The only reporters allowed inside are Chuckles and Jovy," the driver said.

"Great," Ziggy said under his breath.

"I know!" Floyd replied, grinning as the door flew open. "I love Chuckles and Jovy. They always interview the marshals from the winning teams."

Ziggy kept his gaze fixed on his feet as he followed Pepper to the front doors, dogging her every step. *It's okay, Pep, you didn't know. Things moved so fast.* He rehearsed his goodbyes to Pepper and Floyd. *I'm sorry I never played Warlocks and Warlords with you, Floyd. I wish we had more time.* They'd probably be the only ones at his funeral. Was there even a photo of them together? The shouts from reporters blurred together, making them easier to ignore. His mind felt like it'd been ripped out, run through a blender, and poured back in through his ear.

"There's Alexia," Pepper said as they entered the building. Rushing to meet her, Alexia cried. "They're all still alive!" She was more disheveled than Ziggy had ever seen her. The shoulder of her blouse was torn, and her sleek hair was windblown and knotted. Her calf was heavily bandaged, but at least she wasn't limping.

He frantically scanned the room, but Hirofumi was nowhere to be found. Maybe it was the countless hours he had spent watching killers emerge from the darkness, but he was on edge, waiting for Hirofumi to burst out of the shadows and take his revenge.

"Have you spoken to any of the doctors?" Pepper asked.

Alexia nodded, her expression tense. "Only briefly. The Samurai's in critical condition, but they're doing everything they can to keep him alive. Meihua is recovering but still unconscious, so they're monitoring her closely. Carol and Benedict are being treated mostly for exhaustion and dehydration. Carol's also on a seventy-two-hour psychiatric watch. She's been hysterical since she woke up."

"Technically, she's been hysterical since she first stabbed UltraChad," Floyd pointed out.

"What about Big Montana Ice?" Pepper asked, her voice barely above a whisper.

"She's in surgery," Alexia said. "They're trying to fix the internal bleeding and burns, but it's bad."

Taking a quick look at the crowd of press still outside the door, Pepper directed everyone to a more secluded corner of the waiting area. "What do you want to do?" she asked. "Should we give an official statement?"

"Winning teams always give a statement," offered Floyd.

"Absolutely not," Alexia said with a condescending scoff. "We won, but it's only a triumph if none of the killers die. If we give a statement too soon, we'll look like fools if it all comes to nothing."

Everyone turned to Ziggy, waiting for his opinion. Alexia tapped her foot impatiently. "I hate talking to the press," he finally said. "So, I agree with Alexia."

Alexia opened her mouth to object, only to realize that Ziggy had agreed with her. "Exactly," she said. "We say nothing until all our killers have been medically cleared."

Pepper's phone chimed. "I just received word that the veterinarian wants to meet with us so we can make some decisions about the corgis. Two of them might not make it. He's waiting for us on the fourth floor."

"Someone should tell Benedict," Floyd said. "They're his dogs, and I'm sure he wouldn't want them to suffer. He should be involved in the decision."

"They're not his dogs," Alexia said with a glare. "They're Dip-Ship's, which means they're mine. Put them down; he has plenty to spare."

"You and Ziggy go talk to Benedict," Pepper ordered, already moving toward the nearest elevator. "Alexia and I will meet with the vet."

"Wait," Floyd said. "Where's Benedict's room?"

"Ask reception," Pepper said as she stepped through the doors with Alexia.

"Move!" Alexia hissed as the elevator doors closed in their faces.

Floyd sighed but obediently headed to the information desk near the front entrance. Ziggy trailed behind him at a snail's pace, anxiously searching for any signs of Hirofumi or his henchmen.

"Marshal Ghostshade!" a voice bellowed from the opposite end of the lobby. A flurry of people and camera equipment charged in his direction. Chuckles was approaching fast with a determined look on his cheap-suit face, with Jovy at his heels like a dutiful lap dog.

Ziggy turned to run but accidentally bowled over Floyd instead, knocking him to the ground. Floyd landed hard on his backside. "Careful!" he said with a wince, while Ziggy muttered frantic apologies, reaching down to help Floyd to his feet.

"We need to get out of here," Ziggy said, tugging on Floyd's shirt.

"Benedict's on the third floor," Floyd said. "But it's okay. I can go talk to him while you do your interview."

Ziggy balked. "I don't want—"

That's when Chuckles thrust a microphone eagerly into his face. "We're here with Marshal Ziglar Ghostshade, who just proved to the world that lightning can indeed strike twice!" Chuckles said, a grin plastered on his face. "Congratulations to District DipShip on an incredible victory. You must be on cloud nine!"

Ziggy's mouth dropped open, but no sound emerged. Floyd was already halfway to the elevator.

"Look at him! He's in shock!" Jovy exclaimed.

Chuckles laughed. "I think the entire world is in shock! This has got to be the underdog story of a lifetime. Everyone will be talking about you for generations to come!"

"Marshal Ghostshade." Jovy sidled up next to him. "Tell us how you managed to lead team DipShip to such a miraculous victory."

The silence became unbearably protracted, each second amplifying Ziggy's panic. He finally managed to mumble, "It was... unexpected." Sweat beaded on his forehead, and as he sensed their disappointment with his answer, he turned to leave, hoping his awkwardness would dampen their enthusiasm. But Chuckles and Jovy were undeterred, leaning in even closer.

"Come now, Marshal Ghostshade," Chuckles pressed. "Don't be modest. What's your secret?"

Ziggy tried to force a smile but faltered as his stomach emitted a loud gurgle, resonating through the now-silent surroundings. Nausea washed over him as his ears grew hot. The sensation was horrifyingly familiar. Lost in the hellscape of the day, he'd forgotten to take his GlutoBlock. "Please excuse me," he said, struggling to keep his voice steady. "I really need to—"

"Just one more question, Marshal Ghostshade!" Chuckles cut him off.

Ziggy's vision blurred as the nausea intensified. Without another word, he shoved Chuckles aside and bolted, certain he was about to shit himself on camera—a fitting end to the last twenty-four hours.

Corridors and rooms blew by, and Ziggy caught sight of a massive medical ward, filled with cells, the killers undergoing various medical procedures. Doctors performed CPR on a thin, wiry man, his body jolting from defibrillator shocks. Another stitched up a woman's stomach, carefully closing a deep gash in her guts.

Ziggy's stomach cramped as sweat mingled with liquified terror. As soon as he laid eyes on a bathroom door, his sphincter spasmed in anticipation. Clenching his buttocks, he darted forward on tiptoes as if he were crossing on a bed of hot coals. He kicked open the door and bashed into a stall. With only seconds to spare, he let go, releasing his bowels. The stench of fear mingled with the acrid smell of sloppy, putrid shit.

Nature's call was a tsunami, and he couldn't weather the storm anymore. Overwhelmed by weariness, he slumped against the toilet tank. He should've been used to this by now, but the combination of fear, exhaustion, and shame broke him. He put his face in his hands and wept.

Once the storm of emotions subsided, he took the time to clean up and flush, but found himself too drained to leave the stall. The truth was, he belonged there. Who was he to think he deserved anything other than unending pain? For the first time since taking his blood oath in the dump, his shame and grief broke free, trampling through his body. He was part of the shit, cowering in the filth that defined his existence. A toilet man. A parasite that sucked the life out of everything and everyone he grew to love.

He'd drained everything from Gio, Pepper, and Floyd, and with nothing else to bleed, he collapsed inward, consumed by a fiery self-immolation.

Chapter 24

Wake Me Up Before You Cocoa

It seemed like an eternity before Ziggy heard the bathroom door open. He cursed under his breath, hoping it wasn't more emboldened reporters ready to catch him with his pants down.

"Ziggy?" Floyd's voice echoed off the tiles. "Are you in there, Ziggy? Ziglar Ghostshade!"

"For fuck's sake, Floyd, pipe it!" Ziggy barked back. "Someone will hear you!" The last thing he wanted was another run-in with Chuckles and Jovy.

"I knew it!" Floyd's voice was closer now, louder. "I knew you'd be here. You forgot your GlutoBlock again, didn't you?" His sneakers squeaked to a stop in front of Ziggy's stall, and a bottle of GlutoBlock rolled underneath, bumping against Ziggy's feet. He picked it up and shoved it in his pocket. Floyd had basically rolled more than five thousand dollars across a bacteria-riddled bathroom floor.

"What is it with you and Pepper?" Ziggy complained. "Do we really need to have this conversation now? Most people don't want to chat while they're cranking a steamer."

"I heard the toilet flush before I came in," Floyd said matter-of-factly. "And you're the only one in here, so I know you're finished defecating."

"What are you, the toilet police?"

There was a pause before Floyd said, "You're being sarcastic. I know that because there's no such thing as toilet police, and you must know that because you're a marshal."

Ziggy sighed, the sound bouncing off the walls. "Benedict's crying about his dogs," Floyd said. "He's back in his transport cell. I told him about the consultation with the vet, but he was wailing so much he may not have heard me. I didn't stay. It was too loud, and I didn't have my headphones."

"It's fine," Ziggy muttered, not wanting to talk but not wanting Floyd to feel bad about something he couldn't control. "It's okay, really." Silence hung between them, heavy with unspoken words.

"It smells awful in here," Floyd said, and a strange bubble of deranged laughter rose in Ziggy's chest.

"Not much I can do about it now," Ziggy said, fighting back a grin. He opened the stall door. "Besides, you're the one who followed me in here."

"Pepper didn't think I'd be able to find you," Floyd said, his voice tinged with pride. "But I did."

"You do have a knack for sniffing me out," Ziggy muttered, moving to the sink to wash his hands. He dried them on a paper towel instead of using the loud hand dryer—for Floyd's sake. "I'm not going back out there," he said when he was through, glancing warily at the door and leaning against the bathroom counter.

"I know you don't like talking to reporters, but this seems different," Floyd said. "You're not the regular Ziggy level of annoyed. You seem"—his bushy eyebrows knitted together—"afraid."

"Something like that," Ziggy mumbled.

Floyd pulled out his phone and turned it toward Ziggy, revealing an emotion wheel. "Which one of these emotions describes it best," said Floyd. "Anxious, paranoid, distressed, fretful–"

"It's complicated," Ziggy blurted out.

"Pepper told me about your history with Hirofumi," Floyd said, watching Ziggy's face intently and dropping the chart. "How he threatened your life and forced you into hiding after the marshals revolted."

Ziggy felt the sudden sting of tears behind his eyes and quickly blinked them away. He was exhausted—so dog-tired he could collapse right there on the bathroom floor.

"I'm assuming, then, that during the Opening Ceremonies, he threatened you again, and that's why you're so scared," Floyd continued softly.

Ziggy shook his head but couldn't find his voice. His throat felt like it was full of sap. None of it mattered anymore. The damage was done. Hirofumi was coming for him, and he had to end all of this before he dragged his friends down with him.

"Well, are you going to tell me what happened or not?" Floyd demanded, crossing his arms. "There's no point in hiding it." His peevish expression startled Ziggy; Floyd rarely got angry.

"I can't," Ziggy choked. "I want to, but I can't."

"Why not?"

"It's complicated."

"You keep saying that, but you never explain why!"

"Let it go, Floyd. It doesn't matter."

"It matters to me!" Floyd yelled in Ziggy's face. "Why won't you just tell me what happened? I'm not dumb. I can understand complicated things."

"Because I can't lose you!" The words flew out before he could stop them. "I can't go through that again! I won't put you and Pepper at risk."

Floyd's shuttered expression drained away. There was a long silence as he processed, his eyebrows furrowing up and down. His fingers moved like he was typing on an invisible keyboard, analyzing Ziggy's outburst and forming an understanding. "And you don't want to put us at risk because you love us," he said, his eyes twinkling. "You love me."

"No, I don't," Ziggy said mulishly, irritated at the spark of delight in Floyd's eyes.

"Yes, you do," Floyd said. "Admit it. You love me, and I'm your best friend."

Ziggy rubbed his face in his hands. "For fuck's sake, Floyd."

"You know it's true."

"Fine," Ziggy grunted, almost ready to run from Floyd like he had with Chuckles and Jovy. "I admit it. You're my best friend. Now, can we please stop talking about this?"

"I knew it!" Floyd said with a toothy grin. "And no. We're not going to stop talking about it. In fact, you're going to tell me everything." He grabbed Ziggy by the arm and dragged him to the door, peering cautiously around the corner first. "The coast is clear," he said, leading Ziggy down a corridor to the service elevator.

"Where are we going?" Ziggy asked, exchanging a brief nod with the Mongaphalee hospital employee already in the elevator, pushing a cart of linens.

"To the sixth floor," Floyd said. "We'll talk in Meihua's room. She's too tired to wake up, and if she did, she wouldn't understand most of what we're saying. Plus, it's a secure area—no prying eyes, and Pepper can easily find us if she gets worried and comes looking."

"But—" Ziggy began to protest, only to be cut off by Floyd's determined stride as they exited the elevator. Floyd hauled him down a long corridor of rooms, stopping at the one on the far end. With a flash of his DipShip ID, he addressed the guard stationed outside the door.

"We're here to visit Lin Meihua," Floyd announced. "I'm Floyd McNut, Operations Analyst for District DipShip, and this is—"

"Marshal Ziglar Ghostshade," the guard interrupted, his voice resonating with reverence. "It's an honor." The guard rolled up his sleeve, revealing a tattoo that read 'Ziglar GOATshade' in tight, black lettering.

"GOATshade?" Ziggy echoed, both horrified and confused to see a play on his name tattooed on a random guard's arm.

"Greatest of all time," the guard said, a grin spreading across his face. "I may have flunked out of the marshals, but I stood by you in the Red Judas riots."

Ziggy was speechless as Floyd pulled him into Meihua's room. The guard let him pass without even a cursory check of his badge.

Meihua was in her transparent cell, tucked into a comfy bed and surrounded by medical machines. Ziggy sank into a nearby chair, while Floyd dragged another over to sit next to him. He'd been right about one thing. Meihua didn't budge at the sound. She looked like an ancient, sleeping vampire.

"It smells like antiseptic in here, but at least it's better than the bathroom," Floyd said, wrinkling his nose. Turning to Ziggy, he gestured for him to proceed. "Go ahead. I'm listening."

Talking felt futile to Ziggy, a weak attempt to change the march of fate. "What's the point?" Ziggy said, his shoulders slumping in resignation. "If the most powerful man in the world wants me to disappear, there's nothing I can do."

"Why does he want you to disappear?" Floyd asked, his face filled with genuine concern.

Ziggy knew there was no way out of the conversation. If Floyd didn't eventually worm the truth out of him, Pepper would. It wasn't that he didn't want to confide in them. It was that he knew how far they'd go to try to keep him safe, and when it came to Hirofumi, there was no such thing as "safe." Pepper and Floyd would do anything for him, and he didn't deserve it. Guilt gnawed at him. Sacrificing himself to save them made sense. He was a crabby old loner with an entire carousel full of emotional baggage. But allowing someone as kind as Pepper or as loyal as Floyd to do the same for him felt wrong to the core.

The room fell silent, the faint hum of Meihua's machines lending a dissonant backdrop to their conversation. "You must be exhausted from running for such a long time," Floyd commented, breaking the silence.

Exhausted didn't begin to describe it. He'd spent years running, years hiding in a dark well of grief, burying his emotions deep within. Now, his emotional dam teetered on the edge of collapse, the cracks spreading like fractures in his fragile heart, barely containing the flood of sorrow.

"Once, in Warlocks and Warlords, I played as a level 50 wind sorcerer," Floyd said. "I was on a quest with my friends—a battle cleric and a rogue assassin. We snuck into the Ghoul King's lair and stole the Withering Scepter, but on the way out, we accidentally triggered a trap, and a magical wall of necromantic thorns blocked our exit from his tomb."

"Now's not the time to talk about Warlocks and Warlords, Floyd," Ziggy said, but Floyd's intense glare silenced him. "The battle cleric, of course, tried to hack his way through the thorns with Stone Scourge, his longsword," Floyd continued, snorting with disdain. "He took so much necrotic damage that he had to use Healing Meditation to recover."

"Floyd, I don't think this is helping me—"

"Just listen for once!" Floyd snapped. "The rogue used her high dexterity score to try to sneak her way through, but nearly got trapped in the tangle. I even tried to use Fire Storm to burn through the thorns, but my magic wasn't strong enough."

Ziggy tried to concentrate on concentrating. Only Floyd would find a way to talk about video games when Ziggy's life hung in the balance.

"None of us noticed the Ghoul King rising from his slumber until he attacked," Floyd went on, his tone deadly serious. "Our solo attempts to get through the thorns seemed useless when faced with such a ferocious common enemy. We all knew we couldn't win against the Ghoul King. We had no choice but to unite, play to our strengths, and part the thorns."

Floyd's eyes lit up with the memory. "The battle cleric channeled his divinity and lent me his full wisdom modifier to channel my magic into summoning Radiant Strike, a powerful spell that could banish the necromantic thorns and overwhelm them with radiant power. The rogue disappeared into the shadows and landed a sneak attack blow on the Ghoul King, stunning him, and giving us time to escape. You see what I'm saying? We couldn't get through the thorns alone. We needed each other's strengths to compensate for our individual weaknesses."

Ziggy frowned. "I still don't get why we're talking about wizards."

"It's a metaphor, Ziggy." Floyd rolled his eyes. "Not everything has to be taken so literally. This isn't just about you anymore. We're a team, and that means we look out for each other. You may want to protect us, but we want to protect you, too. We're stronger together. We complement each other's strengths and compensate for each other's weaknesses. For example, one of your weaknesses is that you don't think you deserve anything good. One of my strengths is that I always find you and change your mind. If we stick together, we can defeat the Ghoul King."

Ziggy absorbed Floyd's words, an uncomfortable clarity dawning on him. He wasn't alone. And he needed to stop acting like he was. He might not deserve Pepper and Floyd's unwavering loyalty, but he could try to be worthy of it. And it needed to start with him trusting them with the truth.

"Hirofumi's still angry I executed Red Judas," Ziggy confessed. "He thought he could lock me up and no one would give a damn. But the marshal uprising blindsided him. It made him look weak, and now he hates me for it. He's terrified that if I ever challenged him again, the public and the marshals would stand behind me."

"The marshals would for sure," Floyd said. "All the ones I've ever met love you."

"He told me at the Opening Ceremonies he'd kill me if DipShip won a spot in the Championships," Ziggy said, his voice cracking. "I was supposed to force a loss, then go back into hiding as soon as the Prelims were over."

"But that obviously didn't happen," Floyd said. "And there was no way to predict Bear Knuckle's spine and neck being crushed by the Samurai falling on him."

"We won by accident," Ziggy said, "but I doubt that matters to Hirofumi."

Floyd's expression grew thoughtful. "Let me get this straight. Hirofumi wants to kill you because he's afraid you'll rally the marshals against him for a second time?"

Ziggy shrugged. "That's what he said. Even a herd of sheep can trample a wolf."

"That doesn't make sense."

"I know."

Floyd grasped his forearm. "No, Ziggy, think about it. He'd only worry about you rallying the marshals if he's up to something the marshals would want to rally against."

Ziggy eyes widened, his thoughts going into overdrive. "Say that again," he ordered Floyd, who looked at him strangely.

"You mean the thing about Hirofumi?"

"Say it again!"

"Hirofumi would only worry about you rallying the marshals if he were up to something they'd want to rally against," Floyd repeated. "Otherwise, fearing you would be absurd. You're not physically threatening, and you don't have enough power to hurt him financially."

"Maybe I've been thinking about this all wrong," Ziggy murmured. "I assumed it was about pride and politics—that Hirofumi didn't want me to sully his image."

"I doubt it," Floyd said with a shrug. "People with that much money and power don't worry about their image because they control the media. They have entire teams dedicated to changing public perception."

"You're onto something," Ziggy said.

"Onto what?" Pepper chimed in from the doorway. Her eyes shifted back and forth between Ziggy and Floyd. "Did he finally tell you what happened with Hirofumi at the Opening Ceremonies?"

"Yep!" Floyd grinned. "He also confessed his love for us and said we're best friends."

Pepper smirked, her eyes landing on Ziggy. "Took you long enough."

"We need to talk," Ziggy said, but she shook her head.

"First, we're going back to the hotel," she commanded. "Then, we'll eat. After that, I plan to sleep for a day or two. Then, and only then, will we talk."

Ziggy's head was swimming with fatigue. "Good idea."

"We need to vet the Mongaphalee guards stationed outside Ziggy's room," Floyd said, rising to his feet. "I should probably sleep in his room with him, too. Since we're officially best friends." Ziggy didn't object.

"Hirofumi?" Pepper guessed, and Floyd nodded. "He said he'd kill Ziggy if DipShip won a spot in the Championships."

Pepper's eyes shrunk, and Ziggy winced. She had a shot at being CEO, but it came with heavy emotional baggage.

"Hirofumi might have already turned the guards," Pepper said after a tense pause. "And Alexia won't spare any of her personal security. She's paranoid about another Samurai attack."

"What do we do?" Ziggy asked, already hating the trouble he was putting them through.

"The guard outside won't side with Hirofumi," Floyd said. "I'll bet he knows some trustworthy security."

"How can you be sure?" Pepper asked.

"He's a fan of mine," Ziggy said, not wanting Floyd to go into detail about the embarrassing tattoo.

"I'll handle it," Pepper said, marching toward the door.

Ziggy lumbered to his feet to follow his friends from the room, but not before Floyd turned and said, "Just so you know Ziggy, we love you too."

Chapter 25

Comfortably Crumb

Two weeks after DipShip clinched their place in the Championships, Ziggy was perched on Pepper's couch, a bowl of chips balanced precariously on his knee. The atmosphere was deceptively comfortable—cushy couch, cozy room, no social pressure with just the three of them—but the air was so thick with apprehension, he felt like he might choke on it.

Miraculously, all the DipShip killers had survived, but only Benedict, his uninjured dogs, Lin Meihua, and Carol, were able to make the journey back with the rest of the group. Big Montana Ice and the Samurai were recovering in intensive care, too medically fragile to be moved. Still, once the analysts had verified that the DipShip killers were in mostly stable condition, they'd moved forward with the Championship match-pairings.

Ziggy wasn't dumb enough to approach the announcement with anything other than dread, but Alexia had traveled to the press event to shake hands with the CEO of whichever unfortunate team they were destined to face, and Ziggy breathed easier knowing Hirofumi would likely be in attendance as well. No secret Pill Depot assassins had tried to smother Ziggy in his sleep—yet. He'd relaxed more since leaving Mongaphalee, at least as much as a person could relax with a target on their back, but he knew Hirofumi would eventually strike.

He felt some confidence in Pepper and Floyd's constant supervision. Floyd had temporarily moved into Ziggy's apartment, and even now there was a security detail outside Pepper's door. It wasn't an ironclad solution, and he was pretty sure he and Floyd were going to drive each other crazy, but it was secure enough for Ziggy to get some respite.

Floyd plopped down next to Ziggy, nearly upsetting the bowl of chips. "Best-case scenario," he said, taking a sip from his bottle of orange soda, "DipShip pairs against StellarSecure. Their top pick for a Centennial would've been Terminato, but Terminato died from liver failure and their only other qualifying killer is Right-Swiper, and she killed all her victims with poison. But Meihua is better with poison than Right-Swiper could ever dream of, so the match is ideal."

Ziggy did his best to tune out as Floyd delved into the possible match outcomes. His relentless dissection of every conceivable scenario since they'd left Mongaphalee was fraying Ziggy's nerves. Pepper wordlessly handed him a beer and joined them, a smile forming on her lips as she engaged in Floyd's ongoing evaluation of Right-Swiper's proficiency with poisons.

During their conversation, Ziggy's mind wandered to the aftermath of the Preliminaries. Once the chaos subsided and more information came to light, he learned that Alexia, Boomer, and Hirofumi had been rushed to the recovery hospital after the gondola fire was extinguished. Alexia had suffered minor burns and had a small piece of shrapnel lodged in her leg. Hirofumi, miraculously, walked away unscathed. Boomer, however, was in a coma. Ziggy wasn't sure if he'd recover, but if the sickening thud when he hit the ground was any indication, it didn't look good. Then again, he wondered at the resilience of a man who'd survived being impaled by his own severed arm.

Ziggy had braced himself for Alexia's fury. Defying her orders and pulling the team back from the win had been a shocking move, and he'd anticipated an explosive reaction. Instead, they were met with chilling silence. Alexia's icy demeanor was extreme, and she refused to speak to any of them, including Pepper, for days. Winning a qualifying slot did nothing to mend the rift; Alexia felt snubbed by their collective insubordination. Things only got worse when the media labeled DipShip's victory a fluke, suggesting that Alexia had no hand in their success.

Fortunately, a cleverly worded press release and a few cryptic social media posts from Pepper were all it took to turn the tide. The narrative shifted, painting Alexia as a heroine triumphing in the face of disaster. When they arrived back in DipShip, Alexia was swept up in a frenzy of press interviews, social events, sponsorships, and awards. She quickly became the media's darling, the celebrated CEO of a rising star company. It also helped that Alexia viewed their win as a vindication of her superior leadership, and with Pepper working tirelessly to manage it all, the frost between Alexia and the team began to thaw. Alexia had the ABCD in her line of sight, and Pepper, the CEO position in hers.

"They're talking about us!" Floyd said, and Ziggy turned his attention back to the screen, where Chuckles and Jovy were commenting on DipShip. They played the clip of the Samurai's three-person takedown in the Rapist-No-Escapist.

"Just look at that form!" Chuckles exclaimed, flashing his boxy teeth. Jovy nodded along like a bobblehead. "It's no wonder the Warlord was named 'Best New Serial Killer of the Year!'"

"Did you see the limo decapitation?" Jovy asked, her mouth open in exaggerated awe. They played the clip, zooming in on the Samurai's battle-worn face, which held a captivating combination of fury and focus. When he lunged from the side of the ice cream truck, swinging his homemade scythe, even Ziggy got chills. The physical feat was extraordinary, making the Samurai look like he had almost superhuman strength and skill.

Chuckles tittered, slow-blinking at the camera. "As if that wasn't already shocking, the Warlord made a daring assassination attempt on DipShip CEO, Alexia Ito."

The next clips rolled, and Ziggy watched for a second time as the Samurai scaled the Ferris wheel, blew open the gondola door, and then plummeted to the ground, landing directly on top of Bear Knuckle. Jovy groaned as they replayed the action in slow motion, showing the Samurai's lifeless fall, crushing the massive killer into the dirt.

"His life was most likely saved because he was unconscious when he fell," Floyd said. "Plus, landing on someone as big and squishy as Bear Knuckle probably absorbed some of the impact. Any idea when they'll release the Samurai from the hospital?"

"Not for a while," Pepper sighed, kicking off her shiny orange heels with a thud onto the carpet. She settled on the couch, tucking her legs underneath her. "I'm hoping they'll do the Vigilante battles last. He needs time to recover."

"He had compression fractures in five vertebrae, a collapsed lung, a concussion, bruised ribs, a broken leg, a broken arm, and a fractured skull," Floyd listed. "It's incredible he didn't die."

They turned their attention back to Chuckles, who was speculating why the Samurai attacked the gondola. "Some say it was revenge, but earlier this week, DipShip publicist Boomer D'Chango weighed in on the violent and unexpected attack."

Shock flooded Ziggy, and Floyd gasped, "No way!" as the screen shifted to a very bruised and bloodied Boomer, sitting in a hospital bed wearing a full body cast. One leg was held up in a sling, and his head was secured by a stabilization loop anchored to his skull.

"Why else would he have attacked?" Boomer said, somehow managing to look condescending even though only his face was visible. "Jealousy. Lust. High society. Money. The unreachable is an obsession for him. Trash Daddy wants what he can't have, and it's driving him mad."

Pepper sighed, and Ziggy rubbed his temples. Boomer had not only survived, but continued to push the narrative that the Samurai was striving to be everything he actually stood against.

"I hope he never sees that interview," Floyd said, echoing Ziggy's thoughts. "Why would Boomer say that when the Samurai flat-out said he hates everything about the ultra-rich? He never liked that marketing idea."

Ziggy scoffed. "I think Boomer's just bitter that the Samurai doesn't want to be his Trash Daddy.".

"Why *do* you think he attacked the gondola?" Pepper asked. "I mean, I know he hates executives, but he abandoned the team in order to do it. He could've cut down UltraChad in one strike."

Ziggy grunted, doing his best to hide any emotion. He knew exactly why the Samurai had attacked Alexia. She was on his executive hit list. Ziggy didn't know why the Samurai hated her so much, but hers was the life he'd asked for in exchange for his own. *A life for a life.* The Samurai had seen an opportunity to strike in the Prelims, and for reasons Ziggy couldn't fathom, he'd taken it.

Pepper and Floyd didn't know about his blood oath with the Samurai. But now that the Prelims were over, Ziggy was determined to tell them. He just didn't know how to. It was like giving his friends a lit stick of dynamite while they were trying to defuse a ticking time bomb. Pepper wasn't exactly loyal to Alexia, but she didn't want her dead. If she knew how badly the Samurai wanted to kill Alexia, she'd try to intervene, and Ziggy knew the Samurai would do anything for justice—even if it meant collateral damage. Floyd might not be as inclined to intervene, but he'd ask a million questions, and even though the Samurai didn't explicitly state their oath was a secret, Ziggy knew deep down that it was.

"Maybe he wasn't after Alexia," Floyd said practically. "He probably wanted to kill Boomer. Meihua told me they've all talked about murdering him. Except Carol."

Chuckles and Jovy moved on with the program, shifting to interview Ziggy's least favorite analyst, Jomar Santos.

"How do you and the other analysts determine the pairings?" Chuckles asked with theatrical curiosity. "That must be quite a challenging undertaking."

"I know I wouldn't want to be the one making those decisions," Jovy added, so attuned to Chuckles she sounded like a parrot on his shoulder.

Jomar reveled in the limelight, straightening in his seat. "District to district pairings are carefully selected by evaluating each player's strengths and weaknesses, and their performance in the Prelims. Hundreds of analysts contribute to the seeding process. It's important to match districts based on their player-to-player skills and abilities. It's not a random process, but an analytical one that's impossible to manipulate."

Pepper chewed on her lower lip. "Since DipShip performed better than expected, should we be worried about being seeded too high?" she asked.

"Seeding is more for tournaments with multiple games or rounds," Floyd explained. "It's a way to make sure the best teams don't match up until later in the competition. In Super Serial, it's player versus player, but within teams that only have a single match. The seeds are assigned based on strength, pitting last year's winning team against the top seed from the qualifying teams. Since this is DipShip's first year competing, and our scores before the Prelims were low, there's no reason for concern."

"Any standout contestants this year?" Jovy asked, flipping her wavy hair over her shoulder.

"Some surprises indeed," Jomar played coy. "And a few note-worthy teams. The level of performance in this year's Prelims was exceptional. Mongaphalee knocked it out of the park."

"They really did," Jovy agreed. "I couldn't tear my eyes away from the screen."

"Rumors are circulating it might make Super Serial's top ten Preliminaries of all time," Chuckles said as if announcing the world's most important news. "What are your thoughts, Mr. Santos?"

Jomar's response was drowned out by Floyd's skeptical snort. "It's way too soon to make that claim," he said. "People say the same thing almost every year after the Prelims are over. I'm not saying Mongaphalee didn't create an amazing cityscape, but to say it compared to 103rd Prelims in AeroGenco is a bit of a stretch."

Chuckles lowered his voice, adding dramatic anticipation to his next question for Jomar. "I'm sure you know by now that absolutely everyone is talking about District DipShip. Before the Prelims, you made a personal visit there. Did you see anything that might have hinted at their meteoric rise to fame?"

Jomar chuckled, fiddling with his thick jeweled rings. "Ah, Dip-Ship," he began. "I have to confess, outside of Ms. Ito herself, every-thing about that visit was a disaster. I was just as surprised as anyone by their incredible performance."

"Who surprised you the most?" Jovy asked, leaning forward as if every word from Jomar's mouth held a fascination.

"It's hard to say. The MLM Murderer was certainly a shock," Jomar said, and a picture of Carol covered in blood, slashing down at a lifeless UltraChad flashed onto the screen. "After her interview, she almost had me convinced she was innocent. Honestly, she didn't seem like the fighting type."

Jovy laughed with delight. "Isn't that the truth? I don't think anyone saw that coming." The attack unfolded on the screen, and Carol morphed into a blood-soaked demonic figure, relentlessly stabbing UltraChad, all while muttering verses of scripture.

"And it's not just that she killed him," Jomar said, unable to repress a small shudder. "It's the way she killed him. She struck with such precision it's almost impossible to believe she didn't know what she was doing."

Chuckles beamed at the footage as though he were watching a benign game of golf. "Look at all that rage. She just doesn't stop. She truly embodied the Angry White Women category."

"Many are saying that despite the Samurai and the Witch being responsible for most of the points," Chuckles mused, "it was the MLM Murderer who cinched the win."

Jomar pressed his fingertips together, nodding in agreement. "District Taste-E Chicken was poised to win the last spot in the Championships until their run-in with DipShip. Had the MLM Murderer not killed UltraChad when she did there would have been a much different outcome."

Chuckles and Jovy ended the interview with Jomar, and Ziggy forbade himself from blushing when Ejigu joined them on set.

"That is one gorgeous man," Pepper said with a smirk, but when Ziggy turned to glare her into submission, she only laughed.

"Joining us now is Super Serial analyst Ejigu Aman Meba," Jovy said, sounding a bit breathless as her eyes wandered over Ejigu's impressive physique.

"Call me Ejigu," he said, and his warm, rich voice sent an embarrassing jolt of lightning up Ziggy's spine. He was like a schoolboy with a crush, and hated himself for it.

"Ejigu," Chuckles said with a plastic smile. "Analyst Jomar Santos was just commenting on District DipShip. I understand you also were in DipShip prior to the Preliminaries. What are your thoughts on their performance?"

Ejigu crossed one ankle over his knee. "I think it was a remarkable performance," he said. "Not because of their killers, but because of how they communicated with Marshal Ghostshade and the rest of his team in the control room. Individually, they were unimpressive, but together, they were more formidable than I could've imagined."

Ziggy tried not to flush, but his ears felt hot. Pepper beamed, glowing under the shine of his compliments, and Floyd actually clapped his hands.

"Any standouts in particular?" Jovy asked. "A few DipShip killers had very low scores going into the Prelims. Have you changed your mind about any of them?"

Ejigu chuckled. "I've changed my mind about all of them," he said, "but I was the most wrong about Lin Meihua. Even at her age, she performed better than most predicted favorites. The poisonous head cannon was beyond anything I could've ever imagined."

At the mention of her name, Ziggy's mind strayed to Meihua's incredible performance in the Prelims. The press was talking about her almost as much as the Samurai. However, the battle had taken its toll on her frail body, leaving her drained and suffering from exhaustion, bruises, dehydration, and a fractured arm. She ended up needing a pacemaker, so Floyd was by her side during most of her recovery. After the Prelims, Ziggy was a lot less worried about their bizarre friendship. If Meihua wanted Floyd dead, she could have killed him a thousand different ways by now.

Chuckles continued his questioning. "During the analyst interviews, Alaskan Thunder had an incredibly violent outburst. Do you think her impulsiveness hurt the public's perception of DipShip before the Prelims?"

"Without question," Ejigu said, nodding in acknowledgment. "After our visit to DipShip, most analysts felt the team would likely crumble as the competition progressed. We doubted if Tanya could make it through without killing a teammate and disqualifying Dip-Ship."

Pepper gave a scoff of indignation as she muttered, "They clearly missed how loyal Big Montana is to the team during the interview. She treats them all like siblings, and the analysts mistook that for animosity."

Ejigu continued, "The dedication she showed toward her team-mates during the battle surprised me. She still had irrational out-bursts and charged into fights without thinking, but if the Warlord was DipShip's sword, then she was their shield."

Ziggy finished his beer, and Chuckles and Jovy shifted their conversation with Ejigu to other teams and players. His analysis of Big Montana Ice had been spot on. After the Prelims ended, Big

Montana Ice had to be treated for internal bleeding, bruised kidneys, embolism, and broken bones in both hands. But all of that was nothing compared to her burns, which had been so severe she'd needed dermal regeneration on her neck and ear

For the first week, her sickness and injuries had subdued her, but yesterday Mongaphalee doctors said she'd returned with a vengeance, causing more trouble than ever before. She'd even returned to asking nonsensical, demon-determining questions.

Benedict, on the other hand, hadn't stopped crying all week. In the end, eleven of his dogs had died in the Prelims, and one more later from bee stings—leaving him with sixteen for the Championships. He mourned their loss so keenly Ziggy couldn't help but feel sorry for him. Benedict was a serial killer who didn't give a damn about the pain he put his victims and their families through, but even that couldn't make Ziggy completely overlook the suffering caused by the games. That was the problem with the dual nature of Super Serial. Benedict loved his dogs with his whole soul, and even if his pain was based in delusion, it was still real.

Pepper seemed to agree, because she arranged to have the dogs cremated. Yesterday, she gave Benedict a paw-shaped box containing their ashes, and he'd sobbed himself to sleep, clinging to it tightly.

"It's about morale," Pepper said, but to Ziggy, it was like putting a pretty bow on a sheep before sending it to slaughter. Benedict lived through the Prelims because of his team, but in the one-to-one battles, he'd face death alone. Ziggy didn't have high hopes for his survival.

Following Ejigu's interview, Chuckles and Jovy engaged in a continuous stream of conversations with analysts and subject matter experts. Each of them shared their thoughts on the Prelims and speculated on how the results would affect the Championship rounds. Nearly all of them had something to say about DipShip.

Ziggy finished two more beers and was just sinking into a pleasant buzz when Chuckles and Jovy were finally ready to announce the results. Part of him was nervous, but the other was gratefully, comfortably numb. Sitting here on the couch with his friends, he could almost believe everything would be all right. It was a lie, but there would be plenty of time to panic tomorrow when they knew what they were up against.

"Fingers crossed for StellarSecure," Floyd said, sucking in a breath. He crossed his fingers in front of him. "We could actually win against them under the right circumstances."

"Presenting the Championship pairings for the 119th annual Super Serial competition!" Jovy cried, and the pairings flashed on the screen.

At first, Ziggy bypassed the horrible reality, his gaze automatically drawn to the bottom of the list. But when he finally spotted DipShip, his entire existence seemed to disintegrate. DipShip was listed as the number one seed for the qualifying teams, facing off against the top seed from last year's winning districts—Pill Depot.

"Holy cat-humping Secretariat," he whispered, and Pepper gasped, her hand covering her mouth. Floyd's jaw dropped, his eyes wide with shock. "That can't be right. There must be some mistake."

"In a stunning turn of events, District DipShip has been placed in the number one seed!" Chuckles reported with grating enthusiasm.

"I'm sure there are some stunned faces over at DipShip right about now," Jovy said with a tittering laugh.

"This is the first time in Super Serial history a first-year team has been placed in the top seed," Chuckles went on, but Ziggy felt like he was watching through a toilet paper tube. "The closest came twelve years ago when District Climb-Axe was placed in the sixth seed after their first Preliminaries, and if you'll remember, Jovy, they were absolutely annihilated in the head-to-head."

"Let's hope Alexia Ito hasn't grown too attached to her killers," Jovy said with a wry grin. "I heard Pill Depot has a dynamite team this year."

Cameras panned to the executive stage, where Alexia and Hirofumi Ito both stood. Waving to the cameras, Hirofumi smiled, calm as a crocodile waiting to drag its prey into the murky waters. Alexia was pale, and even from the screen, Ziggy could see a deep sadness in her eyes. Hirofumi extended his hand towards Alexia, pausing for the photo op, but she turned away, refusing to shake it, staring defiantly forward until they were both led off stage.

"Drama!" Jovy sang in delight.

"It's rigged," Pepper murmured. "I can't believe this is happening."

"The numbers just don't add up," Floyd exclaimed, his voice growing increasingly perplexed. "Our chances against Pill Depot are lower than winning the Prelims."

"It's because of me," Ziggy said softly.

Pepper turned off the footage. "It's not your fault," she said before they lapsed into silence, each of them pondering the enormity of a head-to-head with the most powerful corporation in the world.

Suddenly, the quiet was shattered by the shrill ring of Ziggy's phone. Fear flashed in Pepper's eyes as Ziggy pulled it from his pocket, his hands trembling as he brought it to his ear.

"Marshal Ghostshade," came the unmistakable voice of Hirofumi Ito.

Ziggy couldn't respond. His tongue felt like it was glued to the roof of his mouth.

"I hope you didn't miss the announcement," Hirofumi said, a tinge of sinister glee on his tongue. "I look forward to facing off with DipShip in the Championships."

Ziggy still couldn't string together a coherent sentence, his mind paralyzed with fear.

"I warned you," Hirofumi went on, his voice growing more congenial and more terrifying with every word, "and now you'll watch as I slowly destroy everything and everyone you love. Your friends. Your family. I've already begun."

Ziggy's heart dropped into his stomach. He could see the horror mirrored in Pepper and Floyd's faces; they could hear every threatening word.

"And when you're broken and clinging to the last shreds of your pathetic existence, begging for a lifeline that will never come," Hirofumi's voice flattened into a hiss, "I'll skin you alive and feed you to the crows. Goodbye, Marshal Ghostshade."

The call dropped.

Epilogue: Famous Last Curds

Light seeped beneath the door of Alexia's office, casting ominous shadows on the floor. Despite the late hour, Ziggy knew she'd still be awake. The guard stationed outside gave him a nod, granting him silent permission to enter.

Inside, Alexia sat at her desk, her forehead pressed against the cold glass. Her breath fogged the surface in sporadic puffs, as if even her sighs were exhausted. Her gaze was hollow, lost in some distant nightmare only she could see. Despite everything she'd done, Ziggy felt a tinge of pity at the look of defeat in her eyes. He wondered what it was like to have a man like Hirofumi as a father. Her chance at happiness was probably slimmer than his own.

"Here to pour salt in the wound?" Alexia snapped, looking up at him. Dark circles ringed her eyes. "Well, save it. I don't need you to tell me how fucked I am."

Ignoring her hostility, Ziggy sat in the seat across from her, the chair creaking under his weight. "The last time we were together like this," he remarked, "you used my husband's ashes to blackmail me."

"Go away," Alexia ordered, sitting up fully, her glossy hair tumbling over her shoulders like a curtain of ink. "I mean it, Ziggy. Get out of my sight before I call security."

"Did you know that at the Opening Ceremonies, your father threatened to kill me if I didn't force a loss in the Preliminaries?" Ziggy said abruptly, slicing through the room's stifling tension. "And the night the match-pairings were announced, he threatened to kill not just me, but everyone I love."

Alexia froze, her sharp facade momentarily cracking. Ziggy could see the wheels in her head lurching into motion. "What's your point?"

"I think we both know he's not the type of man who makes idle threats."

"No, he's not," Alexia rasped after a moment. "You figured out he hates you. Join the club."

"He rigged the match-pairings just to humiliate you," Ziggy said quietly. Commiserating with her softened her expression by a fraction, and she slumped back into her chair. "Nothing I can do about it now," she said. "I have no power and no money."

"I already know that," Ziggy said. "That's not why I came."

"Then why did you come?" she asked, her glare still intense but now mixed with reluctant curiosity.

"I never expected us to find common ground, but here we are," Ziggy said, a frown tugging at the corner of his mouth. "Like it or not, we need each other."

"Need you?" Alexia scoffed. "If we'd matched against any other district, I might need you to win, but it's over. No one beats Hiro-fumi Ito."

"But you did beat him—in the Prelims," Ziggy said, and when she didn't reply, he waited, his silence a patient challenge.

After a stubborn moment, her pride kicked in. "You're right," she said. "I did beat him." Her eyes began to brighten, so Ziggy pressed his advantage, adding, "Everyone was against you, even me, but you still won."

"That's right. I still won."

Ziggy weighed his next words, knowing one wrong move could send the team spiraling into the abyss. "You can beat him again. But you can't do it alone. Not this time."

Alexia's face hardened. "What's the catch?"

"I'll win you a seat on the ABCD," Ziggy said. "And in exchange, you'll keep me and my friends safe from your father."

Alexia tapped her fingertips rhythmically on the desk, engrossed in thought.

"Hasn't he been emperor long enough?" Ziggy said. "Isn't it high time someone new took control?"

Her tapping stopped, but Ziggy saw her teeth clench.

"The only thing you can do to earn his respect is destroy him," Ziggy said. "Beat him at his own game. Win."

She smiled a dark smile, and for a moment Ziggy feared he'd made a mistake. His outstretched hand shook hers, and in that moment, he knew he was trading the tiger's jaws for a viper's fangs.

Other Books by Harker McNair

SUPER SERIAL

Book One of the Super Serial Series

THE RECLAIMING

Book One of the Auction Series

Book One of the Auction Series

About the Authors

Mandy Harker and Preston McNair are pretty good at slinging stories, and they don't care who knows it. Mandy's a dreamer with a passion for hip-hop dancing. She once performed The Cabbage Patch on a yacht, and has seen all but two of the Star Wars movies. Preston's stronger than your Dad, guaranteed. He has mastered twenty-seven bird calls, and he learned how to make fajitas this year. Together, they make the most epic co-authorship the world has ever known.

Find them at: www.harkermcnair.com

Super Duper Serial Music

Spotify

YouTube

Acknowledgements

You probably never expected us to return with more of this nonsense, but it's important to note that we didn't accomplish it alone. Our lives are overflowing with incredible people who support and inspire us; we could easily write fifty pages expressing our gratitude, but we'll try to keep it brief. No promises.

First, to our readers, who always encourage us to keep writing. Thank you for your messages of support, thank you for the laughs, and thank you for understanding that satire runs deep. In the beginning, we worried there wouldn't be a market for something as eccentric as this, but we're forever grateful to have been proven wrong.

A massive shout-out to our developmental editor, Jill Davies. Jill, no one but you would've stuck with us for so long under such annoying circumstances. Your patience, diligence, and equally bizarre sense of humor helped mold this book into what it needed to be. Thank you for seeing everything this series could be and reorienting us when we veered too far off course.

Chris Knight at The Deliberate Page, copyeditor extraordinaire, thanks for your unending perseverance and attention to detail. Sorry for all the times you had to figure out the correct way to write swear words. We couldn't have done this without you.

To our cover artist, Jeff 'TheArt' Smith. We hit the jackpot when you agreed to design our covers. Your enthusiasm, inventiveness, and creativity brought this story to life. Thank you for sharing your talent with us, and with our readers.

Huge props to our incredible assistant, Eric Wimberly. You've been a light in the disorganized darkness, and we're truly grateful for everything you've done to keep this crazy ship afloat. To Jimmy Cooper, our continued criminal guide and greatest champion, thank you for being yourself. To our many sensitivity readers, we're eternally grateful for your input. Being offensive in the right way is no easy task. We appreciate your willingness to take on such an enormous challenge.

To our children, you've been our greatest source of strength and inspiration. We love you more than you can imagine. And last, but never least, to our spouses, Scott and Rachel. We know things are getting weird. Thanks for sticking around. We love you endlessly.